POSSESSIVE MAFIA VOWS

AN ENEMIES TO LOVERS DARK MAFIA ROMANCE

RUTHLESS BILLIONAIRES MAFIA ROMANCE

VIVY SKYS

Copyright © 2025 by VIVY SKYS

All rights reserved.

No part of this book may be reproduced in any form or by any electronic or mechanical means, including information storage and retrieval systems, without written permission from the author, except for the use of brief quotations in a book review.

PROLOGUE

SIENNA

The nightclub. The heavy beat vibrating inside my chest. The sticky heat of too many bodies crammed inside a room, dancing and jumping and swinging each other around like they're having the best night of their lives.

I lose track of time in the bottom of a shot glass that seems to refill itself on demand. I kiss lots of cheeks, I laugh a lot, head tipped back, raucous laughter that accompanies saying goodbye to the old year. Midnight comes and goes in a frenzy of dance moves that are probably nowhere near as elegant as I imagine in my fuzzy head.

Victoria is right behind me as we leave the restroom, and then she isn't.

"V?" I push my way through the crowd that seems to close in on me like water filling a room. Panic creeps into my veins. Not for me, but for Victoria who feels out of her comfort zone if she walks the wrong way around the grocery store.

Then I spot Kenickie from *Grease*.

Or rather, he spots me.

His dark hair is pulled into a perfect quiff that flops over his forehead, but it's the green eyes that hold my attention. Even in the flashing lights and the hazy atmosphere, I know they are the most perfect green eyes I've ever seen. And everything else vanishes.

Apart from the string of beads around my neck. The chunky beads worn by Wilma from *The Flintstones*, that choose this exact moment to break free and pitter-patter across the floor towards the leather-jacketed demi-God heading my way.

Dear fucking God, shoot me now.

He bends and picks up a stray rock, still warm from my skin, and hands it to me, and I instinctively take it.

To our left, a woman in a white vest and panties dressed as Ripley from *Alien*, skids on a bead, her arms cartwheeling as a guy in a floor-length black robe catches her. Ordinarily, I'd have been mortified and simultaneously trying not to laugh out loud. But it seems my body has been drained of every emotion other than rip-my-clothes-off-and-devour-me-now desire.

"Cat's eyes." I'm still staring when he stands right in front of me.

They crinkle at the corners. "Actually, I'm Kenickie." He has a faint accent that I can't place in three words, but I know I want to hear more when I reach up to touch the lines fanning from his eyes.

"You should meet—" I was going to say he should meet my friend Victoria who is dressed as Sandy for the costume party.

But he cuts me off with, "I think I already did."

He places a warm hand on the small of my back and guides me into him so that our hips are touching. Anyone else, and I'd have slapped their hand away and told them to fuck off, but not my green-eyed Kenickie. The word 'my' has already slipped into my vocabulary, and when he raises my hand above my head and spins me around, I focus on the moment our bodies will touch again.

I don't hear the song that's playing. We're dancing to our own tune, every touch of his hand against mine sending electricity through my veins and straight down to my sex. It's inevitable that we will kiss before the night is over.

When we do, I know that one kiss is never going to be enough. I don't think I've ever wanted anyone more than I want him, and it comes to me in a flash of inspiration that we need to get the hell out of there before it's time to go our separate ways.

"We should go watch the sunrise."

I watch his face light up, his eyes glinting like emeralds.

"Where?" he asks.

"Anywhere."

I slide my hand into his, so easily it's like they were made to fit together and drag him towards the exit. I look for Victoria. She has literally vanished, but all that matters is that I have Kenickie until sunrise and I'm not going to waste a moment.

We burst onto the sidewalk like we've just jumped out of a giant cake—*surprise*—dragging the heat with us. Kenickie squeezes my hand. I'm like a magnet unable to resist when he pulls me against him, melding our bodies together.

"Mo leanbh alainn." His lips brush my ear sending shivers down my spine.

I'd never have believed it possible to get so many sensations from my earlobe, but whatever he whispered, I'm already throbbing for him.

"What does that mean?" I can barely hear my own voice over the blood gushing through my veins.

He doesn't answer. Instead, he backs away from the sidewalk and down the alleyway between the nightclub and the building next to it, and I follow. My feet may or may not have touched the ground. It's immaterial.

"Ta tu uaim." His lips brush mine.

Whatever he's saying, he had me at Kenickie back in the club, so I'm not going to question it.

He splays his fingers through my hair and pulls my face closer, those green eyes holding mine in the darkness that has folded us into its cocoon.

We kiss.

Fuck do we kiss.

I wouldn't be aware if a bulldozer ploughed straight through the buildings on either side of us and buried us beneath a pile of rubble.

His hands are somehow underneath my dress, and do I stop him? Nope. I spread my legs wide, my lips still attached to him and embrace the thrill that shoots the length of my spine when he slides a finger inside me.

He sucks on my bottom lip, nibbling it between his teeth. He licks my face, my neck, my jawline. He sticks his tongue in my ear and curls his finger inside my pussy around the spot that sends my heartbeat racing and my already woozy brain cells reeling.

"What dark magic is this?" I tilt my head back against the damp icy wall and whisper to the night.

"It's all you."

He pushes his tongue between my lips and explores my mouth, while his finger rubs and teases and torments my clit, bringing me to the edge and holding me back.

He pulls away, just enough for me to stare into his almond-shaped eyes. "All I'm doing is waking you up. The rest is down to you."

He makes it sound as if I've been sleepwalking all my life. But when he catches the spot again with his finger, it's all I can do to lean on him to keep myself upright.

"Ta tu agam." He kisses me long and hard. "I've got you."

My orgasm explodes over his finger. My body shudders, uncontrollably, like I've just stepped out of a freezer. All I can think about is, if this was all me, why the fuck have I never felt anything like it before?

He holds me close. Patient. Working me expertly until he hears me whimper.

Then he slides his finger out of me and places it in my mouth. He watches me closely as I lick my own juices from his skin, his gaze so intense, I couldn't look away if I tried. Then his tongue joins mine, licking and tasting and probing.

"I've never tasted anything so sweet." He kisses my lips, straightens my dress, and holds my waist as if afraid to let me go in case I melt into a puddle of orgasm on the ground at his feet. "Have you?"

I shake my head. "No."

He takes my hands in his. "Sunrise?"

I'd forgotten all about it, but there is no way I'm walking away from him until we've welcomed the new day and the new year together.

It's an omen. Meeting him in the wee hours of a brand-new spanking-clean year. Like writing the first word on a blank page with a fountain pen. It's a new story, and we are our own protagonists.

A sleek black car is waiting for us nearby. I don't ask where it came from or where we're going. From the first moment I set eyes on him, the world flipped on its axis, and I wouldn't have been surprised if the vehicle grew wings and flew us high above the glass towers and glittering skyline of New York City.

He looks at me as he drives through the city and across the bridge, a smile tugging his lips permanently upward. "Best sunrise you've ever seen?"

He could've asked me how old I am, where I live, what I do for a living. All the regular questions people ask each other on a first date. Not that this can be called a date. He found me in a nightclub and made me come all over his finger, the kind of stuff most people only ever read about in a steamy romance novel. I don't think it qualifies as a date.

He doesn't even know my name yet.

But this is our story, and we're writing it our way.

"The Grand Canyon."

His eyebrows almost disappear beneath the quiff. "You've seen it?"

"I went on a road trip one year. Me and my best friend. Before things..." I shrug and stare straight ahead out of the windshield. "We didn't sleep much that trip. It felt like we were chasing time, you know. Trying to trap it in a net for future use. So, yeah, the Grand Canyon. It felt like we were floating above the rocks in a sea of pink and lilac and gold."

"A beautiful memory." When he speaks, it almost sounds as if he's singing a lullaby. "Mine would be at the Giant's Causeway in Ireland."

That's where the accent is from. I don't interrupt him though; it's haunting to listen to.

"I'll take you there one day. Legend has it that the Causeway was built across the Irish sea by a giant who was trying to reach a rival giant in Scotland."

"Do you believe the story?"

"Sure, why not." He shrugs, flashes an easy smile at me from the driver's seat. "Everyone needs some legend in their life."

So, that's it. We're talking about giants and sunrises when we both hear the screeching of tires across tarmac.

Blinding lights fill the car. Dazzling. I know that the world is dark outside, save for the street lamps lining the highway, but inside, we're plunged into the kind of glaring whiteness associated with heaven in the movies.

Then, through the stark light comes something huge and rumbling and terrifying. A beast on huge heavy wheels. The car seems to slide out from under us, moving with a mind of its own.

Someone screams. And then the sound of metal on metal replaces the screams inside my head before the world turns from white to black as if every light on the planet has been switched off.

1

SIENNA

Six Years Later

Deep breath.

I'm ready. As ready as I'll ever be.

This gallery is literally a dream come true; it's no wonder the butterflies in my tummy are having the wing-fight of the century. I never thought it would happen. I mean, I know you're supposed to tell the universe what you want, visualize it, mood-board it to within an inch of its life, and turn it into reality.

And I did that. Yep. Still have the fading mood boards to prove it.

But opening an art gallery is a big fucking deal. Especially when you're a wannabe artist scraping by on what you earn from other jobs, just waiting for the day someone picks up a piece of your artwork and declares to the world: *This woman is the next Picasso! Or Van Gogh. Or Frida Kahlo.*

Whatever.

Let's just say that kind of epiphany doesn't happen often. Or ever if we're being honest. So, would the universe have listened to me if my best friend Victoria hadn't fallen in love with an Irish billionaire sex-God?

Not a chance in hell.

I glance around the gallery one last time. My eyes linger on my favorite piece, the largest piece I've ever painted, and the one that felt like drawing blood from a piece of marble. It's a self-portrait although no one would ever know. It's all color, swirls of ethereal garnet-red, cerulean, and tangerine, more like an aura-portrait.

An aura-portrait of the woman I was before...

Even if people don't recognize me somewhere inside the splashes of bright acrylic, I hope they'll understand the emotions oozing from the canvas.

I wander through to my office out the back.

My office.

I'll never get used to these words: my office, my gallery.

I sip water from a glass through a metal straw, careful not to smudge my lipstick, and study my reflection in the mirror on the wall opposite the window.

The dress I'm wearing cost more than I used to earn in six months of teaching art at middle school. Victoria insisted on buying it for me. "Call it a happy-gallery-day gift," she'd said with a twinkle in her eye.

She ignored my protests of, "But you and Caleb have already done more than I ever expected, V," and "I don't know how

I'll ever repay you." She spotted the moss-green fishtail dress with the Bardot neckline while I was still eyeing up the racks of clothes I'd need a bank loan to afford, and grabbed it before I could even blink. Then she led me, dazed, into a changing cubicle and sat down in a comfy armchair to wait for my transformation.

Now, I smooth the crushed velvet bodice with the palms of my hands and turn my body this way and that, admiring the way it clings to my hips and trails across the floor behind me. It's giving Morticia Addams vibes, only softer.

But what I'm really doing is avoiding looking at the scars above the neckline. The shiny pink flesh, like ruffles of frosting that tightens the skin between my cleavage and collarbone. I trace them with my fingertips, and the memories come flooding back as they always do.

My face is pale, making my eyes appear huge and dark. All pupil, no iris. My breaths come in rapid shallow gasps, the skin between my collarbones rising and dipping with the effort of trying to fill my lungs.

Even now, almost six years later, reliving the car crash takes my breath away.

It isn't even so much the accident that has this debilitating effect on me. It's knowing that if I allow the memory to keep going, eventually I'd reach the part where I regained consciousness and realized that I was alone.

Kenickie was gone.

I was trapped inside the car. Aside from the safety belt, something heavy and solid was pinning me to the seat. I couldn't budge it. I couldn't unfasten the belt that was cutting into my cheek and neck. I yelled for help, but no one came.

I managed to slide my hand into my pocket and wrap my fingers around my phone. My movements were slow, sluggish, clumsy.

"Please don't drop the phone," I muttered under my breath. "Please, don't..."

I slid my thumb across the surface. I couldn't move my neck to see what I was doing, I just prayed that I'd find the green button from muscle memory and hit the last number I dialed earlier in the day.

Victoria.

That's when the mangled remains of the vehicle went up in flames.

I swallow painfully, my tongue sticking to the roof of my mouth and reach for the emerald silk scarf that I bought to match the dress I'm wearing. Looping it around my neck, I fasten it into a bow to cover the unsightly scars.

That night, I didn't find out that Kenickie's real name was Kyle.

Kyle Murray.

Billionaire bachelor and lawyer to the Irish mafia family.

I didn't know who he was until my best friend Victoria agreed to marry his brother Caleb, in an arrangement designed to get Caleb's crazy ex-girlfriend off his back.

Because this is the kind of world they roll in.

Fake marriages. Casinos. Leaving an innocent passenger to die in a car accident.

Kyle will be at the gallery opening tonight. I can hardly turn him away when it's his family's money that paid for it in the first place.

His brothers rescued him the night of the accident. They told him that I must've died on impact, and he believed them. Victoria believes them too. He wants us to start afresh. Forget what happened. Put it behind us and build on the connection we had in the short time we spent together.

I've told him I can't.

The problem is, I can't walk away either.

2

KYLE

"Are you sure you should be here tonight?" I question Victoria.

It sounds way harsher than intended, but Victoria's due date was a week ago, and she has that funny kind of walk that women have in the later stages of pregnancy, like she's trying to carry a ton of boxes and can't see where she's going.

"Whoa, is this what the family taught you in Ireland, to speak with no filter?" My brother Caleb places his arm around Victoria's waist and steers her away from me.

Victoria laughs. "I'm pregnant. I'm not sick. And I wouldn't miss this for the world."

Her eyes seek out her best friend Sienna who is charming a group of guests in front of a painting that appears to float off the canvas to speak personally to the viewer.

My gaze flits back and forth between Sienna and the artwork. I don't know what it is—I'm no art connoisseur—but there's something familiar about this piece.

"Sienna is stunning tonight." Victoria's voice jolts me back to the room.

I know what I was doing: trying to look anywhere but at the artist in the green velvet dress. But now that Victoria has said her name out loud, I can't drag my eyes away from her. Stunning doesn't cut it.

I've been away for three months, trying to clear my head, and learn to exist with the heavy weight of Sienna's rejection. I came on too strong, too soon after I found her again. She'd been kidnapped because of our family, and I didn't even give her a chance to breathe before I was telling her I loved her and begging her to forgive me.

No other woman has ever had this effect on me.

The night we met, New Year's Eve six years ago, should've been the first night of the rest of our lives. When she suggested we chase the sunrise, I almost added the word first.

First sunrise. First kiss. First of everything two people could possibly want to share.

Then our lives blew up because of a truck driver who didn't know when to say no to a few beers. My brothers pulled me from the wreckage. They did what they thought was right: got me out of the situation before the press got hold of the story. They checked Sienna's pulse, or lack of, and figured there was nothing they could do for her. I still can't forgive them for it.

I tried to find her. I didn't know at the time, but Caleb tried to find her too, only he was searching for a corpse, while Sienna was fighting for her life in a hospital with burns covering most of her body.

"Come on." Victoria links her arm with mine and leads me across the room.

Sienna does a double take when she spots me. She excuses herself from the small group of guests and joins us, her appraising gaze sending signals directly to my cock.

Focus, Kyle.

"You made it, V." Sienna leans across Victoria's swollen belly to hug her. "I was sure you'd go into labor today."

"I warned the baby to stay inside until tomorrow."

Pregnancy suits my sister-in-law. Her skin is glowing, her eyes are bright, and her hair tumbles over her shoulders in thick luscious curls.

"Kyle." Sienna peers at me from beneath lowered lashes. "You look ... different."

My hair has grown while I've been away, and I've cultivated a layer of so-called designer stubble which I decided to keep. I still walk with a limp from my leg being shattered in the horrible wreck that changed our lives forever. But I think what she means is, I've lost the veneer of anxiety that shrouded my life before I went to Ireland. I took advantage of the fresh air, vibrant Irish scenery, and roaring log fires in country pubs while I was away, and tried to let go of everything else going on back here.

"Should I take that as a compliment?"

Her fingers instinctively play with the scarf around her neck, but there's a smile on her lips, nonetheless. I'll take it as a win.

"When did you get back?"

"A week ago."

I wanted to swing by the gallery to see her. Fuck knows, I'd have come straight from the airport if I thought she'd have been pleased to see me. But I didn't spend the last three months promising myself that I'd give her space only to ruin it the instant I set foot back inside the city.

Only now, I can't be certain, but she almost seems disappointed. Her shoulders drop momentarily. Then a server, a young guy wearing smart black pants and a crisp white shirt approaches us with a tray of champagne flutes, and the moment passes.

I sip my drink, the bubbles fizzing behind my teeth.

Now that I'm standing beside her, I feel my resolve and good intentions crumbling. This isn't how it's supposed to be. There shouldn't be this awkward space between us.

So, ignoring my head that's screaming at me to walk away before I cross the flimsy line keeping us apart, I lean my face close to hers, so close I can smell her light, understated perfume, and say, "Favorite piece of art?"

She moistens her lips with the tip of her tongue, and half-turns towards me. It all seems to happen in slow-motion. I can see the shadow of her eyelashes on her cheeks, the freckles spattering her nose, the curve of her lips which are exactly as I remember them from years ago.

But before she can respond, a tall guy in a blue Armani suit swoops in from out of nowhere, and kisses her cheek, raising a faint blush as Sienna pulls away. From both of us.

"Nick?" She blinks furiously as if trying to bring him into focus.

But I don't need to adjust my eyes. The guy's raven-black hair is slicked away from his forehead. His cheekbones and jaw are expensively chiseled to perfection. His eyes are pale-gray, and his smile so wide, I can see his back teeth. I'd wager that he practices his smile in front of a mirror each morning before he leaves home in case he gets caught on camera. Wouldn't want to be seen looking anything less than immaculate.

"What are you doing here?" Sienna asks.

He obviously wasn't on the guest list; this gives me a small thrill of satisfaction.

"You mentioned tonight was your opening night last time we met."

My fists instinctively clench. That was for my benefit, the guy hasn't even looked at me yet.

"I couldn't miss it." Yep, the fake smile isn't going anywhere.

"Nick." Sienna takes a deep breath and glances my way, the color still in her cheeks. "This is—"

"There's someone I want you to meet." Nick takes her arm and guides her away from me, his gaze dragging across my face as though I'm invisible.

Sienna peers at me over her shoulder. She isn't smiling. But my eyes are locked onto his arm which has already snaked its way around her shoulders.

Lower it, I dare you.

My hackles are up. Something about the man makes my flesh crawl, and the thought of Sienna being touched by him makes me feel nauseous.

"Deep breath. I can see your knuckles." Caleb is standing next to me. I didn't even hear him coming.

"Do you know that guy?" I gesture to Nick with a nod of my head.

"No, but I'll find out who he is."

"I'll do it."

The guy obviously wanted to get Sienna away from me. He didn't even bother with introductions. But from the way Sienna has already extricated herself from his arm, I get the feeling that he's a little too close for her liking.

Well, that makes two of us.

"Kyle, I know how you feel about Sienna," Caleb says.

I feel a 'but' coming. I guess it must be easy to hand out advice when you're about to have a baby with the woman you love. I don't feel any bitterness towards Caleb and Victoria; they met the same night I met Sienna, and they got their second chance for love last year when they were reunited. I'm happy for them.

Caleb didn't almost kill the love of his life in a car crash.

"Give her time," he adds now. "She'll see straight through the douchebag when she realizes that he thinks he's the beautiful one."

I clink my champagne glass against his. It's a fair point; I only hope he's right.

The evening drags. It's going well for Sienna, and for that I'm grateful, but every time my eyes seek her out, hoping to get another moment alone with her, Mr. Armani is right beside her, treating her like his property. When I hear laughter, there he is, all white teeth and well-practiced smile. Before Sienna's speech, he's there clinking his glass to get everyone's attention, winking at her like he's got it all in hand.

I swap my champagne for water. Sienna might not want my protection, but someone needs to keep Mr. Up-Close-and-

Personal in check, and I don't want alcohol to cloud my judgement.

Later in the evening, I'm studying the painting I noticed when I first walked in when a faint ripple of commotion reaches me from somewhere near the back of the gallery.

I turn around and spot Caleb helping Victoria into a seat while she clutches her abdomen, face contorted into a grimace of pain.

"Shit!"

I navigate artwork and people, to reach them a second too late. Once again, Nick swoops in, crouching in front of my sister-in-law and speaking to her in his silky-smooth voice. "Has your water broke?"

Victoria's face relaxes a little. Caleb cups her hand in his and raises it to his lips. "No."

"How often are the contractions coming?"

"They were every five minutes."

I pick up on the 'were'. "Were you in labor before you got here?"

Victoria offers me a tight-lipped smile. "The pains were intermittent. I thought I could deal with them so long as they didn't get any stronger, and I wanted to be here, for Sienna."

On cue, Sienna appears beside me, and I force myself to ignore the scent of her perfume and the swish of her dress against my legs. "V?" Her eyes are wide. "Are you in labor?"

Victoria doesn't answer. As another contraction grips her body, she squeezes her eyes shut and inhales deeply, releasing her breath through her button-hole shaped mouth.

Nick waits for it to pass, watching Victoria so closely, I don't know how Caleb hasn't throttled him yet. "Two minutes between contractions. They're getting stronger, aren't they?" At Victoria's nod, he turns to Caleb. "I'm a surgeon not a gynecologist, but I delivered my sister's baby. Long story. But let's just say that I'll do what I can."

Victoria's breathing is already growing ragged, and her knuckles turn white as she grips Caleb's hand. A low groan escapes her lips, and I don't think she even registers it.

"This is going to be quick." Nick's tone is firm, reassuring. He's confident that he's the only person here who knows what to do in the circumstances and he's reveling in being in control.

"I'll get the car brought to the door," I say.

I'm already two steps away when he chimes in, "There isn't time."

Victoria turns huge dark eyes to me.

"We'll get you to the hospital, Victoria." I hold her gaze. "We can alert the gynecologist. You'll be in safe hands."

I've seen the birth plan. Mom made sure we all knew what was to happen in case she or Caleb weren't around when Victoria went into labor. Tonight, Mom and Emily are at a charity event, and one glance at Caleb is all I need.

Victoria gives me the briefest nod.

This isn't a power struggle, even if that's Nick's agenda. This is about delivering my niece safely into the world and ensuring that my sister-in-law gets the medical care she needs. I'm taking no chances. I'm not about to start playing God with my family's lives.

VIVY SKYS

My phone pressed to my ear, I alert the driver, and clear a path through the gallery to the exit. I turn around to find Caleb and Sienna supporting Victoria as she makes her way slowly across the room, Nick trailing behind them as though poised to catch the baby before she hits the floor.

"I'm so sorry, Si," Victoria murmurs. "This was supposed to be your night."

"Hey, don't you dare apologize. This is my goddaughter you're bringing into the world." Sienna glances at me, and I'm relieved to find that we seem to be on the same page: getting Victoria to hospital.

I step outside first and open the rear passenger door of the car that's waiting with the engine running.

Victoria climbs onto the back seat and clings to the headrest in front of her, body bent double as another contraction takes hold.

I pat Caleb's shoulder as he gets into the car, close the door, and stand back, watching the vehicle enter the steady flow of traffic. They're about to meet their baby girl. It's the start of a whole new adventure for them as a family, and excitement gurgles inside my chest.

I turn to Sienna. Swamped with emotion, I want to tell her how privileged I feel to share this moment with my brother and sister-in-law. How happy I am that she's here too. But she has already gone back inside.

Peering through the window, I spot her immediately in her green velvet dress. She has her back to me, so I can't see the expression on her face. She's with a small group of guests, but there's no mistaking the lanky guy in the Armani suit standing right beside her.

Head down, I walk back to my apartment.

My niece, Holly Marie Murray, arrives safely at one minute past midnight weighing eight pounds and six ounces. She's a December baby. A Murray. Although, studying the photos from Caleb that are currently taking over my inbox, and the mop of dark hair on the baby's head, she's going to look like her mom.

I don't sleep. The adrenaline fades, and I'm left balancing the scales between excitement about the baby's arrival and concern for Sienna. Was it my imagination, or was Nick pushing the boundaries between friendliness and slimeball aggression?

And if so, what am I going to do about it?

I rise early. The sky is dark and heavy, the city is already a hive of flickering lights and humming traffic. The long winter nights and gray days that barely make an appearance before darkness descends again, don't usually affect me. But after the vast openness of Ireland, the city is starting to feel claustrophobic.

In my office, I ask the concierge to bring me coffee and fruit, and power up my computer.

Nick, clearly not a fan of formal introductions, said that he was a surgeon. He wasn't on the guest list, and Sienna was surprised to see him. He also injected into the conversation the seemingly casual comment that she'd mentioned the gallery opening the last time they met.

In the moment, I'd taken the bait. I assumed, as insinuated, that he and Sienna were perhaps more than friends. But she seemed uncomfortable with his proximity, and thinking about it now, I didn't see her reciprocate his touchy-feely approach. She didn't lean into him the way two people who enjoy each other's company would.

I'm no expert on body language, but I'm almost certain they know each other on a professional level, and it has nothing to do with art.

Into the search engine, I type in the name Nicholas, cosmetic surgeon, and New York City. There are nowhere near as many results as I'm anticipating, and it takes me less than thirty seconds to locate Nick Morris and open his website.

The first page contains a color image of him smiling at the camera in a silver designer suit, white shirt, and gray tie. All that's missing is a sparkle from his expensive teeth to complete the golden-boy image.

"Okay, let's see what you're hiding, Nick Morris," I mutter to the screen in front of me.

I trawl the Internet, digging deeper and deeper, through Nick Morris's work history, college, and as far back as high school. Nothing. But no one is that squeaky-clean, and this is ringing more alarm bells than if I'd discovered a wife, a mistress, and a criminal record. I know first-hand how unwanted information can be made to disappear.

I don't trust the guy.

I don't know what his agenda is concerning Sienna, but my gut is telling me that it has nothing to do with love. One glance at the guy was enough to tell me that number one on his list is Nick Morris, and perhaps, as Caleb said, I should trust Sienna's judgement, but he'll have to lock me in a cell to keep me from looking out for her.

My suspicions are burning a hole in my chest.

I can't concentrate on work, I can't drag Caleb away from his baby girl, and Mom will already be besotted with her granddaughter too.

So, I do the next best thing. I call Terry, my step-father, and arrange to meet him in the Wraith's restaurant for breakfast.

"What a bonny baby!" Terry's sporting his granddad grin as he takes a seat opposite me at Caleb's regular table. "Have you seen the pictures?"

He doesn't wait around but unlocks his phone and opens an image of Mom cuddling baby Holly in the hospital room. Mom looks young again, as if having a new baby in the family has erased life's creases from her forehead and given her an added roll of the dice.

I can't help smiling.

"She'll break hearts when she grows up." Terry locks his phone, and orders coffee and loaded pancakes. "You're looking well, Kyle. Ireland suits you."

We talk a bit about my trip, but Terry's astute enough to pick up on the fact that I'm holding back, contributing the bare minimum to the conversation.

"What's going on, lad?" He spears maple-syrup covered pancake onto his fork, pops it into his mouth, and sits back.

Deep breath. I know how this is going to sound, but I have to ask. "Ever heard of a cosmetic surgeon called Nick Morris?"

He swallows, cricks his neck from side to side, washes his food down with a mouthful of black coffee. He's thinking. "Should I have?"

"He's Sienna's cosmetic surgeon."

Terry sets his cup down and scratches the corner of his eye. "And?"

I explain that I met the guy for the first time at the gallery opening where he arrived unannounced, and that I don't trust him. "I've done some digging. He's either a saint or he has someone mopping up his footprints."

Terry nods, pensive. "Don't trust him how?"

"He showed up without an invite, didn't wait to be introduced, and then didn't leave Sienna's side. I haven't figured him out yet, but his snub was aimed directly at me."

"Okay." Terry sits forward and rests his elbows on the table. "Let me ask you something. Would you be so mistrustful of the guy if this had been about anyone but Sienna?"

I swallow a mouthful of coffee and wince as it scalds my tongue.

Would I? It's virtually impossible to answer as this does already concern Sienna. But thinking back to the fake smile and the hand on her lower back guiding her around the gallery as if he owned it, I know that this is about more than him touching her.

"Gut instinct: yes."

"Fair enough. You want my advice, tell Sienna how you feel." I'm about to shut this suggestion down when Terry raises a finger. "You can say your piece, and the rest is down to her."

Maybe he's right.

But I'm treading a fine line with Sienna, and I don't want to tip her over the edge and straight into the arms of Nick Morris.

3

SIENNA

Life is good.

I have my gallery. Victoria and Caleb have Holly. It'll soon be the holidays, and the world is already twinkling like the sky spewed fairy lights everywhere.

There was a time when I believed that Christmas was for other people. The ones who still harbored that tiny kernel of belief in their hearts that a man with a fluffy white beard and a red outfit could travel around the planet in one night and spread joy and happiness. But over the years I've grown to enjoy it because I get to share it with people I love.

People I choose to love.

The ones I keep in my life because they're important to me.

The holidays were different when I was a little kid. Instead of waking up at the crack of dawn, too excited to sleep, I would lie in my bed, waiting for the house to reveal whether it would be a day for smiling or a day for hiding in my room, trying not to make a sound.

Images pop into my head before I can stop them.

I wake up on Christmas morning to snarling voices reaching me from the kitchen. I climb out of bed and sit on the bottom of the stairs to listen, shivering from the cold. The living room door is open, but the Christmas tree is dark, the baubles clinging to the branches, waiting for the fairy lights to bring them to life.

"Who the fuck do you think pays for the electricity?" My dad's voice is filled with sickly yellow anger.

"It's Christmas, Hooch." That's what everyone calls him. Hooch. Including my mom. "She's just a kid. Let her have the lights. Just for today."

He snorts. "The stupid fucking lights or dinner. Your choice."

There's a pause before my mom replies. "But we all got to eat. You're gonna make her sit in the living room and go hungry because you don't want the lights on the tree?"

I'm glad I can't see his face when he says, "You'll be sitting right next to her."

"What about dinner?" My mom's voice is pleading now.

"I'm going out. You enjoy your fucking fairy lights. I'm sure the kid will understand that you chose them over putting food in her belly."

"Hooch, you can't do—"

There's a sound like a cupboard door being slammed, and I jump. It's the same sound that always precedes my mom telling me that she walked into the door.

We have fairy lights on the Christmas tree that year. Mom and I sit on cushions in front of it eating cheese sandwiches and orange slices, while the bruise on her jaw turns black and purple and she dabs the blood from her swollen lip with a kitchen towel.

I shiver despite the perfect temperature inside the gallery.

I wish I could go back and tell five-year-old me that it will get better. That it won't be long before he leaves us for good, and that one day, long after my mom's passing, I'll learn that the holidays bring out the best in people. It's probably due to cheesy Hallmark movies, but still, it's the one time of year when people raise their heads from their phones and smile at one another.

I'm still smiling when I go to lock up the gallery and switch off the lights.

The door opens, and someone steps inside, shaking raindrops from his suit jacket.

Kyle.

I never got a chance to tell him at the opening night, but his sabbatical has done him good. His brown hair is longer, wavier, curling around his ears and over his shirt collar, adding to the rock-star look that comes with the ear piercing and the tattoos sneaking out from under his cuffs. His eyes are brighter too, like Ireland managed to put the sparkle back in them.

Now, he's less the suited-and-booted mafia lawyer, and more the man I met in a nightclub years ago. The man who spoke about giants and legends and told me that everything he made me feel, was all me.

"What are you doing here?"

"Can we talk?"

I peer outside at the rain zigzagging like lightning down the windows and catch a glimpse of my reflection on the glass. I look ghostly, drab, barely here beside Kyle's renewed energy, and my confidence slips through the keyhole as I close the door behind him.

Raising my head, I face him and try to ignore the way my pulse races, his green eyes taking me straight back to New Year's six years ago. I swear I can still feel the music thrumming inside my chest.

"You waited till I'm closing the gallery to come and speak to me?"

He shrugs. "I almost didn't come."

I drag my eyes away from him and head through the gallery to my office, away from the windows and the prying eyes of anyone passing by. The butterflies inside my heart are back, the little traitors. *Don't make eye contact*, I tell myself. If I don't meet his eyes, I'll be safe.

I pause in the middle of my office, suddenly hyper-aware of how much space Kyle consumes just standing there. He didn't seem this tall the night we met. Probably because we were in a noisy crowded club where we had to lean in close to hear each other speak.

"I had a lot of time to think in Ireland," he begins, filling the chasm between us and sucking me in.

Seriously, how am I so weak that I can't even be alone in a room with him without my body reminding me of that night?

"I don't expect you to forgive me for leaving you that night, Sienna. I can't even begin to imagine how afraid you must've been when you realized that you were alone. I'd hate me too." He sucks in a deep breath and exhales shakily.

He's right about one thing: it's the scariest fucking thing that has ever happened to me.

"I've never been able to let you go, Sienna."

His eyes lock onto mine and, too late, I try to look away. But I'm already trapped.

"Call it obsession, or survivor guilt, or whatever. I know how I felt about losing you and I know what I want."

I don't speak. I'm transfixed listening to him, my heart drumming its own peculiar beat like it wrote this tune especially for Kyle. I'll hear him out, it's the least I can do, but he just doesn't get it. The last six years were different for him than they were for me. He didn't have to undergo numerous surgeries. Or lay awake at night wondering what kind of man could leave a woman to die alone on the highway. Or watch his physical scars morphing into something that he still couldn't face showing anyone.

Our paths followed different trajectories after the car crash, like pieces of shrapnel from an explosion, and not even all the Murray money can bend them so that they meet again somewhere in the future.

"I want you, Sienna. I've wanted you since the first time I saw you, and nothing will ever change that. Have you ever wondered why I didn't ask your name that night?" he asks, and I chew my bottom lip and shake my head. "It might sound crazy, but I felt as if I already knew you. You could've been called Jane or Greer or Thomas—"

"Thomas?" I smile. The chasm is gradually closing.

He smiles too. "It wouldn't have mattered what you were called because you were already you. You were already the you I see in front of me now."

I shake my head and sniff back tears. "I'm not the same person though. Too much has changed."

"You're right: too much has changed." He shrugs. "But you know what, when I look at you, I see *you*, Sienna."

He steps closer, and I'm rooted to the ground like a centuries-old tree.

"I see what's inside. I see the sunrise over the Grand Canyon, the colors bursting to get out of you and onto canvas, and the fearlessness like a lioness in the wild."

"A lioness?" My voice is barely there.

"A leoin."

He reaches out, so slowly his hand might not be moving at all and touches the dip between my collarbones. His caress is kitten-soft, and my breath hitches in my chest.

"Please don't..." I shake my head, but I don't pull away.

There's no air in the room. His oxygen is my oxygen. His heartbeat is my heartbeat; if his heart were to stop right now, so too would mine.

"Tell me you don't want this." His fingers tilt my chin so that I'm looking directly into his eyes. "Tell me to walk away and never come back, and I will."

My heart is frantically trying to claw its way out of me. My pussy is clenching at his touch. But the fear is still there, like a lump of ice deep in the pit of my stomach, warning me not to trust him. He left me once before; he can do it again.

"Say it, Sienna. Tell me you don't want this, and I promise that you'll never hear from me again."

"*Never?*"

Is that what I'm afraid of? That Kyle will be true to his word, and I'll never be this close to him again? Why does the thought of never hearing him call me *leoin* again feel like a spear poking holes in my chest?

While he was away, I got my life back onto an even plane. No ups, no downs, no distractions. Just me and my work. Kyle has been back for a week, and here I am all over the place like I'm trying to walk across a frozen pond.

What the fuck is wrong with me?

I don't even have to ask. When he's this close to me, I'm transported back to that dark alleyway, every nerve-ending in my body screaming to be fucked.

"Well?" Kyle asks. "It's your call, Sienna. Tell me you don't want me."

"I…"

Kyle's lips are almost touching mine. I can feel his breath on my face, see the bottle-green flecks in his eyes, smell his cologne.

It would be so easy. Tell him to turn around and walk away. It would all be over.

But I already feel the emptiness of losing him like Goldie Hawn's character in *Death Becomes Her* with a hole straight through her middle.

"I can't…"

He cups my face with both hands. His tongue is in my mouth, and I can't even believe the sounds that are coming from me. My body has made the decision for me, and now there's no turning back.

Kyle picks me up and carries me to my desk. The pot of pens rolls onto the floor and lands with a crash. I push Kyle's damp jacket over his shoulders and fumble with the buttons of his shirt, our lips attached, tongues chasing each other around my mouth.

Everything else is forgotten.

Kyle raises my arms in the air and pulls my chunky sweater over my head. I gasp. The overhead light in the office is stark, designed for computer work.

"Kyle, no," I breathe against his neck.

"No?" He pulls away, and I cross my arms over my chest.

"Let's go to the studio." The studio is in darkness. He won't see my scars.

Too late. He's already spotted them.

I try to get down from the desk, and he helps, offering me his hand. I've not felt this exposed or this vulnerable, well, ever. "This was a mistake. I'm sorry."

But he pulls me towards him, his free hand entwined in my hair. "Trust me, Sienna. Please."

I don't speak.

He holds my gaze long enough to know that I'm not going to bolt, and then he traces the scars across my neck and chest with his fingertip. "Don't be ashamed of your body, Sienna. These marks are part of you. They are what makes you so special."

He dips his head and kisses the scar that starts between my cleavage. He traces the puckered skin with tiny fragile kisses, across my chest, around my collarbone, and up to where my jawline meets my left ear.

"Mo leoin, you are so beautiful."

His kisses travel to my mouth and keep going. No part of my face is left untouched. He sucks on my earlobe. My neck. My hairline.

My entire body is tingling, and I realize that my arms are no longer crossed over my chest, and my bra is on the floor.

Kyle unzips my pants and tugs them down over my hips while his lips continue to trace damp patterns from my belly button to my abdomen. He slides my panties down, and I step out of them. No one has seen me naked since the accident, and I'd kind of accepted that it was how it would always be.

I feel his tongue between my legs and instinctively reach behind me for the edge of the desk to keep me upright.

"You're beautiful, Sienna." He peers up at me from between my legs, his eyes greener than ever, while his thumb strokes the livid scar on my inner thigh. "You believe me, don't you?"

I nod. My pussy is dripping, and his tongue has barely touched me. God, I never realized how badly I wanted this. How badly I want *him*.

"Say it." He spreads my legs while still holding my gaze. "I'm beautiful. Say it."

"I'm beautiful," I whisper.

"Say it like you mean it." He watches me closely, eyes narrowed. "You want me to make you come, don't you?"

"Yes."

"I want to make you come, Sienna. I want to suck this pussy dry, but I can't do it until you tell me you're beautiful."

"I'm beautiful."

My breathing is growing ragged, and he still hasn't touched me, but my pussy remembers. It remembers, and now that we've come this far, it's pleading for him to fuck me with his tongue.

"That's better." Without warning, he drags his tongue between the folds of my sex and the reaction is instantaneous. "You taste so fucking good, Sienna. Sweeter even than I remember and fuck, those memories have kept me going all this time."

He spreads my legs even further, and I arch my back, pushing my sex onto him. He licks around the outside of my pussy, dragging his tongue back and forth and teasing me with the tip just far enough inside to promise me the orgasm to end all fucking orgasms.

His tongue comes out, and he kisses the scars above my mound.

I know what he can see. I've studied the shiny skin in the mirror until I could recreate it on canvas with my eyes closed. But for the first time, I don't feel as though I need to hide it.

Kyle inserts a finger inside me. Two fingers. Three. "Don't come yet, mo leoin." He finds the spot and drags his hand back and forth across it while his tongue catches my juices. "How fucking wet are you? You've been saving this up for me, haven't you?"

The fingers slide out. His tongue replaces them, my pussy clenching around him. My breathing is ragged; it was ragged from the moment he opened me up, and the lack of oxygen reaching my brain is making the world spin.

There is only his tongue. Nothing else exists.

"Come for me, Sienna. Come all over my face."

Back and forth, my pussy throbbing, my clit tingling. My orgasm explodes, and Kyle holds my thighs, his tongue relentless. The spasms just keep coming and coming.

I barely have a chance to catch my breath before Kyle lowers me back onto the desk. He raises my legs and rests them over his shoulders while he unzips his pants and releases his cock. Gripping it with one hand, he rubs it around my sex, smothering it with my cum.

"Guide me in." He places my hand around his girth.

He's solid and silky at the same time. I place the head inside my pussy and thrust my hips, pushing myself onto him. Deeper and deeper. Till I think there's nowhere else for him to go, and then he leans over me, raising my ass off the table and giving him the extra space he needs to fill me up.

My eyes widen. I wrap my arms around his neck and kiss him.

I can taste me on his tongue. I still hear Kyle's words from almost six years ago: *All I'm doing is waking you up. The rest is down to you.* His kisses are demanding. There's no air for me to breathe but his, and that's okay. It's exactly as it should be.

His cock pounds into me. Our bodies merge into one happy chaotic mess of cum and pre-cum, and I know that if I could pull him in any deeper, I would.

"I've waited so long for this, Sienna." His words bleed into my mouth, and I'm not even sure if I imagined them.

"Me too."

He pauses, just long enough for me to see the glimmer in his eyes, and then his mouth smothers mine again, and his body judders as he fills me up with his cum.

When we are both still, he smooths the hair away from my face. "You're even more beautiful than in my memories. Promise me that you'll always remember this. No matter what happens, you'll never forget how special you are."

I reach up and kiss the tip of his nose while his dick shrinks inside me, and my pussy squeezes him out. "No matter what happens? Why does this sound like goodbye?"

He nuzzles his nose against mine. "It's only goodbye if that's what you want."

"It isn't." And I mean it.

He supports his upper body on his elbows, and it feels like we're in a tiny cave, shielded from the world outside. Nothing bad can happen to me here. I feel it, and I believe it, and the tiny part of my consciousness that understands this moment won't last forever is thankfully silent.

"Sienna, I—"

I place my finger on his lips. "Don't, Kyle. You don't need to say anything."

"I do." He sighs, and I already feel the outside creeping in, and the moment seeping away like water through a crack. "I know that you don't want to be a part of my world. But I would give it all up for you, Sienna."

"I... No." I try to move out from under him, but he doesn't budge. "I can't ask you to do that. Not for me."

"You're not asking me to do anything. I'm telling you this is what I want."

"It would never work, Kyle. You would always resent me. Your family would never forgive me."

"How could I ever resent you for making me happy?"

"But I..." I'm wasting my breath. I could toss a hundred arguments into the equation, and he'd shoot every one of them down in flames. "What if I don't make you happy?"

He smiles. "You're all I've ever wanted, so it's a no-brainer. We could relocate to Ireland."

His eyes search for a glimmer of hope or excitement in mine, something he can hold onto and mold into a future that belongs to us both.

"Sienna, I would move to Antarctica with you if it's where you wanted to be. I'd be happy on a deserted island, living in a roofless shack with no running water and an endless supply of watercolor paints. I'd even move to fucking Timbuktu if I could wake up to your smile each morning."

I chuckle. "Is Timbuktu even a real place?"

"There's only one way to find out."

The eagerness in his voice is so real that I feel a sharp stab of guilt in my chest. I shouldn't have allowed this to happen, not if it's going to give him false hope. He said all the right things. He made me feel beautiful again, and sexy, and desirable, but it would be wrong to drag him away from everything he knows, even if he believes it will make him happy.

It won't.

If we shrink our world to the two of us and my art, bitterness will inevitably spread through his veins like poison. It will taint everything that he thinks he loves about me until all that remains is a shriveled nugget of bone-dry dust that once resembled affection.

"I don't want to go anywhere, Kyle. This is my home. It's your home too. Now that I have my gallery..." I was about to say that I have everything I want, but I can't bear to see the hurt in his eyes. And it isn't strictly true. "I have everything I want, for now."

"You can open an art gallery anywhere, Sienna. You can have a chain of galleries around the world."

He makes it sound achievable, and I wonder if there's anything that the Murrays' mafia money can't buy.

"Think about it, that's all I'm saying."

Kyle stands and offers me a hand to help me off the table.

He pulls me into his arms, and it would be so easy to say yes. To watch his face light up with joy. To know that he would protect me with his life and that I would never want for anything again.

But the past needs more than a shit load of dollars to wipe it clean.

"I'll think about it."

"Thank—"

Before he can finish, the buzzer sounds beneath my desk for the front door and makes us both jump. Kyle, my nakedness, the feel of his cock inside me, the fact that we just had sex on my desk, it all evaporates as reality kicks back in, dragging me back down to earth with a skull-shattering jolt.

"Fuck!"

I grab my panties from the floor and almost fall flat on my face as I step into them, adrenaline pumping through me. Kyle grips my arm to keep me standing, but I can't look at him.

"Are you expecting a late client?" He zips up his pants and buttons his shirt, and I don't know how his fingers are still cooperating with his brain.

My panties are already saturated with his cum, but there's no time to deal with it now. Not that I keep spare clean underwear at the gallery. I tug my pants up over my hips and drag my sweater over my head, wishing that I wore a lighter outfit to work, one that didn't set my skin on fire where Kyle's fingerprints linger.

"It isn't a client." My mouth is dry.

The bell rings again.

Fuck, fuck, fuck! I should have turned Kyle away while I had the chance.

I catch a glimpse of us in the mirror. Kyle is as immaculate as ever, his damp suit jacket almost dry, not a crease in sight as evidence of what we just did. And there I am beside him, rosy-cheeked, my hair looking like I just climbed off a vertical loop roller coaster in gale force winds.

I push my hair back and fasten it into a messy bun on top of my head. Then I lick my index fingers and try wiping away the dark smudges under my eyes where my mascara has leaked, probably while I was in the throes of the best orgasm of my life,

"You look beautiful, leoin." Kyle meets my gaze in the mirror.

"No one would ever know that my cock was just inside your beautiful pussy."

He comes closer, and I can smell me on him. Or can I smell it on me? I clamp my hands over my mouth and exhale into them, checking out my breath. It'll have to do.

My stomach twists as I switch the office lights off and walk through the gallery. Maybe I should've warned Kyle that I was expecting Nick, but it's too late now. His beige cashmere coat is visible through the window, and as we approach the entrance, his smile fades when he spots Kyle.

Deep breath. I unlock the door.

I only agreed to the date because Nick refused to take no for an answer. But right now, sitting opposite him in a swanky restaurant, feigning interest in his conversation while my body is still tingling from Kyle's touch, is the last thing I want to do.

"Hello, Nick." I can feel the tension emanating from Kyle. "You met Kyle at the launch party."

I have a vague recollection of Nick whisking me away from Kyle when he arrived and somehow manipulating my movements so that our paths didn't cross again, but I tuck it away for later.

"Kyle Murray."

Nick doesn't shake Kyle's extended hand, he doesn't smile in greeting, or exchange any of the pleasantries associated with making new acquaintances. Instead, before I can diffuse the obvious hostility between the two men with a flippant comment, he says, "I had a feeling we'd meet again, although I didn't expect it would be so soon."

His tone is cold, a million miles away from the soothing cadence of the voice he has perfected for anxious patients.

"Kyle popped in to see how I'm getting on," I say.

"I'm surprised he didn't just do some digging or get one of his cronies to check up on you. That's what guys like you do, isn't it?"

My gaze flits between the two men. I've no idea what he means, but the chill in his voice has just obliterated the contentment I felt in Kyle's passionate embrace a short while ago.

"What are you talking about?" I ask.

Nick arches a well-groomed eyebrow. "Your friend here has been making inquiries about me. Perhaps you should've warned him that you don't need his permission, or anyone else's for that matter, to date other men."

4

KYLE

Date? Is Sienna dating Nick Morris?

It feels as if the revelation has wrapped cotton candy around my brain and sealed it inside a polythene bag.

Why didn't she say anything?

I gave her the opportunity to let me go. I said that I would walk away, and she'd never hear from me again. Was it too much pressure, or did she want me as badly, as desperately, as whole-fucking-heartedly as I want her?

"Kyle?" Sienna's voice slices through the spun sugar in my head and lodges in my throat. "What's he talking about?"

"It sounds worse than it is." Jesus fucking Christ, and I sound like a kid who just smashed the flatscreen TV and is trying to kid his parents that they can still watch *The Simpsons*. "We didn't get introduced, and I was curious. I'd do the same with any new acquaintance."

"How many other background checks did you carry out after the gallery opening?" The eyebrow is still quirked at an awkward angle, and I wonder if he has a resume of poses that he refers to for various occasions.

"The other guests were considerate enough to introduce themselves. But you…"

I sense Sienna flinching beside me. But this guy's moral compass is all over the place, and I refuse to sit back and let him cozy up to her over a steak meal and fine wine, when I haven't yet figured out his motive. Had he been rude and dismissive to every other guest at the gallery, I'd be more inclined to let it go, but he singled me out as the threat to his alpha status, and I want to know why.

"…You were trying to control the board without first meeting your opponent."

Nick's smile is smug, one corner of his mouth raised, while his eyelids are hooded, hiding what lays behind them. Sienna is listening, open-mouthed. I know that this will require some explanation later, but if I can sow the seeds of mistrust where Mr. Morris is concerned, it will be worth it.

"Opponent in what exactly?" he asks.

"Whatever game you're playing."

"Okay." Sienna stands between us, palms facing outward like she's the referee at a boxing match. "Will someone please tell me what the fuck is going on here?"

Her eyes have darkened, the flush on her cheeks has vanished, and I have to accept some responsibility for that.

"Sienna, I didn't get a chance to speak to you at the opening party."

"So," Nick steps in, "you thought you'd do some snooping, make sure I file my tax returns on time and check that I wasn't kicked out of college for inappropriate behavior towards my science professor."

"Kyle?" Sienna blinks slowly as if she can feel a migraine coming on. "Is this true?"

"I ran some checks. For my own peace of mind."

Nick squares his shoulders. He's not about to confess that this is still a power struggle between two men who desire the same woman, but his body language says otherwise. If we were peacocks, he'd be parading his feathers right about now to prove that he's the cool kid on the block.

"Why don't you tell her what you found?"

If it wasn't for Sienna, I'd wrap my fist around his throat and squeeze that smarmy neck until he turned blue in the face, but after what occurred between us earlier tonight, I won't risk losing her all over again. Especially not for this arrogant asshole.

"Why don't you explain how you know all this?" Because I'd like to know how a cosmetic surgeon knows who has been keeping tabs on him.

"Seriously?" Both eyebrows are lifted now. *Questioning pose number two.* "That's what you're going with: tit-for-tat?"

"No."

I ignore Sienna's pleading eyes and step closer. In this instance, I have to accept that what I'm about to say won't win me any points with the woman I love, but it will give me a sense of satisfaction.

"I'm going with this." I keep my voice low and steady. "If I find out that you've ever so much as raised your voice to Sienna or touched a hair on her head, you'll regret it."

I turn to Sienna, snatching away his opportunity to retaliate. If there's one thing I learned from my brothers, it's that you always make sure you have the last word, even if that word is spoken on your dying breath.

"Remember what I said, Sienna. I meant every word."

Her crushed expression melts my heart but touching her now in front of this asshole will be like claiming a prize, and Sienna isn't an object to be paraded around by the winner. I have no intention of *winning* her. She'll come to me of her own free will or not at all.

And I'll live with it either way.

I walk away.

My car is waiting for me at the corner of the block. I climb into the back seat and slide my phone out of my pocket as Seamus, my driver, puts the car into gear and pulls into the road. The fuzziness in my head has cleared with my renewed determination to do whatever it takes to protect Sienna.

I can't think about him touching her. If I allow the images into my head, I'll stop the car, sprint back to the gallery, and give the guy a reason to prosecute me, and I can't look out for Sienna from a prison cell.

Instead, I call Terry and ask him to put a guy on their tail. Discreetly. If Sienna realizes that they're being followed, she'll know who's behind it, and I can kiss goodbye to her considering my proposal to leave the city and make a life elsewhere.

Together.

But the guy is like toxic gas that has seeped into my nervous system and gotten me rattled. Terry asked how I'd feel if this wasn't about Sienna. But it's irrelevant. This *is* about Sienna, and Nick Morris sets my back teeth on edge—something about him just doesn't sit right with me, and I will find out what it is.

It's late. I haven't eaten. But I can't face going back to the Wraith.

I could go to Cash and Bash. But I already know how they'd deal with the situation, and my chances of ever having Sienna in my life will shatter to smithereens when she finds out that her cosmetic surgeon has suddenly vanished.

Peering out the window at the city lights, I realize that we're almost at the Dragon's Den, the nightclub and casino owned by Mateo Dragonetti, leader of the oldest Sicilian mafia family in New York. There was a time when the name alone would've raised the hair on the back of my neck and inspired me to seek an alternative route. But after his daughter kidnapped Sienna and Victoria's brother Mason, the mafia leader agreed to the alliance our family had been looking to arrange for years.

I ask Seamus to stop outside the Dragon's Den.

Renovations were recently completed on the aging building, and it gleams like polished glass when I walk inside. The concierge waves me through to Don Mateo's private room above the casino, and I find him seated at a table overlooking the main floor below, a glass of Cognac in front of him.

He gestures for the bartender to fix me a drink as I take a seat opposite him. "How was the trip?" he asks.

"Much needed."

He studies me coolly. "And I should imagine it already feels like a distant memory."

He sips his drink and sighs as the liquid goes down. He's still a good-looking guy. Craggier than he would've been in his youth, but his white hair is still thick, and his eyes have retained their blue despite the bloodshed he must've witnessed in his time. Even so, his daughter's selfish antics have aged him prematurely, and I wonder how much blame he has shouldered himself for raising her to be so self-absorbed and so utterly devoid of compassion.

The bartender returns with an ice-cold beer for me, condensation dripping down the outside of the glass.

I sip the liquid; the bubbles do nothing to relieve the niggling questions buzzing around inside my head. "Six years ago," I begin, "I met a girl."

The old man sets his glass down and sits back in his seat. "I'm listening."

I tell him about the accident, and the part my brothers played in rescuing me from the situation, and he remains silent.

"The girl I met that night is Sienna Walker, Victoria's best friend."

I've no idea how much, if anything, he knows about Sienna, but I know that he and Victoria have become close while she helped design the new Dragon's Den.

"For five years she believed that I left her for dead. I don't expect her to unpack those emotions and fold them in my favor overnight of course."

"She's the reason you went away." It's a statement not a question.

"She is. But my feelings haven't changed."

He spreads his hands wide. "Did you expect them to?"

I smile. "No, I went away to give myself some breathing space."

Mateo nods. "And now that you are back?"

"There's another guy on the scene."

I don't know where Nick fits into her life given that I had my cock inside her a couple of hours ago, but this is the simplified version for Mateo's benefit.

"Is it serious?"

"Not from what I've seen so far."

He drains his glass and waits patiently for me to continue. If his daughter had an ounce of her father's composure and dignity, things might've turned out very differently for our families. Caleb might've married her when they were younger and secured the alliance that would've set us all on different paths.

What ifs and maybes.

"My gut is telling me not to trust this guy," I say.

"Your gut or your heart?"

"Both?" I shrug. "He's clean. There's not even so much as a parking ticket against his name."

"Too clean." The bartender brings Mateo another drink and swaps the new glass for the empty one in one fluid movement. "What were you hoping to find?"

"A motive for dating her now, when he has been her surgeon since the accident."

The old man rubs a hand across his jawline. "You think this has something to do with you?"

"I'm almost certain of it."

"My motto is: if you're looking for dirt, you will find it."

I raise my glass to toast him. The motto's meaning isn't lost on me; if you're looking for dirt, why not spread some of your own. But going down that route defeats the object and will only prove to Sienna that I am the person she thinks I am, a mafia lawyer who can bend the law to his own advantage.

"No can do. I'm missing something. No one is that impeccable."

He smiles. "You're looking in the wrong place."

"Where should I be looking?"

"If you want to know what the branches are doing, you must first look at the roots."

"His family?" Because with the analogy comes the realization that there was no mention of Nick Morris's family in any of the information that I uncovered.

"You're looking for a motive." Mateo swallows a mouthful of cognac and studies the glass as if gauging how long it will take him to finish his drink. "I trust your instincts. When it comes to affairs of the heart, there is no greater muscle than your gut. So, to understand how someone works, you must first find out where they came from."

"Back to his roots," I mutter to myself.

"We are all shaped by the paths our ancestors trod before us. Sure, we find our own way. We meet our own crossroads and choose our own directions. But your choices will be different to mine. His will be different to yours." He shrugs. "You get the picture. Find his baby photos and you will almost certainly find his motivation."

I finish my beer with the don and thank him for his advice.

"I am honored that you came to an old man such as me for advice," he says, and I can see the sadness in the fine red lines crisscrossing the whites of his eyes.

I head straight to my office when I get back to the Wraith, remove my jacket, and sit at my desk.

I spend a huge proportion of my time sitting at my desk, staring at the same computer screen in front of me now. But there's a sense of serenity to be found in the evenings when the world outside the window is a myriad of blurred lights fighting for their place against the darkness and the rain. Is it the knowledge that the city is slowing down and preparing for slumber? Or is there comfort to be found in normality and solitude?

Powering up the computer, I resume my search for Nick Morris.

I didn't go any further back than high school the first time around. Now, I take my time, focus on the information on the screen instead of on him and Sienna gazing at each other above a flickering candle in a strategically lit restaurant.

I check the records of the middle schools that feed into the John F. Kennedy high school that Nick Morris attended. His name is there, Nicholas Morris, date of birth: 27 September 1983. Nothing extraordinary to be found.

But when I check out the kindergartens in the same area of the Bronx, I draw a blank.

Plenty of kids with the name Nicholas, but none with the surname Morris. I cross-reference the other children called Nicholas with the names of kids who attended high school in the Bronx, and they all check out. Which means that Nick Morris either didn't attend kindergarten or his family relocated to the area in time for him to join middle school.

I fill the coffee machine and switch it on.

Time to go back even further.

The first mouthful of coffee is so hot it burns the roof of my mouth, but it helps me to focus. I have a feeling it's going to be a long night.

I go back to the relevant high school records. From there, I take Nick Morris's date of birth and, using a fake police identity, research New York state institutions for a birth certificate. As I suspected, he wasn't born in New York State.

Systematically working my way through the states of America in alphabetical order, I reach the final one with no success. No record anywhere of Nicholas Morris born on 27 September 1983.

He was adopted. Or his name was legally changed before he started middle school.

I refill my cup with steaming black liquid; the coffee has barely hit my system yet, and I'm operating on adrenaline alone.

If you want to know what the branches are doing, you must first look at the roots.

Mateo Dragonetti may have been closer to the mark than he realized with his philosophical comment.

Accessing adoption records is more cumbersome, for obvious reasons, but if there's one thing that I've learned from the casino's resident IT programmer, it's that nothing is impossible. No system is infallible. You simply need to find another way in, by thinking like a cypherpunk, by thinking like someone who understands how to protect information.

I lose track of time. The jug in the coffee machine empties, and I refill it with bottled water. My mouth is dry. My palms are sweaty. The muscles in the back of my neck are burning from sitting in one position for too long, but I've come too far to give up now.

When I finally find a way into the system I need, I fist-pump the air.

The sky outside the windows is still black, but swathes of violet and mauve are bleeding upwards from the horizon. My eyes are gritty with tiredness. And I still have a long way to go.

I pace my office to get the blood circulating through my limbs.

Then, rolling up my sleeves, I resume my seat, and start scrolling through every adoption record for the relevant date.

I'm so close. I sense it in the heavy rhythm of my heartbeat.

I told Mateo Dragonetti that I was hoping to find a motive. Evidence that Nick Morris isn't just a cosmetic surgeon attracted to a patient. Proof that dating Sienna Walker will benefit him in some way aside from the obvious.

Nothing could've prepared me for what I eventually discover as the city is waking up and the streets fill with noise.

Nick Morris entered the care system in Chicago when he was eleven months old. He was discovered in a rundown apartment when a neighbor alerted the police department to the baby that had been screaming for hours. According to his records, his mom's body was found on the bed beside the baby's crib—she had been beaten to death.

The temperature in my office feels as though it has dropped a couple of degrees, and I rub my hands together to keep them warm.

I open an image of the birth certificate. Nick Morris was given his mother's maiden name at birth: Scanlan. The line reserved for the father's name is blank.

My gut clenches. I could leave it here. Nick Morris had the kind of start in life that reads like something from a horror movie, potentially witnessing his mom being brutally murdered while he screamed from inside his crib. His recollection may have been buried beneath the vivid autobiographical memories that children start to form as they grow older, but that bloody scene will have scarred his psyche for life.

The panic trying to beat its way out of my chest goes way deeper than Nick Morris's trauma though. This hits too close to home. Chicago. His mom bludgeoned to death. The child abandoned.

Ignoring the message from Lauren, the PA that I share with Caleb, letting me know that she's in the office, I search for the court records regarding the case.

This time, I know what I'm going to find. It doesn't stop the bile from rising in my throat when I read the name of the prime suspect in the murder investigation.

Caelan O'Reilly.

The police launched a nationwide investigation to find Sally Scanlan's killer, with no success. They followed leads that had them scurrying like insects from Canada to Mexico. While

Caelan O'Reilly, having changed his name to Caelan Murray, was worming his way into the life of a young woman named Moira. A young woman he would almost kill seven years later. An attempted homicide for which he is currently serving a life sentence.

My brothers and I share the same biological father as Nick Morris.

Coincidence?

The voice inside my head is shrieking at me that there's no such thing as coincidence.

Nick Morris is here for a reason. Now I need to figure out exactly how Sienna fits into the puzzle.

5

SIENNA

Shortly after I arrive at the gallery the following morning, I receive a delivery of flowers. A hundred white roses. The card reads simply: *Kyle*.

I take them through to the office, place them on my desk, and sit back in my seat. The fragrance fills the room, and I find myself turning the card round and around between my fingers. They're beautiful. Pure and innocent and delicate.

But I wish he hadn't sent them.

I don't want flowers. I cover my face with my hands and press my palms into my eyes making them burst with firework displays of color.

I don't know what I want but sending me flowers isn't going to change anything or help me to make up my mind.

Is he trying to buy me? I mean, isn't that what people like the Murrays do, buy whatever they want, including people? Do they ever stop to consider that there are people out there who want different things? People who maybe don't want to live in a glass tower and eat Michelin-starred food every night and get photographed by the paparazzi every time they step foot on the sidewalk?

"Ugh!" I groan out loud and then catch my reflection in the mirror.

The glow I felt when Kyle was here yesterday has vanished, and with what happened after, I can't even rekindle it with vivid memories of his face buried in my pussy. Because whenever I think of Kyle, a warning sign flashes in my head: *He was investigating Nick's background.*

Why? If he'd discovered anything incriminating, he'd have told me, wouldn't he? Or he'd have threatened Nick to keep his distance. So now, I can't help wondering if he somehow knew that I was going on a date with Nick and came here to distract me.

My face floods with heat. Was yesterday just a game to him? Making the first move before Nick arrived. Filling my pussy with his cum and my head with promises to take me anywhere in the world I want to go.

I move the roses onto the floor. I can't think straight with them winking at me in the glare of the overhead light. Then I take my tablet out of the drawer and power it up.

Into the search engine, I type the name Nicholas Morris. I've seen the framed certificates on the walls of Nick's clinic, highlighting his qualifications, the years of studying that preceded his current position. *Trust me.* That's what those certificates say to his clients. *Your life is safe in my hands.*

So, why did I feel so uneasy while I was with him yesterday evening?

Sure, the conversation flowed. Okay, so it was mostly about Nick, but there were no awkward silences bringing the date to a standstill. He spoke about his collection of handmade Venetian mirrors (from Venice), his favorite vacation (skiing in Vermont), his golf handicap (twelve). And I listened.

If I'm honest, I was grateful not to have to talk about myself. My thoughts were still spinning after the altercation between him and Kyle, so it wasn't Nick's unwavering ego and relentlessly charming smile that grated on my nerves. Kyle sowed the seeds of mistrust, and I bought it without questioning why.

"What am I doing?" I tilt my head backwards, close my eyes, and inhale deeply.

Turning back to the tablet, I wiggle my fingers above the keyboard. I know what I'm doing. I'm not lowering myself to Kyle's level, I'm giving Nick the benefit of the doubt. At least that's what I tell myself, when I ignore his professional website and dig deeper.

Thirty minutes later, I slide my tablet away from me and sit back in my seat.

Of course I didn't find anything. What did I expect? To find his name on an old-fashioned wanted poster with a sketched caricature of his gleaming teeth and aquiline nose? WANTED, NICK MORRIS, SERIAL SMILER.

If it wasn't for Kyle, I would never have even checked him out. I allowed Kyle's jealousy to infect a perfectly acceptable surgeon-patient relationship, when I should've just let his comments wash over me.

Kyle is the first person to touch me since the accident. I've never even come close to wanting anyone else, but all he had to do was look at me, whisper *"Leoin"* in my ear, and there I was opening my legs and pulling him inside me like my entire future depended on it. I let him in. I dropped my guard and played right into his hands where Nick is concerned.

So, why do I still feel like I'm missing something important?

I replay snippets of last night's date in my head. Nick was a perfect gentleman. He held the door open for me, he pulled the seat out at the table and tucked it under me, he didn't expect me to pay half the bill. He didn't even pressure me for a kiss when he dropped me off outside my apartment.

I reflexively flinch when I get to the part where Nick tried to kiss me.

The car engine was still running. He unfastened his seatbelt, checked out his teeth in the rearview, and then leaned closer. "I've enjoyed tonight, Sienna." His voice was suitably low, the perfect pitch for following up with a goodnight kiss.

"Me too," I said. It wasn't a complete lie; it simply wasn't the whole truth.

His face moved closer. I saw the faint shadow of stubble on his upper lip and jawline, pale freckles across his nose and the tops of his cheeks that were not visible from a distance, smelled his cologne and coffee on his breath. It made me feel nauseous.

I turned away from him, opened the passenger door and tried to climb out without unbuckling the safety belt. It pulled tight across my chest, the edge of the strap slicing into my neck, and my hand brushed his as we both tried to free me at the same time.

"We should do this again," he said, moving back into his seat. If he realized how desperate I was to get away from him, he covered it well.

"Yes." I was already on the sidewalk, my apartment building looming behind me. I leaned into the car, forced a smile, acted like I didn't almost strangle myself on the passenger seat belt. "Thank you."

In the safety of my apartment, I guzzled a glass of cold water from the tap and waited for it to cleanse me of the experience.

It didn't.

I leaned against the counter breathing heavily and tried to regulate my pulse. He has the classic looks and charm of a Hollywood movie star from the 50s. Dark hair, high cheekbones, smoldering eyes. So, why, in the heat of the moment, had I found him so repulsive?

As if sensing where my thoughts are wandering right now, my phone vibrates with a message. I slide it out of my pocket and unlock it.

Kyle. *Can we talk? It's important.*

Not even an apology for the way he behaved with Nick.

I wish they would both leave me alone. It's obvious that I'm not attracted to Nick in the same way that he is attracted to me. It's equally obvious that I can't be trusted to be alone in a room with Kyle without wanting to rip his clothes off and fuck him on every available surface.

Which is why I'm better off single.

I message Kyle back: *I don't think that's a good idea.*

I massage my temples. I want to lock myself in my studio, drag an acrylic-splattered shirt over my clothes, and paint until nightfall. Creating art clears my head. Twenty-four hours of me and my canvas, and I might be able to see things a little more clearly.

My phone vibrates a second time.

I open the message, expecting to see Kyle's name, and realize, too late, that it's from an unknown number.

Sienna, it's Dad. I'm back in NYC and would really like to meet up.

I stand outside the Rinse, hands shoved inside my coat pockets, and peer at my reflection in the window. The glass is tinted a smoky brown, making me look like some kind of dirty ghost, the outline of my face distorted and hazy.

I shouldn't be here.

I don't want to be here.

So, why am I still standing on the busy sidewalk, avoiding the staring gazes of passers-by, unable to make the decision to turn around and walk away?

My father left us the day after my sixth birthday.

I remember how he walked into the kitchen, saw the remains of the chocolate cake Mom made for me, six used candles still lying on the side of the plate, and turned his face into a rubbery mask of pure hatred. I didn't even see it happen. One moment, my mom was sitting next to me at the small table where we ate dinner, and the next, she was on the floor, eyes bulging, face turning puce while his fists tightened around her neck.

I can still hear the screams now. *My screams.*

Maybe that's why he let my mom go and walked out. Or maybe he was scared that if he stayed any longer, the cops would come for him, and he would have to take his punishment like a man.

That was the last time I saw him. His face stopped appearing in my nightmares a long time ago, and I'm not even sure I'd recognize him if he was standing right beside me. I don't even know how he found my number, but I guess he heard about my gallery, and his curiosity was piqued. Perhaps he thinks that I've come into some money, and I'll be generous enough to share it with him.

I turn around and walk a few steps away from the Rinse, head down, hands balled into fists inside my pockets.

My mom never spoke about money; she didn't need to; it was obvious she struggled her whole life to keep us going. She never mentioned my dad at all once he was out of our lives. But it doesn't take much to figure out that he's the kind of man who would accept handouts from his own daughter.

I'm torn.

I don't want, or need, him in my life, but if I don't give him the benefit of the doubt just this once, it will always haunt me. Be the bigger person, that's what my mom would say if she was here.

Deep breath.

I turn around, open the door, and step inside.

I've never been inside the Rinse before—I know it's owned by Kyle's brother Bash—but my dad had already booked a table. I walk through the lobby wide-eyed at the Hollywood-style glamor, the huge gilt-edged mirrors, the spanking clean black-and-white tiled floor, the sleek gold reception desk.

I'm struck once again by how different Kyle's life is to mine. This is normal for him. He wakes up every morning in the sheer black-glass monument that is the Wraith, makes coffee, takes a shower, and never once thinks that someone in the city is staring at his home, gap-mouthed at the unimaginable opulence of a lifestyle like his.

My dad is waiting at a table in the Rinse's glitzy restaurant when the concierge asks me to follow him.

My stomach lurches sickeningly when I see him. I thought I wouldn't recognize him after twenty years. I was wrong.

He raises brown eyes to meet mine, and my body reacts from muscle memory. My pulse races. Heat spreads through my body and sets my cheeks on fire. My legs tremble so violently, I almost collapse onto the seat pulled out for me by the concierge.

"You came."

His shoulders are round and hunched, his neck jutting out at a ninety-degree angle like the retro nodding dogs people used to put on the parcel shelf of their car years ago. He hasn't aged well. His skin is slack and pasty, his bottom lip juts out, and there are deep creases across his forehead and around his mouth. My gaze drifts to his hands which are folded in front of him, and I swallow bile at the sight of his long uneven fingernails.

He looks like a man who has abused his body all his life. But my body is refusing to listen to my brain. I'm still the little girl who hid in her room whenever he came home drunk and cried herself to sleep with a pillow over her head to drown out the sounds of her mom's screams.

The server comes to the table to take my drink order, and I ask for water.

"How have you been?" my dad asks when the server has walked away.

Um, I've been alone since Mom died. Struggling to make enough money to pay the rent. Or how about undergoing more surgeries than I can remember, to repair the burns I suffered in a car accident one fateful New Year's Eve.

"Fine." I can't meet his eyes.

"Sweetheart."

Fucking sweetheart?

Anger starts to creep in, slowly replacing the anxiety triggered by his reappearance.

He isn't here to apologize; he is probably unaware that he has anything to apologize for. He's here because he thinks that popping up uninvited into my inbox and calling me sweetheart will erase the years he's been missing and give him a fresh start. I don't for one second believe that this has anything to do with me, unless he wants a piece of my gallery.

Well, I'd like to see him fucking try.

"What do you want?" I ask.

We're not the only people in the restaurant this lunchtime, but it feels as if I'm trapped inside a bubble with him, one that I need to pop as quickly as possible so that I can escape before he seals it.

He swallows a mouthful of his drink. Is it whiskey? Dutch courage. Not that men like my father need it—they're bullies, and bullies only ever pick on people who are weaker than they are.

"I wanted to see you. I know I've not been a part of your life, and I don't expect to waltz back in and pick up where we left off."

Thank fuck for that.

"But, well..." Tears well in his eyes. "...I've realized what I've been missing. I know I can't turn back the clock, but it isn't too late to put things right. Is it?"

The server returns with my glass of water, eyes up the untouched menu, and backs off again.

I raise my eyes; I need to see this. "How?"

The frown lines across his forehead deepen, his eyebrows lower. He looks genuinely perplexed, as if he expected to say, "Surprise! I'm back!" and receive my undying gratitude while we do some sightseeing and catch up on old times.

"How will you put things right?" I repeat.

"I thought we could spend some time together, you know. Get to know one another." His voice is infuriatingly calm, placating, like he's talking to a six-year-old who doesn't understand what they've done wrong. My shoulders bunch up tighter with every word. "I've missed you, sweetheart."

"Hell, no!" The words are out in the open before I can stop myself, and I hear the chair legs scraping the floor as I stand up. "You don't get to say that. You don't get to sit there and call me sweetheart, and you certainly don't get to tell me that you've missed me."

"Sienna, I..." He shakes his head; his bottom lip is still rolled out like a petulant child. "I know I fucked up."

"You don't say!" My chest is heaving. I know the people sitting at the other tables are probably gaping at us, but I'm past caring about what anyone else thinks. "You didn't at any point over the last twenty years wonder how I was? Didn't it occur to you to pick up the phone and call me? Or maybe apologize to Mom for what you did to her?"

He nods and sniffs loudly, twisting his nose from side to side. "I know I should've, Sienna. You can't tell me anything I haven't already figured out for myself. I was a selfish asshole. I'll hold my hands up to that." He shows me his palms to prove the point. "I wanted to see you. I don't expect you to believe me, but I did. I just ... didn't think your mom would allow me back into your life."

His voice is clogged with emotion, but something inside me, the tiny piece of my heart that was probably afraid to let go of my father, solidifies. I feel it resting deep inside me like a pebble on the riverbed.

"You still can't do it, can you? You still can't accept responsibility for your actions and say sorry."

"I..." Brown eyes blink back at me. "Sit down, sweetheart. Please?"

I sit heavily in my seat. Not because it's what he wants but because the adrenaline pumping through my veins is making me feel lightheaded, and I refuse to let him see how his presence is affecting me. I will not give him that.

I swallow a mouthful of water and instantly feel it trying to eject itself from my trembling body. "I'm listening."

"Despite what you think of me, there hasn't been a day go past that I haven't thought about you."

I suck in a deep breath and hold it in my lungs. I'm starting to see a pattern here: everything that comes out of his mouth is about him. Not me or Mom. Just him.

"I was a fucking idiot. I had everything I ever wanted, and I let it slip through my fingers. I was too self-absorbed to realize what I had until it was gone."

That old cliché.

"I was young, Sienna. Too young to be a father, I know that now."

"Is that your apology?"

His lips twitch into a half-smile. "I'm sorry. There, I've said it. I'm sorry. I regret what I did, but I'm not the same person I was then."

"You'll have to forgive me if I don't take your word for it." I watch him sip his whiskey, and wish I'd ordered alcohol too.

"I know."

It's still there, the condescending tone. I'm the grown-up, and you're the child. I'm right, you're wrong. I'm clever, you're stupid. Like a scene from *Matilda*.

"You know Mom's gone, right?" I ask.

His eyes grow large with fresh tears. He's good. He knows how to switch it on for the desired effect, but it feels like this is all for show. There's nothing underneath the surface.

"I heard."

"Why didn't you look for me then?"

"I thought it would all be too raw. I thought... I thought you'd blame me."

"You're right. I did blame you."

He smiles. "At least you're being honest."

That makes one of us.

"But you said you *did* blame me. Past tense. I'll take that as a win."

I want to get up, walk out, and never look back, but I have one more burning question. "Why now? You didn't try to find me when Mom died, so why are you back now?"

"I heard about your art gallery." He strokes the side of his almost empty whiskey glass. "I'm proud of you, Sienna. But it made me realize that you are your own person now. I thought that if you at least heard me out, you'd make up your own mind about me, and then perhaps we could move forward."

Predictable. I guessed it was the gallery that had drawn him out of the woodwork.

"You still haven't said how you want to put things right."

"It'll take time, sweetheart, I know that. Just, please, give me a chance. That's all I'm asking."

I swallow. "Are we done here?" I can't sit across the table from him and eat lunch. He'll instinctively believe that he has won.

"Is that a yes?"

"I'll think about it."

He drains the rest of his drink in one mouthful and raises the glass to me in a toast. "That's all I wanted to know, that you'll give me a chance."

Before I can reiterate that I only said I'd think about it, a man approaches the table. My father's face smooths into an expression of pleasant greeting, and I turn around expecting to find the server waiting to take our order.

"Kyle?" I can't hide the surprise from my voice.

No point asking him what he's doing here; the Rinse belongs in the family.

"Everything okay here?" His gaze takes in the empty whiskey glass, my barely touched water, and the lack of food.

My heart is racing. Nick. My father. Kyle. I feel like they're all closing in on me.

I grab my purse. "I was just—"

"Everything's great," my father interjects. He extends his hand for Kyle to shake. "Hooch. I'm Sienna's father."

I don't know if it's sheer bravado or if he simply has no conscience because he introduces himself as if he and I have been meeting for lunch every week for the past twenty years.

Kyle's eyelids flicker between me and my father, but his expression remains neutral. The professional demeanor automatically kicks in. "Pleased to meet you. I'm Kyle. Kyle Murray. My brother owns the Rinse."

This information doesn't register in my father's eyes. "So, how do you know my daughter?"

I balk at his use of the word daughter. Has he still not learned that his name on my birth certificate doesn't make him my dad? He relinquished that title long ago, long before he even walked out on me and my mom.

"Sienna's best friend is my sister-in-law."

Maybe Kyle has sensed the tension between us as the response is instantaneous and noncommittal. He's giving nothing away.

"You're almost family then." The crocodile tears are gone, and the smile firmly fixed in place is all for Kyle. "It's great to see my baby girl surrounded by people who'll look out for her."

My flesh crawls all over the baby-girl endearment. What the actual fuck!

It's a step too far, and I stand up, grateful when Kyle steps aside for me to leave.

"I'll call you, Sienna," my father says as I walk away.

I want to yell at him not to bother, to stay the fuck away from me, but Kyle is right behind me, and I just need to hold it together until I'm outside.

"Sienna?" Kyle's voice is gentle as he reaches for my hand in the lobby of the Rinse, and that's when the tears start spilling.

6

KYLE

I don't even think about the consequences. Sienna is upset, and I can't leave her like this, so I call Seamus, usher her into the back seat of my car, and take her back to my apartment.

She rests her head on my shoulder, and I give her a handkerchief to wipe her eyes, grateful to my mom for making sure all her sons carry freshly laundered handkerchiefs in their suit pockets.

The ride is silent as I give her time to calm down.

When the car pulls into the basement lot of the Wraith, I ease Sienna away from me just enough to open the door and climb out with her. The dim yellow lighting must penetrate whatever is going on inside her head because she peers around, fat teardrops clinging to her eyelashes. I quell the urge to catch one on my fingertip.

"Wh-where are we?" she stammers.

"The Wraith." I guide her into the private elevator. "No pressure, Sienna. I thought you could use some breathing space."

"What gave it away?" She tries to laugh, and the sound is muffled by the sobs still loitering under the surface.

In the elevator, she tries to mop up her tears, sniffing occasionally. We don't speak.

When we reach my apartment, I settle her on the sofa and fix her a brandy, neat, in a crystal tumbler. "Drink this. It'll make you feel better."

Sienna doesn't hesitate. She takes the drink, swallows it in one mouthful, and then splutters into the handkerchief as it goes down, producing more tears.

"I needed that," she says finally.

I go to the liquor cabinet and fix two more drinks, both with a splash of soda. Removing my suit jacket, I sit opposite her, keeping my distance. She sips her second drink with caution.

This isn't how I anticipated this conversation going. I wanted to warn her about Nick. I have nothing concrete to prove that his intentions towards her are anything other than a guy wanting to date a beautiful woman, but I can't sit back and say nothing. I'll never forgive myself if my suspicions are correct and he hurts her.

The mere thought of him laying a finger on her makes my jaw clench.

But now is not the time.

"Do you want to talk about it?"

She raises puffy eyes to me. "Not really. I should never have met him."

I sip my brandy and soda. I never touch liquor during the day—I don't have the liver for it like my brothers and my mom—but if I don't dampen the sharp edges of this overwhelming need to protect Sienna, I'll end up doing something I regret.

"Why did you?"

She puffs up her cheeks and releases a shaky breath. "I was trying to be the bigger person. Ha!" She shakes her head. "I didn't want to spend the rest of my life wondering what he wanted to say."

I sit forward on the sofa and rest my elbows on my thighs. I don't know much about Sienna's life—I've only gleaned snippets of information from Victoria—but I can imagine how the conversation went. She wanted an apology, and he would have skirted around a sorry, blaming everyone else for his mistakes until she forgot the reason why she was even there.

"And all he did was leave you with the sour taste of disappointment in your mouth."

"So fucking disappointed." She tips her head back and finishes her drink. "Can I get another one of these? They're not even touching the sides."

"Are you sure?" I stand up and take the empty glass from her. Our fingers brush, and electricity shoots down my spine.

Not now, I tell myself.

As if reading my mind, she quirks an eyebrow and smiles. "Don't worry, I won't accuse you of trying to get me drunk."

She slumps back against the cushions, kicks off her boots, and curls her legs under her.

I refill her glass with my back to her. When I look around, she's back on her feet and standing by the floor-to-ceiling windows, peering out across the city.

I stand beside her, and she accepts her drink with a grateful smile.

"Do you still see the skyline when you look out the window?" she asks.

I follow her gaze. The sky is heavy, ominously gray with the threat of snow. "Every day. I like it best when it's stormy outside. It gives me a sense of serenity. Like whatever is going on in my life is nothing compared to the howling wind and the torrential rain."

She turns to face me. "But do you ever feel like a prince in a gilded tower? Like you're untouchable, you know? Removed from the real world."

I smile and sip my drink. "Is that how you see me?"

"I guess. I mean, you never have to worry about paying the rent, do you? Or catching the bargains at the grocery store before they sell out. Or getting stuck in traffic on your way to work." Her eyes have softened; the brandy is taking effect.

"Sometimes, I think it would be easier to have those kinds of problems." She opens her mouth to protest, and I stop her. "I'm not looking for sympathy. But the higher you grow, the longer the fall on the way down."

"Unless you jump."

"I hope you mean figuratively speaking."

Sienna rests her forehead on the glass and studies the ground below. "I hope you're not scared of heights."

"I'm not, but it took some getting used to when I first moved in."

"Kyle, what are we doing?" She turns to face me, her eyes searching mine.

"We're taking some time out. That's all."

I know this isn't what she means. She wants to know what's going on between us, and my throbbing cock is asking the same question, but after the altercation with Nick, I'm determined to sit back and wait for her to come to me. If I push now, it'll send her running straight into his arms, and it'll make it even harder for me to protect her.

"Some time out?"

She moves closer. Her eyelashes are still wet, and her cheeks are flushed from the brandy, and I have to resist the urge to cup her face with both hands and press my lips against hers.

Closer. Her lips are almost brushing mine. I can smell the faint tang of brandy on her breath. Feel the heat emanating from her.

"Do you want to kiss me, Kyle?"

All or nothing.

"More than I've ever wanted to kiss anyone in my life." My voice is husky.

"What's stopping you?"

I set our glasses down on the floor at our feet. The instant my fingers entwine with her hair, my intentions to give her space fly out of the window and are swallowed up by the heavy gray clouds.

She parts her lips to let me in. She closes her eyes, tilts her head backwards, and melds her body to mine.

"Sienna," I murmur between kisses. "If you want me to stop, tell me now."

Our tongues meet. Her arms wrap around my neck, pulling me onto her as though any distance between us is too much. I'm not about to give her a second chance to push me away.

I pick her up, and her legs curl around my hips. I carry her to the sofa and set her down gently, one knee between her legs while I loosen my tie and unbutton my shirt.

Sienna's fingers are already fumbling with the zipper of my pants.

"No." I move her hand away. "Not yet."

"Are you always this bossy?" She slants her eyes at me, and I smother her mouth with a long, deep kiss.

"Always."

I pull away long enough to tug her sweater over her head. I slide my hands beneath her back, unfasten her bra and toss it onto the floor with the sweater. Then, I sit back on her legs, pinning her beneath me so that she can't move, and raise her arms behind her head so that I can study her body.

"*An-alainn.* So beautiful."

"Kyle..."

"Don't say a word."

Starting with her collarbones, I trace a pattern down her body with my fingertips, circling her breasts, her nipples, her ribs, and her belly button. Goosebumps pop on her arms, and her nipples grow erect.

"Hello." I lean forward and suck her left nipple, tugging on it until it swells. I move onto her right nipple, squeezing her breast with my hand.

When I raise my eyes, Sienna is watching me with a small smile.

"What do you want me to do, leoin?"

Her eyelids are heavy. "I want you to fuck me. I want you to turn me over and fuck me from behind, and then I want you to fuck me again."

I hold her gaze while I unzip her jeans. Underneath, she is wearing black lace panties that accentuate her pale skin. I climb off the sofa and pull off her jeans but leave her panties on. Still standing where I can see Sienna reclining on the sofa, naked apart from the black lace panties, I remove my shirt and pants.

My erection bulges inside my boxers, and Sienna's eyes drop and widen. She instinctively licks her lips. This will be the first time I'll have fucked her skin-on-skin, and my cock is aching to get started.

I drop my boxers, springing my cock free, and step out of them. Then, kneeling between Sienna's legs on the sofa, I rub the end of my cock around her pussy. She arches her back, pushing herself onto me.

"Do you want me, leoin?" I spread her legs and press my cock into her pussy through the black lace.

She gasps. "Yes."

"Show me."

Her eyes open wide. Without missing a beat, she hooks one leg over the back of the sofa, and pulls her other leg towards her chest, holding her knee and opening herself up for me.

"Good girl."

Gripping her inner thighs, I lower my face to her sex and suck her folds through the panties. "You're dripping, Sienna. Did you come without me?"

"No." She raises her head so that she can watch me. "This is what you do to me, Kyle."

Blood surges through my veins, engorging my cock some more. "Say that again."

"This is what you do to me, Kyle." Her voice has risen a notch.

"Do I make you wet?" I pull the panties aside and insert a finger.

"Yes."

I slide a second finger in, hooking them around her clit. "You can get wetter for me though, can't you?"

"I..." Her breathing is already growing shallow. "Yes."

"I can't hear you, leoin."

"Yes."

A third finger goes in. I can feel her juices dripping down my hand as I work her clit. "Nope. Louder. I want everyone in the fucking building to hear you."

"Yes, I can get wetter for you," she cries out.

I pull my fingers out and stick them in her mouth while I lick her sex. The combination of her sucking on my fingers, and my tongue inside her, forces pre-cum from my dick.

"Sienna." I stop licking and peer up at her from her pussy. "You are so fucking sexy. I could fuck you for the rest of my life…" I part her sex and push my tongue in as far as the hilt.

She stops sucking her taste from my fingers momentarily as my tongue finds the spot. Then she grips my hand and sucks them all the way in, gagging as her mouth fills, while her pussy clenches around me. I lick until her orgasm explodes into my mouth and dribbles down my chin, but I don't stop. She releases my wrist, but I leave my fingers in her mouth while her body writhes beneath me.

I lose track of time. All that exists is my tongue inside her, and her cum trickling down my throat.

But she told me what she wanted, and I'm not about to let her down.

Sitting back on my haunches, I flip her over, dragging her ass towards me. Her upper body is limp, her face squashed against the sofa cushion.

I slide my cock into her dripping wet sex and lean over her so that I can whisper in her ear. "Is this what you wanted, leoin?"

"Yes."

"You want me to fuck you from behind?" I ram my cock into her, my balls slapping against her pussy.

"Yes."

I pull out. "Not yet."

A low groan escapes her lips as I spread her butt cheeks wide and lick her. I want to taste every part of her. I drag my tongue from her pussy to her butt, until she pulls a tasseled cushion over her head.

Then I give her what she wants.

I fuck her from behind, gripping her hips tightly, and pulling her onto me. Then I flip her over, close her legs and fuck her again, her tight pussy sucking me in until I fill her with my cum.

After, I lay beside her on the sofa, tracing her nipples with my finger.

She turns her face to look at me. "Do you remember what you said to me before, Kyle? That this... This is all me, and you were only waking me up?"

I smile. "I remember."

"I never forgot it. I dreamed about it at night. You were there, with your hair in a quiff, and I always felt like I was the most beautiful woman in the world."

"You are."

She shakes her head and stares at the ceiling.

I tweak her nipple. "Hey. You promised you wouldn't go back there."

"My scars—"

"Your scars are part of you." I lean on one elbow and press butterfly kisses to the scars across her chest. "Even if the skin healed perfectly, they would still be part of you."

She faces me again and kisses me lightly on the lips. "Thank you."

"Oh no. Don't you dare thank me. Thanking me means that you don't believe me, and I'm not letting you go until I know that you do."

She chuckles. "I should go."

I lean over her, smoothing her hair away from her face. "Do you believe me?"

"Yes."

I wrinkle my nose. With her naked breasts pressing against my chest, my cock is already springing back to life. "I'm not convinced."

She sucks on her bottom lip. "You want me to convince you?"

"Aye. I'm not sure how though."

"I think I might know a way."

Pushing me off her, she sits up and strokes my erection. "Prepare to be convinced," she says before she goes down on me, her tongue pushing into the slit and her teeth nibbling the head.

It's one of those days that doesn't fully wake up before night crawls back in again.

It's almost evening before we pull our clothes on and stand in front of the window with our hands wrapped around mugs of steaming black coffee. Our distorted reflections peer back at us.

I don't want to let her go, but I know that I have no choice. No pressure. That's what I promised her and myself.

I still need to warn her about Nick, but that will be the quickest way to kill the moment and today has been too special to deflate it like a popped balloon before it's even over.

I remember that she didn't eat lunch with her father.

"We could get dinner," I suggest. "Anywhere you like. Room service if you're not ready to face the world yet."

She smiles, but I sense her pulling away from me. "I think I should just go home."

"I'll take you home."

"No, Kyle, I can walk."

I tug a lock of glossy red hair over her shoulder and wind it around my thumb. "Humor me, Sienna. What kind of man would I be if I made you walk home when there's a car sitting in my parking lot doing nothing?"

"You're not making me walk home. I enjoy it."

"Now I know you're lying."

"Kyle, I don't need a chaperone or a bodyguard or whatever. I'm a big girl now. I can—"

Her cell phone rings, cutting her off. She pulls it out of her pocket, checks the caller ID, and averts her eyes. "I should take this."

Walking away from the window, she keeps her back to me as she takes the call.

My hackles are up when I hear her say, "Hello, Nick."

The man chooses his moments. I'm starting to think he has his own people trailing me.

"Sorry," Sienna keeps her voice low and her head down. She still has her back to me; it's obvious that she'd rather be taking this call anywhere but in my apartment. "I met my father for lunch."

I try to imagine Nick's reaction. Has Sienna told him about her father? I can't bear the thought that the man knows more about her than I do, but I guess that's his professional style: get to know the patient so that they trust him with a scalpel.

"Twenty years."

Sienna's shoulders are already bunched up around her ears. An hour ago, she was relaxed in my arms while I fucked her. I fight the urge to snatch the phone out of her hand and hurl it out the window.

"No, it was completely out of the blue."

She freezes, and my pulse picks up speed.

"Do you think?" She glances at me then, catches my eye, and turns away.

Whatever Nick Morris is saying at the other end of the call, it concerns me, and I'm angry with myself for not telling her sooner what I know about him. Because if I tell her now, it will sound like I'm retaliating. Again.

I'm not playing Nick Morris at his own game.

I need to rewrite the rules, get one step ahead of him, and stay there.

7

SIENNA

There must be something unnatural in the water. Either that or the universe has decided it's time to throw some more curveballs my way. I can picture the stars huddled together up there, murmuring, *"Sienna Walker has had it too easy for a while. Let's liven things up a bit."*

After Nick's phone call yesterday evening, I didn't even finish my coffee. I had to get away from Kyle. I needed the time and the space and the oxygen to think.

He knew something was wrong. Maybe it was the way I couldn't meet his eyes, or how I grabbed my purse, coat, and boots, and finished dressing in the elevator as if we were running through an emergency fire drill. He still insisted on his driver taking me home, so I sat in the back of the car, my purse clutched to my chest like a lifebelt.

Outside my apartment building, I waited for the black car to merge back into the traffic before I started walking.

Head down. One foot in front of the other. Nick's words replaying inside my head like captions on a social media video.

Don't you think it's a coincidence that Kyle comes back from Ireland and then your father is on the scene again?

It would never have occurred to me. Maybe my brain doesn't think about things logically or laterally or whatever. I'm an artist, not a problem solver. I look for beauty not ugliness. But now I can't unsee it.

This morning, Central Park is decorated with a fine film of sparkling frost. I walk to work—I wasn't lying when I told Kyle that I like to walk—my breath forming delicate white clouds in front of my face. I let myself into the gallery and lock the door behind me. I don't have any appointments until this afternoon, so I'm going to drink coffee, eat croissants, and paint. On repeat.

I've barely shrugged my vintage Afghan coat over my shoulders when my phone vibrates inside my purse. I don't need to open it to know that it's from my father. He hasn't stopped messaging me since I walked out of the Rinse with Kyle yesterday.

The anticipation of picking up a paintbrush and transferring my emotions onto canvas seeps through my pores, leaving me feeling bone-weary and wooly-brained from lack of sleep. I read the messages. Plural.

I have a surprise for you, sweetheart.

I'll swing by the gallery later to tell you all about it.

I know this is hard for you. It's hard for me too. But I told you I've changed, and I'm determined to prove it to you.

He's fucking persistent, I'll give him that.

I know what he's doing. He's bombarding me with messages so that I can't forget about him. He'll wait an hour and message me again. Regular as clockwork. Allowing me no time between contact to resume normal life without him in it.

I don't respond.

I haven't replied to any of his messages, I haven't even added his number to my contact list, he's still sitting there in my inbox as UNKNOWN.

"Unknown, just the way I liked it," I mutter to myself.

But the thing that's niggling away at me, and the reason I need to spend the morning painting, is my father's non-reaction to Kyle's announcement that his brother owns the Rinse. Like he already knew this. Or another way to look at it is that he already knew who Kyle was.

I press my fingertips to my eyebrows as if I can push the brewing headache back inside my skull.

What reason would Kyle have to find my father and then reintroduce him into my life? None. Victoria would've told him that we're estranged and that I had no desire to reach out to him. But I can't ignore the timing.

Or can I?

My father will get bored when he realizes that I'm not interested in putting things right or getting to know him. He'll only put in so much effort with zero return, and then, if the universe is listening to me, he'll crawl back inside his rathole and forget all about me.

Yes. Boredom is the best I can hope for.

Or death. Maybe he'll get run over by a yellow taxi, or assassinated in his bed, or pushed off the top of the Empire State Building.

I'm still smiling to myself when I open my tablet and check my emails.

My pulse gathers speed as I read the most recent correspondence from an art collector. He wants to buy a painting. No, scratch that; he wants to buy my favorite piece. Apparently, he saw images attached to the article in the *New Yorker* magazine after the launch and would like to come and view it in person later today.

I don't respond immediately. Instead, I wander through to the gallery and stand in front of my aura-portrait, soaking up the vibrancy.

I guess, when I painted it, I never expected to sell it. Selling my artwork was a pipe dream, a fantasy, something that only ever happened to established artists, not part-time middle school teachers. I want people to see my art, of course I do. But the idea of this piece hanging on someone else's wall... I'm not sure how I feel about it.

What if they're purchasing it for all the wrong reasons?

What if ... they want it because it matches their color scheme, or reminds them of Great-Aunt Mabel, or fits a space on a wall that they've been trying to fill for a while?

Maybe I'm overreacting. But I'm emotionally attached to my art the way authors are emotionally attached to their books and actors are emotionally attached to their movies.

Besides, I need the money. If I don't sell my work, I'll never be able to pay Caleb back for the money he put into the gallery.

I'm so lost in thought that my heart pounds when the doorbell rings. I turn around and instantly recognize the face peering through the window at me.

It's Bash. Kyle's brother.

I unlock the door and let him in. He has Kyle's eyes and the same smile, but his hair and neatly trimmed beard are darker with flecks of copper when they catch the light.

"I wasn't sure if you'd be here." He surveys the gallery, lips stretched into a permanent smile. "Wow. Victoria was right. This is exactly what I'm looking for."

"Victoria sent you?"

"Not exactly. We talked about your artwork, and she suggested I come and check it out before I shop elsewhere." It takes him a couple of beats to realize what he said. "That sounds worse than it is. I only meant—"

"It's fine." My gaze lingers over my favorite piece briefly. "Do you want coffee? I've not had anywhere near enough caffeine today."

"And it's only—" he checks the Rolex on his wrist "—nine-twenty-three."

"Yep. Don't ask."

He follows me through to the office, and my cheeks grow hot when I think of what Kyle and I did on the desk. He takes a seat, leans back, one leg crossed casually over the other, and helps himself to a croissant.

"I'm opening a new nightclub. Are you open to new commissions?"

Am I ever!

It feels good to discuss art with someone who knows what he wants. I don't know Bash or Cash that well, but it's like talking to Kyle without the sexual chemistry bouncing around between us.

When we've agreed on four pieces, to begin with, and my brain is still trying to process the zeroes this will add to my practically empty bank account, he throws in: "Have you seen Kyle since he got back?"

My heart jumps on the bandwagon, prodding my ribs like I might've missed the name. "Yes." What does he know? Has Kyle told his brothers about us? "Why?"

Jeez, that's one way to draw attention to the heat in my face.

"No reason." Bash stands up. "He's been quiet."

"Maybe he's been busy." *Digging for information on my cosmetic surgeon.*

"Maybe." His eyes flicker back to his watch.

"Has he said anything to you about…" I leave the sentence hanging.

What am I doing? Bash is a member of the same mafia family as Kyle. It's bad enough having one brother on Nick's case without alerting the rest of the family to his existence as well.

"About?" His expression is unreadable.

"Did Kyle ask you to come here and check up on me?"

"Nope. Kyle stopped telling me what to do a long time ago when he realized that I would automatically do the opposite."

I think about it. "So, he told you to stay away?"

Bash laughs, the kind of laughter that would be infectious in a crowded room, easy and charming and loud. "I'm not saying a word."

I walk with him through the gallery and open the door.

Bash hesitates on the threshold and turns to face me. His expression is so like Kyle's when he's being serious, that it takes my breath away momentarily.

"Kyle's one of the good guys," he says. "Would it be such a bad thing if he had people looking out for you?" Before I can answer, he shrugs and walks away.

A black car is waiting for him, the engine idling, and hazard lights on. The Murrays must have a fleet of expensive black cars complete with chauffeurs at their beck and call. Fancy a McDonald's? No sweat. Send the chauffeur to pick it up.

But I bet they've never even tried McDonald's classic Big Mac Meal.

I watch the car drive off. I'm about to go back inside and close the door, when a man dressed all in black standing outside a store on the opposite side of the road, turns his face away from me and studies the window. Neither of us moves.

Was he watching me?

I linger outside, but it's cold, and my teeth are chattering, so I go back inside and close the door as gently as I can, holding my breath until I hear the faint click. Within moments, the guy turns around, checks out the gallery, and then walks away.

Anger bursts inside my chest.

What the actual fuck does Kyle think he's doing?

Back in the office, I type a message—it takes three attempts to get it right because my fingers are trembling—and send it to Kyle.

Get your man away from my gallery or I'll call the police.

I refill my coffee cup. It's too late to get my paints out before my afternoon appointment, and I'm not sure that I'd produce the kind of piece I could sell right now anyway.

A message comes back before my first mouthful of coffee has gone down.

Sienna? What's happened? Can I call you?

I suck in a deep breath and type, my fingers jabbing so hard at the keys I'm surprised I haven't punched a hole in the screen.

Bash was here, but you already know that don't you? I don't want your men following me. I don't want your protection.

My phone rings, and I pick it up. I don't wait for him to speak.

"Why are you having me followed?"

"Hey, sweetheart."

The voice makes the hairs on the back of my neck stand on end. I didn't check the caller ID. *Fuck!*

"Who's following my baby girl?"

"No one. And I'm not your baby girl."

A chuckle reaches me through the handset, and I instinctively hold the phone away from my ear, as if his fingernails will appear at any moment and scratch the side of my face.

"You'll always be my baby girl, Sienna."

Why is he still talking?

"I'm busy. Can I call you later?"

I could just hang up, but he'll only call me back. Best to just get the conversation over and done with, finish my coffee, maybe put my earbuds in, close my eyes, and listen to some meditational rainfall on Spotify. Cleanse the rest of the world from my system.

"Too busy to open the door and let me in?"

Fuck!

"You're here?"

"Didn't you get my message?"

He knows I did. He can see that it's been read even if I didn't reply.

"Yeah…" I'm trying to find an excuse not to open the door, but it wouldn't surprise me if he watched Bash leave too. Resigned, I say, "I'm coming."

He's standing outside blowing exaggeratedly into his cupped hands to keep himself warm when I open the door. He's wearing a beaten-up brown leather coat that looks as if he bought it in the 70s, and square-toed lace-up shoes that have probably never been polished. I notice for the first time, his shiny, liver-spotted scalp peering through his thinning gray hair.

"Thought you'd never open the door." He steps inside without waiting to be invited, and peers around at my artwork, rubbing his hands together like a miser from an old fairy tale. "This is classy, sweetheart."

I close the door, shutting me in with him.

I don't want him here. He hasn't moved. He hasn't touched anything. But the thought of him breathing on my paintings sets my teeth on edge like he's swallowed something noxious and has come here to destroy everything he sees. I find myself studying his mouth, waiting for a puff of dirty green gas to appear.

Deep breath.

I've let him get to me, and that's exactly what he wanted. Any attention is better than none, right?

"Is this the piece?" He steps closer to my self-portrait, and I'm jolted into action.

I scurry across the room, heart pounding. "I think that painting is sold."

Did it sound like I was saying: *Touch that canvas at your own peril*? I fucking hope so.

Maybe he picks up on the threat in my voice.

He stops a couple of paces away from the painting and turns to me with a smug smile, still rubbing his hands together. "I know."

Wait. What?

"What do you mean?"

"Someone is coming to look at it this afternoon, right?"

I swallow. The last coffee I drank with Bash is buzzing through my veins. "How do you know about that?"

He grins at me, revealing large front teeth. "I found the buyer for you. He's a friend of mine. When I told him about your gallery, he said he'd buy a piece or two. You know. To help you find your feet."

I'm trying to process this. *My father. A friend of his. My favorite painting.*

"Why?" I shake my head. "Why would you do that?"

"Because you're my baby girl, and I'll do anything to help you."

His bottom lip rolls out again, and I realize that this must be his go-to expression of hurt. The sympathy-call. Next, he'll say: *I was only trying to help.*

"I was only trying to help, sweetheart."

Ugh! I forgot the sweetheart.

"I don't need your help."

He glances around the gallery, his eyes settling pointedly on every painting before returning to me. "That's not how it looks from where I'm standing. How many pictures have you sold?"

"A couple." *Why am I even telling him this?* "I've only been open a few days."

I'm still justifying myself to the man who tried to kill my mom and walked out on me when I was six years old. I don't need his validation. I don't need anything from him.

"Which is why I'm trying to give you a head start." He steps closer to me, and I move backwards. "Hey, there's no crime in getting some help from your family."

You're not my family.

It's on the tip of my tongue, but I don't say it out loud. I'm acutely aware that no one knows he's here, and I left my cell phone on my desk in the office. If he tries to hurt me, I'd never get to it in time to call for help. I don't like that this is how I feel when I'm around him, but he's never given me a reason to trust him.

"So, this guy, your friend ... he's not an art collector?"

"Not exactly."

"Not exactly?" I'm already working myself into a rage of I'm-never-letting-this-piece-go levels, and he isn't doing anything to salvage the situation.

"He collects beautiful things."

"Beautiful things?" I'm repeating his words like a fucking parrot, my voice growing shrill. "Come on, give me something I can work with here. Are we talking statues, Faberge eggs, women?"

He wrinkles his nose from side to side like I'm the one out of place in my beautiful gallery. "Sweetheart, something is wrong. You shouldn't be this stressed over a painting."

He's still talking to me the way he did in the Rinse, slowly, his voice low and measured as though he recognizes that a word out of place will send me careening over the edge and into an abyss.

"That's just it." I match his tone—two can play at this game, and if he wants to treat me like a kid, I'll react accordingly. "It isn't only a painting. It's *my* painting. No one else on this planet will ever be able to recreate it because only I know what went into it. And it isn't the *painting* that's stressing me out. It's you."

He blinks, fluttering his eyelashes like a cartoon character. "Me? What have I done?"

"Why are you interfering? Why are you even here?" I throw both arms up into the air as though posing the question to a higher being.

"You know why I'm here, Sienna, and I didn't think I was interfering. I thought I could help you make some money. That's why you opened the gallery, isn't it? To sell your work."

He furrows his brow like he's having a hard time understanding his new-found daughter.

I shut my eyes briefly. It makes no difference what I say, he'll always turn this around to him being the loving father trying to make amends.

"I want to sell it on merit. I want people to look at my work and feel compelled to buy it because it reaches out to them. I don't want a friend of a friend handing over some cash as a favor."

"Sure, I get it." He nods, and his head keeps right on nodding like it has somehow worked loose from his neck. "I'll speak to him. Tell him the piece is no longer for sale."

Relief floods my chest. "You will?" Maybe he is trying.

"Anything for my baby girl." He licks his lips. "On one condition."

There it is: the hidden clause.

"Tell me who's been following you."

"What?" It takes several beats for me to work out what he's talking about. My shoulders slump. "It's nothing. I was just being paranoid."

"People don't get paranoid for no reason. You sounded pretty adamant on the phone."

"It's fine. Nothing I can't handle."

He watches me for a long time, and it's obvious that he doesn't believe me. Finally, he says, "Have it your way. But I want you to promise me that you'll let me know if it gets out of hand."

"Okay." I'm not promising him anything. An awkward silence settles between us, and I glance at the door. "I'm busy…"

"I know." He walks to the door, the coat flapping around his legs. "If I find out someone is hurting my little girl, I'll—"

"They're not. I'm fine. Everything is fine."

"That's a lot of fines for someone who looks as if she's about to cry."

He reaches out a hand to touch my face, and I back away, tears stinging my eyes right on cue.

"Please go."

I want him to leave so that I can lock myself in my studio and breathe again. My chest feels tight, and my head is spinning, and I don't think I've taken a deep breath since he walked through the door.

"I'll call you, sweetheart. I'm never going to stop trying."

He walks away, and I follow his retreating back with my eyes. He's almost at the corner of the block when another man walks towards him in a beige coat with a red woolen scarf around his neck. They exchange a few words, and I head back inside, checking that the man in black has gone.

I don't even make it to my office before the doorbell rings again.

Sucking in a deep breath, I go back and open the door expecting to find my father standing there looking apologetic. But instead, I'm peering into the cool gray eyes of Nick Morris.

He smiles and steps inside, unwinding the red woolen scarf

from around his neck. "I was passing by and thought I'd take you for lunch."

8

KYLE

Sienna isn't reading my messages. I try calling her, and she doesn't pick up, so I type one final message and hit send.

I don't know what you're talking about. Five minutes. If I don't hear from you, I'll come to the gallery.

Five minutes drag by so slowly it feels like five hours. I'm already in the elevator and on my way down to the parking lot before the time is up.

I call Bash from the car en route to the gallery. "What did you say to Sienna?"

"Huh?" I picture my brother scratching his head and messing up his hair. "What did she tell you?"

"Nothing. That's the problem. She isn't even reading my messages now."

I hear Bash suck in a deep breath at the other end of the call. "Chill, man. She's probably chewing on the end of a paintbrush right now, oblivious to your panic attack."

"I'm not having a panic attack. You didn't tell her that I sent you, did you?"

"Hmm..." Bash goes quiet.

I peer out of the passenger window. I'm still nowhere near the gallery.

"Why? She'll never believe that buying some of her work was your idea now."

"It was only a bit of fun, Kyle. I didn't think she'd fall for it."

I pause, repeating her messages in my head. "She said someone was following her. Did you see anyone hanging around when you left the gallery?"

"Only the bodyguard."

"Bodyguard?" My heart rate quickens. "Who was he? Did you recognize him?"

"I wasn't paying attention. I assumed he was there on your instruction—"

I hang up.

Sitting forward in the back of the car, I ask Seamus to take a shortcut to the gallery. He's been driving around New York City his entire life; I don't pay him to keep me sitting in traffic.

It's hard to keep still. Someone has posted a bodyguard outside Sienna's gallery, and it isn't me.

I call Terry. He answers almost before the phone rings. "Kyle."

"Have you got a guy following Sienna?"

"No. You didn't ask me to put someone on it, did you?"

"Shit!"

"Kyle? Do you need me to send someone straight over?"

"No, it's fine. I'm on my way there now."

Someone is watching Sienna. But the question is: who?

The first name that springs to mind is Nick Morris. But unless I missed a huge chunk of information regarding his current status online, he doesn't have access to a personal security team. Maybe the person Sienna saw is a private investigator. So, whatever Nick Morris is hoping to find out about her is something that he doesn't want to ask her personally.

The traffic seems to be moving more slowly than ever.

I'm almost tempted to get out of the car and walk the rest of the way when Seamus pulls up outside the gallery, and I watch Sienna climb into the back of a taxi with Mr. Morris. The guy is determined not to let her out of his sight.

"Follow that cab," I say to Seamus.

Am I way off-track with this? Is the guy genuine, and I'm simply allowing my feelings for Sienna to cloud my judgement?

Before the thought fully materializes though, I know that isn't the case. It's too convenient that he waited for me to come back from Ireland before he started pursuing her, and now I have the name Caelan Murray waving red flags inside my head as well.

I keep my eyes firmly fixed on the taxi ahead of us, mentally urging Seamus to drive faster.

My phone starts ringing, and a picture of my mom appears on the screen.

Terry told her about our conversation.

I press the green button. "Mom."

"Where are you, Kyle?"

"Right now?" I'm stalling. I can't allow my mom to distract me before I know where Nick is going with Sienna. "I'm in the car."

Silence.

Then Seamus stops the car and says, "The eagle has landed."

We're outside a restaurant in Brooklyn. I can see Nick holding the passenger door of the taxi open for Sienna. She climbs out, folds her coat across her chest, and stares at the white columns flanking the entrance and the gold lettering on the windows.

"I'm outside Gage and Tollner, Mom," I speak into the handset. "Can you meet me for lunch?"

I make a reservation and wait for Mom to arrive.

By request, we're directed to a table near the back of the busy restaurant, where I can see Nick Morris's profile. Sienna is obstructed by a huge potted fern. I'll know if she stands up, but until then, I'm more interested in her companion.

"You need to visit Caleb and Victoria." Mom doesn't even glance at the menu. "You haven't seen your niece yet. She won't be a baby for long."

"I know. I will. I'm waiting till they're home and settled in a bit."

It's an icebreaker; this isn't the reason she called.

"What's going on, Kyle? You looked so well, so ... happy when you came back from Ireland."

"I'm still happy."

I order a pitcher of water from the server. She orders a brandy, neat. The smile fades as soon as he walks away. "This is me you're talking to, Kyle. You're back a week and already asking Terry to make inquiries about a cosmetic surgeon."

"I didn't ask Terry to make inquiries ." My eyes instinctively slide Nick's way.

"I take it this is the guy sitting at nine o'clock with Sienna now." Her expression doesn't alter. I should've known she would register everyone in the restaurant before we sat down.

"His name is Nick Morris. He's Sienna's surgeon."

"They're not discussing invasive procedures over a steak and a bottle of red wine though." She clasps her hands in front of her on the table. "Why are we here, Kyle? What's bothering you?"

This is one of the things I love about Mom. She might not always agree with what her sons get up to, but she'll listen to our reasons and form an opinion once armed with all the information.

I talk her through my first meeting with Nick Morris at the gallery opening.

"I wish I'd been there." She shakes her head and follows the server's progress as he returns with our drinks. "I'd have pulled him up on it." She sips her brandy and studies me closely.

"Something doesn't sit right with me." Aside from the fact that we share the same violent asshole father.

I can't mention Caelan to her. I haven't even decided if I'll mention him to Terry yet. The name is too close to home for all of us, and we need to remain objective about whatever the hell Nick is playing at.

"Okay." Mom sits back in her seat. "I believe you. What do you want me to do?"

I shake my head. "Nothing. I can handle it."

She flattens her lips together. "Firstly, whatever this is, we handle it as a family. Come on, Kyle. When have any of you ever had to resolve a problem alone?"

I fill my glass with water and drink half of it, tracking the cold liquid inside me. "Never."

"Secondly, we make sure she's being watched around the clock. We don't want a repeat performance of what happened with Olivia Dragonetti."

"Someone else is already stalking her. And she thinks it's for me."

"Okay." She's unfazed. "Terry will deal with that one." She hasn't glanced around at Sienna and Nick, but she'll know the instant they move. Mom has a built-in antenna for this kind of thing.

I swallow. My tongue sticks to the roof of my mouth as Nick's hand snakes across the table to touch Sienna's. She moves her fingers out of reach, and I exhale slowly.

"And thirdly." Mom waves a hand in front of my face to get my attention. "I don't want you sliding back into the way things were before, Kyle. You've come too far."

"I won't." I don't even sound convincing to my own ears.

"Sienna will come to you when she's ready. What's for you—"

"—won't go by you." I finish the idiom for her. "I don't trust him, Mom."

Mom covers my hand with hers. "We'll get to the bottom of it. I promise." She arches an eyebrow. "I could always go over there and introduce myself right now."

I smile. "I don't think that will be necessary. The less he knows about us the better."

"Do you think this is about us then?" She narrows her eyes.

"I didn't." *Until I discovered who his father is.* "But I do now."

"Go on."

"Call it a hunch."

Mom drains her brandy in one go. "That might work on Terry and your brothers, but you're the lawyer of the family, Kyle. My steadfast tin soldier."

"Didn't he only have one leg?"

"You're missing the point. He fell in love with the paper ballerina and stayed true to her despite everything that happened to him. What I'm trying to say is, you wouldn't risk losing Sienna over a hunch. So, either there's something you're not telling me, or the Irish contingency did a better job on you than I imagined they would."

I glance across the restaurant, but Nick is no longer there. I half-stand, knocking the table with my thighs and making the vase of flowers in the middle rock precariously. Sienna is still seated, her chin resting on her steepled fingers.

"Looking for someone?" Nick sneaks up on me without warning. The smile is still fixed firmly in place, but his eyes are cold like the Irish Sea on a winter's day.

"Hello." Mom is on her feet. She shakes Nick's hand, dragging his attention away from me. "Moira Keegan. But you already know that don't you?"

It isn't lost on me that she dropped the Murray from her name when she introduced herself.

"Nick Morris." If Mom caught him off-guard, he recovers quickly. "I met your sons at Sienna's gallery."

"I'm sorry I couldn't be there. Sienna is like family to us."

His eyes flicker, but otherwise, his face is devoid of emotion. "That will explain the reason why you followed us here. You should've joined us. Sienna would've been only too happy to invite you to sit with us."

"Oh no," Mom says brightly. "We didn't want to intrude. Besides, Kyle and I had family matters to discuss." She keeps her eyes fixed firmly on him. "Good to meet you. Say hi to Sienna for me."

She sits back down. Nick, recognizing when he has been dismissed, returns to his table.

I watch him sit down. He doesn't look my way, but I sense that he knows he's being watched. The fake smile returns the instant his ass hits the seat. I wait for him to tell Sienna that he spoke to us, but she doesn't glance around, and within minutes, he signals the waiter for the check.

Mom is busy reading through the menu. She takes her time, trying to decide between the steak and the lobster. She doesn't look up when she says, "Has he gone?"

"Aye."

She closes the menu. "There's something familiar about him. I don't know what it is, Kyle, but you're right not to trust him."

9

SIENNA

There's an envelope waiting for me in my mailbox when I get home this evening. It crinkles in my hand with the weight of another problem. My legs feel sluggish as I climb the stairs up to my second-floor apartment.

I should still be buzzing from the gallery opening. This should be the most exciting time of my life—I finally have everything I ever dreamed of. Well, almost. But it feels as if the men in my life are conspiring to keep me from reaching my happy place.

I only wish I knew why.

Are they in this together? Do they have a group chat on WhatsApp where they confirm their plans for me over the next twenty-four hours?

Kyle must've sent Bash to the gallery to keep an eye on me. *I think*. I'm not sure, but I can't ignore the timing. Then my father showed up. And Nick... It feels as though Nick isn't giving me a moment to think, whisking me away on a lunch date before I'd even had a chance to process my father's visit.

Did Nick speak to my father on the street corner, or did I imagine it? He knew that Kyle had been doing some background research on him, but how? I'm no tech whizzkid, but it doesn't all add up to the Nick I thought I knew.

Then, I hit a mental brick wall when I think about my father.

He displayed zero emotion when he was introduced to Kyle, and I can't even begin to consider the kind of people he associates with. I'd rather burn my painting than allow it to hang on his friend's wall.

I switch on every light in my apartment as I walk through to the narrow galley kitchen and drop my purse and unopened mail onto the counter. I open the refrigerator, pull out the bottle of prosecco that I was saving for the opening night, and pop the cork. I didn't open it before because Victoria was in labor, but tonight, I feel like I need it.

I take a huge glug before easing out of my coat and draping it over the end of the counter.

The letter is staring at me. I could leave it till morning, but it'll be a bug crawling through my dreams all night. Best to open it now, even though I sense it isn't good news.

Here goes. I try to empty my mind as I slide my finger underneath the flap and rip the envelope open. It's from my landlord. He's giving me two months' notice to vacate my apartment.

Deep breath. I fold the letter in half with shaky fingers and stuff it back inside the torn envelope.

Two months. Plenty of time to find somewhere else to live...

Who am I kidding?

Aside from the fact that *affordable* apartments are scarce in the city, I don't have the money for a down-payment. Sure, Caleb's money funded the gallery, but I still put every cent I'd ever managed to save into it myself, and who knows when I'll see any profit from my work. My father kept his word and cancelled his friend's appointment, but my other meeting didn't result in a confirmed sale either.

The only good thing to come out of today was Bash's commission, but even that was manipulated by Kyle.

The intercom next to my front door buzzes, and I take my glass of prosecco with me to answer it.

"Sienna, it's Nick. Can I come in?"

My stomach drops. Why can't he leave me alone?

Then I remind myself of all that he has done for me since I was first referred to him, how vulnerable I was, his endless patience trying to minimize my scars and restore my confidence. Guilt blossoms inside my chest. Nick is a good guy. It isn't his fault that I'm not attracted to him in the same way he's attracted to me, but the least I can do is give him a chance I suppose.

"Sure." I hit the button to open the external door downstairs.

Moments later, Nick appears in my doorway with a bunch of flowers, vibrant orange gerbera, red and purple anemones, and white stephanotis.

"You brought flowers?" I take them and instinctively bury my face in the bouquet and inhale the scent. "They're beautiful."

"Like you."

I flinch. It's so smarmy, so cheesy, that I have to compose my features before I stand aside and let him in.

"How did you know where I live?" The question bursts out of me.

"Your medical records?" He fills the space in the airless hallway. Too close. Squashing the flowers between us. "It's confidential information, but I figured that we're friends. Aren't we?"

"Sure." The uneasiness is back, swirling around inside my gut.

I walk back to the kitchen, put down my glass of prosecco, and busy myself arranging the flowers in the only vase I possess.

"Prosecco?" His voice and his eyes follow me from the other side of the kitchen, which isn't far. "What's the occasion?"

"The gallery." I don't look up from the flowers. "Art. Life."

"Very philosophical."

I sense rather than see his smile as I stand back to admire my arrangement. "Shit. I didn't offer you a drink. Sorry. It's been a long day." I take another glass from the cupboard and fill it with bubbly liquid for Nick, then I refill my own glass.

"Anything I can help with?"

I lean back against the counter, sip my drink, and shake my head. We could go into the living room, but I feel exhausted suddenly with the weight of the landlord's notice hanging over me, and I want to go to bed.

Alone.

I don't want Nick to get too comfy or get the wrong idea that he can stay.

"It's fine." That word again: *fine*. Anyone in their right mind can see straight through it; it's the word we all use when life is a million miles away from fine. "I'll manage."

Nick's eyes flicker across my face as though he can access my thoughts through my pores. "Sienna, you don't have to do everything alone, you know." Pause. "I want to help."

I smile. "Thank you, but I don't think you can."

"Try me." His eyes hold mine, but he doesn't move any closer.

"I need to find somewhere to live." I shrug. "My landlord has given me notice to get out of my apartment."

"Okay." His expression is bland. "Do you have somewhere in mind?"

"Nope." I sip my prosecco. The bubbles are not helping to blur the edges. Yet.

"Look, I already know what you're going to say, but there's a spare room in my apartment if you want it. Even if it's just temporary. Until something more permanent comes along."

"I can't." I shake my head, my thoughts drifting with the movement like bees following pollen in the breeze. "It's generous of you, but you've already done enough."

Too much.

"Well, it's not entirely selfless." He watches me coolly. "I have a vested interest in you, Sienna. I enjoy your company."

Here's the part where I'm supposed to reciprocate the compliment and say that I enjoy his company too, but I can't bring myself to put the words out there.

Unfazed by my gap-mouthed silence, Nick adds, "I hope that we can spend more time together. No pressure though. The offer is on the table if you want it."

He downs his drink and leans over me to place his empty glass next to the sink. He's close enough to kiss me, and I press my lips together, willing him to back off. I don't want to kiss him. It's the first time I've admitted it to myself, but now that I have, I need to figure out what this revulsion has to do with Kyle.

He does back off, and I release a shaky breath.

"Think about it, Sienna. That's all I'm asking."

My dad's words pop into my head unbidden. *Just, please, give me a chance. That's all I'm asking.*

"I will." I feel numb.

"I'll see myself out."

I don't move. I'm rooted to the floor, those four words flashing like a neon sign inside my head. That's all I'm asking. That's all I'm asking. *That's all I'm asking.*

Maybe it's time to leave the city.

But I don't want to leave. I've lived in New York all my life, and I shouldn't be forced to move away because of Nick. Or my father. Or Kyle.

Perhaps I could sleep in the studio behind the gallery until I find a place that I can afford to rent. It isn't designed to be lived in, and my stuff would have to go into storage, and what if it took six months to find another apartment?

No. I'm not encroaching on my studio space.

I miss Victoria. Swallowing another mouthful of bubbles, I message her:

Hey, how are you doing? How's my beautiful goddaughter?

Then I add: *Are you awake?*

Within moments, Victoria is video calling me.

"Of course I'm awake." She angles the phone so that I can see the baby suckling on her nipple. "I've forgotten what sleep feels like."

She looks tired, dark bruise-colored smudges under her eyes, and her hair scrunched up into a messy bun on top of her head. But her happiness oozes down the phone.

"I can't wait to meet her."

"When are you coming over, Si? I miss you, and honestly, Holly is already changing. She's so alert. Her eyes follow her daddy around, and she settles the instant he holds her in his arms."

I smile. "She's going to be a daddy's girl."

"I'm gushing, sorry." Victoria scrunches up her face in apology, but the grin isn't going anywhere. She's smitten. "What have you been up to? How are things with the gallery?" She glances at the wall, and adds, "Why are you calling me so late?"

"You called me, remember."

"Did I? Wow, my brain is even foggier than I thought it was."

"The gallery is great."

Her eyes narrow, and she lowers her voice. "What's wrong, Si?" She knows me too well.

Where do I start?

"My father is back from the dead."

She blinks back at me. "What does he want? I hope you told him to get lost."

"He wants to put things right." I twist my mouth into a lopsided smile.

"I repeat, I hope you told him to get lost." Victoria holds the phone closer to her face. "You didn't, did you? Please don't tell me that you've spoken to him in person."

"I had to, V. I wanted to hear him out."

"And?"

"And now…" I tilt my head back and sigh heavily. "He turned up at the gallery yesterday."

"Sienna." Victoria's voice is firm. "You don't have to do anything you don't want to do, you know. I'll speak to Caleb about it in the morning."

"No, please don't. I don't want any trouble."

"Do you want him in your life?"

I thought the answer would be simple. A straightforward no. But it turns out only people like my father find it easy to walk out on family. I know I don't owe him anything. I know I don't need him in my life, so why is it so difficult to say it out loud?

"Promise me that you'll stay away from him, Si," Victoria says. "Men like that never change."

"I know."

We're both quiet, both watching the sleeping baby in Victoria's arms.

"Have you seen Kyle?" she asks.

Before I can answer, the baby starts fidgeting, and Victoria drops the phone. Her face reappears briefly. "Sorry, Si. Gotta go. I want to hear all about it when you come over." She ends the call.

I can't ask them for help with finding somewhere to live. They've done enough already. I refill my glass and toast myself. "You're on your own this time, Sienna."

Kyle's car is waiting outside my apartment block the next morning.

I put my head down and start walking, but the driver's door opens, and Seamus gets out.

"Sienna?" He calls me back. "I can give you a ride."

"I don't need a ride." I glare at him and keep moving.

His footsteps follow me.

I freeze, turn around, and grip the strap of my purse over my shoulder.

"I know you'd rather not get in the car with me," Seamus says, keeping his voice low, "but Kyle asked me to get you safely to work, and I'm just following orders."

I inhale deeply, filling my lungs. "Tell Kyle you missed me. Tell him I left before you got here, or, I don't know, I wanted some exercise."

He nods once. "Don't look around now, but the guy sitting in the black car with tinted windows has been watching your apartment for the past three hours."

I go to look around because it's human nature; someone tells you not to do something, and you instantly have to do it.

"Don't look," he hisses under his breath.

I stop myself. "If the windows are tinted, how do you know he's watching my apartment?" I don't even know why I'm letting myself get dragged into this conversation.

"Maybe it's because every time he has a cigarette he gets out of the car, leans against the hood, and stares at your front door."

I swallow. "Maybe he's waiting for his girlfriend."

"That would explain why he rolled his window down when you walked outside." Seamus's eyes twitch. "I don't want to frighten you but—"

"You could've fooled me."

He inclines his head, conceding the point. It doesn't make me feel any better. "But, another guy has jogged past your building more times than I can remember since I got here. And before you say he's just jogging, ask yourself why he would take photographs of your building as he passed by?"

I stare at him, trying to reassemble my thoughts. "How did Kyle know they would be here?"

"You told him that you were being followed yesterday."

Did I? So much happened after I saw the guy in black, I'd pushed it from my mind.

"Okay. Can you take me to the Wraith?"

Seamus smiles, making his ginger moustache twitch. "I thought you'd never ask."

"What the fuck is going on?" I don't hold back once the door to Kyle's office closes behind me. "Who are those people following me around?"

"Sienna." Kyle makes the mistake of raising both hands to calm me down.

I bat his hands away. "Don't tell me that you don't know who they are. That's what you do, isn't it? Find out information and make it go away."

"Can we sit down and talk about this calmly?"

"How can I be calm when there are strange men watching my apartment?" My voice is already shrill, and I've barely started.

Kyle gestures to the coffee machine, and I nod.

While he fills two cups with steaming black coffee, I sit on one of the couches in his office, which is almost as big as my entire apartment. His computer screen is locked. His desk is neat, not a piece of paper or a stray pen in sight. If anyone had asked me to describe his office without seeing it, that's probably how I'd have pictured it.

Kyle places a cup in front of me and sits on the sofa on the other side of the low, glass coffee table.

I swallow a mouthful of the black liquid too quickly and my eyes water. "So, do you know who they are?"

"I think I can hazard a guess." He cradles his cup in both hands as if trying to keep warm.

"Are you going to enlighten me, or is it on a need-to-know basis?"

"Sienna, I'm trying to protect you."

"Why do I need protecting? Until a week ago, I was perfectly happy in my little apartment, grabbing a coffee-to-go from Starbucks on my way to work, and not a tinted window in sight."

His lips quirk into a half-smile.

"Until you came back from Ireland," I add.

He flinches. But he doesn't deny it. "I think you should move into the Wraith for a while."

I almost choke on my coffee, and liquid splutters across the glass surface of the table. "What the actual fuck! We fuck a couple of times, and you want me to move in with you?"

Way to go, Sienna. I see the hurt in his eyes, and I don't even try to suck the words back in.

"No, I told you there was no pressure, and I meant it. You can have one of the executive suites. It's not ideal, but I'll feel better knowing that you're safe."

I put my cup down, too hard, and wince as it clangs against the glass. I stand up and pace the room. My landlord serves me notice to vacate my apartment, and now this. It's all a little too convenient. Too much at once. It's almost as if Kyle planned this so that I'd be closer to him. First stop, an executive suite, next stop his bedroom.

I stop pacing and face him. "Did you tell my landlord to write to me?"

Kyle furrows his brow. "No. Why did he write to you?"

My jaw is still clenched so tightly it hurts, but I think I believe him. "I need to find somewhere else to live."

It hits me then like I've been slapped with a wet towel: I thought I had two months' grace, but Kyle is making it sound as if I need to get out now.

"That's settled then." His voice jolts me back to the increasingly painful present. "I want you to move into the Wraith today. I'll ask Lauren to get a suite allocated to you."

A week ago, I had my gallery opening to look forward to, and now... Now, I feel as though I've slipped through a glitch in the galaxy and ended up in a parallel universe where everyone looks the same, but underneath the surface, they've turned rotten.

"No, Kyle. I can't stay here."

"Why not?" His eyes scrunch up in confusion.

"I can't afford to pay for a room here let alone an executive suite."

"I'm not asking you to pay for it, Sienna. I'm trying to keep you safe."

"That's just it though." I run my fingers through my hair. "You shouldn't need to keep me safe. I don't even know what's going on. Do they want to hurt me? Are they trying to kill me? What have I even done?" The questions come tumbling out all at once.

Kyle rises and crosses the room to stand in front of me. "I-We think that they're being employed by Nick Morris."

A snort escapes my nostrils before I can stop it. "Nick!" My voice sounds incredulous. "That's what this is all about? You and Nick? He's a cosmetic surgeon for fuck's sake. He's not a mafia assassin."

"Okay, maybe not Nick then. Whoever Nick is working for."

"No." I step away from him, shaking my head. "What evidence do you have?"

"Sienna, I need you to listen to me, and I'll try to explain."

"Oh, please do." My breathing is shallow, and my brain is spinning, trying to keep with this new revelation.

"Nick was right, I was investigating his background." Pause. If he's doing it for dramatic effect, it's working. "It turns out that we share the same father. Nick's father is Caelan Murray. He murdered Nick's mom and tried to murder our mom too."

"I... What does this have to do with me?"

"That's what I'm trying to find out."

10

KYLE

Her face grows pale, her eyes larger than ever. She doesn't belong in this world. I knew it when I first met her, but I understand it far more clearly now. Which is why I want to take her away from the city, away from the family, and start over somewhere new. We could be different people in Ireland. Maybe then we'd have a chance to make this work.

"No." She shakes her head. "There must be some mistake."

"I wish I was wrong, Sienna. My father is serving a life sentence in jail; the last thing I want to do is rake up the past when it's best left buried. But whatever Nick is up to, it's connected to my family."

"But I've known him for years."

I want so badly to fold her into my arms and make this all go away, but I'm acutely conscious that one wrong move will send her fleeing. And I need to keep her close.

"Sienna, did he ever ask you on a date before?" I try to keep my tone devoid of emotion. She already believes that this is a rivalry between me and Nick Morris, and I'm not adding fuel to that blazing fire.

"No, never. He never ... looked at me that way before."

"Ask yourself: why now?"

She's picking at the skin around her thumbs without even realizing what she's doing. "What do you mean?" Her voice is tiny. Vulnerable.

I clench my fists to stop myself from taking her hands in mine and kissing the pulpy flesh around her thumbnails.

"Why did he never ask you on a date before? Why didn't he ask you last week, or last month, or last year?"

Her eyebrows lower and her bewilderment morphs into narrow-eyed mistrust. "You think he only wants me because of you?"

"No, that's not what I'm saying."

"What are you saying then, Kyle?" Her voice has become brittle.

"I'm saying that he waited till now for a reason."

"And the reason is you?" Her eyes are all over the place. "I've been busy with the gallery in case you forgot. Maybe Nick was waiting for the gallery to open before he asked me on a date. He's been a perfect gentleman. Unlike you."

"I'm not going to argue with you about this, Sienna. I'll make sure you're safe, but I'll keep my word. No pressure. This is not some fucked up ploy to trap you."

"Fine." She squares her shoulders, but her breathing is a dead giveaway of the turmoil going on inside. "I'm leaving then."

She turns around and crosses my office to the private elevator.

"No, wait, Sienna." I reach the door before she can open it and cover the control panel with my hand.

"Move your hand, Kyle."

"I can't let you go back to your apartment."

"I'm going to work. Some of us don't have the luxury of knowing the billions in our bank accounts will keep a roof over our heads." Her gaze is steady.

"Are you always this stubborn?" I try to lighten the mood, but my timing is clearly way off-target.

"Only when it involves making my own decisions."

I lower my hand. "Seamus will take you. But you're coming back to the Wraith tonight when the gallery closes. I'll leave the key to your suite with the concierge."

"I don't work for you, Kyle. You can't tell me what to do."

I nod. "Please will you come back here tonight?"

The elevator door opens, and she steps inside. When she turns around to face me, her expression has softened a little, the haunted look that appeared in her eyes when I told her about my father having been smoothed away.

"Okay."

"Thank you."

I watch the door close, taking her away from me as the numbers on the control panel start counting down.

I unlock my phone and call Seamus. "She's on her way down. Don't let her out of your sight."

She doesn't want my protection, but I'm hoping she has at least accepted that it's what's best for her.

I go to my desk and call Lauren. "Can you allocate a suite to Sienna Walker and leave the key with the exec concierge?"

"Sienna Walker? Is that the—"

I cut the call. Seamus is ringing my mobile.

"I lost her."

My gut clenches. "What do you mean, you lost her? She was in the elevator."

"She ran before I could stop her. Sorry, boss."

"Find her. I'll cover the gallery and her apartment."

I call Terry and explain the situation. "I'm calling a family meeting. How soon can you get here?"

By the time Terry, Cash, and Bash are seated on the couches in my office, Seamus and two members of Terry's security team have tracked Sienna to an apartment building in Queens. When she left the Wraith, it seems she ran straight into the arms of her father as he stumbled out of the casino after pulling an all-nighter.

I let her go. My men are under strict orders to notify me the moment she leaves the building.

What I really want to do is go straight there, bang on every apartment door until I find her, and bring her back here with me, but I promised I wasn't trying to trap her, and at least she isn't alone. I'm not sure how proactive her father will be in keeping her safe, but I'm consoling myself that while she's with him, Nick can't get to her.

The lesser of two evils.

"You must promise me that what I'm about to tell you doesn't reach Mom." I kickstart the meeting with a bang.

Bash knocks back a whiskey shot. "You have to tell us what it is before we can agree to that."

"Bash is right," Cash joins in. "I mean, if you're about to tell us that Holly isn't Caleb's daughter, well…" He shrugs. "I'm not withholding that kind of information. Mom will string us up by our bollocks and leave us to—"

"Lads, I think we get the picture," Terry interjects.

Deep breath. I thought I could handle this without involving Terry and my brothers. I was wrong.

"Nick Morris. Cosmetic surgeon. He's been treating Sienna since the accident."

I have their attention. The twins might wind each other up and mess around a lot of the time, but they know when it's time to stop the banter and get serious.

"I met him at the gallery opening. Something about him was off, and when I did some digging, it was obvious that his people had been doing a shit load of cleaning up behind him. Turns out…"

My pulse is racing. This isn't the kind of conversation you want to have every day. Or at all.

"...he was born in Chicago and entered the foster care system when his mom was murdered. No father's name was recorded on his birth certificate, but the man suspected of killing his mom was called Caelan O'Reilly."

Terry is on his feet, hands wrapped around the back of his neck. "You're sure about this, Kyle?"

"Aye. I wish I wasn't."

"Fuck!" Cash drains his drink and refills their glasses.

"Does this guy, Nick Morris, know who his father is?" Terry's eyes are distant. He wasn't around when our father tried to kill our mom, but he knows the score, and he's been keeping our mom safe, and alive, ever since.

Bash hasn't spoken a word.

"If he didn't before," I say, "I'm guessing he does now. He's all over Sienna like a fucking dose of the shingles."

"What does Sienna have to do with any of this?" Bash is working it out in his head, slotting the pieces together, so that he can formulate a plan.

"Jeez, I must've gotten more than my fair share of the brains when we shared our mother's womb," Cash says. "You're looking right at the reason Sienna is involved." He points to me.

"She's his way in," Bash says, catching on quickly. "The gatekeeper. He obviously knows our bloodlines are connected."

"Do you think he's after your mother?" The color has been sucked from Terry's face, and his hand instinctively seeks out the gun tucked inside his jacket pocket.

"No, I think it's me he's after." Now that I've started, I have to tell them everything. "Mom met him yesterday. He was in a restaurant with Sienna. He knew that I was trailing them, so he came over and introduced himself. Mom said he looked familiar."

The door opens then, and Caleb walks in. "What have I missed?" He sits on the couch next to Cash and helps himself to a glass of iced water.

"Get yourself back upstairs to your wife and baby, lad." Terry gestures with a nod of his head towards the door. "Everything is under control."

Caleb's gaze slides around the room. "Okay. You look like you've seen a ghost, Terry. My twin brothers haven't been this quiet since Cash almost decapitated Bash with a golf club when they were six years old. And Kyle's worried about Sienna because her scumbag father is back on the scene."

"How do you know that?"

He shrugs. "Victoria spoke to Sienna last night." His eyes are puffy with lack of sleep, but an aura of peacefulness and contentment is clinging to him like a fine mist. "He should be easy enough to handle. The guy is a loser according to Victoria. We can make him go away."

"Oh, it gets better." Cash studies his empty glass. "Seems our father couldn't keep it in his pants before he met Mom."

Caleb's fists clench. His shoulders stiffen, and he sits forward, resting his elbows on his thighs. He might be two years younger than me, but he was the one who shielded us from our father's fists before he got arrested. Because of my asthma, Caleb made himself the alpha, and that's exactly what he's doing right now. He's on high alert, ready to strike.

"Talk to me," he says.

When I'm finished telling him about Nick Morris, he stands up, dragging himself to his full height. "Let's go speak to him, find out what he wants, and send him on his fucking merry way."

"Whoa." Terry raises his hands. "We need to think about this. We already know that he isn't operating alone."

"And Sienna knows about his father," I add. "I had to tell her. Nick has men following her. I've allocated her a suite here temporarily, until this is resolved."

"So, we'll be doing everyone a favor by getting rid of him." Caleb shrugs. "Win-win."

"Sienna will know I'm behind it."

"She'll thank you in the long run," Caleb says.

"I'm with Terry on this one." I stand up too. "No one wants him gone more than I do, but I don't want Sienna caught in the crossfire."

"She won't be." Caleb addresses Terry. "The guy at least needs a warning, Ter."

Terry's shoulders slump. "I hear you. If your mom finds out..." He leaves the sentence hanging. "But it's not going to be that simple. I had a couple of my men on his tail yesterday after your mom met him. Don't worry, she doesn't suspect the truth."

"She won't find out," Caleb mutters under his breath. "He'll be long gone before that happens."

Terry doesn't react. "He went to Sienna's apartment yesterday evening. He took flowers."

I flex my fingers. If I thought he'd laid a finger on Sienna, I'd wring his neck with my bare hands before handing his corpse over to my brothers to bury.

"He didn't stay long." Terry must sense my overwhelming urge to cause the man some serious harm. "Fifteen minutes max."

That's fifteen minutes too long.

"They lost him after he left."

"Lost him where?" I ignore my brothers' eyes on me. They know how I feel about Sienna, and Caleb, more than anyone, will understand the instinct to protect.

Terry shakes his head. "That's just it. My men said it was like he evaporated into the night."

"What the fuck." I'm pacing now, the way Sienna did when she was here earlier. "Someone is protecting him. Someone knows where he is."

"We'll find him, lad." Terry motions with both hands for me to settle.

"Meanwhile," Caleb says, "I got a report on Sienna's father. Robert Carlton Hooch. Grade A loser who targets women with kids, uses them for somewhere to kip for a while and then moves on when his creditors catch up with him."

"How much debt?" I've been so busy focusing on Nick's past, I didn't stop to check out Sienna's long-lost father. "He was in the Rinse a couple of days ago. With Sienna. He didn't seem surprised when I told him that it belonged to my brother."

"He'll have done his research," Caleb says. "He was in the casino all night, throwing money at the roulette table."

"Any trouble?"

"Nope. But it seems our friend Hooch has a string of debts with a casino run by a bratva family."

"The Petrovs?" Ivan Petrov was involved in Sienna's abduction earlier in the year. The family has apologized since, but I don't trust him.

"A new mob," Caleb says. "Does the name Bogrov mean anything?"

"It does to me." All eyes turn to Terry. "They're trying to run the Petrovs out of town."

11

SIENNA

My father's apartment isn't much bigger than mine, but it's in an area of Queens that I don't know well, which, by my erratic thinking, will hopefully mean that I'll be harder to track down.

He caught me off-guard outside the Wraith. He couldn't have timed his exit any better if he tried; I literally collided with him as I was running away from Seamus.

"Hey, sweetheart." He instinctively grabbed my arms to keep me on my feet and dropped them when I pulled away from him. "What are you doing here?"

I don't remember what I said. I probably wasn't making much sense at the time, and before I knew it, we were climbing into the back of a taxi and heading away from Manhattan.

It isn't until I'm standing in his living room, watching him pick his laundry up off the floor and trying to hide some empty liquor bottles, that I realize how rough he looks. His face is sagging, his skin gray. His eyes are bulging, and when he turns to face me with an armful of dirty clothes, I can see that the whites have been overtaken by swarming red lines.

"I wasn't expecting visitors."

"It's okay, you don't have to tidy up on my account."

I shouldn't be here. I understand the mixed signals I'm giving him: one moment I'm telling him I want nothing to do with him, and the next I'm hopping into a cab and coming home for breakfast. But despite the grubby carpet, and the scorch marks on the arms of the threadbare sofa, I kinda feel like I'm on neutral territory.

At least here I don't have to think about Kyle or Nick. So long as I make it clear to my father that I just need some breathing space, he won't get ideas that we're rekindling our non-existent father-daughter relationship.

"Don't be silly, sweetheart." He stops in the middle of the room and stares at me as if he can't remember how I got here. "I never thought... Well, I hoped that one day you'd come to visit me. You've made an old man very happy."

Fuck!

"Sit down, Sienna. I'll make coffee. I don't know about you, but I could do with some. It's only instant. Not sure if you've got a taste for the expensive stuff."

He talks to me from the open-plan kitchen. I've no idea where he deposited the laundry and bottles, but he's no longer holding them.

"Instant will be fine."

I check out the sofa cushions. They're smeared with something that was probably greasy and has now left dirty gray smudges in the weave of the fabric. I find a clean spot and sit down still wearing my coat. I feel uncomfortable standing in the middle of the room like I don't belong here.

I don't belong here. But I'm trying to think of it as a haven. A harbor in the storm. For now. Just while I get my head around what Kyle told me.

I realize as I watch my father hunched over the kettle on the counter, spooning coffee granules into two mugs, that when Kyle was talking about his father, I automatically confused the story with my own. His father almost killed his mom. I watched this man hurt my mom more times than I could count.

But they're not the same person.

I keep this in mind as he comes into the living room and hands me a cup of coffee that has too much cream in it. I cradle it in both hands, and stare at the milky swirls on the surface of the liquid.

"You want to tell me why you were in such a hurry this morning?" He eases himself into an armchair and slurps his drink.

"Not sure I know where to start."

"It's easy. Start at the beginning." He wipes his nose on the back of his hand and sniffs loudly. "Sorry. I'm a fucking idiot, I know. The beginning is the last thing you want to remember."

I'm not reliving the car accident for him. I'm not telling him about Kyle or Nick either; I might as well sit here and spill my heart onto the floor and let him sift through the pieces. No. He doesn't get to know everything, especially not the vulnerable parts.

"I need to find somewhere to live."

Last night, this was a disaster. A bomb thrown into the middle of a chaotic bonfire, just to shake things up a bit and see which way the sparks would fly. This morning, it feels like the easy part. There must be plenty of affordable apartments out there even if their location isn't exactly desirable; I've already made up my mind not to stay at the Wraith.

Call it pride. Call it stubbornness. Whatever.

I'm already indebted to Caleb and Victoria for the gallery. I'm not sure how much more debt I can shoulder before I crack beneath the weight.

"Why? What have you done?"

"Nothing."

Maybe if I was thinking straight, I'd have considered the oddness of the question. But I'm not, and it fades into insignificance compared to everything else that is going on in my life.

"My time is up." I shrug.

"Lucky for you, I came along when I did then."

I stare at him blankly.

"I have a spare room. You can stay here, sweetheart." He guzzles his coffee in one go and licks the dregs from his upper lip.

"I..." My pulse is racing. I walked straight into this one, and I need to dig my way out of it before it's too late. "No, I can't. Thank you, but—"

"Why can't you?" He scratches his eyebrow like I gave him a

conundrum to solve rather than telling him I can't use his spare room.

"I just can't."

I wish I could muster some conviction in my voice, but I'm still battling the notion that someone is having me followed. I've been abducted once already since Victoria met Caleb. How do people like the Murrays live with this constant threat of danger? Or do they become anesthetized to it over time? And this is the world that Victoria has brought baby Holly into.

"It wouldn't work," I add as an afterthought.

Because you tried to strangle my mom to death and then walked out on us.

"We want to get to know each other." The scratching shifts to his left ear.

I don't remind him that *he* wants to get to know *me*, and that this is one of those instances where it doesn't work both ways.

"I can't think of a better way, can you?" He raises a crooked eyebrow in my direction.

I feel the energy draining from me as if a plug has been pulled. "There's too much going on right now. It wouldn't be right. I need to handle this myself."

He sits forward in his seat. "You said you were worried about being followed, sweetheart. That's not the kind of situation I want my baby girl to handle alone. Not while I still have breath in my body."

Hysterical laughter gurgles inside my chest. He's serious, and I'm starting to wonder if he's been in a drug-induced coma for the past twenty years.

"There's nothing you can do about it."

"Have you seen me?" He stands up and straightens to his full, unimpressive height. He'd probably be as tall as Kyle if his shoulders weren't quite so bowed, but he speaks with the confidence of Andre the Giant. "They'll have to get through me first."

"I don't even know who *they* are."

"Does it matter? I don't see anyone else stepping up to help my little girl."

I almost chuckle at this. I wonder what he'd say if he knew that Nick was the first to offer me his spare room, while there's an executive suite with my name on it at the Wraith.

I know that Kyle lives in the building. Victoria and Caleb live there too with their baby daughter. So, why do I feel less exposed here in this dingy Queens apartment?

"Think about it while I make another coffee." He peers at the cooling liquid in my cup. "You haven't touched yours."

"I'm not thirsty."

He doesn't wait around. While the kettle chugs to life in the kitchen, his phone rings. He checks the caller ID on the screen, glances at me, and says, "I have to take this, sweetheart. Make yourself at home."

I expect him to go into the bedroom and shut the door, but instead, he goes outside and leaves me alone in the apartment.

While he's gone, I look around the living space. The walls were probably magnolia once upon a time, or ivory, or Chantilly lace: a pretty color with a pretty name. A generic painting hangs slightly askew on one wall, a country scene with haystacks and an old-fashioned horse and cart in the foreground. The shelves are home to a tiny vase containing some dusty silk flowers, a plastic clock showing the wrong time, and a book with a cracked spine, *The Richest Man in Babylon*. It's the only personal object in the entire apartment.

I hear the key turn in the lock.

"Sorry about that, sweetheart." He drops his phone back into his pocket. "So, when do you want to move in?"

"I don't know…" I stand up. "I should get to work."

"Have you got appointments scheduled for today?"

"No, but I—"

"That's settled then. Look, stay here today. I'll leave you alone, I promise. We can go and pick up some of your stuff later, see how you feel in the morning. Maybe then, you'll feel comfortable enough to tell me what's going on."

"Just for today," I find myself saying without fully considering the implications of spending twenty-four hours in my father's company.

Perhaps it's the view from the window of concrete apartment blocks. Or the sound of cars rumbling past outside. Or the Reggae music blasting from a neighbor's stereo. Regular noises; regular lives. People running errands, preparing for their shift at work, and wondering what to cook for dinner.

I take off my coat and make myself a black coffee.

True to his word my father does leave me alone.

He showers and then disappears into his room. Within minutes, his snores are loud enough to rattle the walls.

I roll up my sleeves and clean the kitchen. I can't sit in the living room doing nothing all day, and cleaning is therapeutic. I clear my head and convince myself that twenty-four hours will give Nick and Kyle sufficient time to back off. I don't know if Seamus followed me here; I haven't checked outside for fear I'll find another jogger running back and forth and a car with tinted windows parked up on the curb. I'm hoping that if he did, he'll report back to Kyle that I'm with my father.

This is the scariest part: everyone—*Kyle and Nick*—seem to have more information at their fingertips than should be legal. The fact that I haven't seen a laptop or tablet in my father's apartment is some small consolation.

Later that afternoon, we exit the building via the back way and take a taxi to my apartment. My father waits outside while I hastily pack a bag and then we go straight back and order a pizza takeout. We eat in front of the TV, a game show I've never watched before. My father guesses the answers and gets them wrong and then shakes his head every time I guess correctly.

"How did my little girl get to be so clever, huh?"

"I worked hard at school."

The comment settles between us like a line that says DO NOT CROSS. We've deliberately skirted around the past, trying to keep this situation as normal as possible, but I guess it's unavoidable.

"Your mom must've been so proud of you." There are tears in his eyes again, and this time they almost seem genuine.

Almost.

"She was." I fold stringy cheese into my mouth and wipe grease from my chin with a paper napkin.

"I wish I'd gotten to tell her how sorry I was."

Deep breath. "Why didn't you?"

"I waited too long." He bites off half a slice of pizza. "Then, there never seemed to be a right time, and I thought it best to leave your mom in peace."

"What about me?"

"You were better off with your mom. I wasn't in a good place, sweetheart. You didn't need me walking back into your life with all the shit that was following me around."

He replaces the lid on his empty pizza box and rises. "I've got to go out. Keep the door locked, and don't wait up for me."

He dumps the box on the kitchen counter and grabs his keys.

"Where are you going?"

"To see a man about a dog."

The door closes behind him, and he locks me inside.

I can't sleep. The bed is uncomfortable, my feet feel like blocks of ice, and I can't figure out how to turn the heating on. And my father isn't home.

I shouldn't be concerned about him, but it feels wrong that he asked me to stay when he knew he wasn't going to be here. He promised to look out for me—were they just words to him? A means to an end to convince me to stay?

Or do the lies trip off his tongue so easily that he doesn't bother to keep track of them and follow through with actions?

Pulling on an extra pair of socks, I wrap my coat around me and wander through to the kitchen. I boil the kettle and make a cup of coffee to keep me warm; sleep is eluding me anyway, so the caffeine won't make any difference.

Back in my father's spare room, I sit on the bed with the pillows propped up behind me and power up my phone. On my father's advice, I switched it off when I arrived so that I couldn't be tracked, but thinking about it now, even with my foggy brain cells, I'm sure that cell phones can be traced by their most recent activity.

I've had three missed calls and twenty-seven messages from Kyle.

Victoria tried calling six times; no doubt Kyle alerted her to my falling off the radar. I open her last message: *Si, I'm worried about you. Call me!*

Nothing from Nick.

I shouldn't be disappointed. Didn't I send a private message to the universe requesting that they both leave me alone? But it leaves me with a sense of uneasiness, nonetheless. He has texted me relentlessly since the gallery opening, turning up unannounced to take me to lunch, rocking up at my apartment with flowers.

And then silence.

I check the time on my phone. 04:57. I can't call Victoria in the middle of the night, and I already know what she'll say when she finds out where I am: *"What the fuck, Si! Are you insane?"*

I hear a crash from somewhere in the apartment, and my heart starts racing.

Fuck!

Hands trembling, I place the cup of coffee on the nightstand, and tiptoe across the room to the door. My blood is gushing in my ears so loudly I can't hear anything else. Then, a dull thump reaches me, closely followed by, "Shh."

I peer around the room for something I can use as a weapon, and my gaze settles on a length of curtain pole propped up against the corner of the opposite wall. I grab it quickly and go back to the door, opening it a crack, barely wide enough to allow the cool air of the apartment to brush my face.

All I can see is the dingy darkness of the hallway. Whoever it is, they haven't switched the lights on, which means they don't want to be seen. My mind latches on to the man in black loitering outside the gallery, and the car with the tinted windows parked outside my apartment. They know I'm alone.

Where the fuck is my father when I need him?

I lean back against the door. I wish I'd gone home, but there's no point regretting it now. I have two choices: I wait for them to find me, or I try to catch them off-guard and use the element of surprise against them first.

My pulse is galloping. My internal temperature has gone through the roof. But I don't consider the consequences of what I'm about to do.

I open the door and peep through again.

Nothing.

I'm about to fling the door wide open and race along the dingy hallway yelling at the top of my lungs when my father stumbles out of the kitchen with a pint glass of water in one hand and practically falls through his bedroom door.

I don't move. I stare at the closed door until my eyes water. I'm still wielding the curtain pole in my hands like a lightsaber, waiting for him to re-emerge or for someone else to pounce on me from the shadows. But nothing happens.

There was no intruder. No man in black with a pistol in his pocket. No pretend jogger wearing a black suit under his sweatpants.

My father had clearly been drinking. He didn't even notice me with a metal pole in my hand, and I can already hear him snoring.

I go back into my room and close the door. I drag the nightstand in front of it—it won't stop anyone from getting in, but it will at least make a noise if someone tries to open the door. Then I sit upright in bed, drink my coffee, and wait for morning to come.

I play Candy Crush Saga on my phone until my eyes feel sore.

I scroll through social media.

I avoid reading Kyle's messages; I don't have the bandwidth for them while I'm still in fight-or-flight mode. They'll have to wait until daylight at least.

My eyes feel gritty when I climb out of bed, shower, and make coffee. I find an old radio and turn the music up loud. I eat a slice of leftover pizza, cold, because I'm running on empty, but it sticks in my throat and makes me feel nauseous.

I want to get out of here, go to the gallery, immerse myself in paint and cleanse myself of the past twenty-four hours. But I'm not leaving until I've spoken to my father.

It's almost lunchtime when he eventually emerges from his room like a mole burrowing out from its underground tunnel. He wanders into the kitchen scratching his head and yawning loudly.

"Morning, sweetheart." He refills his glass with water from the cold tap.

"Where were you last night?"

He tilts his head back and drains the glass without coming up for air. "I met up with some friends." He burps loudly.

"I thought you were an intruder."

He blinks at me slowly. "You're safe here, sweetheart. I wouldn't let anything happen to you; I told you that."

"But you weren't here. I couldn't sleep. So, when I heard a noise, I thought someone had broken in."

"Now, you're being paranoid." He opens a cabinet, pulls out a loaf of bread, and sticks two slices into the toaster.

"Stop being so fucking paranoid! You're the reason I don't come home because I can't deal with the fucking interrogation!"

The memory flashes into my head, and it's so vivid it takes my breath away. I've never thought of it before. It must've been buried beneath layers of happy memories that I made with my mom before she died, but now that it's there, I can't shake it off.

That's what he used to say to my mom. Whenever they had a fight, he'd accuse her of being paranoid, like she was the one in the wrong.

"I'm not being paranoid." I keep my voice calm. "You didn't come home till 5 a.m. I thought someone had broken in."

"What are you talking about, sweetheart?" He's holding a tub of spread from the fridge in front of him. "I was home just after midnight."

"No. I made a coffee and checked my phone. I was waiting for you to come home. You went into the kitchen, filled a glass of water, and went to bed."

"I always take a glass of water to bed with me. But I can assure you that I was home a little after midnight. I peeped into your room, and you were sound asleep, so I didn't wake you. You must've heard me when I got up in the night because I was thirsty."

The toaster pings, and he catches the slices of bread as they pop out. He turns his back on me to spread the butter.

I'm confused. I was awake all night and I didn't hear him come in. And I'm positive that I'd have heard him open my bedroom door.

"I didn't sleep." I'm frantically trying to recall if I did doze off or not. "My brain wouldn't switch off."

He grins at me from over his shoulder. "Next time, I'll record your snoring."

"I don't snore."

"I've got news for you, sweetheart: you do."

I'm too tired to argue with him. I know what I heard, and I know what I saw, but now I'm questioning whether he's telling the truth, and I did maybe doze off for a while without even realizing.

"I'm going to the gallery." I grab my purse.

"Wait for me to finish my breakfast. I'll come with you."

12

KYLE

"I went to Nick Morris's clinic this morning." Mom's gaze flits between me and Terry from the couch where, for once, she has a cup of creamy, sweetened coffee in front of her. "He isn't there."

"Okay, Mom. Firstly, what the hell were you thinking?"

When I discovered Nick's identity, my initial reaction was that he was coming after his half-brothers. Jealousy maybe? He has his own clinic, a lot of his clients are wealthy women, and while he doesn't move in celebrity circles, his reputation means that his income will keep him in regular Caribbean cruises and skiing vacations.

But it doesn't compare to the Murray fortune. So, I convinced myself that this wasn't about Mom. If, however, he's looking for a way in and Sienna isn't playing ball, Mom might be next on his list of targets, and that's another risk I'm not prepared to take.

"I needed to see it for myself." Mom raises her coffee to her lips, a distraction from what she knows is coming.

"See what?"

"Him. Caelan's son."

My chest tightens. I didn't need to use my inhaler while I was in Ireland. I've not been back for two weeks, and already I feel that restriction in my lungs, as though they shrunk in the wash.

I glance at Terry. His expression is unfathomable, but his eyes register a mixture of emotions: fear, surprise, resignation. Guilt blossoms inside my chest, adding a little extra strain to my wheezing airways; I should never have asked her to meet me for lunch. If I'd kept her away from Nick, she'd have been blissfully unaware of my half-brother's existence.

"How did you know?"

"There was something in his eyes. Something cold." She's looking straight through me to the past, to memories of the man we've spent our lives protecting her from. "I knew that he looked familiar, but I couldn't attach a name to the face. It was the feeling in here—" she places a hand over her tummy "—that jogged my memory. That sickly sense of foreboding that something bad was coming."

She blinks, snapping herself out of her painful reverie.

"I'm sorry, Mom."

I slide my inhaler from my pocket—I've carried it with me ever since my last asthma attack when Sienna was abducted by Olivia Dragonetti and Ivan Petrov—and place it between my lips. I suck in a deep breath and hold it in my lungs.

"I understand why you didn't tell me, but it wasn't your secret to keep, Kyle. Or yours, Ter." She faces my stepfather. "How can I protect myself when I don't have all the information?"

"We thought it was for the best." Terry rubs his jawline with one hand. "You know I won't let anything happen to you. I made that promise when I met you, and I've never let you down, have I?"

"No," Mom concedes. "But this is different. This is personal. That man is here for one reason, and it isn't to reduce women's breast sizes."

"Mom, we don't think that this is about you," I say.

"How many meetings have you had without me?" Her eyes narrow.

"One." One too many, I realize now. "We think that he's using Sienna to get to me."

She finishes her coffee and grimaces; all my life, she has added too much cream to her coffee because it's too bitter and then doesn't drink it because it cools too quickly.

"From his disappearing act," she continues, "I'd say that he's already gotten what he needs from Sienna."

"Did you speak to anyone at the clinic?"

"Uh-huh. They said he's taking some leave to deal with a family crisis." She pauses. "That's professional-speak for he's lying low until he's ready to make his next move."

"We just need to figure out what that is," Terry says.

"Well…" Mom stands. "While you're figuring it out, I'm going to get my daughter as far away from here as possible."

One glance at Terry tells me that he knew nothing about this decision either. "Where are you going?"

"Ireland." Mom's shoulders slump. "I don't want to split the family up for Christmas, but we made a pact to keep Emily out of the family business, and that's what I'm going to do."

"Moira." Terry steps closer and folds her hands in his. "I can't protect you both when you're on another continent."

"You won't need to, Tel. Where we're going, no one will ever find us."

"But—"

"It's final," Mom snaps. "You take care of my boys, and I'll take care of our daughter."

My phone vibrates then with a message from Seamus. *She's on the move.*

I message him straight back: *You know what to do.*

"What is it?" Mom asks.

"Sienna has just left her father's apartment in Queens. I wanted her to stay here, but she's too stubborn to listen." I'm already heading for the door.

"Kyle." Mom's voice halts me. "Maybe Queens is the best place for her right now. While she's with her father, she's removed from whatever is going on with Caelan's son."

The only problem with that is I don't trust her father either.

Sienna doesn't question why I'm at the gallery. She closes the door behind me, turns the key in the lock, and I follow her into her office.

Nothing has been moved. The gallery is still clean and fresh and bright, but something oppressive is hanging in the space above our heads, casting a whole new light over the vibrant artwork. Twilight has come early, and it isn't going anywhere.

Not until I make this situation with Nick Morris go away.

When she turns to face me, her eyelids are heavy, her face ghastly pale.

"Talk to me, Sienna." I try to hide the dismay at her tired appearance from my voice. I'm clambering over precarious rocks here, an obstacle placed between us by a man who has now disappeared off the face of the earth.

"I doubt I can tell you anything you don't already know." She fills the coffee machine, and hovers next to it, waiting for the aroma to fill the room.

"You stayed in Queens last night, with your father."

"Ha! You're not even going to pretend you're not having me followed."

"You left the Wraith in a hurry. I was worried about you."

"So, Seamus has been sitting outside my father's apartment all night?" Her voice has lost the accusatory edge.

"Not all night."

She straightens two cups on the tray next to the machine. "What about the men who were outside my apartment? Are you still denying any knowledge of them?"

"Sienna..."

I want to take her home with me. I want to tuck her up in my bed and watch her sleep peacefully, safe in the knowledge that no harm will come to her while she's in my care. But she isn't ready to trust me, and so far, my attempts to gain her confidence keep backfiring.

"If they were my men, you wouldn't have known they were there."

Her lips twitch at the corners. "Did Seamus have anything to report back in the night?"

There's something she isn't telling me, but I'm conscious that I need to tread carefully. She let me into the gallery this morning. The moment she stops talking to me will be the time I start truly panicking. If she doesn't keep me in the loop, I can't protect her.

"Like what?" I hesitate, unsure how far to push it. "I know you got a pizza takeout."

"Ah, but do you know what toppings and sides we got?" Finally, the smile reaches her eyes.

"You've got me there." I allow my shoulders to drop just a fraction, enough to let her know that I'm still not here to put pressure on her. "I know that you picked up some clothes from home and then didn't leave the apartment until you came here today."

Her expression immediately turns serious again. "What about my father? Did you have him followed too?"

"I know where he was if that's what you're asking."

Sienna furrows her brow. "Where?"

Okay, so either he hasn't told her where he's been, or she doesn't believe him.

"He was in a casino."

"Which one?"

"Does it matter?"

My mom said that she couldn't protect herself and her family if she wasn't armed with all the relevant information. But this is different. Sienna's father is a loser with a gambling addiction. He's easily handled. Unlike the illusionist cosmetic surgeon whose pièce de résistance is vanishing into thin air.

She inclines her head. "Did he win?"

"No." I'm hoping she doesn't ask me how much money he lost.

She fills the two cups with strong black coffee and hands one to me. "So, he'll be desperate to win some money back, huh?"

"That's how it usually goes."

"Shall we sit down?" It isn't really a question.

She slides the chair out from behind her desk and sits down. She rests her elbows on the desk and cups her face with both hands as though her head is too heavy to hold up.

I sit opposite her.

"What time did he get home?"

"What's this all about, Sienna?" I don't spell it out: she spent the night in his apartment, but she's asking me about his movements. Something isn't quite right.

She blows the surface of her coffee to cool it down and takes a tentative sip. "I only want to know what time he got home." Her bloodshot eyes are all over the place, and that's before the caffeine hits.

"Around 5 a.m."

She chews her bottom lip so aggressively I'm worried she'll put her teeth straight through it. "You're sure about that?"

"Aye."

"Did you see anyone else enter or leave the building?" Her voice trembles.

"Neighbor on the first floor went out at twelve-thirty and came back with a carrier bag filled with liquor and smoking a joint. Another neighbor left earlier in the evening to start a night shift at the hospital."

Sienna sits upright. "How do you know this?"

"She was wearing a nurse's uniform, and she didn't look like she was heading to a costume party."

She puffs up her cheeks and releases a steady breath. "That's that then."

"You'll have to let me into the secret, or I can't help you."

"It doesn't matter." She strokes the side of her cup with her thumb catching a stray drop of brown liquid.

"It does to me."

For the first time since I arrived, she looks at me properly. "I heard him come home. I couldn't sleep, and I thought it was an intruder. But when I questioned him about it this morning, he said he was home by midnight."

"Maybe he was confused."

"He was drunk, you mean?"

I spread my hands. "Aye. Or maybe he felt guilty for leaving you alone all night and hoped that you didn't hear him come in."

"I guess..." She doesn't sound convinced.

I feel as if I'm being torn in two. Part of me wants to sit here until I've convinced her to take advantage of a suite in the Wraith. While the other half of me, the half that isn't controlled by my heart, is trusting my mom and Terry's advice to keep her safe in Queens. For now.

"Sienna, do you feel safe with your father?" I can't let this question go unasked.

She closes her eyes and inhales deeply. "I shouldn't feel safe with him after what he did to my mom, but I don't think he would hurt me. Besides, I have a curtain pole."

"A curtain pole?"

"Long story." Her lips quirk into a weary, lopsided smile. "I'll keep it next to my bed."

Her gaze holds mine, and it feels as if she has a whole lot more to say but doesn't know where to begin.

"You know that you can call me any time."

"I know."

"I'm not going to pull my men, Sienna. I know you don't like the idea of them knowing your every move, but until... Well, until I'm certain that you're not in any danger, they're staying."

"You think I'm in danger?"

"I'm simply being careful." I swallow a mouthful of coffee. "Have you heard from Nick?"

Her hands instinctively curl into fists, and I want so badly to unfurl them, kiss them all over, and ease the tension in her spine.

"Not since he... Not since he came to my apartment with flowers." Pause. "Why?"

"No one knows where he is."

She arches an eyebrow. "You mean *you* don't know where he is."

"He isn't at his clinic. His assistant claims that he's busy with family matters."

She shakes her head vehemently, and I feel her slipping away. "Maybe he wanted a break from being followed too."

"No, Sienna, that isn't what this is all about."

"What is it all about then? You can't keep dropping cryptic hints without telling me what the fuck is going on. You don't like each other, I get it. But you can't go around forcing innocent men to skip town and then shift all the blame onto them."

"Sienna, he isn't innocent. He isn't the person you think he is."

"Go on then." All traces of weariness have gone from her voice. "What has he done that's so bad?"

"I don't know yet."

"Well, be sure to come and tell me when you find out. Or maybe just ask Seamus to knock on the door and recount the message on your behalf."

"Sienna, please listen to me. I don't want to leave you in Queens, but my family believes that you'll be safe there. They—"

"Your family? So, what, you all sat around a boardroom table and decided that I can't look after myself? That I'm a gullible artist who doesn't recognize a con man when he asks me on a date?"

"No, it isn't like that."

"Was Victoria invited to this meeting? Did she agree with me staying with my father? Because that sure as shit wasn't how it sounded the last time I spoke to her. Or does she have to go along with the family decision?"

Her cheeks are growing flushed. I don't know how but whenever we're together, the conversation always spirals out of control. But I do know that it always revolves around Nick Morris. Every goddamned time.

"No, Sienna. Victoria doesn't know about any of this." I stand up. "But I do know that she would want me to protect you, and that's what I intend to do."

I walk back through the gallery, and she doesn't follow me. It takes every ounce of my self-control not to turn around, run back to her, and take her home with me.

But I don't.

When Sienna Walker comes to me, I want it to be on her terms.

Until then, I will do everything in my power to keep her safe. Even if it means following her backwards and forwards to Queens myself.

13

SIENNA

I spend the rest of the day painting, transferring all my niggling insecurities onto the canvas where I can make better sense of them.

I don't message Nick. If the information given to Kyle is correct, and he's dealing with family matters, he won't want to be disturbed. I intend to take advantage of his silence by shutting him out of my mind completely.

Him and Kyle.

I was almost ready to take Kyle up on the generous offer of using an executive suite at the Wraith temporarily.

Almost.

Until he dropped his bombshell about the family conference in which I was the main topic of conversation. Does he have any idea how it feels to know that people are talking about your life as if they're the ones in control? Or is being in control such an intrinsic part of his life that he can't see it from my point of view?

I block my father from my thoughts too.

But when I'm cleaning my paintbrushes at the end of the day —one of my favorite jobs as it's so therapeutic—the uneasiness creeps back in.

Kyle's suggestion that my father felt guilty for leaving me alone in his apartment all night sounds feasible, but the niggling feeling like an itch behind my eyeballs is telling me he's wrong. Guilt has never featured in my father's vocabulary before, so why now? And if he felt bad about leaving me knowing that I was being followed, why did he go out at all?

No, the lure of the casino was greater than his daughter's needs.

Which brings me full circle back to why he lied about what time he got home.

My stomach twists when it occurs to me that he might not have been lying. What if he snuck in at midnight as he claimed, but with company? What if he brought a woman home with him, and the sounds I heard at 5 a.m. were her trying to leave before I woke up?

I don't know which is worse. Him lying to me, or the mental image of him fucking a woman in the other room while I'm there. And if that's the case, is it going to be a regular occurrence?

Closing the gallery for the night, my movements grow sluggish as lack of sleep catches up on me. I've always been independent. I had to grow up fast when my mom died, and I've always looked after myself, but I feel like a lost and lonely sixteen-year-old again. I'm afraid to go home, but the thought of going back to my father's apartment for a second night doesn't exactly fill me with holiday cheer.

I retrieve my coat and purse from the office and check my messages. They're all from Victoria, begging me to call her back. I know I should. She has a newborn baby to look after, she doesn't need her best friend adding to her already overloaded stress levels. But tiredness is crashing through me in waves, and I don't have the energy to tell her everything that has happened.

I message her instead, to stop her from freaking out:

Sorry V, been super-busy. I'll call you tomorrow. Give the baby a big kiss from me.

I haven't even met Holly yet.

My best friend is experiencing the most momentous, life-changing experience, and I've not been there for her. I'm a bad friend. I've let the situation with Nick and Kyle get out of hand and I've taken a backseat in my own life.

Well, not anymore.

I've got this.

I'll go back to my father's apartment, grab my stuff, and then I'm going home. Kyle promised to protect me, so now's his opportunity to show me what he can do.

I feel like a bird released from its cage, and I practically float towards the door. I don't know why I didn't think of this sooner—there's no reason for me not to stay in my own apartment if Kyle's men are guarding me. I don't need to be in the Wraith. Wherever I go, they'll go too.

I take a taxi to Queens. It's an expense that I could do without, but I'm still riding on the buzz of taking charge of my own life again. The holidays are almost here. I've given my dad more effort than he deserves. And there's no possibility of Nick turning up at my apartment with a reservation for dinner in some swanky Manhattan restaurant.

Tonight, I'm going to make some grilled cheese and sleep.

Tomorrow, refreshed, I'll start looking for another apartment.

"Didn't your key work?" my father asks when he opens the door to let me in.

"What key?"

He stands aside, and I join him in the narrow hallway. No lights are on in the apartment, I notice, and I can see the flickering lights from the TV in the living room.

"I gave you the spare key this morning." He closes the door and turns the key with a click that jangles my nerves.

"No, you didn't. You must've forgotten."

He stands too close to me, and I can smell his stale breath.

"I left it in the kitchen for you." He sniffs loudly.

"It's probably still there. Shall we go and check?"

I lead the way. I need some time to think without having to stare at his hunched shoulders.

I've no idea how old my father is, but I would guess he's in his mid to late sixties. Is he too young to start showing signs of early dementia? Or was he simply suffering from a massive hangover this morning and there's an enormous black hole where his memory should be?

Something spicy is simmering in a pan on the stove and my

stomach growls, reminding me that all I've eaten today is a slice of cold pizza.

I turn around to face him. "Where did you leave the spare key?"

"In the fruit bowl." He gestures to an empty dish with nothing but dust and fluff collecting in the bottom and then stirs the food in the pan with a wooden spoon.

"Maybe you left it somewhere else."

"I remember giving it to you, sweetheart. We swapped keys. I've been to your apartment today to collect some more of your stuff like you asked."

My heart starts thudding sickeningly. "I didn't ask you to go to my apartment. I've still got my key."

I pull my keyring out of my purse and fumble through them to find the one I'm looking for. The silver key that fits my front door, and the heavier key that lets me into the building. They're both gone.

"Did you take my keys?" My breathing is speeding up, and I'm too hot in my coat with the heat from the hob.

He half-turns, dripping Bolognese sauce onto the floor. "You gave them to me, sweetheart. You stood right there and—"

"No." I shake my head. Why didn't I notice sooner that they were missing? Because now I realize how light the bunch of keys in my hand feels. "I didn't give them to you. I'm going home. Why would I have asked you to bring my clothes here?"

His bottom lip droops. "But I've made spaghetti Bolognese. Your favorite. I used to make it for you when you were a little girl."

I have a vague recollection of sitting at the kitchen table when I was a kid, pushing pasta around a bowl because it tasted like tomato, and tomatoes make me gag. They still do.

"I can't stay. I only came to collect my stuff."

"I made it especially for you."

"I don't like spaghetti Bolognese."

"But it was your favorite." His face scrunches up in confusion.

"It wasn't. I only ate it because…"

Because I was afraid that you would hurt me if I didn't.

He stares at the wooden spoon in his hand, and the steam hovering above the pan. Then his expression crumples. "I fucked up again, didn't I?"

"It's okay. I'm not hungry." Liar. "I just want to get home and go to bed."

"I'll cook something else. I can run down to the bodega on the next block. Tell me what you want, and I'll go and get it." The desperation in his voice bites into my already jagged nerves.

"No, please don't. I'm tired. It's been a long day. Can I have my keys back?"

I hold out my hand, and he rummages in the pocket of his loose-fitting jeans. I don't breathe until he drops them into my palm. They're warm from his body heat, and I try not to think about it as I reattach them to the keyring. I still have no idea how he got them, but I park that problem for now.

"Where did you put my stuff?"

"In the spare room."

I don't waste a beat. My father's proximity and the smell of the tomatoey sauce are making me feel claustrophobic. I can't even remember why I came here last night, and it's even more unthinkable to me why I accepted his offer to stay.

Twenty-four hours, I said. Or is that another memory that will differ to his?

A black sack is on the bed in the spare room. I open it and peer inside. Sure enough, it's filled with my clothes, and I'm tempted to leave them here because now I have to live with knowing that he rummaged through my closet while I was painting in my studio.

What else did he touch while he was there without my permission?

He said that I asked him to collect my stuff. I know I'm tired, but I'm pretty fucking certain I'd remember exposing myself and everything that I possess to the man who hurt my mom.

Securing the black sack with a knot, I drag it into the hallway. I peer around the kitchen door at my father who is glugging beer from a bottle.

"I'm going now."

He wipes his lips with the back of his hand. "I wish you would stay. I won't go out tonight. We can get noodles or a kebab, whatever you want."

"I can't." I soften my tone, but I'm not apologizing for leaving him.

I never asked him to come back into my life, but all I want to do now is draw a line under the past and move forward. Alone. And he can congratulate himself on putting things right which is no doubt how he'll remember this.

He walks with me to the front door.

Outside, I hesitate. Will he accept that this goodbye is final? Or should I walk away and then block his number?

"You can return my spare key when you find it, sweetheart." Before I can remind him that I don't have it, he adds, "And the next time you need to borrow some money, all you've got to do is ask."

Then he closes the door in my face.

That night, I sleep for twelve hours. I wash all my clothes to cleanse them of the smell of my father's apartment. I paint. I throw myself into PR for the gallery.

I don't look for Kyle's men outside my building.

I don't dwell on my father's parting comment that I stole money from him. I'm not angry or frightened. I don't feel sorry for him—I don't feel anything at all—but I realize now that he needs medical assistance, and that I don't owe him anything.

A couple of evenings later, I have a meeting with a client at the gallery, a restaurant owner looking for some pieces to hang in their foyer. The woman, who is in her forties with fine, pale hair caught up into a sleek ponytail, and the casual elegance of someone who knows the clothes that suit her, is approachable and talkative. Within minutes of entering the gallery, she tells me that I'm the artist she's been looking for all her life.

I feel my smile growing wider as the meeting progresses. She wants to commission enough pieces for me to put a downpayment on a new apartment, and I finally feel as if the world has started spinning the right way again.

Until my phone rings, and I see Kyle's name on the screen. He has kept his distance, as promised. If he's ringing me now, he must have a good reason, and I instinctively know that it won't be good news.

"Please excuse me," I say to the client as I hit the green button.

"Sienna." Kyle's voice sends a shiver of excitement down my spine, and I hide my face from her. "I need you to come to the Wraith."

"Now?" I switch my phone to my other ear. "I'm in the middle of—"

"I'm sorry. I didn't want to call you, but your father insisted."

"My father?" I lower my voice. "Kyle, can I call you back?"

"I wouldn't have bothered you if it wasn't urgent. If you don't want to get involved, just say the word. But I'll have to let my security team deal with him."

"Why?" I glance at my client who is studying her own phone and pretending politely not to listen. I can't afford to lose her, but I need to know what's going on. "What has he done?"

"I'll explain when you get here. He's refusing to cooperate until you arrive."

Is this how it feels to have someone like my father in your life? Does trouble follow him around or does he not know any other way to exist?

"I'll get there as soon as I can."

I end the call and face my client, who is already sliding her phone into her purse and rising to her feet.

"I'm so sorry," I say. "It's a family emergency."

"I understand. Family must always come first." She produces a gold-embossed business card and places it on my desk. "I'll be in touch. It was a pleasure meeting you, Sienna. We'll be seeing a lot more of each other in the future."

I breathe a sigh of relief. At least I haven't lost the first promising customer to walk through my door since Bash.

I watch her climb into a red sports car and drive away before I lock up and hail a passing taxi to take me to the Wraith. I'm not sure why Kyle didn't involve his security team before calling me, but I guess he must have his reasons.

When I arrive, the concierge ushers me straight through to a private room in the casino where I find my father seated at a table with his head in his hands, and an empty brandy glass in front of him. A guy with long gray hair tied back into a low ponytail sits opposite him. I can't see his face, but from the broad shoulders, thick neck, and black suit, I guess he must be security.

Kyle comes rushing over to me and pulls me into a booth so that we can speak in private. "I'm sorry, Sienna. Your father was escorted from the casino earlier." Pause. "He was cheating."

At this point, nothing surprises me, but then I recall his forgetfulness and his allegation that I'd stolen money from him.

"Kyle," I keep my voice low, "do you think he understands what he is being accused of?"

Kyle's eyes flicker momentarily. "He understands. This isn't *Rain Man*. You don't count cards and then plead ignorance when you get caught."

"He was counting cards?" I don't know what this means exactly—my knowledge of card games is restricted to Rummy for beginners and Crazy Eights—but I do know that cheating will never be tolerated. "Will you ban him?" Maybe it would be the best thing that could happen to him.

"It isn't that simple. He owes a lot of dangerous people a lot of money, and I can't just let him walk out of here with a verbal warning to stay away. I have to let these people know, do you understand?"

"I think so. Is it some kind of casino-owner code? You know, like a pirate code?"

Kyle smiles. "Something like that."

"Why am I here, Kyle?"

"He refused to go anywhere until he saw you again."

I shake my head. "He does realize that I'm not responsible for him, right?"

"That's why I wanted to speak to you in person."

My phone vibrates then. It isn't a call. It's something I've only heard once before, when the new alarms in the gallery were being tested.

I stare at the screen. "Fuck. I've got to go, Kyle." I'm already sliding out of the booth. "Someone is trying to break into the gallery."

14

KYLE

"I'm coming with you."

Her gaze instinctively slides towards her father, who is sitting with his head in hands like he has no idea where things went so wrong.

"What about—" she begins.

"Terry will take care of it, Sienna."

I recognize the look in her eyes. It's despair. Overwhelmed. Weariness.

She doesn't deserve this.

I lead the way through the casino and down to the basement lot where Seamus is waiting for us with the car engine running.

Sitting in the back seat with Sienna, the brightly lit store windows flashing by in a blur, I berate myself for not insisting that she stay in a suite at the Wraith when I had the chance.

Too many coincidences. Nick's disappearance. Her father somehow convincing her to stay at his apartment and then getting caught cheating ... *in our casino.*

It's all connected. But despite throwing every second of my time at it, I still don't know how.

Sienna's face is turned toward the passenger window. Her shoulders are tense. Her fists are clenched by her sides. Her reflection in the glass is ghastly pale.

I cover her hand with mine. "You're cold."

She turns to look at me, and her eyes plead with me to tell her that everything will be alright.

"The NYPD will already be on the scene. Any damage that has occurred: I'll get it sorted tonight, Sienna."

I hope that she can read between the lines and know how much I love her. It's my fault that she has to rebuild her trust in me, and I'll give her all the time in the world if that's what it's going to take.

She doesn't speak. We spend the rest of the journey with my hand over hers, and her hazy reflection haunting me from the passenger window.

What is the point of wealth if I can't take away her pain? The question slides back and forth behind my eyelids like a mantra. *What is the point...?*

The revolving blue lights come into view as we pull into the road housing Sienna's gallery. My pulse races. I'd hoped that it might be a false alarm, a glitch in the system, or a mouse scurrying across the floor inside. Now, the best I can hope for is that the damage is minimal.

Sienna's door opens before Seamus can bring the car to a halt.

I don't miss a beat. I jump out, circling the car in a few strides. I'm not letting her do this alone.

A uniformed cop greets us at the doorway.

I can see more uniforms inside, but my gaze has already settled on what appears to be the remains of a shredded canvas, and hot, stinging bile rises in my throat.

"This is Sienna Walker," I speak for her.

Sienna is frozen to the spot, one hand hovering over her mouth while her gaze darts back and forth, trying to see the destruction and not wanting to see it at the same time.

"She's the owner of the gallery."

"I'm sorry, ma'am." The cop's faint smile is apologetic. "I'll need to see some ID before I can let you inside."

"Kyle...?" Sienna's voice is barely audible. Her eyes are large with tears.

I slide my wallet from my jacket pocket and present my own ID to the cop. "My family owns the Wraith, the Rinse, and the Titan."

I'm not above using our reputation when the situation calls for it, and right now, I'd bribe him with a Caribbean cruise for him and every member of his extended family, and his neighbors, if it would help Sienna.

The cop's eyes hardly graze my ID before he waves us inside.

I hear him confirm our entry to a colleague, but the words hardly register in my brain as it tries to process what my eyes are seeing.

The floor is littered with strips of canvas, long jagged splinters of broken easel, splashes of color ripped out of context. Some paintings remain on the wall, but the torn artwork hangs from them in tatters. Nothing has been left untouched.

I feel numb, but when my eyes land on Sienna, she resembles a waxwork of the beautiful woman I know. Her face is ashen. Her expression is twisted into a combination of grief and disbelief. If someone broke into the Wraith and trashed the casino, I'd be gutted, but it doesn't compare to the loss of Sienna's artwork. She must feel as if her heart has been ripped from her chest and shredded into a million tiny irreparable pieces.

A female cop approaches us, flinching as she follows Sienna's gaze to the painting that held pride of place at the launch, and is now torn straight down the middle, but still standing.

"I'm sorry, ma'am," she says. "I realize how difficult this must be for you, but I need to ask you a few questions."

Sienna turns huge, tear-filled eyes towards the woman, but doesn't acknowledge her. She sways a little, and her hand instinctively reaches for mine. I squeeze it and slide my other arm around her shoulders. It's all I can do for her in the moment.

It's the least I can do.

If I hadn't called her to the Wraith…

The police officer slides a small notepad and pen from her jacket pocket. "There were no obvious signs of a break-in. Can you tell me who else has a key to the property?"

Sienna's breathing is shallow, and I give her another squeeze. "No one," she whispers.

"Are you sure about that, ma'am?"

"Did you give Victoria a key?" I prompt.

"No." Her voice is filled with panic like this is a test, and she's scared of getting all the answers wrong. "Not with the baby. I didn't want to put any pressure on her."

"And does anyone else have access to your keys?" The cop's gaze slides between me and Sienna.

"No." Sienna chews her bottom lip and releases a heavy sigh. "It's just…"

"Just what? Any information that you can give us will be helpful, ma'am."

"My father. He took the keys to my apartment…" Sienna leaves the sentence hanging. "But I was here. I had the gallery key."

"What about the spare?" I ask.

"The spare?" She blinks several times, processing the question.

"Did your father have the spare key, Sienna?"

It's all starting to come together inside my head; just a few pieces left to connect. Her father got caught cheating at the Wraith because he needed an alibi. He needed witnesses to prove that he was at the casino while the gallery was being ransacked, and what better proof than being held in the private lounge by the owner? Demanding Sienna's presence was the finishing touch, a foolproof way to ensure that the gallery was empty.

"I don't know." Fresh tears spill over her bottom lashes as she peers around at the destruction.

"Do you know where your father is now?" The cop scribbles on her notepad.

Sienna's expression is blank, so I answer instead. "He's at the Wraith. He's currently being held by my head of security."

"And can you tell me what time he arrived?"

"I can get the time from our CCTV cameras."

I know where this is going, and I don't want the NYPD to discount the man without at least considering the circumstances.

"Sienna's father got caught cheating in the casino. I was dealing with the situation in-house, and he demanded to see Sienna. If he hadn't, if I hadn't called her and asked her to come to the Wraith, she'd have still been here."

"But he has an alibi for the time of the break-in," she reiterates.

"Yes, but it's all a little too convenient, don't you think?" I maintain eye contact, waiting for a hint of recognition that what I'm saying makes sense and that she'll follow it up. "He coordinates the perfect alibi while an accomplice breaks into the gallery."

She addresses Sienna. "Can you think of a reason why your father would want to do this to you?"

"No." It's obvious that Sienna is holding back tears, and my heart cracks open for her. "I hadn't seen him in twenty years. He said he wanted to make things better."

"And do you believe him?" The woman's voice has softened just a little.

"No." Sniff. "I don't know." Sienna snatches her hand away from me and covers her face with both palms. "It's all ... just wrong. I don't even know what's going on anymore."

Her shoulders shudder as she finally succumbs to the sobs that she has been trying to contain.

"Sienna..." I fold her into my embrace and stroke her hair while she lets it all out. "I'll make it all better. I promise I'll find out who did this, and I'll make it all better."

"How?" She pulls away and stares at me, damp-cheeked, and teary-eyed. "How can you make it better? I can't reproduce those pictures. They'll never be the same because I'm not the same person I was when I put my heart and soul into painting them."

"I know." I'm finding it hard to swallow. "I know, Sienna, but I'll do everything in my power to help you start over."

"I just got a commission." She shakes her head, talking out loud. "What about all the money I owe Caleb?"

The officer's ears keen at this. "Who is Caleb? Can I ask how much money you owe him?"

"Caleb is my brother." My shoulders slump with the increasing enormity of what it will take for Sienna to start over again. "He's the investor behind the gallery."

"How much money do you owe Caleb, Sienna?" she presses.

"I don't know exactly." Sienna dabs under her eyes with the back of her hand. "A lot."

"And is he putting pressure on you to repay him?"

"No." Sienna shakes her head vehemently. "It's not like that."

"What is it like?"

I know the cops have a job to do, but while she's standing here asking questions about money, the perpetrator is out there somewhere and probably feeling zero remorse for having destroyed a young woman's life work.

"My brother is married to Sienna's best friend." I step in. "He doesn't want or expect Sienna to pay back the money he put into the gallery."

The cop arches an eyebrow. "That's very generous of him."

I ignore the comment. "Will you question Sienna's father?"

"I can't disclose details of the investigation." She flips her notepad shut and slips it back into her pocket. "If you remember anything else that might be relevant, here's my number." She hands me a business card. "Have you seen anyone loitering about while you've been in the gallery, Sienna?"

"Only the bodyguard."

"Bodyguard?" Frown lines crease her forehead.

Sienna scoffs in my direction. "Where is he when I need him, huh?"

"Okay, would someone like to explain what this is all about?" The notepad comes back out of the pocket.

"Someone has been having Sienna followed," I explain. "I was concerned for her safety, so I had a member of my security team keeping an eye on her."

"Where are they now?"

"Outside in the car. Sienna came with me from the Wraith."

"That's convenient too." Sienna's tone is dull as if she doesn't like where her thoughts are leading. "Why didn't you have someone watching the gallery?"

I sense the cop paying close attention, but I focus on Sienna. It suddenly feels as if the entire situation has been flipped on its head, all arrows pointing in my direction. "Because I was more worried about your safety. I never expected this to happen. Never in a million years."

"Have you ever had a key to the gallery in your possession, sir?" I can't see the cop's notes, but it's obvious that she has written down my name.

"No. I've been in Ireland for three months. I only got back last week." I want to add that I shouldn't have to justify my actions. I'm not the bad guy here.

But I keep it to myself.

"You could've set up this entire scenario." Sienna appears to shrink away from me. "You wanted me to stay at the Wraith. You wanted me to believe that I was in danger."

"Sienna." I reach for her hand, but she snatches it away from me. "You're upset. It's understandable given the—"

"Upset? No." She shakes her head. "Upset doesn't even come close to what I'm feeling right now."

"I know. I wish that I could make it better, Sienna." My chest is starting to feel tight, but I need to tell her how I feel before I use my inhaler. "You must know that I would never do this to you. When you're hurt, I'm hurt. All I've ever wanted is for you to be happy. You believe that don't you?"

I stepped back when she asked me to.

I gave her the chance to let me walk away, and she didn't take it.

"You're not thinking clearly," I add. "You're in shock, Sienna. Let me—"

I don't finish what I started. We all hear the commotion outside the entrance, and my gut clenches when I spot Nick Morris trying to convince the cop on the door to let him in.

"Nick?" Sienna spots him at the same time. But instead of ignoring his arrival, she tells the officer that she knows him.

"I came as soon as I heard." Waved inside, he joins us with his cashmere coat buttoned up against the cold and his wide cheesy smile accentuating the movie star looks. His gaze takes in the ruined artwork and the chaos, and his shoulders slump theatrically. "What happened? Did they get away?"

Sienna is crying again.

Nick stands protectively beside her. My only consolation is that Sienna isn't crying on his shoulder.

"How did you hear about it?" I demand. There were no reporters outside when I arrived with Sienna, and neither of us spoke to anyone else once the alarm was raised.

He doesn't miss a beat. "A colleague saw the police cars parked outside the gallery and called me straight away."

No mention of where he has been.

"What can I do, Sienna?" He holds her gaze so that her attention is on him.

"It's all in hand," I say. "I'll get a team in to repair any damage and salvage what we can."

He scans the gallery. "Did they…" his voice breaks. "Did they destroy everything?"

Sienna covers her face again as fresh sobs erupt.

This time there's no stopping him. He wraps his arms around

her and turns his back on me so that I'm blocked from her view.

"I'm so sorry, darling," he murmurs against the top of her head. "I'm so sorry that this has happened to you. I know how much hard work you put into opening the gallery."

"Why ... did this ... happen?" Sienna manages between sobs.

"People are cruel, Sienna." He turns his face to the policewoman while trapping Sienna against his chest. "Are there any leads? I trust that you'll be checking CCTV cameras."

"Of course, sir." Her tone is neutral, and I wonder if she'll add the name Nick Morris to her notepad, along with an observation about how he blustered in and took control of the situation. "May I ask how you know Ms. Walker?"

"We've known each other for several years. I was her surgeon, before our relationship became personal."

My heart tries to perform a somersault, and my breathing quickly catches on when it crashes against my ribs. I use my inhaler to ease the wheezing in my lungs.

Nick releases Sienna. He holds her at arm's length and lowers his face to her level. "Why don't you come back to my apartment, Sienna? I can't bear the thought of you being alone tonight, after this. Kyle will close the gallery for you once everything is sorted, won't you?"

He doesn't even glance my way.

"Sienna, you don't have to do anything you don't want to do," I say.

I can't be certain that she even hears me because Nick is

already leading her outside, one arm draped across her shoulder.

Neither of them look around before they climb into a waiting taxi and drive away.

15

SIENNA

Kyle was right about one thing: I'm not thinking clearly.

It feels as though I'm having an out-of-body experience.

I watch someone else climb into the back of a taxi with Nick. It's another woman, strangely familiar, who presses her face up against the passenger window and watches the city flash by in a blur of fairy lights and shiny tinsel and gigantic red ribbons. The same woman is trying not to inhale and commit to memory the overpowering scent of Nick's cologne and the vanilla air freshener swinging from the cab's rearview mirror.

All my artwork ... trashed.

I think my brain is blanking out what I saw—I can't recall specific details—but I'm left with a gaping hole in my chest that I've no idea how to fill.

Every single painting that was destroyed held a special place in my heart. They all contained a piece of me, a thought, an emotion, a glimmer of an idea that, once brought to life on canvas, was set free. Released into the universe like a fragile bird finding its way home.

They will never exist again.

They're all gone.

It's this finality, this loss, that I don't know what to do with. I know it isn't like losing a loved one. I know that there are people all over the world dealing with far greater loss, but this knowledge doesn't stop the tears from flowing.

I might not have lost someone I care about, but I have lost a part of me, and that's why I feel so numb.

"Sienna, we're here." Nick's gentle voice barely penetrates the fuzziness wrapped protectively around my brain.

I look at him. His eyes are filled with concern, his hand on mine is warm. A surgeon's hands. Strong but delicate. Sensitive but steady.

He pays the driver, climbs out of the taxi, and walks around the car to open my door.

My body is moving from muscle memory.

I get out of the car, stand on the sidewalk, and wait for him to tell me what to do next.

"This way."

He places an arm around my shoulders, and we enter his apartment building together, our shoulders and hips bumping awkwardly against one another. I follow him up the stairs, trapped in the moment. The crime scene is lurking inside my head, just waiting for me to stop functioning so that it can send all those horrible heart-wrenching images flooding back.

Nick unlocks the front door to his apartment, and gestures for me to step inside first. I do. My feet are still moving. I must still look like me, I probably still sound like me too, but I'm not really here.

I'm back there in the gallery, fractured into a million brittle shards that will need to be glued back together again to make me whole.

Nick faces me inside the entrance hallway of his apartment. It's wide enough for him to keep his distance, and for that I'm grateful. I don't want him to touch me. I don't even know why I allowed him to bring me here when I should be clearing up the mess in the gallery, but I feel powerless to take back control of my life and plan my next move.

"I think we could both use a drink." It's a statement, not a question, but I nod anyway.

He takes off his coat, hangs it on a hook near the front door, and then gestures for mine. I obediently turn around so that he can tug my coat over my shoulders, before following him through to the kitchen.

Nick pulls a chrome and red leather stool out from under the breakfast bar and waits for me to sit down. From one of the wall cabinets, he removes a bottle of Jack, and two chunky crystal glasses, then pours a generous slug into each. He hands one of the glasses to me.

"You probably don't want it," he says, "but it will help with the shock."

I sip the liquid and grimace as it goes down.

Nick leans against the opposite counter watching me closely. "Sienna, I know that no one can replace the work that you've lost tonight, but I want to help. And before you tell me there's nothing I can do—" his eyebrows slide upwards creating faint creases below his immaculate hairline "—just remember that you don't have to deal with any of this alone."

I swallow a mouthful of Jack this time, hiding behind the glass because it's easier than thinking.

"What I'm trying to say," he continues regardless, "is that I'm here to support you any way I can."

"Thank you." My voice is thick with emotion.

"Do you have any idea who might've done this?"

The liquor is still burning inside my gullet. I vaguely recall Kyle accusing my father of creating an alibi for himself in the casino tonight, but somehow, I can't connect him to the person who trashed my work.

Why would he do this?

What would he achieve by destroying everything I've worked so hard for when he has only just come back into my life?

But the thought that he had my keys is niggling away inside my head, scratching at the surface to make me search deeper. He didn't have the gallery keys. I had them. But he also lied about what time he came home that night, so maybe he stole the key and got a replica made while I was trying to sleep.

I don't understand what possible motive he might have though.

"Do you think someone is jealous of what you've achieved?" Nick is still pursuing the subject.

"I-I can't think of anyone."

He knocks back his drink and refills his glass. He hasn't told me where he has been or why he didn't call—not that he owes me an explanation—but I can't help thinking that it's another coincidence that he just happens to come back the night the gallery is broken into.

"Look, Sienna, it pains me to say this, so I'm just going to get it out there and then we can move on, okay?" I don't speak, and he continues anyway. "Do you think Kyle Murray is involved somehow?" He flinches theatrically as Kyle's name hangs between us.

A vivid image of Kyle telling me that I'm beautiful pops into my head, and my heart does this weird fluttery thing that sends knee-trembling signals down my spine at the same time. *Tell me to walk away, and you'll never see me again.* Kyle went to Ireland to give me space. Why would he come back and then do the one thing that would hurt me the most?

I try to picture Kyle giving the order to destroy my artwork and stage it to look like a break-in. He might be part of a ruthless and successful mafia family, but I know he isn't a monster, despite the way my thoughts were spiraling earlier.

"No." Too feeble. I clear my throat. "No, he would never do something like that."

Nick's glass hovers in front of his lips. "Okay, I believe you." His tone implies the opposite. "I won't mention it again."

"Do you know my father?" The question bursts out of nowhere.

"Your father?" His lips twist into a bewildered smile; I'm sure it's supposed to be endearing, but inexplicably it reminds me of Kaa the python snake from Disney's *The Jungle Book*. "Should I know him?"

Deep breath. My pulse is racing, pumping some heat back into my body. Or maybe it's the alcohol that's making me warm.

"You spoke to him outside the gallery one day. It looked as though you knew each other."

He shakes his head and spreads his hands wide. "I don't remember speaking to anyone. Perhaps we exchanged a greeting in passing."

"Perhaps." It's entirely feasible, so why is my gut telling me that he's lying?

"Are you hungry, Sienna? Have you eaten?"

I haven't, but I can't face the thought of food.

"I appreciate you bringing me back here, Nick." I set my glass down on the counter, if I drink more, I'll be sick. "But I think I should go."

"Why?" His eyes are wide, and he rubs one hand across his smooth chin. "Where will you go? My offer of the spare room still stands, Sienna. I don't think that you should be alone, even if it's only for tonight."

"I'll be fine. I just want to crawl into bed and forget about everything for a few hours." I can't even summon the energy to smile.

"Please stay." He moves closer. "I won't get in your way, I promise. I'll feel better knowing that you're not alone, and if you decide that you want to talk, I'll be here for that too."

"I don't know, Nick."

I want him to leave me alone. After what happened at my father's apartment, I simply want to go home, pull on some comfy pajamas, and bury myself under my own comforter, but I still can't bring myself to be openly rude to him; he's only trying to help.

"One night, Sienna. Give yourself a break and allow me to take care of you for one night."

I smile despite my misgivings.

He takes another step closer.

"Nick, I can't…"

I can't what?

I can't share your bed because there's someone else.

I can't kiss you because I know how it feels to be kissed by Kyle.

I can't pretend any longer that you'd be the perfect boyfriend because no one makes me feel the way I feel when I'm with Kyle Murray.

Without warning, Nick slides a tiny box from the pocket of his pants and drops onto one knee. He snaps open the box to reveal a diamond ring that glints as it catches the overhead light. I'm blinded by it momentarily. Not by the diamond itself, all I can see is the glimmer like a star exploding in the palm of his hand, but by what's about to follow.

"Sienna, will you marry me?"

Yep. There it is. The unexpected proposal by a man who's so sure of himself that he hasn't considered my response might not be what he wants to hear.

I'm still staring at the diamond.

What the actual fuck is going on here?

My heart is galloping, making me breathless.

"Nick, I wasn't expecting…" My brain can't form a coherent

thought and transfer it to my mouth. "I don't know what to..."

That's untrue. I do know what to say.

No!

What is wrong with me that I can't say it out loud? I'm not afraid of how he might react to being rejected, but I am afraid of hurting his feelings. He would never willingly hurt me, I'm certain of it, he has simply made a terrible error of judgement regarding our relationship.

"You don't have to say anything right now, Sienna. I realize that I've caught you by surprise, and my timing is probably way out with what happened tonight. But I know how I feel about you and..."

He inhales deeply, his face lighting up with his smile and making me feel even worse.

"...well... I know that I want to spend the rest of my life with you. Take as long as you need. We have all the time in the world."

He rises, and I follow his movements with my eyes still on the diamond in his hand.

Trembling, he closes the box and leaves it on the counter. Then he refills our glasses, clinks them together, and downs his drink in one.

"I don't think I've ever been so nervous." He leans back against the opposite counter, giving me space, and demonstrates his trembling hands with a shaky smile.

I'm uncomfortably aware that I haven't spoken, but I don't trust myself to let him down gently. "I wasn't expecting this, Nick. I haven't heard from you in days."

His smile broadens. "I wanted to speak to my family before I proposed. I guess I wanted their blessing. Not that I needed it. But I wanted this to be perfect for you, Sienna."

He pauses, "Then some fucker went and ruined it by breaking into your gallery."

I avoid looking at the box containing the diamond ring. I try not to think about Kyle fixing up the gallery.

Nick and I have only dated a few times. Sure, I've known him for five and a half years, but as a doctor and patient. It's hardly the same as building the foundations for our future together. I always thought this kind of spontaneous proposal only happened in the movies.

I guess I was wrong.

"I'm going to shower; it's been a long day." He straightens, fingers flexing as if undecided whether he should leave the engagement ring where it is or move it out of sight. "Please, make yourself at home, Sienna."

Home?

The thought of making this my home, a home to be shared with Nick, makes me feel slightly queasy. But I put it down to a combination of recent events and the Jack Daniels on an empty stomach.

"The spare room is ready for you," Nick continues, oblivious. "There's wine in the fridge. Takeout menus in the letter rack." He gestures to a gleaming chrome rack on the end of the counter. "Tonight is yours, Sienna."

He takes my hand, raises it to his lips, and then leaves me alone in the kitchen while he makes his way to the bathroom.

I can feel the imprint of his lips on the back of my hand. I try rubbing it on my sweater, but it makes no difference. His cologne is clinging to my clothes. I can't breathe without his scent filling my lungs and making me choke.

I can't stay here.

I jump off the stool. With one final glance at the jewelry box on the counter, wishing that I'd imagined the whole thing, I tiptoe along the hallway and past the bathroom. I unhook my coat and drape it over one arm, holding my breath as I open the front door. I can still hear the shower running as I let myself out and close the door behind me.

The night is bitterly cold. The sidewalk sparkles with the first layer of frost, and my footsteps crunch as I walk along the streets of Manhattan. I don't put my coat on. The biting chill is grounding me, blowing the fog from my head, and making my cheeks sting.

I don't understand Nick's proposal out of the blue. He hasn't even tried to kiss me on a date yet, but I guess he has old-fashioned principles, which is why he sought his family's blessing first. Even with this in mind though, I still can't make it all add up.

Then there's the gallery.

My heart does a backflip each time I think about it. Kyle will tidy the gallery and make it secure, but no one can replace the artwork that I've lost. It's a mammoth task, starting afresh, but I have my own art studio now. If I have to concentrate on new commissions to begin with, that's what I'll do.

The despair I felt when I saw the broken canvases isn't quite the big black hole that I felt myself sinking into when the police officer was questioning me. It's still there. I know that I could slip into it at any moment, but right now, I need to figure out what to do about Nick.

I walk until I can't feel my fingers and toes, and my thighs are stinging from the cold. But I keep moving. Each step is taking me closer to the one person who will help me make sense of my emotions, because I understand that the problem with Nick's proposal isn't Nick. It's me.

Standing outside the entrance to the sheer black tower known as the Wraith, I check the time on my phone. Ten-thirty. It feels like it should be hours later. Maybe I should have called Victoria in advance, but I'm praying that she'll be awake with the baby and will be happy to see me. Besides, it's about time I visited my goddaughter.

The heat inside the lobby is stifling after the sub-zero temperatures outside.

The concierge eyes up my clothes and smudged makeup and approaches me before I've taken a few steps. He's naturally suspicious when I tell him that I'm visiting the penthouse apartment, and I almost cry out loud when Victoria answers his call. I haven't seen her since Holly was born less than a fortnight ago, but it feels as if it has been years.

My legs are shaking as the elevator carries me up to the fiftieth story.

I haven't eaten since breakfast, but the thought of food makes my insides churn, and I clamp a hand over my mouth as the elevator glides to a halt.

The doors open into the apartment, and I hear voices coming from the living area. Low voices, so as not to disturb the baby, but I recognize them instantly.

Victoria and Caleb are not alone.

VIVY SKYS

Kyle is here.

16

KYLE

"Sienna!"

I'm on my feet the instant the elevator door opens, but Victoria beats me to it.

She crosses the living room, her feet barely touching the floor, and throws her arms around her best friend. They stay that way, locked in an embrace forged on years of friendship, until eventually, Victoria releases Sienna and leads her into the living room, where Caleb and I are waiting for them.

A huge part of me is relieved that Sienna is here and not in the arms of the slimeball Nick Morris. But one look at her puffy eyes and pale skin fills me with guilt that I'm still putting my own feelings first.

Her expression crumples when she spots me, and everything I wanted to say evaporates like condensation on a window.

"I should go." Sienna's shoulders drop. "I don't want to interfere."

"Not without meeting your goddaughter first." Victoria's eyes meet mine briefly as she goes to the bassinet currently parked at the end of the couch, and lifts baby Holly into her arms. She coos at the infant, nuzzles her nose, and then hands her over to Sienna. "Holly, meet your Auntie Sienna."

I watch Sienna cradle the baby in the crook of her arm and study the tiny pink face, tears welling in her eyes. Happy tears. Not the hopeless tears that she'd shed at the gallery earlier. And my chest swells at the sight of her with a baby in her arms.

Sienna deserves happiness.

She deserves to have everything that she's ever wanted, everything that she's worked so hard for.

She sure as fuck does not deserve to have it all crushed right in front of her eyes, by a man who wants to reclaim his 'father' title after twenty years' absence.

He had to be involved in the break-in. *He had to be.*

"She's so beautiful," Sienna whispers.

Victoria's proud smile lights up the entire room. "She is."

Caleb rubs his hands together. "Time to open that bottle of Moet we've been saving, now that you're both here."

"Decaf coffee for me." Victoria stands on tiptoes and kisses my brother lightly on the lips before sitting beside Sienna on the couch. "I don't want to get our daughter drunk."

I've never been jealous of my brother, of any of my brothers, but this scene of domestic bliss, of normality and love and warmth, tugs at something deep inside. I want this.

More importantly, I want this with Sienna.

Caleb busies himself in the kitchen, his eyes constantly seeking out his wife and daughter, and I hear the gentle pop of the cork from the champagne bottle. He returns shortly after with three slender flutes filled with bubbles and a cup of steaming coffee for Victoria.

"To family," Caleb says, raising his glass.

"To family."

Finally, it is Victoria who brings up the subject of the gallery. "Kyle told us what happened, Si." Her voice is gentle. "You know that you don't have to deal with this alone."

Sienna lets out a tiny snort before she can stop herself. Then, realizing how it sounded, she shakes her head, heat flooding her cheeks. "Sorry, V. That wasn't aimed at you."

I replay in my head all that I can remember from our conversation at the gallery, and the warmth in my chest subsides when I realize that it was aimed at me.

"I was trying to help, Sienna. I've secured the gallery, and I've got a team of men working in there through the night to repair the damage. I only wish I could do more."

I set my champagne glass down on the coffee table between the couches and rest my elbows on my thighs. Sienna and I both keep our eyes firmly fixed on the baby, and it occurs to me then that Holly is acting as a kind of diffuser to moods and tempers that might otherwise have been running riot around the penthouse apartment.

"I know." Sienna's gaze meets mine and something seems to connect between us; it's fragile, as delicate as butterfly wings, but the fact that it's there at all gives me hope. "It's been a long and eventful day."

The roller coaster reaches the apex and plummets towards the ground. My hands ball into fists, every fiber of my being suddenly on high alert. I ignore the warning glance from my brother.

"What did he—"

"What else has happened, Si?" Victoria interjects, her voice low, reminding me that there's a baby in the room.

"I..." Sienna sucks in a deep breath, eyes closed momentarily. "It's nothing. Nothing I can't handle anyway."

"Sienna." I wait for her to give me her full attention. "Do you want me to leave, so that you can speak to Victoria in private?"

It isn't the first time that I've given her the opportunity to let me go, and I doubt that it will be the last. I'll keep throwing the ball into her court until she understands that I mean what I say. Until she understands exactly how I feel about her.

Her eyes linger on mine. Then, "Nick proposed to me tonight."

My pulse quickens. I suppress an image of Nick Morris going down on one knee and slipping a diamond ring onto Sienna's finger. My gaze tracks to her left hand, which is still ring-less. For now.

Victoria almost chokes on a mouthful of coffee. Caleb reflexively leans closer and rubs her back while she grabs a tissue from a silk-covered box on the table.

"Where the fuck did that come from?" Victoria's hand flies to her mouth. "Sorry," she whispers to the room in general. "I know I shouldn't swear in front of the baby, but what the actual *fuck*!"

Sienna smiles for the first time since she arrived. "You're only saying out loud what I was thinking when I saw him go down on one knee."

She deliberately avoids meeting my gaze, and I don't know if it's because she's embarrassed after what happened between the two of us, or if she's about to shatter my heart and toss it straight back to me.

"So, you had no idea that it was coming?" Victoria asks.

"No." Baby Holly wriggles in Sienna's arms, distracting her temporarily, before settling down again. "I mean, literally, no. We've been on a few dates. I know I'm out of practice, but if there were any signs along the way, I totally missed them."

She's saying everything that I want to hear, but my skin is still crawling at the thought of that man proposing to the woman I love. I don't know him. I've spent very little time in his company, but what I have seen doesn't resemble a man who is besotted with a beautiful woman.

"You didn't miss them," I say, and all eyes are on me. "Do you honestly believe that he's in love with you? Has he told you that he loves you?"

"Okay." Caleb is wearing a sweatshirt and jogging pants, and his stubble is longer than I think I've ever seen it. He's comfy and contented. But his eyes are still alert. "Sienna, I think what my brother is trying to say is, trust your instincts. If you didn't see it coming, it's because you were not supposed to."

Sienna's gaze slides around the room, settling on each of us in turn.

"Caleb is right, Si," Victoria says. "If it was what you wanted, you wouldn't be here right now without a ring on your finger."

"There's too much going on." Sienna's voice is clogged with emotion. "I don't even know what to think anymore."

"Hey." Victoria places her arm around her friend's shoulders and wipes the tears from her cheek with her thumb. "It's hardly surprising with your father rocking up out of the blue and then the gallery. If you want my opinion, the guy's a fucking asshole for proposing to you tonight when you're clearly struggling."

"I'm starting a swear-box," Caleb chimes in.

"Sorry." Victoria wrinkles her nose. "But he is. I've never met the guy, and I already don't like him."

"You've never met him?" I blurt out.

Sienna and Victoria have been best friends most of their lives. They tell each other everything, they practically raised Abigail together, and yet Sienna has never introduced Nick to her. The more I learn about the man, the more I see him as a shadow lurking in the background of Sienna's world just waiting to reveal his true colors.

Caleb's eyes flicker my way. He's thinking the same as I am.

"The opportunity never arose." Sienna shrugs. "I never thought…"

"You never thought that he would propose to you one day," I complete the sentence for her.

"What did you say to him, Si?" Victoria poses the question that I've been trying to swallow.

"I didn't. He didn't give me a chance. He told me to take as much time as I needed to think about it, and then he took a shower. That's when I came here."

Victoria furrows her brow. "He took a shower? The jerk proposed to you and then jumped in the shower? What the actual fu—" She sucks on her bottom lip and swallows the expletive. "What did you do with the ring?"

"I left it on the kitchen counter." Sienna peers at the baby in her arms, a wistful smile appearing on her lips. "I couldn't wait to get out of there."

Yes!

I stop myself from fist-pumping the air.

He proposed, and Sienna isn't there; she's here, with us, and I'm not letting her out of my sight again.

"That's your answer then, Si," Victoria says. "You know my motto: if it isn't a definite yes, it's a no."

"What should I do?" Sienna puffs up her cheeks and releases a steady breath.

I'm hoping Victoria will tell her to say no. Let him down gently, or not so gently; either way, the answer should remain the same.

Instead, she says, "I think you should take some time out, Si. Caleb and I have been talking about it."

She deliberately avoids making eye contact with me, because whatever it is they've been discussing, no one thought to include me.

"We'll pay for you to go to Ireland." Before Sienna can protest, Victoria continues, "You need some time and space to breathe. Without anything getting in the way."

"There's an annex connected to the Murray family home,"

Caleb joins in. "You can have the entire place to yourself. No one will interfere."

"You can paint all day and all night if you want." Victoria smiles. "This is what you need, Si. You've needed it for a long while, only I couldn't help you before. But I can now. Go to Ireland. Paint. Sleep. Drink Guinness every day if you want."

"It's full of iron," Caleb adds.

"Just learn to exist again, and everything will fall into place."

Sienna's eyes fill with tears again. "I don't know... I'm not sure I have the energy..."

"Which is exactly my point!" Victoria's lips press together in the kind of stern expression I always associate with one of my middle-grade school teachers. She turns to me. "Kyle, help me sell it to her, will you?"

Where do I start?

"It's the best place in the world to relax, Sienna. Fresh air. Green fields. More cows than people." I can't contain my smile when I see her mouth curving upwards.

"I'm grateful," she says, "truly I am, but I can't."

"Why not?" Victoria is still wearing her school marm look.

"The gallery—"

"Is taken care of," I say. "Apart from the artwork, and you're the only person who can solve that problem." I pause, picking up on Victoria's enthusiasm. "Try to imagine setting up your easel with a backdrop of snowy mountains, trees, and streams filled with salmon."

"I won't find many clients in an Irish field filled with cows."

"They have Internet in Ireland too."

"What about my apartment? I have to vacate it soon." She's running out of steam, and I wonder how many arguments with Victoria she has lost in the past.

"That's sorted then." Victoria finishes her coffee and eyes up the glasses of champagne on the glass-topped table. "Vacate it now, then there's nothing holding you back."

"It's not that easy." Sienna slumps back against the sofa, and the baby lets out a feeble cry.

"It's absolutely that easy." Victoria checks the time on her watch. "Three hours. My baby is hungry." She scoops Holly out of Sienna's arms and sits back down, placing a muslin cloth over the baby's face while she prepares to feed her.

Sienna still hasn't touched her champagne as if she's afraid to let the bubbles go to her head. "I've never traveled that far on my own. I've never traveled anywhere on my own."

"Si," Victoria says, "you're the strongest person I know. You're not going to let a flight to Dublin beat you."

"It isn't just the flight though."

She doesn't need to say anything else. I can see it in her eyes that this isn't about the flight. She's overwhelmed by the curveballs that life keeps throwing at her whenever she believes that she's finally on the right path.

"I'll travel with you." The words spill into the room before I can think this through. "I'll introduce you to the Murrays, make sure you're settled, and then I'll fly back to New York. Victoria is right. A week in Ireland will make you wonder why you stayed in the city for so long."

Caleb is quiet.

Victoria knows how I feel about Sienna, and she gives me a smile that says she'd hug me if she wasn't currently feeding her baby.

"You're needed here, Kyle," Sienna says, shaking her head. "I can't ask you to do that."

"You're not asking. I'm offering. No strings attached."

There's nothing I'd enjoy more than staying in Ireland with her. But the first hint of me pulling a stunt on her like the one Nick Morris pulled tonight will have her packing a suitcase and leaving the city behind in a cloud of grimy polluted dust.

It could go either way. After what Sienna has been through, she could thank me with a dazzling smile and ask me to prepare the private jet, or she could dash into the elevator before any of us can stop her and run straight back to the surgeon with the ulterior motive. If it's the latter, I expect I'll be serving a prison sentence soon for hurling him from the top of the Wraith.

"How long could I stay?"

The question sends a surge of adrenaline through my veins.

We're traveling to Ireland together.

Me and Sienna.

Sienna and me.

I'm finally going to get her out of Mr. Morris's sleazy clutches and somewhere safe, somewhere that she might hopefully reevaluate our relationship without the pressures of the city weighing down on her.

"As long as you like." Caleb picks up the conversation while my heart performs a tap dance inside my rib cage. "As long as it takes."

Sienna stands and sways on the spot, sitting back down on the couch heavily. She raises a hand to her temple and closes her eyes.

"Sienna?" I crouch on the floor in front of her, acutely conscious that I'm the second man to go down on their knees for her tonight. "What's wrong? Are you sick?"

"I'm fine. I just came over a little dizzy. I should go."

She grips my hand tightly and tries to stand again, still wobbly.

"It's the champagne. I haven't eaten."

"You're coming with me." I link my arm with hers; she's shaking, which is hardly surprising after the day she has had. "You can have my spare room for tonight. We'll discuss the trip to Ireland tomorrow once you've had some sleep and some food."

She doesn't even argue.

Victoria's eyes follow us across the room. "I'll come and see you in the morning, Si."

In the elevator, we stand side by side and stare at the door. My apartment is on the level below the penthouse, and barely sixty seconds pass by before we're both standing in my living room, the New York skyline winking at us through the floor-to-ceiling windows.

The lights activate as we enter the apartment.

It's warm inside.

But Sienna still looks like a deer stunned by the headlights of a rapidly approaching truck with a carcass clinging to the front bumper.

"Here, let me take your coat." My fingers brush her shoulders, sending sparks of electricity directly to my brain.

I can't ignore them. I can't ignore her perfume, or the curve of her cheek, or the way her hair sweeps across my chest as she turns around to face me. But I force my hands to remain by my sides, her coat tucked into the crook of my arm.

"Sienna, you know I had nothing to do with the break-in at the gallery. Don't you?"

Her eyes dart around the apartment, but at least she has stopped trembling. "Yes." It's barely more than a whisper. "What happened to my father?"

"He won't be returning to the Wraith."

"Should I be worried about him?"

Is it my imagination or has she moved closer to me? So close. It would be so easy for me to lean in and kiss her neck, the dip between her collarbones, her earlobes.

My cock is already halfway there.

"Only if you feel that he's worth your energy."

"All my stuff is still at my apartment."

Now the huskiness in her voice is unmistakable, and I allow myself a glimmer of hope that she ran away from Nick this evening because of me.

"I'll take care of it."

"Why are you doing all this for me, Kyle?"

"Sienna." My own voice matches hers, and my hand entwines itself around a lock of her fiery hair, almost of its own accord. "Haven't you figured it out yet?"

Tiny dimples appear either side of her mouth when she smiles, and I can't believe I haven't noticed them before. "I think I have."

"*Mo leoin*. You are the most beautiful woman I have ever met."

I toss her coat aside. No distractions.

I cup her neck with one hand and pull her towards me. She doesn't resist. I lower my mouth to hers, and she parts her lips to let me in.

Her kisses are hungry. Frantic. Feverish almost. Tiny whimpers escape as she slides her fingers through my hair.

"Kyle, what are we doing?" she whispers, her oxygen mingling with mine.

"We're trusting our instincts. I want you, Sienna." I pick her up and wrap her legs around my waist. "I've wanted you since the first moment I set eyes on you."

She silences me with her tongue.

She grips my hair tightly, holding me against her like her life depends on never letting me go.

Her passion matches mine, pumping my blood around my veins and engorging my already throbbing cock.

I cross the room blindly, relying on my senses to get me to the couch where I set her down and start fumbling with the zipper of her pants. I feel Sienna's fingers tugging at my waistband. Frantic. Desperate.

"Tell me you want me, leoin."

"I want you." Breathless.

"Show me."

She releases my cock from my boxers and wraps her fingers around the girth, teasing the head, rubbing the leaking pre-cum around it. I pull away just enough to drag her pants down over her hips and drop them onto the floor. A quick glance. White lace panties.

White has never looked so fucking good on anyone.

She guides my cock down to her pussy, and I push it through the soft fabric, feeling the lace tighten around me as I try to find my way deep inside.

"Do you like that?"

"Yes." Her voice is breathy, her eyes glittering.

I kiss her long and hard, while I fumble with her panties. Too impatient to remove them, I pull them aside and drive my cock in all the way. "I've got to have you now, leoin." I slide out again, her juices clinging to me.

I want to take her so fast that she forgets to breathe. I want to take it slowly, savoring every single part of her, tasting her all over, watching her orgasm carrying her away from the rest of the world.

"I'm going to fuck you like you've never been fucked before." I probe her mouth with my tongue and nibble her bottom lip while she watches me wide-eyed. "I'm going to fuck you till you beg me to stop."

She smiles. "Never."

I ram my cock into her sex, and she instinctively arches her spine. I want to chew her nipples. I want to brand her with my kisses, but that will have to wait.

Cradling her head with my arms, I pound her pussy, deeper and deeper, until it's all that exists. Her hips meet mine. Her wetness seeps onto my balls. At some point we roll off the couch and Sienna is on top of me, but we don't stop.

"Ride me, leoin."

I bounce off the floor as I thrust my cock up and into her. My pants are tangled around my legs. We're a sweaty mess of colliding limbs and hips and mouths, and I grip her hips tightly, guiding her sex up and down my cock.

"Is this what you want?"

"Yes," she gasps. "Yes!"

"Take me in your mouth, Sienna. Now." I lift her off me and position her body so that the head of my cock is rubbing her lips.

Sienna slants her eyes. Her lips close around me, and she starts sucking.

"Don't stop." My breathing is growing ragged. I'm so close. "I'm coming, leoin. Suck me dry."

My entire body judders as I ejaculate down her throat.

17

SIENNA

I'VE BARELY SWALLOWED THE LAST OF KYLE'S CUM before he is on his knees.

He tugs my sweater over my head, and unclasps my bra in one fluid movement, dropping them onto the couch. Then, without speaking, he removes his shirt and studies my body before cupping my breasts in his hands.

Kyle sucks my nipples, nibbling them between his teeth, sucking on the soft flesh surrounding them, leaving behind a daisy chain of kisses.

He is all I can taste.

He is all I can feel.

This—*Kyle*—is the reason why I ran away from Nick and his unexpected proposal, and the instant I allow this thought to materialize, my pussy begins throbbing for more.

"Kyle..." I lower my head and drag my fingers through his hair.

His cock is still hard. I can feel it bobbing between my thighs as if waiting to come home.

"Yes?" His mouth smothers mine, and I feel myself drifting away on a vessel of mingled breaths and overpowering lust.

I can't even remember what I wanted to say.

He lowers me gently back onto the floor and pulls off my pants. He spreads my legs wide and sucks my pussy through my panties. It shouldn't feel this sexy, but my orgasm starts to build the instant he tugs them aside and starts sucking on my clit.

"Nu-huh." He raises his head, his trim beard glistening with my juices. "I know you want it, but you're gonna have to wait."

"I-I can't."

"Okay, perhaps we need a lesson in how to be patient."

A low gurgling chuckle escapes my throat before I can stop it. "And you're going to teach me?"

So quickly, I barely register his movement, he snatches my sweater from the sofa, wraps it tightly around my wrists, raises my arms above my head and fastens them securely to the leg of the coffee table. I could probably free myself if I tried, but I don't. The excitement coursing through my veins and the wetness seeping between my legs is enough for me to play along.

"What are you doing—"

He smothers my mouth with his. His tongue is everywhere, his teeth are biting into the soft flesh around my lips, and my pussy starts thrumming wildly.

"Did I ask you to speak?" The gleam in his eyes as he pulls away and looms over me is wicked.

"No."

"Do you know what happens when you speak out of turn, leoin?"

"You'll fuck me harder?" My voice is playful, the excitement evident.

His lips quirk upward at the corners. "Only if you're a good girl." I've never heard his voice sound this husky before.

His lips brush mine. He drags his tongue along my jawline until it finds my ear. "Do you trust me?"

His breath on my neck is warm, and shivers travel down my spine. I instinctively open my legs. My panties are saturated.

"Yes." I don't even question it.

His shirt appears from nowhere. He rolls it into a long narrow strip of cloth and places it over my eyes, fastening it at the back of my head.

His mouth crushes my lips, his tongue probing.

I don't know how it's possible, but being blindfolded heightens the sensation by a hundred times. I sink into the lights popping and flashing behind my eyelids and return his kisses.

The instant my tongue meets Kyle's he pulls away. There's a stinging sensation in my nipple, and he leans in close to my ear again. "Naughty leoin. I didn't tell you to kiss me back."

"But..." I lick my lips, and he tweaks my nipple again.

"Your lips are mine. I'll lick them when I'm ready."

He pulls away, and his absence raises goosebumps on my skin. My ears keen for a whisper of his movements, but I don't hear a thing.

Then he rubs my lips with the end of his cock, and I can taste him all over again. I instinctively open my mouth to take him, and he rolls my hips sideways, slapping my ass with the palm of his hand. It stings a little. And my sex reacts, drawing me closer to my orgasm without him even touching me.

His cock is back, and this time he pushes the end between my lips. "Lick me, leoin. Lick me like I'm the best popsicle you've ever tasted."

I lick around the head, tasting the residue of his cum. I drag my tongue along his length, circling the rim, and forcing it into the slit. He pulls away, just enough to make me follow him with my mouth, and I do, like a groupie chasing her favorite rock star.

His mouth closes around my tongue without warning. He sucks, and a low groan escapes my lips.

"Good girl."

He licks my lips. The dip between my collarbones. The scars tracking their way across my chest. My nipples. My belly button.

Not being able to see him means that I'm following him by the trail he leaves behind on my body. My pussy is waiting. And fuck does he know it.

So, he keeps going. He kisses my hips. I know what he can see, the puckered flesh, the shiny pink ridge of the scars resulting from the car crash, but I focus on his tongue instead. Where he's going. What he's going to do next.

He rolls me sideways and traces damp swirling patterns across my butt cheeks making me flinch as he finds a spot that I never knew was ticklish. He's quiet. He doesn't want me to preempt his next move.

He raises my right leg. His kisses travel down the back of my thigh. He sucks on the skin at the back of my knee, and keeps moving down to my ankle, the tender flesh on the sole of my feet, my toes. His tongue flickers in and out, and I barely have a chance to wonder how there can be so many sensitive nerve endings between your toes when he slides my legs apart and pushes my knees backward, raising my butt off the floor.

He rips my panties from me and supports my legs easily with his shoulders. "You're learning. Keep being a good girl and I'll make you come, leoin. Would you like that?"

I'm panting just at the thought of his tongue dragging across my clit. "Yes."

"You'll have to try harder." His accent is even more lilting than usual.

"Yes, I'd like that." The words tumble out.

He slides a finger inside me. "You're wet, Sienna," he drawls. "Are you a little bit excited?"

"More than a little bit."

The finger comes out and his cock lands heavily between my legs. My pussy clenches expectantly. But Kyle is enjoying the game too much. He thumps my sex with the end of his cock, rubbing it between my folds, covering it in my juices.

And I lay there with the flashing lights behind my eyelids and the eerie image of me naked and blindfolded on Kyle's living room floor, with my hands tied behind my head.

I've never felt so vulnerable or so sexy before.

I gasp out loud when Kyle's mouth sucks on the outside of my sex. He sucks and licks, his tongue exploring every part of my exposed pussy, teasing my clit with tiny gentle licks before sucking my juices from me some more.

I thrust my hips towards him. Desperate. And his palm slaps my other butt cheek.

"What did I say?" He sits back, but keeps my legs raised. "I'm starting to think that you don't want me after all."

"I do."

"You do what, Sienna?"

"I do want you." My heart is racing. "Please, or I'll come without you, Kyle."

His low chuckle reaches my ears. "Much as I'd love to see that, I'm not letting you have all the fun without me."

My pussy is suddenly filled with his fingers. He's sliding them in and out of me, and my legs start trembling. I'm too close.

"Lick me, Kyle."

His fingers pull out. Without warning, they're in my mouth, and I can taste myself, and I'm whimpering without even realizing.

Then he's gripping my thighs with both hands, and I can hardly breathe with my knees crushing my chest. But his tongue is inside me, and I'm already spiraling towards the orgasm that has been waiting to explode since we entered his apartment.

"Come for me, leoin. Come all over my face."

I don't respond. My body is already spasming, my eyes rolling back into my head, as the orgasm takes over.

It keeps coming and coming.

I'm still in the throes when Kyle lowers my legs and rolls me over, my wrists still bound to the table leg, my eyes still covered. He pulls my hips towards him and fucks me from behind on his knees, drawing his cock all the way out and ramming it back in again until we finally collapse into a messy panting heap on the floor.

Kyle is heavy on top of me. His face is close to mine, when he whispers in my ear, "You're so fucking amazing, Sienna. My beautiful lioness. My love."

"I meant what I said, Sienna. No pressure. The guest room is yours until you're ready to leave the city and travel to Ireland."

We're sitting at the breakfast bar in the kitchen of Kyle's apartment. We're both wrapped in comforters. We're both naked underneath.

I've lost track of time. The sky outside the window is still black despite the city lights adding their glow to the view, but a hint of gray is already seeping through. I'm sore and tender, every part of me still tingling from his touch.

Kyle kept his word. He fucked me and then fucked me some more.

Neither of us slept, and now we're sipping black coffee in comfortable silence eating buttery scrambled eggs that Kyle made.

"Victoria sat right there eating toast with me one time." He gestures with his eyes to the stool that I'm sitting on. "That's when she first realized that I was in the car with you that New Year's Eve."

He's changing the subject before I can decline his offer to use the guest room.

"I wish I could go back to that night."

"Kyle, don't." I set my fork down on the plate.

I'm ravenous, but even now, after all this time, I still find it difficult to eat whenever my memories of that night wriggle their way to the forefront of my mind.

"Sorry." His expression crumples.

He's like two different people at times. There's the Kyle who blindfolds me and tells me to lick his dick, and then there's this guy scrambling eggs and trying his hardest to put things right between us. I don't know where the mafia lawyer fits into the equation.

"How soon do you want to leave? I need six hours' notice to get the private jet ready. My mom and my sister are already in Ireland." He opens his mouth to say more and closes it again.

"Where are they staying?"

I've met Moira and Emily. They're lovely people, but Victoria didn't mention that I'd be spending time with them too, and right now, I'm not sure that I can face speaking to anyone else. Especially Kyle's mom. I feel like it's my fault that the gallery got trashed, and although it's highly unlikely that she'll accuse me of negligence, it's what I'll be thinking every time I look at her.

"I can't tell you." Kyle pushes his eggs around the plate with his fork.

"Can't?" I frown. "Or won't?"

His smile reappears, and butterflies leap about inside my chest. "Can't. It's such a closely guarded secret that even her sons don't know where she's staying."

"Will she be there for the holidays?"

"Aye." There's something he isn't telling me.

"What's going on, Kyle?"

Moira might be part of a mafia family, but I've seen the way she is with her sons and daughter. Family is everything to her. So, why is she spending the holidays in a secret location in another country? Then it dawns on me that perhaps she and Terry are separating, and my stomach churns for Kyle.

"Forget I asked," I quickly add. "I didn't mean to pry."

Kyle is quiet, eating his eggs before they get cold. Finally, he says, "Something has happened to remind her of the past." His voice is low. "A past that she has spent years trying to forget."

"Is she alright?"

She's surrounded by a team of security guards and four sons with the kind of connections that most people associate with movies like *The Godfather* and *Goodfellas*, so I don't understand why she chose to leave her family behind. During the holiday season.

"Sienna, you don't need to worry about my mom."

I hear him, but why do I still feel like he's hiding something?

18

KYLE

I should never have suggested that Sienna stay in the guest room. I guess part of me was hoping that she'd turn me down, so I only have myself to blame when she curls up on the king-size bed, with the comforter wrapped around her, and closes her eyes.

I shower, dress, and study my reflection in the bathroom mirror.

I can still taste her. Even if I never get to see her again, this is a taste that I will never forget. I remembered it all those years following the accident, as if I was subconsciously waiting for her to come back into my life and fulfill me.

My mate in every sense of the word.

My soulmate.

Sienna is still sleeping when I let myself out of the apartment and head into my office. I open my laptop and instinctively retrieve the files containing Nick Morris's personal information.

Why did he propose to Sienna?

I refuse to believe that he loves her. So, what was he hoping to achieve? Was it simply his way of hurting me by stealing the woman I love out from under my nose? Then what? Once he had her, how long would their marriage have lasted?

My attention settles on the name Caelan O'Reilly.

My brothers and I didn't inherit our father's violent mood swings and sociopathic tendencies. We're probably typical examples of nurture over nature. But our mom saw something in Nick Morris that caused her to pack a suitcase and run.

Should I have told Sienna the truth?

I saw how disturbed she was when she arrived at Caleb and Victoria's apartment, and maybe I'm being overly cautious when it comes to mentioning his name around her, but there's too much at stake. I can't risk losing her again.

I won't risk losing her to him.

Although last night would never have happened if she had any kind of feelings for him.

My cock twitches inside my pants at the memory of Sienna blindfolded, her pussy in my face, dripping wet and ready for me.

I'll stay with her in Ireland if that's what she wants, but I can be patient. Knowing that she's safe, I'll wait as long as it takes.

I call Terry and ask him to update me on the situation regarding Robert Carlton Hooch. Sienna's father.

"No movement since last night. I've got men posted outside his building."

"Did you inform the other casinos?"

"Sure did." Terry pauses. "Seems the guy has ramped up more debts than we thought. If the Bogrovs don't get him first, the Sicilians will."

"Why is he still hanging around?" I'm thinking out loud. If I was carrying that kind of baggage, I sure as shit wouldn't be frequenting the big casinos and getting caught cheating... "Is he on Bash and Cash's radar?"

"No. Seems last night was his first attempt at testing the Murrays."

"Because of Sienna?" My mind is still hopping between Sienna sleeping naked in my guest room, and the incident at the gallery. I'm still trying to connect all the dots. "Anything on CCTV from the break-in?"

"The fuckers knew what they were doing."

"So did he."

"You still think he needed an alibi?" I can hear Terry's thoughts buzzing at me through the handset.

"I'm certain of it." I only wish I knew why.

"Where's Sienna now?"

"In my guest room." Yep, my cock is right there with the image.

There's no reaction from Terry, but snippets of my conversation with Sienna flash into my head. She heard her father come home in the wee hours of the morning, which was confirmed by Seamus, but her father insisted that he was back by midnight. Why did he lie about it? Or did he?

"Are you sure you've got his building covered?" I ask Terry.

"What are you thinking? You want him checked out?"

"If you owed the big boys a whole load of cash, would you still be showing your face in the casinos?"

Terry's quiet. Then, "Reckon I'd be slumming it underground."

"So, why isn't he? Is he depending on Sienna sharing an insurance payout from the gallery with him?" This doesn't sit right with me either though.

"Three days after a twenty-year self-imposed hiatus?" Terry sniffs loudly. "Smells more to me like he wanted an introduction to the Murrays."

"That makes two of them." My voice had dropped and the hair on the back of my neck is standing to attention.

"Him and the surgeon?" Terry asks.

"Do you still have a tail on him?"

"Do you really need to ask?"

"Tel, can you get an exact location on them? I mean can you make sure they've not left via the laundry chute while your men were eying up the front door?"

"I know exactly what you mean." He ends the call.

Fifteen minutes later, Terry calls me back to inform me that neither man is at home.

My next call is to Nick's clinic, where the receptionist informs me that he is still on compassionate leave.

"Like fuck is he," I mutter under my breath.

I'm not expecting to see Caleb, but I almost let out a sigh of relief when the door to my office opens, and he walks in. He's wearing a suit, and the widest grin I've ever seen on my brother's face.

"Did you miss me?"

This is the thing with me and Caleb. We're close to the twins, but they have their own connection which comes from sharing our mom's womb, so our bond is different to the one that we have with them. Caleb has always had my back. Ever since we were little kids cowering from our father's fist, it's as if he instinctively knows when I need him and pops up like a guardian angel sporting his brotherly halo at a jaunty angle.

"Does Victoria know that you're here?" They have a new baby, and I'll send him back upstairs if it means keeping Victoria happy.

"I'm here on her orders."

I can't help smiling at the mental image of Victoria shoving him into the elevator and warning him to get out from under her feet. I remember Mom doing the same to Terry when Emily was a baby.

"She wants me to make sure that Sienna is safe."

"Safe?" I arch an eyebrow. "Is that a euphemism for in my bed?"

Caleb laughs out loud. "I distinctly recall you insisting that she should take your guest room."

"She did." I raise my hands in mock surrender. "This morning."

When Caleb speaks next, his tone is serious. "What's the deal with the asshole surgeon?"

"Terry's currently hunting him down. Sienna's father has conveniently vanished as well."

"So, the sooner we get her away from here the better. Then we can resolve this without any distractions. Can you be ready to leave tonight?"

"You managed without me for three months. Another couple of days isn't going to make much difference."

Caleb doesn't respond, but I can see in his eyes that he doesn't agree.

"What is it?" I ask.

"We both know this isn't about Sienna. I never thought I'd see the day when Mom left the city because she was afraid for Emily."

I should stay, but I promised Sienna I'd travel with her and make sure that she was settled. Am I always going to be torn in two if we make a life together here in New York? Is this how Caleb feels now that he has a wife and a child?

"I'll stay."

Caleb shakes his head. "No can do. Victoria would never forgive me. I just need you to promise me that you and Sienna will leave tonight."

"What about you?" It feels as though I'm abandoning my family when they need me the most.

"What about me?" He shrugs.

"You should be spending time with Victoria and Holly."

Caleb comes to me and places his hands on my shoulders. "Don't worry about me. It'll all be taken care of. I'm Superman, remember?"

"Spiderman."

"Was it Spiderman?" He furrows his brow. "Jeez, I need to catch up on some sleep."

He cups the back of my neck with one hand and pulls our foreheads together.

"Go. Convince her to get on that plane tonight. Tell her that I'll drag her there myself if I must."

Sienna is still asleep when I let myself back into my apartment. My pulse races as I nudge open the door to the guest room; I was half-expecting to find her gone, and an empty jewelry box left behind on the pillow.

I stand there for a while, watching her sleep.

I would give everything I have to go back to New Year's Eve six years ago and not climb into that car with her. We could've watched the sunrise from the roof of the Wraith. I've watched it many times since, and it never fails to aim a sucker punch to my gut when I recall her smile. "*We should go watch the sunrise.*"

Six words that altered the course of our lives in ways we could never have imagined.

I'd swap places with her in a heartbeat.

I'd give her back her life. Her freedom. Her confidence.

Snuggled up inside the comforter, she wriggles, and a bare arm appears. She stretches, arching her back, jolting me out of my reverie.

She should know how beautiful she is.

I will make her believe me if it's the last thing I do.

"Sienna."

I keep my voice low, but she still jumps visibly. She sits up, pulling the comforter up to her chin, yawning widely. "How long have I been asleep? Have you been standing there the whole time?"

I smile. "No." I wish I had. I'd still be oblivious to the two men lost somewhere in the maze of New York City with the woman I love in their sights. "We're traveling to Ireland tonight."

"Tonight?" Her eyes narrow. "Why? Something has happened. Is it my father?"

Strange that her instinct is to name her father instead of Nick. She still trusts the surgeon, and this knowledge seems to suck all the air from the room.

"Nothing has happened to your father."

The less she knows the better. I don't want her to change her mind at the last minute out of some misguided obligation to check up on him.

"The jet is ready. There's no point delaying it." I try to keep my tone light-hearted, but I'm sure that she can see right through me. "Besides, Caleb is under orders from his wife to make sure that you're on a flight tonight."

Her eyes soften at the mention of Victoria, but they quickly cloud over, like the heavy sky outside. I could add that I want to leave the city before the threatened snowfall hits, but she'll get suspicious the more pressure I apply.

"I should speak to Nick."

My hackles are instantly raised.

"I haven't spoken to him since I ran away last night, Kyle. I should at least apologize for leaving without a word."

I nod, thin-lipped. "I'll give you some space." Even though giving her space to speak to him is the last thing I want to do.

I wander back to the kitchen and switch on the coffee machine, straining to hear her voice, to know what she is saying to him even though it feels like a knife straight through my chest.

The coffee pot is only half-full of steaming black liquid when she follows me into the kitchen, still clutching the comforter around her. "No answer." She chews her bottom lip. "I've messaged him to say that I'm going away for a while."

Now is my chance to tell her that she doesn't have to go. We've forced this trip on her. She would never have considered taking a break if Victoria hadn't suggested it. But I can't.

Whatever Nick's intentions, this isn't over yet.

"Thank you," I say.

She smiles. "For what?"

"For letting me help you."

She comes closer. Her lips part to reveal perfect white teeth. Her eyes lock onto mine.

"I've never been on a private jet before." Her voice is husky.

"It beats economy class."

Closer.

"Do we have time...?"

"Time for what?" My cock responds by knocking against my pants, fighting to be set free.

Sienna drops the comforter.

She's still naked. I can see the faint marks on her breasts from where I sucked on her earlier, the flush on her abdomen, the raw patches on the mound of her pussy left behind by my beard.

She reaches for my hand and sucks my index finger before inserting it inside her. My mouth closes on hers while I work her sex to a frenzy, supporting her against my chest until her shudders subside.

We order food from the Wraith's restaurant and get it sent up to my apartment. We shower together. Seamus collects Sienna's clothes from her apartment, and we pack our bags in silence, sharing occasional glances across my bedroom.

She hasn't mentioned Nick Morris since she messaged him earlier. I've seen her checking her phone several times, but I don't think that he has replied.

"I feel like a little girl again." She zips up her luggage and stands it upright on the floor. "My mom's friend had a lodge on Greenwood Lake. She would let us use it in the summer, and I'd get so excited whenever we packed our suitcase even though I knew what to expect."

"Sometimes it's better to know where you're going." I smile.

I know what she means. I have the same sense of exhilaration gurgling through my veins at the thought of traveling to Ireland with her. I can't wait to show her around. To throw open the sliding back doors of the annex and watch her inhale the view. To see Ireland through her eyes for the first time.

"Kyle. What if I can't paint again?"

I place a folded sweater inside my case and cross the room to stand in front of her. I hold her hands; she's trembling.

"What's brought this on? You have an amazing talent, Sienna. Don't let the selfish fuckers who broke into the gallery destroy your confidence. You're better than that."

She nods and sucks on her bottom lip.

"You are, Sienna. We all believe in you."

My phone vibrates then, and I slide it out of my pocket expecting to find Seamus's name on the Caller ID.

It's Caleb. "Where are you?"

"I'm still at home. We're about to leave." My pulse is racing.

"The Titan has just been raided."

What the fuck! Cash's resort hasn't been raided since the alliance with Don Dragonetti was formed. The don saw to it that the Commissioner left the Murray establishments alone in return for the little arrangement regarding the police commissioner's vacation homes and annual allowance.

"How bad is it?"

"Cash has been arrested."

19

SIENNA

"What is it?" Kyle's face has been drained of color. "What's happened?"

The excitement that I'd been feeling about the trip to Ireland evaporates, leaving me feeling weak and unprotected all over again. Whatever it is, the expression on Kyle's face is enough to tell me that our plans are about to be rewritten.

"It's Cash. The Titan has been raided."

"By the police?"

Okay, I know I'm not helping, but although I know what the Murrays do, and I'm aware that some of their activities are probably illegal, I've never connected their businesses to being on the wrong side of the law. Until now.

"What does this mean?"

"I have to stay and help him. I can't leave him, Sienna." He stares at the phone as if awaiting another phone call to pile on the bad news. "I'm the family lawyer."

"Yes of course." My hand finds the handle of my suitcase and I lean on it for support.

I should've known better than to allow myself to get excited. The instant something good comes my way, the universe waggles its finger and says, "*Nu-huh. This is not for you Sienna Walker.*"

Meeting Kyle at the nightclub on New Year's.

The gallery.

The trip to Ireland.

I swallow. This isn't me. I don't lie down and take whatever shit gets thrown at me. I don't wallow in self-pity and wait for someone else to come along and bail me out.

I get back up and I keep on fighting.

Don't let the bastards grind you down—isn't that how the saying goes?

Deep breath. "I understand. Family comes first."

He meets my eyes, and I can see the disappointment in them. While I'm thinking about myself, he's trying to do what's right for everyone.

"I'll go home, Kyle. It's okay. You don't need to worry about me."

Kyle rubs a hand across his jawline, and my brain automatically pictures his face buried between my legs.

"No. That's not what I'm saying. I'll get Seamus to take you to the airport. The family jet is waiting for us. I'll meet you there."

"But what if you get held up?"

"I won't. I'll be there, Sienna." His eyes widen; he wants me to believe him.

"How? What if this can't be resolved tonight?"

I'm disappointed at the vulnerability in my own voice. Is this what Kyle has done? Has he thrown a protective arm around me, promised to take care of me, offered me bodyguards and safe passage to Ireland so that I lower my barriers and stop fending for myself? Anyone can climb into the back of a chauffeur-driven car, board a private jet, and disembark at the other end, clean, well-rested, and woozy on expensive champagne.

So, why am I making such a big fucking deal out of it?

"It will. I promise. It'll all be a misunderstanding. The NYPD won't be able to pin anything on Cash."

It isn't lost on me that not being able to pin anything on him isn't the same as saying he has done nothing wrong. I'm reminded all over again that this way of life... This isn't what I wanted.

I can't spend the rest of my life waiting for a phone call to inform me that someone I love has been killed.

"And if it isn't a misunderstanding?" My voice is small.

I have no idea what Cash has been arrested for, but it isn't going to be for something as mundane as shoplifting or failure to stop at traffic signals.

"I'll sort it." He pulls me into his arms and kisses the top of my head. I can feel his heart beating in sync with mine. "I'll be there."

He releases me and checks his phone again.

"I have to go. The flight is cleared for take-off between eleven-thirty and midnight."

"If you're not there by midnight?"

I already feel myself pulling away from him. Rebuilding the wall that he'd so easily demolished last night. Self-preservation.

He left me once before...

"I want you to stay on the plane and go to Ireland. I'll make sure that someone is waiting to meet you at the other end, Sienna, I promise. Go to the family home and wait for me there."

"Sounds as if you already know that you're not coming with me tonight."

I feel inexplicably crushed. Stupid, stupid, stupid, for letting him in, so that he could hurt me all over again. How do I even know that he didn't plan this down to the last detail: the phone call just as we're about to leave for the airport, the disappointment in his eyes.

I have to stay, Sienna. I can't leave now.

"No, that isn't true. Please believe me. I *want* to be there. I want to travel with you tonight, Sienna. I want it more than you'll ever know. I love you."

I see it in his eyes, and I realize that I've known it all along.

Because I feel the same way about him. It's as if he tethered my heart to his in the nightclub six years ago, and the silk ropes knotting us together have been there ever since.

"It's just, this is family..."

Despite the knots, this is the way that it will always be...

"Okay. I'll wait."

"Good girl."

It's hard to believe that these two words have sent tremors of excitement down my spine before and made my pussy drip with anticipation. Now, they sound flat.

"I'll send Seamus up for your luggage. Promise me that you'll wait here for him."

"What about your luggage?" I hate the accusation in my voice.

But something inside me seems to curl up into a tiny ball and die when his eyes flicker back and forth between me and his open suitcase. He had no intention of coming with me.

"Seamus can bring my luggage too." It feels as if he has already checked out. "I don't want to leave you like this, Sienna."

Like what?

With a promise that you know you can't keep?

With your cum still trickling out from between my legs?

"Go. Your brother needs you."

There appears to be a whole bunch of stuff perching on the tip of his tongue, waiting to dive into the room and convince me that he'll be there.

But instead, he turns around and walks out of the bedroom, his phone already pressed to his ear. It's like watching him morph into a different person as he leaves, every footstep erasing another tiny piece of the man who whispers to me in Gaelic when I'm lying contented in his arms and replacing it with the Murray family lawyer.

An hour later, I'm sitting on the Murray's private jet at Teterboro Airport, peering out of the window at the city lights in the distance. I haven't heard from Kyle since he left his apartment. I don't know if he is handling Cash's incarceration from the comfort of his office in the Wraith, or if he's sitting with the Police Commissioner pleading his brother's case over a bottle of brandy.

I check my cell phone again.

Nothing.

The aircraft belongs on a movie set. The seating area is ivory, the cushions upholstered with ivory velvet, the trimmings polished mahogany, the strip lighting understated and classy. Seamus showed me the bedrooms when we boarded.

Fucking bedrooms complete with ensuite shower rooms!

No chance of having your knees crushed by the seat in front or turning into a contortionist while you try to wash in the poky restroom, not when you travel by private jet.

How did Victoria keep this to herself?

How does anyone ever learn to take this for granted?

It's another reminder that Kyle and I exist in different universes.

The steward—because the Murrays employ their own private fucking airline staff as well—has stopped trying to offer me a glass of champagne. I've barely touched the ice-cold water served in a crystal tumbler that he served with a selection of 'nibbles' when Seamus and I first boarded.

My mouth is dry. My palms are sweaty. My brain hasn't been able to focus on anything other than the minutes ticking slowly by towards take-off.

He isn't coming.

He promised that he would do everything in his power to make this flight, but if he was coming, he'd be here by now.

My hopes keep soaring and dipping like a gull trying to navigate a sea storm, but each dip is sinking lower and lower, until the moment of truth arrives. Then, the doors will close, and the steward will tell me to buckle up during take-off, and I'll be leaving behind the only home I've ever known for a strange country. On my own.

Eleven-twenty-five.

The flight is cleared for take-off between eleven-thirty and midnight.

Is Kyle sitting in a dingy police department somewhere in the city trying to convince the cops to release Cash, and panicking that he isn't going to make it in time? Or is he waiting for an alert to inform him that the flight has taken off without him so that he can forget about me for a while?

I unbuckle the safety belt and pick up my purse and my phone.

I don't even know how I allowed myself to be talked into this situation. This is where I belong. I should be at the gallery, overseeing the repairs that Kyle requested, reading emails, and getting back into the art studio.

Seamus is already on his feet before I can go anywhere. "Mr. Murray has just arrived." His lilting accent is more pronounced than Kyle's, but there's no mistaking the relief in his tone. "You might want to fasten your safety belt. Once he boards, the pilot will prepare for take-off."

"Kyle is here?"

Anticipation, joy, the thrill of knowing that Kyle kept his word and got here as soon as he could all surge through my veins, making me feel giddy.

He came!

My heart starts skipping as Seamus leaves me to go and welcome his boss. I should never have questioned his promises. I should've trusted him the way I did the night we met.

Sunrise over the Giant's Causeway here we come.

I peer back out of the small oval window at the city lights. Perhaps I will ask the steward to open that bottle of champagne after all.

I'm still smiling when I turn back to the cabin to face Kyle.

My stomach plummets like I'm riding the Tower of Terror in Disney World rather than sitting comfortably in a private jet that hasn't even left the ground yet.

It isn't Kyle who takes the seat opposite me.

It's Nick.

He's wearing a black polo-neck sweater and black pants, his cashmere coat draped casually over his arm as if this were a regular vacation that we'd planned together. His hair is a little ruffled and his cheeks are tinted pink from the chill of the night air, but the smile hasn't altered. It's the same smile with which he greeted me at my first appointment. The same smile that accompanied his unexpected proposal.

And now this.

"Nick?" I can barely find my voice to speak. "What are you doing here?"

I glance at the cabin entrance, expecting Seamus to follow Nick on board, but there's no sign of him. My pulse is racing through the scenario, trying to pinpoint the exact moment when Kyle and Nick switched places, and failing epically.

"I know you weren't expecting me." He places his coat on the seat next to him and fastens the safety belt around his waist as if traveling by private jet is his preferred mode of transport, and one that he enjoys regularly. "Kyle has been otherwise detained."

He hasn't answered the question. My brain picks up on the way he skirted around it, waving red flags behind my eyes, but my body isn't cooperating.

"He finally came to his senses."

Nick slides his phone from the pocket of his pants and unlocks it, and I watch him. My fingers grip the handles either side of my seat. My throat clicks as I try to swallow.

"Here. This is the message I received from him earlier this evening."

Nick turns his phone around so that I can read the words on the screen, but they're just a bunch of jumbled up letters to my confused brain.

"What does it say?" I whisper.

He takes the phone back and reads the message out loud.

"I realize now that Sienna deserves better than the only way of life that I can offer her. She's an amazingly talented beautiful woman, and I wish her nothing but the best of everything life has to offer her. She told me about your proposal. At first, I was angry, but I can't stand in the way of her future anymore. Take care of her. You have my blessing."

He locks the phone and peers at me from across the polished table between us.

I can't meet his gaze. Instead, I stare at the phone, at the black screen behind which Kyle's words are screaming at me that he's a liar.

Liar.

LIAR!

"I-I don't understand." My head feels bunged up with tears that I refuse to shed over Kyle Murray, and I sniff loudly. "Why... Why would he do that?"

"He wants what's best for you, Sienna." He smiles. "At least on that we both agree."

I stare out of the window.

My thoughts can't seem to get a grip on anything and make sense of what's going on.

Kyle wanted to get me away from Nick. He was holding stuff back from me, I know that much, but Victoria's suggestion that I spend some time in Ireland played right into his hands. It would get me away from Nick, my father, and the gallery, and leave him free to do what exactly...?

No. I mentally shake myself. None of that sits right with me.

He calls me *his leoin*. His lioness.

He said *he loves me*.

When I'm with him, I feel like I'm the most beautiful woman to have ever graced this planet, and he wouldn't do that if he didn't care about me. Would he?

Was it all a joke to him? A distraction until he'd had his fun and was ready to hand me over to Nick?

I can't believe it.

But the truth is, I don't want to believe it, and my heart is still trying to keep that faint glimmer of hope alive, even when faced with reality.

What about Victoria though? She would never have suggested the trip to Ireland if she'd known about Kyle's plans. She'd have warned me to stay the fuck away from him instead of trying to push us together.

"No. I can't do this." I unbuckle the safety belt and stand up. "I need to speak to Kyle."

"It's too late, Sienna. We're already moving." Nick's eyebrows slide upwards, his eyes flickering across my face as though he's afraid that I'll try to leap from a moving aircraft.

I stare at the runway lights alongside the plane, the city moving slowly by, at the airport growing steadily smaller as we coast along the tarmac. In my bewilderment, I didn't register the engines powering up or the door closing. I was trapped in a moment with Kyle. The moment when I handed over the piece of me that I'd shut down since the accident.

I should've heeded the warning in the song that's been playing on repeat in my head since Thanksgiving.

Last Christmas, I gave you my heart, and the very next day, you gave it away.

"I need to get off. Stop the plane, Nick."

"Darling, I can't. We're already in the air."

Right on cue, the aircraft's nose tilts towards the sky, and I stumble back to my seat, sitting heavily. This feels all wrong. Kyle said that he would arrange for someone to meet me at the airport. He said that he would join me there later if he missed the flight.

"Where's Seamus?" Finally, I face Nick. "He should be on board."

"Kyle recalled him." Nick shrugs. "There was no need for him to accompany us now that I'm here."

"But you don't know where I'm staying." I know that Kyle would never have agreed to Nick staying at the Murray family home.

"We'll check into a hotel, Sienna. We can go wherever we want."

I feel the pressure against my chest as the aircraft takes off. Gravity. Pinning me to my seat. Trapping me on board with the wrong man.

We keep climbing, climbing, climbing.

And my thoughts keep spiraling.

This was supposed to be a break for me. Time to relax, breathe, and paint. It's what Kyle wanted for me too; how can I do that with Nick by my side?

The aircraft reaches a certain height and then lists sideways as we circle the airport to pick up the correct flight path. I stare down at the ground. There's the runway, lit up to keep us on track. The airport terminal. The buggies that carry the luggage out to the waiting aircraft.

Then I spot something else that draws my attention. A car. In the parking lot. It takes a few seconds for me to figure out that it's the private bay where Seamus parked the car when we arrived earlier. But it isn't the vehicle that's making my stomach flip over and over.

If Kyle had recalled the driver as Nick said, the car would be gone. But it isn't. There's no sign of anyone else in the lot, but there is something on the ground next to the car, hidden from the view of any other vehicles entering the compound. I squint, trying to bring it into focus before we climb any higher and it becomes a speck of dirt on a terrestrial map.

My breath sticks in my throat.

It's a figure.

A body.

And it isn't moving.

I fixate on it until the plane leans the other way, and I lose sight of it.

My opportunity to call Kyle has passed now that we're in the air. I can't ask him if Nick is telling the truth, but I don't really need to.

"Sienna, is everything okay?" Nick's voice jolts me back to the present.

His eyes search mine, his expression unreadable. He's waiting for me to tell him what I've seen on the ground. But then what? Will he tell me that I'm being paranoid, imagining things because his presence came as a bit of a shock? Or maybe he'll laugh and tell me that I've spent too much time in the company of a mafia member and am turning shadows into corpses.

"Why didn't Seamus come and tell me himself?"

"There was no time. The plane would've missed its time slot."

"Would that have been such a bad thing?"

He smiles. His smile has always been so dazzling, so practiced, that it draws the eye to his perfect teeth, but now, I notice for the first time that it doesn't reach his eyes. Sure, smile lines appear at the corners, but his eyes remain cold. Untouched.

"I guess not. But, well…" He presses his hands together as if in prayer and gazes at them, pensive. "I was worried that Kyle Murray would change his mind at the last minute and spoil everything again."

"Again?" I can't keep the revulsion from my voice, but if he notices, he covers it well.

"I've waited almost six years to tell you how I feel about you, Sienna, and now that I've plucked up the courage, he's hanging around like a bad smell."

He leans forward and reaches for my hand. I don't stop him.

Being trapped mid-air with a man I don't trust isn't exactly ideal. I don't want to antagonize him. I have no choice but to play along, for now, and pray that Kyle will know what's happened when he gets to the airport and discovers that the flight has taken off without him, and Seamus.

Perhaps he'll find a way to turn the aircraft around.

Will Nick even notice if we start heading back towards the city?

I force my lips to move. It's the best I can hope for. "Well, he's not here now."

His smile stretches. Looking at him now, I can't believe that I ever found Nick Morris attractive. The smile is slimy, like a serpent who knows how poisonous he is and feels absolutely no remorse about attacking his prey.

"You didn't give me an answer, Sienna." He sighs. Everything that he does, every word spoken, every action, is rehearsed, delivered for effect. "I know I told you to take your time, but—"

"Why don't you ask me again?" I feel nauseous saying the words out loud.

He fumbles in his coat pocket and drops the tiny jewelry box, which rolls under his seat. He unbuckles himself and drops onto his knees to retrieve it, then, perfectly placed, he swivels around and holds my left hand.

His fingers are trembling. There are tears in his eyes.

But I feel nothing but repugnance, knowing that this is all an act.

I swallow painfully. My heart is throwing itself against my ribcage as if screaming at me to get away from this man, to say no, to yell at him that he'll never be Kyle. But I suck on my bottom lip and breathe deeply.

"Sienna, will you marry me?"

It's laughable. Hysteria is bubbling inside my chest, and I know that if I acknowledge it, the plane will be filled to bursting with my messy, choking sobs. Where's the declaration of love? Where are the terms of endearment or the well-chosen words that express his feelings for me? Where is the gleam in his eyes?

"Yes." I squeeze it out, a brittle sound like a dry twig being snapped.

He slides the ring onto my finger. It feels cold, heavy, unnatural. The diamond winks at me in the overhead lighting, and all I see is a tiny rock with the power to crush my future.

"Do you like it? Does it fit? I guessed your ring size, but I can have it made smaller if it's too large."

"It's ... perfect," I manage.

"This calls for champagne." Nick is back on his feet. "Where's the steward when we need him?"

He leans over me and kisses my cheek, and it takes all my willpower not to recoil. I feel queasy. His lips have no right to touch my skin, to kiss my face where Kyle's lips have been.

Unfazed by my lack of enthusiasm, he marches off towards the rear of the cabin where the steward sits. "Don't move. I'll be right back with champagne."

It's only when he disappears and I'm left alone with my erratic heartbeat and the blood gushing in my ears that I wonder how he knew there was a steward on board.

20

KYLE

Caleb, Bash, and Terry are waiting for me when I enter Caleb's office at 3 a.m. Their faces are ashen. Their eyes are bloodshot. Bash and Caleb are still suited up, but their ties are loosened, and crystal tumblers stained with whiskey litter the coffee table between them.

They all stand while I close the door behind me.

"What's going on?" Caleb is the first to speak. "When are they releasing Cash?"

"It isn't going to be that simple."

I sit heavily on one of the couches and accept a shot of whiskey from Terry.

"What do they have on him?" Caleb remains standing. He's running on adrenaline.

I sip the liquid in my glass; it burns, and my eyes water. I've had a couple of hours' sleep in the last forty-eight hours, but more importantly, I'm acutely aware that in putting my brother first, I've let Sienna down. She's currently on our private jet, traveling to Ireland with Seamus, probably having convinced herself that I was never going to make that flight.

Her disappointment cannot come close to matching mine.

"Supplying narcotics, money laundering." I'm leading with the easy stuff.

"Tip-off?" Bash is a live wire tonight, his facial expression and his muscles twitching in sync with his thoughts.

"Don Dragonetti is working on it." Pause. "We suspect the Bogrovs."

"Caelan's fucking son." Caleb starts pacing. "Has to be. We should've taken him down when we first found out where he came from."

"Can't be that hard to track down." Bash aims this at Terry.

Terry is quiet. He has been a mafia enforcer for almost his entire adult life. He knows how this works. There's more to come.

"Not to mention the homicide of Luca Benito last month."

This one sends jagged spears of panic through my chest. The police commissioner's wrists must've been bound with razor-wire and a gun to his temple for him to act on this one, which means that he'll be satisfied that the NYPD can make the accusation stick.

"What's Cash's alibi?" Caleb stops pacing momentarily. His eyes look haunted.

"He was in his apartment."

"With?" Bash asks.

"With a woman whose name he is currently refusing to mention."

"Fuck!" Bash stands too.

We all think better on our feet.

"Stupid fucker! I knew this would come back to bite his ass one day."

Caleb's eyes narrow. "You know who it is?"

"I can guess."

"I'm assuming that she's married." Terry's voice is steady.

His brain is already working behind the scenes, figuring out his best options for destroying whatever evidence the Bogrovs have planted with Cash's name on.

"To a sick bastard who would liquidize Cash's balls and feed them to him through a straw if he ever found out."

I swallow the rest of my drink and fill a tall tumbler with water from the jug on the coffee table. "We can't let it get that far. Terry, can we apply pressure to the Bogrovs? Find out their connection to Nick Morris?"

He must have a role to play in this. The proposal. Cash's arrest on the night I'm due to leave the country with Sienna. It's like one of those jigsaw puzzles where you have no picture to follow; we're aimlessly jiggling the pieces around to make them fit, and his name keeps cropping up bang in the center of the picture.

"And any update on Sienna's father?" I ask.

"He's a slippery bastard." Terry scratches the back of his neck. "Has more connections than we gave him credit for. Either that or the Bogrovs have already buried his feet in cement and tossed him into the Hudson."

"We can't rule him out." I still can't figure out why Sienna let him back into her life, but it isn't important right now. "Robert Hooch and Nick Morris. We need to find out their connection. There's a reason why he was here at the Wraith while the gallery was being trashed. But where was Nick Morris?"

"I'm heading over to the Titan. I'll sort Cash's alibi." Bash already appears lost without his twin in the room.

The Titan's staff were handpicked by Cash; loyalty is the driver in this world. Bash will choose someone he can trust and make them an offer they won't be able to refuse, but we still need Don Dragonetti to shovel some dirt the Bogrovs' way. Attack the charges from all angles.

Terry's phone rings. He doesn't check the Caller ID but raises the handset to his ear without speaking. His eyes instinctively slide my way.

My heart thumps sickeningly. He doesn't need to say a word for me to know that this is bad news and that it involves Sienna.

"I'll be right there." He ends the call.

"Is it Sienna?" My breaths are already growing too shallow to pump sufficient oxygen to my lungs. "What's happened?"

I haven't heard from her. I was informed when the private jet departed and assumed that she was on it.

Fuck!

I should've cancelled the flight. Kept her safe in my apartment until this situation with Cash was resolved and I could travel with her. She didn't want to travel alone. She told Victoria that she'd never been anywhere alone, and I dismissed it. I'm part of a fucking mafia family—we quickly learn to trust our gut instincts, and yet I didn't trust Sienna's.

"Seamus's body has been discovered at the airport," Terry says.

"What about Sienna?" My legs wobble as I stand up, and I raise my inhaler to my mouth.

All eyes are on me.

"She's en route to Ireland as planned."

"But Seamus isn't with her."

My chest is tight. The whiskey and lack of oxygen is making me feel lightheaded, but I can think clearly enough to understand that Seamus was killed because someone wanted him out of the way. They wanted him out of the way so that they could get to Sienna.

"Find out if anyone else boarded the aircraft." My voice sounds dull even to my own ears. "See if we can get it turned around."

"How was Seamus killed?" Caleb asks.

"Slit throat."

Terry and Seamus had known each other all their lives; this murder will hit Terry hard, but his expression remains neutral. There's a job to be done. Revenge first, grief later.

"I'll lead a team across to the airport," Terry continues. "I'll pull whatever fucking strings I need to pull to get that aircraft back to New York City."

I sense the unspoken 'but' at the end of that sentence.

Before I can question Terry, my cell phone rings, and my heart leaps with joy when I see Sienna's name on the screen. I'm so relieved that I don't question why she is messaging me from several thousand feet above the ground.

I open the message and my stomach lurches, nausea crashing through my body.

It takes several beats for me to understand the image on my screen. At first, all I can see is pale skin, a blanket, and blood. Then the shape comes into focus, and I realize that it's Sienna. She's slumped across two seats on our private jet, a blanket thrown over her as if she's napping during the long journey.

But it's the blood-smeared face that causes my pulse to race and every muscle in my body to constrict. Her eyes are closed. Her lips parted. I zoom in to find the source of the blood, but there's nothing visible. Head wound perhaps.

The question is: how bad is it?

Another message pings through:

If you want to see her alive, you'll hand over the Titan by midnight. Instructions will follow.

"Kyle?" Caleb's voice brings me spiraling back to the room, clutching my phone tightly.

"They have Sienna. She's hurt." I feel numb.

"Who?" Caleb presses. "Where is she?"

"Still on the jet." I need to mentally shake myself; I'm useless to Sienna if I can't think straight, if I'm functioning on autopilot.

Terry heads into the boardroom with his phone pressed to his ear and closes the door behind him.

"Okay." Caleb takes control; this is his forte, seeing the situation and being the first one to cross the starting line. "Terry will turn the plane around, and we'll scour every fucking CCTV footage the airport can give us. The fucker who killed Seamus will lead us to the assholes who thought they could steal our aircraft, hurt Sienna, and get away with it."

"What do you want me to do?" Bash is still here, but I can see the conflict playing out behind his eyes. His twin is in trouble. The ropes binding them together are stronger than any other family ties.

"Go to the Titan as planned."

My cell phone is heavy in my hand. "There's more," I add before Bash can leave. "They want the Titan in exchange for Sienna."

"They can fuck right off," Bash growls, his jaw clenched so tightly I can hear his back teeth grinding. "If they want my brother's business, they're gonna have to go through me first."

"They won't be getting anything." Caleb is outwardly still calm. Inwardly, I imagine him to be a seething, bubbling mass of molten lava. "The Titan is a stepping stone to taking everything that we own. They're testing the waters, and we're going to show them what a big fucking mistake that is."

"Why the Titan first?" Bash asks.

"Good question." Caleb stares at a spot somewhere above and behind my left shoulder. Thinking. "They must've known they could frame Cash. We need to tread carefully where that's concerned, but I'll speak to Mateo Dragonetti. Bash, run a background check on every member of the staff at the Titan. I don't care who they are or who they know. No one gets overlooked."

"You think these people have already infiltrated the business?" I ask, finally finding my voice.

"This is all a little too convenient, too flawless for it to have been actioned on a whim. Bash, who else knows about Cash's alibi?"

"Apart from the woman in question? I'm not sure she'd even risk telling her best friend."

"Suits us better that way." Caleb turns his attention back to me. "Find her. I want to know everything about her. What toothpaste she uses. Where she buys her groceries. Who else she has messed around with behind her husband's back. She'll do whatever it takes to stop her husband from hearing about her infidelities, which makes her our best chance right now of getting Cash off the hook."

The boardroom door opens, and Terry comes back into the room. "I can't turn the jet around."

"Why not?" My heart rate immediately spikes.

"The pilot has dropped contact with Teterboro and Dublin."

"Last contact?" Caleb jumps in before I can speak.

"Dublin. Seems the pilot was still following the flight plan until I started asking questions."

"What about Sienna?" I don't need to spell it out.

She's currently on a hijacked aircraft that may or may not be preparing to land in Dublin in a couple of hours. She's injured and is being held to ransom against the Titan. Additionally, my instincts are screaming at me that Nick Morris is the man we need to find, because I wouldn't be surprised if he killed Seamus and took my place on board that flight.

"We'll do everything that we can to locate the plane." Caleb's voice softens just a little. "Terry, we need our men to be the first ones on the scene. Wherever they're headed, they're sure to have a welcome party waiting for them."

"I want to be there," I blurt out.

"Cash needs you here." Caleb flinches as he says the words out loud.

"Would you stick around if it was Victoria's life on the line?"

We already know the answer to this one. When Olivia Dragonetti abducted Victoria, Caleb didn't wait around. He jumped onto his Harley and reached the abandoned warehouse before Terry could get there with his team. He walked into that hostage situation, alone, and without a second thought for his own safety because the woman he loved was in danger.

"That's what I thought." I take my time.

I'm still battling the same question: what's the point of our wealth and our connections in high places if I can't protect the woman I'm in love with? The woman I want to spend the rest of my life with.

"I won't let Cash down. But I can't let Sienna down a second time."

She'll never forgive me.

There'll be no going back if I'm not there to save her this time.

Caleb nods once. "Speak to Mateo Dragonetti. His private jet will get you to Dublin before the next scheduled flight out of Newark.

I'm already crossing the room and heading for the elevator.

"And Kyle?" Caleb causes me to stop. "Be careful."

21

SIENNA

My eyelids are heavy. Without opening my eyes, I can tell that the room is dark. Still night. Although my brain can't seem to make sense of what time it is, as if I've been woken from a deep sleep too soon.

I shift in my bed.

It's hard. Something—a coil from the mattress maybe—digs into my hip and drags me unwillingly back to consciousness. I'm shivering. My face is squashed up against a pillow that smells like it wasn't dried properly when it was last washed.

My nose is cold, and my feet feel like blocks of ice. They're always the first parts of me to feel the cold in the winter; Victoria laughs at me for wearing thermal socks in bed and pulling the comforter over my head when I'm sleeping. But this is a different level of cold. This is the kind of cold I imagine whenever I walk past a homeless person huddled inside a grubby sleeping bag in a store entrance in the city.

I open my eyes. It requires way more effort than it should.

Another tremor travels through me when I find myself staring at a brick wall, slick with moisture.

Perhaps I'm still asleep and this is a nightmare. This is my first thought. It happens. My dreams are so vivid that I often wake up with tear-soaked cheeks or the overwhelming sense of relief that the man chasing me through an empty hospital with a bloody knife was only a figment of my imagination.

But with my heart thumping clumsily against the uncomfortable mattress, and the distinct aroma of damp and mold assaulting my senses, I know this isn't a dream.

I try to sit up, but my muscles are heavy too. I feel drained, lumpish, hungover.

Then, the memories start pouring into my head like an unblocked dam.

The private jet.

Checking the time on my phone and waiting for Kyle.

He didn't show. He was never going to make the flight, and he knew it.

Pain crashes through my skull like a tsunami when I recall Nick sitting opposite me in the aircraft cabin, his coat folded neatly beside him, his smile that was going nowhere.

The ring.

I wiggle my frozen fingers. The diamond ring isn't there.

Did the fucker take it back like a prop that's no longer needed when the play ends?

Was that all it was to him: a prop?

I close my eyes again. It's the only thing that makes sense of his proposal. The lack of any kind of emotional interaction between us. The timescale between our first date and him popping the question.

Ask me again.

I said that, didn't I? I said it in the cabin of the Murrays' private jet. But I must've had a reason because thinking about Nick now makes my entire being want to crawl away from him and hide.

Seamus.

Tears sting my eyes, and my breathing grows shallow.

"*Keep it together*," Sienna, I mutter under my breath. I don't know for sure what happened to Seamus, but he should've traveled with me and Kyle, and he didn't.

Instead, Nick Morris was my travel companion.

And now I have no clue where I am.

I try to sit up. The room spins out from under me, and I lean over the side of the bed and retch onto the floor.

My head… It feels like a bowling ball with a sinus infection.

It doesn't take much effort to figure out that I've been drugged. This is like no hangover I've ever experienced before, and there have been more than a few.

I remember Nick going off to find the steward because he wanted champagne to celebrate our engagement.

Engagement. What a fucking joke. The pretense was obviously for my benefit.

He came back with two glasses and a bottle of Dom Perignon in a silver ice bucket. I went along with the game because I had no choice. Not much I could do about his presence mid-flight short of opening the door and shoving him out, but he has at least six inches on me and a lifetime of pumping iron at the gym.

So, I sat back, sipped champagne, and smiled back at him when he planned our vacation in Ireland.

"We don't have to stay in Ireland," he delivered with a cheesy smile and a casual shrug. "We can go wherever you want, Sienna. This trip is all about you."

He omitted the part where this trip was all about me being drugged, kidnapped, and hidden away inside a dank moldy basement in fuck knows which part of the planet.

It must be a basement.

I stare at the walls until my eyes are stinging and fat teardrops roll down my cheeks. The room is dark, but I can smell the damp clinging to the slimy bricks. It has to be underground. The chill brushing my exposed face is not like the chill that seeps into my apartment during the night when the heating is switched off. This room feels, and smells, as if it has never received a blast of heat since it was built.

So, where am I?

The flight was due to land in Dublin around breakfast time. Did Nick provide a little detour for the pilot, or was Ireland his intended destination too?

The Murrays were supposed to be meeting me at the airport. Did someone inform Kyle that I wasn't alone on the flight, or is he still in his office, waiting to hear that the flight landed safely? How long before his extended family confirms that I was a no-show?

Or ... *shit* ... it occurs to me then that maybe they were included in Nick's plan all along. Maybe this is their basement. A secret basement in a secret hideaway, someplace that even Kyle isn't aware of.

I retch onto the floor again.

How will he find me if he has no clue where I am?

The jet must've obtained clearance to land though, right? Airplanes don't just take off and land as they please; the flight paths would be carnage, and there would be steaming great hunks of aircraft debris all around the world. So, if anyone can track where the plane touched down, it's Kyle.

I take deep breaths and try to ignore the stench of mold seeping through my pores and incubating inside my lungs.

Kyle will know which country I'm in, but unless the Murrays saw me being carried, unconscious, off that private jet and followed us here, he'll still have to find me.

Unless I can contact him myself.

I already know that I'm no longer wearing the fake engagement ring, but I haven't tried moving my arms and legs.

Starting with my feet, I slide them across the lumpy mattress, wincing at the bite of cold as I leave behind the part of the bed warmed by my body heat. My ankles are not bound, so if I can stop the room from spinning, I'll be able to stand up and walk.

It's better than nothing.

Next, I try flexing my fingers.

They feel like something bony pulled out of the freezer, but my movement isn't restricted. Using my hands, I support my upper body on the mattress and push myself upright.

My brain cells swim, making me feel even more nauseous. The pounding ache inside my head shifts to the top of my skull; it feels as though someone's fist has grabbed a hold of my brain and is squeezing it like a sponge.

I've no idea how long I sit there, waiting for the thump-thump-thump to subside. When it finally eases enough for me to open my eyes and survey my surroundings, I'm even more convinced that this is a basement.

The stone floor is as slick as the walls. I can't see any furniture other than the bed upon which I'm sitting. In the dense gloom, I can't even see if there's an overhead lamp. I scan the room until my eyes finally settle upon a gray mass with a different consistency to the rest of the wall. The door.

My escape route.

Gripping the edge of the mattress, I haul myself into a standing position. The room sways violently, and I instinctively reach for the wall to keep me upright. My stomach twists at the slimy touch, but I force myself to lean on it to stop me from falling over. If I want to get out of here, I need to keep moving.

Si, you're the strongest person I know. You're not going to let a flight to Dublin beat you.

I can hear Victoria as clearly as if she were standing next to me.

"No, I'm not going to let a flight to Dublin beat me," I say out loud. I grit my teeth. "Do you hear me, universe? I'm Sienna Walker. I survived the car crash you threw at me, and I'm going to survive this too."

I take a tentative step away from the bed and the slippery wall. I feel weak, like I'm convalescing following a serious illness. Every part of my body aches. I'm shivering uncontrollably, and it isn't only from the cold.

I have no idea what's on the other side of that door. All I can hear is my blood pumping around my veins. But I have to try. Curiosity didn't kill the cat; it gave it a pat on the back for trying and rewarded it with a cozy cushion in front of a roaring fire and a dish filled with fresh cream.

This is the image I keep in mind as I make my way slowly across the dingy room.

A brightly lit room. A roaring fire. A mug of steaming coffee.

An image of Kyle's green eyes flashes into my head, and I pause to regulate my breathing. "He's coming for me. If he meant what he said, he'll keep his promise, and he won't let anything bad happen to me."

I keep moving. One foot in front of the other. My heart and my head are pounding.

I'm almost there when I hear a faint click.

My heart skips. I swipe the clammy air frantically for something to support me and find nothing. I'm still floundering like a fish out of water when the door opens, and I'm greeted by a swatch of dull artificial light.

I blink. Even this sickly yellow light is bright after the intense darkness, and when I manage to squint at the doorway, a man steps into view.

"You're awake." It's Nick. He isn't smiling. "Turn around and walk back to the bed, there's a good girl."

Good girl.

"Where am I?"

"I said 'sit down'." His voice is snappy, brittle, cold. Gone is the gentle tone reserved for his patients.

He moves closer, blocking the weak light from the dingy corridor outside, and I'm flooded with fear that he's armed. I might be stronger than I realize, but I'm not reckless, and I'm getting out of here alive, no matter what it takes.

Because seeing him like this has rammed home to me that people like Nick Morris don't deserve to win. They don't play fair. They see a prize, and their sense of entitlement takes over, triggering the belief that they should have whatever they want. Like the world owes them.

Well, fuck you!

I stumble back across the basement to the low bed which is little more than a lumpy mattress on a cot and sit down before my legs give way. I grab the blanket and drag it around my shoulders. It provides a little warmth, enough to stop my teeth from chattering and for me to glare at Nick as he follows me into the room and shuts the door behind him.

We're plunged into darkness again, and I focus on the shape of him silhouetted against the wall to stop myself from crying out.

He flicks a switch on the wall and a small lightbulb swinging from the ceiling produces a feeble light. His shadowy face is gray, his eyes like empty sockets, his lips almost non-existent.

"Why am I here?" I try an alternative question.

He stands facing me with his arms folded across his chest. I hope that the cold is getting to him too. It's a small comfort.

"You're here as leverage, Sienna. If you've done what we hoped you would do, Kyle Murray will meet our demands in return for your life."

There are so many points to take from this statement that I hardly know where to begin.

"What am I supposed to have done?"

He has been in the room for less than a minute, and it's already starting to feel like a sick dystopian reality show, where the contestants are supposed to guess their next move. Get it wrong, and—*bad luck*—you're dead.

"Make him fall in love with you. Give him just enough to keep him wanting more. Dangling the proverbial carrot so to speak."

"You're sick, do you know that?"

A sinister lopsided smile turns his expression ugly. "Oh, I'm not the one who's sick, Sienna. There are far more dangerous people in the world than me, and some of them are right here in this building."

Nausea rolls my stomach like I'm on a boat, and I swallow bile, the burning sensation in my throat making my eyes water.

"What demands?" I ask.

"The Titan ... for starters. It will be enough to keep you alive. For now. Then we'll move onto the Rinse, and finally the monstrosity known as the Wraith."

"Why?" I can hear the incredulity in my voice. "Why can't you open your own casino? Why do you have to steal someone else's?"

"Oh, I don't want the casinos." He studies his nails as if he has just realized that dirt is collecting underneath them. "The people who are paying me can do whatever the fuck they want with them. They can take a wrecking ball to them for all I care."

"The people who are paying you?"

Anger blooms inside my chest, red and hot and punchy. Kyle and his brothers have worked hard to build their businesses from the ground up. Sure, they might have mafia connections, and they might get their money from illegal practices, but right or wrong, it's their livelihood. The casinos and hotels belong to their family. They live and breathe the family business, something that men like Nick Morris would ever understand.

These people Nick is working for, they won't care about the Titan or the Rinse or the Wraith the way Kyle and his brothers do. They won't put their heart and soul into making them successful. He already said he doesn't care if they demolish them. So, why are they so desperate to steal them?

"Their name is Bogrov," he says, slicing through my simmering rage. "I don't expect you to have heard of them. They're Russian bratva."

Bratva? The word rings alarm bells inside my head.

"Mafia to me and you." Nick answers the question for me.

"I-I thought there was some kind of code between the mafia families."

He snickers. "Only in the movies. It's dog-eat-dog in the real world. The Bogrovs have come along and decided that they want a slice of the Murray pie. Who was I to refuse them?"

This conversation is making me feel physically sick.

He is making me feel physically sick.

"What's in it for you?"

Nick shrugs. "Money. A private island. A lifelong vacation. The kind of bank account that will buy me anything I want."

I don't speak. I never realized until now that his silky voice was balancing on a tightrope between sensuality and sleaziness. Seems his sleazy roots are finally beginning to show.

"You see, women like you, Sienna, make me sick. You expect me to fix you with a scalpel. You're constantly chasing beauty that will never be yours, and never once do you ever consider accepting defeat. How do you think I feel looking at your scars, huh? How do you think it feels when I have to tuck in a woman's sagging jowls and tell her that I can make her look twenty years younger?"

My breathing is speeding up, trying to suppress the nausea swirling around my gut. With every word he utters, my brain is screaming at me to get away. To put as much distance between me and this monster as possible. Only then can I think about what he's saying. If I let the words affect me now, I'll never get away from him.

"Sorry to disappoint you, Sienna, but I never wanted you. I could never be attracted to someone like you." His mouth turns down at the corners with disgust.

You're so beautiful, leoin. Promise me that you'll never try to hide your scars again. They're part of who you are, part of what makes you so beautiful.

I cling to Kyle's words. I cling to the way Kyle makes me feel when I'm with him as if it's my life raft out of this place.

"I'm not disappointed." I'm surprised at how strong I sound. "I could never be attracted to someone like you either, Nick. You see, you're chasing a lifestyle too. You want a bank account that will buy you anything you desire, but you'll never be satisfied."

I stand up. My legs are still trembling, the blanket is still clutched tightly to my chest. But I realize that my scars are still visible above the neckline of my sweater, and I jut my chin towards the ceiling.

"That's the difference between me and you," I continue. "I know what will make me happy."

"Ha!" He scoffs, his expression ugly. "You think Kyle Murray will make you happy? Think again, darling. He won't be so desirable without the Wraith behind him. Will you still find him attractive without his expensive suits and a chauffeur-driven car to beat the city traffic? What about when his brother sells your precious gallery for a downpayment on a shitty apartment in the Bronx?" His laughter is mirthless.

"The answer is yes. I'll be happy in a shitty apartment in the Bronx if I'm with Kyle."

"He'll have to find you first."

The strength I found when he was belittling 'women like me' wanes a little. "You said that when they hand over the Titan…" I can't remember the exact wording he used, but he implied that they would let me go.

"I said you were leverage. Perhaps I didn't explain myself clearly." He waits for me to fully process his words before continuing. "Collateral damage. Once the bratva get what they want, they'll probably have no further use for you, so they might decide to leave you here. I certainly won't be sticking around once I've gotten my cut."

"Where am I, Nick?" He never answered my first question.

"Oh, we're in Ireland, we're just nowhere near the Murray family home." He lowers his arms and checks the time on his wristwatch. "I should go. I'm sure our friend Kyle would've enjoyed our scintillating conversation, but I'm growing rather bored with it now." He yawns to emphasize the point.

"Can I get some water?"

"I'll get some sent down to you with some food. Don't expect it to meet the Wraith standards though. I wouldn't want to raise your hopes only to have them dashed again."

Sent down to me?

"Why am I being kept in the basement? Are you afraid that I'll try to escape? Or do you think I'll recognize where I am?"

His stretched and twisted smile reminds me of the Joker from the *Batman* franchise. "You can try to escape if you wish. Be my guest."

He takes a couple of strides back to the door and opens it wide, gesturing with a sweep of his arm for me to leave.

"I'm free to go?"

This must be a trap, but the thought of leaving this room behind and breathing clean air, of being warm again is irresistible.

"Sure." He shrugs. "You won't get far, and if you do, it will almost certainly result in a horrific and painful death."

I gulp. My mouth is dry, and more bile is lurking at the back of my throat.

"Wh-what do you mean?"

"This property is built on the edge of a remote clifftop. The owner must've had a death-wish, or perhaps he simply wanted to deter other people from visiting. I can't say that I blame him; making small talk can be so tedious."

My thoughts are scrambling around inside my head like beetles hunting for food. What did Kyle say about the Murray property? He mentioned fields and cows and streams, but I don't recall him talking about cliffs.

There's only one way to find out if Nick is telling the truth.

"I don't believe you."

"You don't have to believe me. Go see for yourself."

He's testing me, but I haven't moved.

"I said, '*Go see for yourself*.'"

"I heard you." I hold his gaze.

Without warning, he grips my wrist beneath the blanket and drags me from the room.

We're in a narrow corridor. Naked bulbs hang from the ceiling, casting eerie shadows between puddles of light. The walls are plastered, unpainted, grubby. It's only marginally warmer than the room I've just vacated.

"You're hurting me." I try to wrestle my arm free of his hold, but his fingers are digging into my flesh, and he's determined to hold on tightly.

"Maybe next time you'll do as you're told."

We pass through a heavy metal door at the end of the corridor. Up a stone staircase. Through another door.

We're standing in another corridor that must run parallel to the one on the basement level. Nick hurls me towards a window framed by dusty green velvet drapes held back by gold ropes.

My heart is galloping, but I don't have time to register the pain in my ribs where I collided with the window frame. I'm mesmerized by the view outside.

The house overlooks the sea which is storm-gray, choppy, foam dragging across the surface and hurtling towards us. But it's the sheer drop below the window that has stolen my breath and run away with it. I can hear the waves crashing against the jagged, lethal rocks below.

22

KYLE

Mateo Dragonetti clears his private jet for take-off at 6 a.m.

I'm already six hours behind Sienna.

Six hours.

With the image of her bloody face in my head, I can't sit around waiting for the flight. I have to keep busy. There's nothing else that I can do for Cash until we have more information on his alibi, so instead, I go with Terry to Hooch's apartment.

We already know that someone is covering Nick Morris's tracks, but has Sienna's father been as careful or as clever? His perfectly timed alibi for the break-in at the gallery was premeditated, meticulously planned even, but I get the feeling that someone else was pulling all the strings behind the scenes. Robert Hooch has a history of gambling addiction, petty crime, and assault charges against women, but now he's messing with the big boys, and I believe he's in way over his head.

Terry's team of men are breezing through Hooch's apartment like ninjas. I stand in the middle of the living room and watch them rolling back the carpet to reveal dusty floorboards, lifting the lone picture frame from the wall and taking it apart, ripping open cushions and pulling out the stuffing.

It's hard to picture Sienna in this dingy space. She doesn't belong here. It's too stifling, too decrepit, too dull, like locking a peacock inside a cave and telling it to shine. There are no personal touches inside the apartment, which tells me everything I need to know about Sienna's father.

He's a drifter, following the money and trying to avoid getting caught.

Until now.

Pressure leads to panic, and panic leads to mistakes, and Hooch made the biggest mistake of his life when he involved his daughter.

I wander through to the kitchen. Sienna said that he took her keys. It would've been simple enough to make a copy of the gallery keys and replace them without her noticing that they were missing, but he didn't. He also lied to her about what time he came home from the casino the night she stayed with him. Why?

I call Caleb and ask him to find out where Hooch was that night. I should've done this sooner, but I was so fixated on Nick Morris that I didn't figure on Hooch being a prominent player in whatever game this is. My mistake. He blundered into Sienna's life, making sure that we all saw him, and added the finishing touches to Nick Morris's plan right under our noses.

"Feels like the guy was living out of a suitcase." Terry joins me in the kitchen. "This place isn't lived in. It isn't a home."

"Do you know how he got out without being spotted?"

"Best guess is that he broke into an empty ground floor apartment and climbed out through a window. He clearly had someplace to be."

"Men like Hooch normally run at the first sign of trouble, but I don't think he's done here yet."

Terry's eyes are scanning the room as we speak. "So, what's keeping him here?"

"It isn't Sienna."

"Whatever they're paying him, it was too good to turn down." Terry pauses. "More importantly, he believes that they'll deliver."

The image of Hooch in my head suddenly grows clearer, like the tiny picture inside the autorefractors used by opticians to measure light bouncing off the back of the eye. The lies. The brazen way in which he flaunted meeting Sienna in the Rinse. His accusation that she stole money from him.

He was gaslighting her. Terry is right: Hooch is convinced that whoever is paying him will follow through because he believes that he is untouchable. He preys on people who are weaker than him—generally women—and systematically breaks them down until they can no longer fight back. Then he moves on.

Hooch believes that he is worthy of payment.

He doesn't care who he destroys in his wake because he is the center of his own universe. He doesn't even care that he has put his daughter's life in danger. If Hooch is okay, that's all that matters.

"I need to know if he is on the flight with Sienna." I flex my fingers.

I've never wanted to hurt someone so badly, to the point where Nick Morris is going to have to wait in line until I'm finished with Robert Carlton Hooch.

"If there's anything here, we'll find it." Terry lays a warm hand on my shoulder.

I wander through to the bedroom. The bed is mussed up as if Hooch left in a hurry. The closet is empty apart from a rolled-up sock and a crumpled subway ticket. I unfold the ticket. It tells me that he took the subway to Fifth Avenue/53rd Street station.

It isn't what I'm looking for.

He must've dropped some breadcrumbs along the way. He's untouchable. He got away with hurting Sienna's mom and walking out on his family, and God knows how many other women he has treated the same way. So, to him, this must be just another situation that he'll walk away from unscathed when his bank account is looking a bit healthier.

The nightstand is empty.

The bookshelves are bare.

On impulse, I get on my hands and knees and check under the bed, sneezing when I inhale dust. My airways start to clog, and I cover my mouth and nose with my hand while I scan the carpet that's thick with fluff-balls.

I'm about to stand up and open the window when I spot what appears to be a crumpled note. Turning my face away to help me breathe, I slide my arm under the bed and retrieve the folded paper. Only it isn't a note, it's a well-worn paper coaster, the kind used in traditional Irish pubs.

There's a faded image of a pint of Guinness on the coaster and a name printed across it in bold red font. The first letter is missing, erased with use, but the remaining letters spell out ARREN'S BAR.

Darren's bar?

Terry appears in the doorway, and I hand him the coaster.

"Does this mean anything to you?" My phone is already out of my pocket.

"Darren's Bar?" Terry jumps to the same conclusion as I did.

"No search results." I start systematically working my way through the alphabet until I reach the letter F. "Farren's Bar, Malin Head, Donegal. Why would he have a coaster from an Irish bar?"

"Souvenir?" Terry suggests.

I pocket the coaster. "It's as good a place to start as any."

I stand a little taller, buzzing with the find. It might be unimportant, but there are too many coincidences surrounding Hooch's reappearance in his daughter's life for me to let this go.

I check the time on my phone. If I don't leave now, I'll miss the flight.

Terry's right-hand-man joins us in the bedroom. He's taller than Terry, broader, more solid, his hair turning rusty silver in patches. Patrick has been around for as long as I've known Terry, and in all that time, I've never known them to be more than a few miles apart at any given moment.

"Patrick is going with you," Terry says.

"No, Tel. You need him here."

"This isn't up for debate." Terry smiles. "Your mom would never forgive me if I let you do this alone. And besides, Patrick has more connections in the Irish mafia than I've had hot dinners."

Terry pulls me in for a hug. He was always tactile when we were growing up, but it's one of those things that you wake up one day and realize it's been years since you last hugged. He still makes me feel safe.

It's also a stark reminder of the danger I'm flying into.

Patrick talks. A lot.

He talks about the first sheep he ever sheared as a young lad growing up in rural Ireland. The time he and his pals stole a bottle of whiskey from his pa's stash and got drunk in a forest where they used to spend weekends camping. His grandma's soda bread which she was apparently famous for in the village where he grew up.

By the time we reach the airport, I'm mentally acquainted with every member of his family, including cousins, second cousins, aunts and uncles, grandparents, and even their neighbors when he was growing up.

We're on board the Dragonetti private jet when he mentions a name that raises the hair on the back of my neck.

Sinead.

I trawl through my memories for the name, knowing that I've heard it recently, but unable to place it into context. Until I recall the conversation with Sienna's father in the executive room at the casino.

He said that he wasn't going anywhere until I called Sienna.

"Sienna or Sinead. Take your pick." He'd peered at me with bloodshot eyes and added, "I'd pick Sienna if I were you. Just saying."

He was drunk. I didn't question the name Sinead at the time. He'd been rambling on about the drinks being watered down in the casino bar, and I thought it best not to entertain him. But now, I'm not so sure. Was the name another breadcrumb dropped into the palm of my hand to see if I'd notice?

"I have to make a call." I apologize to Patrick and call Bash from my cell phone, grateful that the aircraft hasn't taken off yet.

"Bash." I don't even wait for him to say hello. "What does the name Sinead mean to you?"

Silence.

I hear my brother walking with the phone clamped to his ear. I hear him close a door behind him, then, "Who told you?"

"Told me what?"

"Sinead Duffy." His voice is hushed. "She's married to Sasha Bogrov."

He doesn't elaborate.

It takes me approximately two-and-a-half seconds to figure out where this is going.

"Shit." I glance at Patrick who is following the one-sided conversation with narrowed eyes. "Cash's alibi."

"Got it in one."

"Have you managed to get hold of her yet?"

Bash hesitates. "Seems she's left the country for a while. Gone home to spend the holidays with family while her husband signs her lover's death warrant."

"Find out where she is. I'm heading to the airport, but if you can get the details to me while we're in the air, I'll pay her a surprise visit when we land."

I end the call, and stare at my blank screen.

What the fuck was Cash thinking?

If Sasha Bogrov finds out what's been going on, there'll be nowhere for my brother to hide.

For a large man with the hugest hands I've ever seen, Patrick's thumbs are flying nimbly across his cell phone's keypad. He peers at me with a smile.

"I've arranged for a friend to meet us at Dublin airport. He'll take us to Sinead Duffy."

We find Sinead Bogrov nee Duffy in the spa at Lough Eske Castle.

Patrick's friend, a giant of a man with a scar puckering his top lip and a missing front tooth, gains us entry to the spa, whilst ensuring that the staff allows us some privacy for our 'surprise reunion with the cousin we haven't seen in years'.

"Sinead Bogrov?"

Her face is buried in the hole at the head-end of the massage bed, a towel covering the lower half of her body. The room is bright, airy, and serene. Relaxing music plays through an invisible speaker. The temperature is perfect, conducive to falling asleep while the masseuse works her magic on strained back muscles.

Her shoulders bunch up, and I almost feel sorry for spoiling the massage before it has even finished.

Almost.

She rolls over, covering herself discreetly with the towel, and slides her legs gracefully over the side of the raised bed.

Sinead Bogrov is an attractive woman. Her hair is darker red than Sienna's, thick curls framing a pale freckled face, and clear blue eyes the color of the sea on a summer's day. Her face is makeup free. Flawless. I'd guess her to be in her mid- to late-thirties, but she is obviously a woman who takes care of herself.

"You know that I can have you removed from here in a heartbeat." Her Irish accent has been tamed, but there's no mistaking the gentle lilt.

"Yet you haven't." Patrick holds her gaze. "Because you know that it would get back to Sasha, and the less he knows about what goes on here the better. Am I right?"

Her eyes harden. "What do you want?"

"My brother Cash has been arrested for a murder he didn't commit." I step in. "You know that he is innocent."

A flush appears high on her cheeks. "I don't know what you're talking ab—"

Before she can finish, Patrick twists her arm behind her back and tilts her neck sideways, his fingers hovering over the Vagus nerve on her throat.

The blue eyes grow stormy, but she doesn't lower her gaze or beg him to stop.

Patrick nods for me to continue.

"We know that you were with Cash the night that Luca Benito was murdered."

"So, what do you want me to do about it? Stand up in court and confess to fucking your brother while my husband was growing his empire? Do you really want to be responsible for Cash's death?"

Her voice cracks when she speaks his name out loud. I might be wrong, but I believe that she cares about him, and Cash's silence, even though she could provide him with an alibi, indicates that he might feel the same way about her.

Or perhaps jail is simply a better option than death at the hands of her psychopathic husband.

"That's not the reason why I'm here."

She blinks several times, trying to figure out what comes next. "I'm listening."

"The woman I love has been abducted by someone who is working for your husband. She is being held somewhere in Ireland."

"Ireland is a big fucking country, you know." There's the Irish accent I was waiting for.

"But who better to tell me where she might be than Sasha Bogrov's wife?"

Her chest rises and falls with the effort of breathing, while Patrick's hand is around her neck, and her arm is forced behind her back. "Sorry, I can't help you. I'm sure you can find the way out by—."

Patrick applies pressure to her throat, and she groans out loud.

I motion him to release her.

Her hand instinctively flies to her throat as tears trickle from the corners of her eyes. "Fucking bastards."

I move closer. Gripping her chin between my thumb and forefinger, I raise her face so that she is looking directly at me. "Do you love your husband, Sinead?"

"What the fuck is it to you?"

"I want to know what you would do if his life was threatened. How far would you go to save him?"

"That's what he pays his bodyguards for."

"Okay." I change course. "How far would you go to save Cash?"

She swallows and looks away before recovering quickly and meeting my gaze again. "I won't let my husband find out about him if that's what you're asking."

It's a start.

"So, you understand where I'm coming from. Your husband is using the woman I love as leverage to steal Cash's business. I have a picture of her on my phone."

Her eyes track my movements as I slide the cell phone from my pocket, unlock the screen, and turn the image of Sienna's bloody face around to show her.

"Now, I know you probably don't care what happens to Sienna, but I do, and I'm going to save her with or without your help." I lower my voice and speak clearly so that she understands I'm not messing around. "A word of warning though. It will get messy without your help because there's no fucking way I'm handing over everything my family has worked so hard to build so that your husband can reap the rewards. Do you understand what I'm saying?"

She nods.

"If I have to throw your name into the mix to save Sienna, I will."

"What about Cash?" She isn't quite so belligerent now.

"Cash is a big boy. He'll figure it out."

"I didn't know this was going to happen, I swear."

I believe her, but she's involved in this whether she likes it or not, hence the reason she's hiding out in an Irish castle. "Where is your husband holding Sienna?" I exchange glances with Patrick to remind her that he could break her neck in a heartbeat.

"I don't know for sure."

"Go on." My pulse spikes.

I'm standing on the same soil as Sienna. It's only a matter of time before I find her, and once I know that she's safe, I'm going to blow Sasha Bogrov's growing empire apart brick by fucking brick.

"He's trying to acquire a property on the Donegal coastline. A fucking mansion, don't you know." She rolls her eyes dramatically. "Because the big bad bratva boss wants to prove that he's invincible."

The scorn in her voice is unmistakable.

"Where is it?"

"It's built on a fucking cliff. Perfect for tossing the enemy off the roof when they get a little too close."

"Who else knows about this?"

My mind is already connecting the dots between Sasha Bogrov, Nick Morris, and Robert Hooch. One of them is holding Sienna on the bratva's orders, and I don't care who it is. They'll be the first to learn what happens when they try to harm someone the Murrays care about.

"I don't know." She shakes her head. "But I can tell you how to get there."

23

SIENNA

Nick drags me away from the window by my hair. I try to free myself, but his grip is too tight. I can feel my scalp stinging and the tears streaming from my eyes.

I lose my balance on the staircase, my foot sliding out from under me. Pain shoots through my ankle and travels the length of my leg as it twists awkwardly, the bone colliding with the back of one of the stone steps. I fall the rest of the way, the ground hurtling towards my face, but Nick yanks on my hair to keep me upright.

I'm obviously more useful to him without a mashed-up face.

I can smell the rotten air as we approach the basement, and my stomach instantly revolts.

"Nick, please," I plead with him. "Don't lock me in the basement. You know I can't escape."

"Shut up, Sienna. Begging doesn't suit you."

He grabs my arm with his free hand and shoves me through the open doorway. My ankle is throbbing. I stumble across the slimy stone floor and land heavily on my knees by the end of the cot. More pain. I roll into a sitting position, dragging my knees to my chest, and rub them to ease the pain shooting up my thigh to the base of my spine. My right knee is wet, and blood seeps through the leg of my pants.

The floor is icy, so I drag myself upright, tentatively putting my weight onto my ankle to test its strength. It buckles, and I have to bite my lip to stop myself from crying out.

"You really should be more careful." Nick watches me from the doorway. "In your condition."

My gaze snaps towards him. "M-my condition?"

The twisted smile is back. "You're pregnant, Sienna." Lines appear between his lowered brows. "Don't tell me you didn't know. You're having his baby, so you see, I couldn't have married you even if I'd wanted to."

He's lying. He's worried that I'll still try to escape. Despite the risk of falling over the edge of a cliff and either dying on the treacherous rocks below or drowning in the Irish Sea.

"Why would I believe you?"

My right knee is starting to swell; I can feel the skin stretching over the knobby bone, the flesh growing spongy to protect the kneecap from further damage.

He shrugs. "Believe me or not, it's irrelevant."

"Why are you doing this, Nick? What did I ever do to you?"

"You got lucky, Sienna. Caleb Murray came along and handed your dream to you on a plate. Although things are not going your way right now, are they?"

"I-I'm going to pay him back."

I'm stalling. My thoughts are still unpacking the comment about me being pregnant, and I'm stuck on it, trying to figure out why he said it. What was he trying to achieve?

"How?" His eyebrows arch upwards. "You no longer have any artwork to sell."

I freeze. My thoughts screech to a halt as his words sink in.

"It was you?" I whisper. "You destroyed all my work?"

"Well, not me personally. Why would I get my hands dirty when someone else will do it for me?"

His frame fills the doorway. I have the overwhelming urge to lunge at him, to headbutt his diaphragm and send him hurtling backwards into the wall on the opposite side of the corridor. With the demonic red-hot rage I'm feeling inside, I could beat him to death with my bare hands or strangle him with the neat leather belt holding up his pants.

But that would make me as bad as him, and I'm better than that.

My mom once said that the sweetest revenge is success.

I didn't understand it at the time, but I do now. I need Nick Morris to stick around long enough for me to get my gallery up and running again and fulfill my dream of becoming a successful artist.

"Oh, and in case you still don't believe me—" he takes his phone out again and slides it around to show me the picture on the screen "—the blood on your face is yours. I performed a portable i-STAT pregnancy blood test on you while you were sleeping. I tested it out of curiosity, not because I was trying to save you. It's simply more leverage for us."

"You did a blood test without my consent?"

I'm still numb. I'm cold. I'm in pain from my ankle and my knee, and now this...

"Seriously, that's what you took from this conversation?" He chuckles, the sound setting my back teeth on edge. "You're pregnant, Sienna. And your lover has until midnight GMT to save you by handing over the Titan."

With that, he slams the door shut and locks it behind him.

I lose track of time in the dingy windowless room.

My knee has swollen to twice its size, but the dull throbbing ache is nothing compared to the thoughts swirling around inside my head.

I'm pregnant.

I'm having Kyle's baby, and he doesn't even know.

I lay on my side on the cot, shivering beneath the blanket, my arms cradling my belly. I try counting back the days to my last period before the gallery opening and realize that I'm overdue. With all that has happened, it was the last thing on my mind, but I'm never late.

Ever.

I'm still in the fetal position, bloody knees pulled up to my chest to conserve as much body heat as possible when I hear the key in the lock.

I sit upright, clutching the blanket to my chin as the slice of meager light enters the basement.

It isn't Nick.

I don't recognize this man. He's shorter than Nick, his muscles are so pumped that his arms don't touch his sides, and his legs are bowed. His hair is thick, jet-black. His dark eyes are deep-set beneath protruding eyebrows. He's wearing a black sweater and black pants. It's hard to imagine him in any other color.

I start shivering again, although it's hard to tell if it's from the rush of icy air on my back when I sat up or this man's appearance.

He kicks the door closed behind him, shutting him in with me.

"Food." He comes closer and sets a plastic tray down on the floor next to the cot.

I don't move. I feel his eyes on me, raking my body through the thin blanket.

"Eat." He slides the tray closer with the toe of his boot.

"I'm not hungry." I'm ravenous, but I won't be able to swallow food in his presence.

"You want me to feed you?"

Something cold and slimy slithers down my spine and makes my heart race. I shuffle backwards along the cot until my spine hits the wall.

"I can feed myself."

"I'll wait." He has a heavy accent. Russian? He seems totally unfazed by the chill in the air.

"Why? What do you think I'm going to do with it?"

He grins. "Why don't you show me?"

"I told you I'm not hungry. I'll eat later." My voice trembles, and I can tell when his mouth lifts in one corner that he heard it too.

"And I told you to eat now." He crouches beside the bed, picks up a triangular sandwich, curling at the edges, and offers it to me.

"No." I hold his gaze.

I could make a dash for the door, but my ankle is probably sprained, and my knee is going to hold me back. He'll reach the door before me, and then he'll know that I'm afraid.

Without missing a beat, he grabs my hair, tilts my head backwards, and shoves the sandwich into my mouth.

I can't breathe. I try spitting the food out, but my tongue is sticking to the roof of my mouth, and my neck is burning. I can't swallow. I try pulling the food from my mouth, but he slaps my hand away and pushes the food down my throat with his index finger.

I start choking. Food splutters from between my lips. Tears well in my eyes.

But he clamps a hand over my mouth and peers into my eyes. He is so close that I can smell his garlicky breath, and it makes me retch. My lips stick to the palm of his hand and are dragged away from my gums. I can taste him, and my mouth fills with bile.

"Show me how you swallow." The innuendo isn't lost on me.

The rage ignited by Nick is back. It sparks somewhere deep inside me, fanned by this man's foul breath and clammy hand.

I bare my teeth behind his palm, snarling like a vicious dog. I ignore the stale bread clogging up my mouth, clamp my teeth around the soft pad of flesh between his thumb and forefinger, and bite down as hard as I can.

My mouth is too full to do much damage, but I have the element of surprise on my side. His hand jerks away. But in one fluid movement, he slaps my face with the back of his hand. My skull would've bounced off the wall had he not been gripping my hair; instead, his knuckles take the brunt of the force, holding me still as his face lowers towards me.

I start hammering his chest with my fists as his intentions become clear, but it's like pounding a brick wall. He's solid. His lips brush mine, and in blind panic, I throw my weight backwards, my knees coming with me, and lash out with both feet aimed directly at his groin.

The pain from my ankle shoots the length of my spine and jars inside my skull.

He lets out an *oof*, but he's still gripping my hair tightly. He drags me off the bed and crushes me against his chest. I can't free my arms to push him off me, and his other hand is sliding over my buttocks, grinding our groins together.

I try to scream, but all I manage is a dry choking sound.

Then he's being dragged away from me, and I shriek as a handful of my hair comes away in his hand. Someone—another man—throws him across the room, but he lunges back again, fists raised.

Until the new arrival produces a gun.

I shrink back against the wall. They can kill each other for all I care, but if Nick is telling the truth, and I'm pregnant with Kyle's baby, I'm not getting caught in the crossfire.

"No harm done." The first man, the Russian, raises both hands in a gesture of surrender.

The other guy has his back to me. "Only because I stopped you. Get the fuck out of here, and don't fucking come back."

I must be delirious. Perhaps I imagined the whole thing, and will wake up any moment now, because this new guy, the man holding the pistol, sounds exactly like my father.

The Russian glares at me one last time like it's my fault that he got caught attacking me and leaves the room. He doesn't close the door behind him.

My chest is heaving. I'm still clutching the blanket to my chest.

The man with the gun turns around, and I know even before his face comes into view that I'm not imagining it.

"Are you alright, sweetheart?" he asks. "Did he hurt you?"

My gaze flickers back and forth between him and the door. I'm half-expecting Nick to jump out and yell, *"Surprise! Had you fooled, huh?"* but no one else is coming.

"Wh-what are you doing here?"

"What, no 'thanks for saving me, Dad,' or 'I'm glad you're here'?" He rolls his bottom lip like he's seriously disappointed in me.

I can't help staring at the weapon in his hand and shrinking even further against the wall. My knee and ankle are screaming at me to sit down, but nothing about this situation is encouraging me to get comfortable.

His eyes follow mine to the gun. "Yeah, sorry you had to see this. Lucky I was packing though, huh? Lucky for you, I mean."

He still hasn't explained his presence in a cliff-top property in Ireland, when the last time I saw him, he was trying to wriggle his way out of a cheating accusation in the Wraith's casino.

"How did you get here?" The image of him speaking to Nick on the sidewalk outside the gallery pops into my head. "Did Nick bring you here?" My voice is finally trying to cut and run while it still can.

"I don't work for Nick. If he had his way, I'd be long gone, and he'd be rubbing his hands together over my share of the rewards."

"Who do you work for?" I already know the answer, but I need to hear him say the words out loud.

"The Russians. I ran up a little gambling debt, and they offered to help me clear it if I found them a way in with the Irish lot."

I watch the puzzle slotting together before my eyes. All the pieces were there, I just didn't look hard enough for them, because I was afraid of what I might find. I knew what he did to my mom, but I still gave him the benefit of the doubt, I still believed that people are not born with evil in their hearts.

I was wrong.

It's this realization that causes me to sit back down.

"You were never interested in putting things right," I say dully.

"Don't sound so disappointed, sweetheart. You never reached out to me. It works both ways, you know."

Something snaps inside me. "I wasn't the one who tried to kill Mom."

"I never tried to kill her, sweetheart. If that's what she told you, then she was lying."

"I saw you!" I stand up again. I need to be level with him; I refuse to be intimidated by this man ever again. "I fucking saw you strangling her. Me! I was there. Or have you blanked that bit out of your warped version of events?"

"I remember." He wrinkles his nose as if the memory is distasteful to him. "But you have to put things into context. She—"

"Oh no!" I'm shrieking now. "Don't you fucking dare blame her for what you did."

"Keep your voice down, sweetheart. If they hear you, it won't be pleasant."

"Ha!" I scoff. "You call this pleasant? You fucking sold me out to clear some gambling debts. After everything you've ever done, you still can't accept responsibility for your own actions, can you?"

"Sweetheart…" He motions with the gun for me to lower my voice. "This is for your own good."

"No, Dad, this is for *your* own good, because that's all that matters to you, isn't it?"

I no longer feel the bite of the cold air in the basement. His patronizing tone is filling my head with excuses and lies.

"Help!" I yell as loud as I can, projecting my voice towards the open doorway. "Nick! Someone? I need help!"

My father raises his fist and pulls it back over his shoulder ready to let it go. My heart is hammering. Then, with one final sidelong glance, he says, "Have it your way," and walks out of the room.

I wait for the key to turn in the lock before I collapse onto the cot and start sobbing.

I need to get out of here.

Kyle won't let them get away with this, but if my father is armed, then the others must be armed too, and if there's one thing I've learned from the Murrays, it's that the mafia always honor their word. Nick said Kyle has until midnight to hand over the Titan.

He won't.

The Titan belongs to the Murray family.

So, then what?

I'm not sticking around to find out.

This building, whatever it is, is built on the edge of a cliff. But what about the other three sides? It stands to reason that the entrance will face inland; all I need to do is get out of the basement, make my way upstairs without getting caught, and let myself out.

Easy.

I practice walking around the basement—I refuse to acknowledge that it's a cell—putting my weight on my ankle and ignoring the throbbing ache in my knee. If my life depends on it, I'll run a marathon, even with a sprained ankle.

I check the door. It's locked. I knew it would be, but I wanted to be sure.

There's only one way I'm getting out of here: I wait for someone to unlock the door and distract them long enough for me to slip out unnoticed.

I stand in the middle of the room and replay various scenarios in my head, none of which lead to me overpowering an armed guard and escaping before they can stop me.

I won't even attempt to get past the Russian.

Nick guards the doorway like he's just waiting for me to bolt.

My best chance is to somehow trick my father into setting me free. The same father who tried to kill my mom and has handed me over to the bratva to avoid paying his gambling debts. The same father who's now carrying a weapon around like it's a cell phone.

He isn't going to smile, stand aside, and wish me luck.

But what other options do I have?

I keep limping around the basement. If I sit down for too long, my ankle and knee will seize up, and I won't be going anywhere.

I just need to find a chink in his armor. Sure, he's a calculating narcissistic asshole, but everyone has a weakness.

I force myself to eat the remains of the sandwich and wash it down with the bottle of water the Russian brought in on the tray. It doesn't seem to go down, lodging in my throat and making me feel queasy, but I focus instead on my father, dragging up memories from my childhood that I've suppressed until now.

In all of them, I'm aware of myself cowering in a corner of the room, or listening from the stairs, or hiding behind my mom. I have no memories of him, *not even one*, that fills me with any kind of warmth or affection. No memories that make me smile. What kind of person chooses to leave behind a legacy like this?

Focus.

I'm not wasting time figuring out what makes my father tick; he doesn't deserve my energy and consideration. I just need to know how to beat him.

Beat him...

I've no idea where the memory comes from—I've never recalled it before—but it's so vivid that it takes my breath away. I stop near the doorway on a circuit of the room, bent double, waiting for my breathing to regulate itself.

I must've been four years old, one of my earliest memories. My mom took me to the park. I was being careless, riding high on the buzz of the swings and my mom pushing me higher than I'd ever been. I went on the merry-go-round, my mom making it spin faster and faster until some other kids wanted to join in. Bigger kids. They ran around the outside of the merry-go-round, pushing it as they went.

I wanted to be like them.

So, I climbed off, held on tightly to the bar, and ran as fast as I could around the apparatus. Which, it turned out, wasn't as fast as the other kids. My feet got tangled up with another kid's legs, I stumbled, and then I was flung sideways, unable to stop myself from landing on my elbow. I scraped the skin off it. My mom carried me home sobbing, sat me on the kitchen counter and cleaned the wound with antiseptic wipes, telling me fairy tales to keep me distracted.

When my arm was clean and dry and covered with a large Band-aid, she said, "Lucky your father isn't here. He can't stand the sight of blood." Then, thoughtful, "That would be one way to beat him, I guess."

My father can't stand the sight of blood.

It isn't much, but right now, it's all I've got to work with.

My knee has stopped bleeding beneath my pants; I can feel it crusting over, rubbing against the fabric as it continues to swell. Would it be enough of a distraction?

I doubt it.

It must be cringe-worthy. Something that's going to turn his stomach on its head and make him want to vomit. I need him to be looking the other way when I run out of the door and lock him inside.

A wave of nausea crashes through me at the mental image of me making myself bleed in front of him. Am I strong enough to do it? How deep does it need to be to halt him in his tracks? What am I even going to use? What if I cut too deep and then I can't stop it from bleeding?

Now I've set the questions in motion, my head is spinning. I've hardly eaten over the past few days, and whatever drugs Nick gave me on the plane are still wearing off.

A horrible thought slams into me, causing me to lean against the locked door for support.

If I'm pregnant, will the drugs affect the fetus? I didn't plan on having a baby right now, but I can't bear the thought of something bad happening to take it away from me.

If I should lose it...

I can't believe where my thoughts are going. I once read in a book that your thoughts have to be controlled or else they tumble into a downward spiral, and mine seem to be sinking to an all-time low. *Alice in Wonderland* has nothing on me right now because my warped brain has figured out how to get past my father.

My entire plan depends on my father returning with more food later. If it's Nick, or the Russian, I'll have to wing it and pray that they're either unarmed, or unwilling to kill me until Kyle has given them what they want.

The inside of my thigh feels sticky and sore. I smashed the plastic tray against the wall and used the jagged edge to slice the tender flesh at the top of my leg. It'll probably scar, but I've learned to live with worse.

I sit on the bed and wait. My ears strain for the sound of footsteps outside the room. When I finally hear the key clicking in the lock, my heartbeat grows so loud, it drowns out everything else.

Please let it be my father.

Please let it be...

I stop myself from crying out loud when he appears in the doorway carrying another tray of food..

This is it. I'm only going to get one shot at this, so I have to make it count. If I fail... I can't even contemplate the alternative.

Hugging my knees to my chest, the blanket covering my legs, I start rocking back and forth. I cover my face and surreptitiously poke myself in the eye. It stings. But I barely register the pain.

"Sweetheart?"

The anger is gone. I question briefly whether he believed his own lies when he said that he wanted to get to know me but instantly shut it down.

Focus. Track his movements. Wait for the right moment.

"Are you sick?" He steps closer.

I should've checked if he was armed, but it's too late now. No turning back.

"Sweetheart, what is it?"

His boots come into view near the bed.

One more step, that's all I'm waiting for.

I keep rocking, and tense my shoulders, groaning as if I'm in pain.

I hear his footsteps. He's approaching me cautiously, but I convince myself that it's because he doesn't want to have to deal with a sick prisoner rather than fear that I'm trying to trick him.

It's now or never.

I shove the blanket off me and raise blurry eyes to him. "I-I think I'm having a miscarriage."

He recoils.

I stand up and peer down at the blood staining my pants

between my legs. More blood than I thought there would be, but there's no time to worry about it now.

"Help me, Dad." I touch between my legs. My fingers come away bloody, and I hold them up to show him.

He gags. Turning his face away, he retches, his entire body shuddering.

He's making me gag too, but I fight it.

The instant he starts vomiting, I lunge at him, my hand reaching for the handle of the pistol tucked inside his waistband.

It's heavier than I expected it to be. I drag it out and, holding it with both hands, I point it directly at him, and back away to the door, as he swipes his mouth with the back of his hand. He sniffs loudly, spit clinging to his bottom lip.

"Put the gun down, sweetheart." The patronizing tone is back, like I'm a naughty child who ate cookies before dinner.

"Don't come any closer." My legs are trembling violently. I still need to reach the door, but I don't want him to try following me.

"Have you ever used a gun, sweetheart?"

I don't answer.

"It's not as easy as it looks." He moves towards me, and I back away.

"Stay where you are."

"Or what? We both know that you won't shoot me. You don't have it in you. Little goody-two-shoes Sienna."

My arms are shaking. I slide my finger onto the trigger. "Try me."

He closes the distance between us with two strides. I don't even see his fist arcing towards my face until pain shoots through my jaw and fills my skull.

It feels as if I'm flying away from him. My feet leave the ground, and my skull collides with the wall behind me. I feel something warm and wet trickling down the back of my head. But all I can hear is the gunshot that went off when he punched me.

The world is spinning. Tiny silver stars spiral behind my eyelids, and I can't tell which way is up. I force myself to open my eyes. I need to get back on my feet before he hurts me again.

The gun falls from my hand, and I don't try to stop it.

I can't see clearly. Feeling my way across the floor with my hands, I use the wall to keep my balance and drag myself upright. My brain is pulsating inside my skull, my eyes are heavy, and I'm scared to move my bottom jaw.

I can see the doorway. The door is still open. He hasn't closed it.

"Sweetheart..." His voice penetrates my foggy thoughts.

Dazed into moving in slow-motion, I turn around. My eyes find him sitting on the floor, propped up against the side of the bed. He's sitting in a puddle of dark liquid. The scene gradually comes into focus, and I realize that his hands are clamped over a wound in his thigh, blood oozing between his fingers.

"Sweetheart..." His breathing is shallow. His skin is deathly pale. "Help ...me."

It takes several long, slow beats for me to understand that the bullet must've hit a major artery. He's bleeding out. And he wants me to help him.

"Sienna..." He tilts his head back against the bed. "Get ... help."

I swallow. It looks bad, but he would kill me to save himself.

That's what pulsates through my pounding head as I shuffle through the doorway and lock the door behind me.

24

KYLE

Patrick and I switch the rental car we took from the airport with another vehicle parked outside a railway station. Patrick drives. An hour later, we're pulling up outside a secluded property buried deep within the countryside of Donegal.

We're gathering a team. Apparently, it's more than Patrick's life is worth if he lets me out of his sight and I end up getting myself thrown off a cliff in the process. His words.

The property belongs to an Irish mob that have a reputation for smashing kneecaps first and asking questions later, and they're already aware of the cliff-top mansion purchased by Sasha Bogrov.

"The man who built it was a mad fecking scientist." The speaker, a man called Damon O'Hara, has thick silver hair and a walrus mustache that twitches when his lips move. His accent is stronger than any I've heard before. "Ye'd have to be to build a house on the edge of a fecking cliff."

"The place gives me the heebie-jeebies," his brother, Aiden, says. "Says a lot about the fecker who bought it."

"What do you know about them?" I ask.

We're in a secure underground room that contains an arsenal of weapons: pistols, revolvers, shotguns. While the women are upstairs watching TV in the kitchen and preparing dinner, chatting about their favorite shows and the Christmas gifts they're yet to buy, the men are choosing ammunition to raid the mansion where Sienna is being held captive.

"New mob. They've not been active in Ireland, until now. But their rep doesn't exactly fill me with confidence. They're thieves, and no one likes a fecking cheap, nasty crook."

I fill the men in on the bratva's demands for the Titan.

They don't react, but I spot the tic pulsing in Damon's temple. "I don't care who the feck they are, they don't get away with stealing a good man's work." He opens a canister of bullets and tips them into the palm of his hand.

A younger lad joins us. He looks like Damon, but with a mop of strawberry-blond hair and golden stubble on his chin and upper lip.

Cillian hands his father a drawing. "I downloaded the layout of the property. There are three levels, but I'm guessing they're holding the woman captive in the basement."

"Is there a way into the basement from underground?" I ask.

It will make life a whole lot easier if we don't have to go through the house to reach Sienna.

"I checked." Cillian shakes his head. "I couldn't find any plans."

"What about the cliff?" Patrick studies the drawing spread across the table. "Could we gain entry that way?"

"Not unless you can grow some fecking wings before we get there." Aiden chuckles, a dry throaty sound, the product of a lifetime spent smoking cigars.

"It's blowing a hoolie out there now." Cillian helps his dad load weapons into an oversized rucksack. "Not the kind of weather I'd go abseiling in."

"Don't worry, lad." Patrick looks me in the eye. "We'll get her out of there."

Aiden claps me on the back. "You're with the O'Haras now, boy. The bastards won't even see us coming."

I've heard the term 'blowing a hoolie' before. I never really understood what it meant until now.

The entire county is on red alert for Storm Humphrey. The government has issued a warning for folks to stay inside, shut away or lock down any freestanding garden equipment, and prepare for loss of power. It's a short distance from the O'Hara property to the waiting, blacked-out vehicles, but the gale-force winds have us walking head-down, almost horizontal into the squally gusts. We're saturated by the time we load up the trunks and climb inside.

We drive in silence.

The closer we get to the coastline, the stronger the gales become. The rain is torrential; the windshield wipers are working at double-speed, and visibility is still practically non-existent. The vehicle we're traveling in is getting buffeted about by the wind, and my stomach lurches each time the driver has to wrestle with the steering wheel to keep us on track.

I try to picture Sienna in the basement of the mad scientist's mansion. What's down there? An image of shelves filled with glass jars containing pickled body parts and rodents swimming in formaldehyde pops into my head, and I shove them away.

I hope that she knows I'll save her.

I don't even know if she has regained consciousness or if the bastard Nick Morris is feeding her with drugs.

"We get Sienna safely out of the house," I say to the group in general, "but you leave Nick Morris to me."

"Goes without saying, lad." Damon glances at me over his shoulder from the front passenger seat. "Ye've got a score to settle. Ain't one of us going to stand in your way."

The terrain begins to climb.

There are no streetlamps, and it's impossible to see anything other than the rain lashing the vehicle's windows.

So, I sit back and think about Sienna.

The way she pants when she's having an orgasm. The way she tastes when I'm eating her pussy. The way she arches her back and pushes herself onto me when she's about to come.

The twenty-four hours she spent in my apartment were exactly how I envisaged it would be to live with her. As a couple. I can't help smiling when I picture her padding around my kitchen with the comforter wrapped around her like a cocoon. Her rosy cheeks. The easy conversation over scrambled eggs and black coffee.

It's everything I want.

There's only one person standing in my way.

Nick Morris.

Sure, he isn't working alone, but I'm unfazed by the new Russian bratva. They dared to try stealing my brother's business, and they'll get what's coming to them. I've yet to figure out the best way to deal with Nick Morris.

He isn't a member of the bratva. He's a slimeball playing on the periphery of the mafia world without having first learned the rules. A worm who needs to be crushed underfoot.

My mom recognized the cruelty behind his eyes the instant she saw him.

Men like Nick Morris never learn from their mistakes. They simply duck under the radar, throw their accomplices under the bus to save their own skin, and find a new target. They prey on the weak. Only Sienna is a lot stronger than he has given her credit for.

As am I.

I'm aware that he chose to attack my family through me: the one he recognized as the weakest link. It's no secret that I took a three-month sabbatical from the family business and came to Ireland, or that I underwent years of therapy following the accident. If he has done his research, he probably knows that I'm asthmatic too.

But I'm in love with Sienna, and I will not let her down a second time.

I doubt that Nick Morris has ever been in love, apart from with himself. I doubt that he's capable of putting someone else's interests before his own. But his lack of empathy is my advantage, it's what will ultimately make me stronger than him.

The vehicles converge outside a ten-foot-high brick wall, and the drivers kill the engines and the headlamps.

Damon addresses Patrick and I in the back seat.

"We'll make our way on foot." He unfolds the plans for the mansion and raps it with hairy knuckles. "There's a gravel drive that leads to the entrance. The rest of the land is wooded—the guy who built the place clearly wasn't a people-person. We'll stick to the trees until we reach the edge here." He taps the diagram a second time.

"Lights?" I ask.

"Attached to the soffits. They're sensory activated, but the storm will work in our favor. Even if they pick up our movement, the bratva mob will think it's the rain lashing the equipment."

I nod. "We're going through the entrance or is there another way in?"

"There's a door here at the side. Mud room. We'll split up once we reach the property. My Cillian will lead his team through the side door and Aiden will cover us through the front. Once you're inside, you head to the staircase at the rear of the building. It will take you down to the basement."

He folds the diagram and stashes it inside the glove box.

The icy rain stings my face when I climb out of the vehicle. The wind is driving it into us in diagonal sheets that slap our faces and drench us from head to toe. It might work in our favor when it comes down to the security lights but invading a cliff-top mansion in sodden clothes when you can't feel your fingers isn't how I would've chosen to do this.

The wall surrounding the property is topped with razor-wire. Cillian and another young lad scale the wall like cats and snip through the wire to allow the rest of us access to the ground. We follow them using ropes and drop down to the ground on the other side by bouncing off the trees and using the branches to slow our fall.

This is the easy part.

The treetops provide some shelter from the torrential rain, and we make our way towards the property, which appears to be in total darkness, not a glimmer of light peeping out from behind closed windows. A security light pops on, activated by the gusting wind and we all freeze. The original owner clearly trusted that few people would attempt to either scale the cliffs or climb the razor-topped wall. The lights are the old-fashioned static type that cast spotlights across the grounds, leaving the rest of the area in darkness, exacerbated by the blinding lights.

I make a mental note of where the lights fall, tracking the fastest and easiest route to the imposing entrance without getting caught in the spotlight like an actor who forgot his lines.

We move stealthily through the woodland until we're almost in the clearing.

From here, the mansion looks even more sinister and formidable, the kind of property movie directors scour the planet for to feature in their horror movies. I squint against the rain trickling into my eyes and scan the turrets on each corner of the rooftop for the obligatory bats silhouetted against the full moon.

A glimmer of movement near the front façade catches my attention. I wipe my eyes with my sleeve, and peer through the rain, but I can't see anything, and the security lights remain off.

"Ready?" Damon asks.

25

SIENNA

My head feels as though it's going to explode. My vision keeps blurring, and my footsteps are clunky like I'm on one of those festival fun-house attractions where the floors keep rearranging themselves between footsteps.

But I keep going. One foot in front of the other. There's no room inside my head for anything else.

At the end of the corridor, I stop. I try to retrace the route Nick took when he dragged me upstairs to show me the cliffs and the roiling sea from the window, but my mind can't quite grab hold of it. I try to take a deep breath, my hand curled around the doorknob, but my lungs are not cooperating either.

I twist the doorknob and crack open the door, just enough for me to rest my forehead against the frame and view the staircase.

It's clear.

I'm moving on autopilot.

One step at a time, wincing whenever I put my weight onto my twisted ankle. I almost can't believe it when I reach the top without getting caught.

Convinced that the universe is smiling down on me, I open the door at the top of the stairs tentatively, my breathing coming in short, painful bursts, my heart playing a new irregular tune. Dizziness causes me to stop and lean against the door. I feel nauseous again, but I can't be sick—I don't think my head could take the strain.

I swallow. Inhale. Count to three.

If they catch me here, they won't give me a second chance.

I hobble through the door and close it behind me with a gentle click. It's a little warmer here, only a little. There's floor covering underfoot, and the walls have been plastered and papered, even if the pattern has faded over time.

A few awkward steps, and I can see the window that overlooks the sea.

I jump when rain batters the pane of glass and instinctively back away, turning around to face another long corridor. There are doors on either side. All closed.

But my heart skips when I spot what must be the entrance at the far end.

This corridor is all that stands between me and freedom.

I've just got to get there.

Another step. My ankle holds. I can do this.

Then, voices.

Panic batters my ribcage, and my head screams at me to find

some Tylenol and sleep until this is all over. Where are they coming from? Which room?

Closer. Laughter. A man speaks in a language that I don't recognize, and then I hear the click of a door handle being turned.

Shit!

What do I do?

Where do I go?

My heart feels as if it's trying to escape, but self-preservation kicks in. I open the door closest to me and step into a darkened room. There isn't time to check out my surroundings. I push the door gently, using it to support me, and study the narrow sliver of a gap between the edge of the door and the frame.

Someone strides past, and my breath hitches in my chest.

I didn't see his face. Is he going down to the basement to check on my father? He'll raise the alert, and then it'll be too late. I have to get out of here now.

I count to three and, when he doesn't return, I open the door again.

I step out into the corridor.

The voices are still there. Loud. Banter. Jovial almost.

It's my cue to leave.

I stumble along the corridor, limping on my sore ankle, the front entrance firmly fixed in my sight. Closer. Closer still. The voices fade into the background behind me.

I don't look behind me when my hand closes around the doorknob. I turn it, and relief floods my chest; I didn't even consider that it might be locked. But my captors were confident that I wouldn't escape.

Their failure.

Then, I'm outside in the slanting rain, and my clothes are immediately soaked through, mingling with tears of relief. Sticking close to the wall, I make my way around the building in darkness, my saturated hair clinging to my face and drifting into my eyes. The wind snaps at my skin, raising goosebumps, the building providing little shelter.

I reach the corner and stop.

The trees are my only option, but I have to clear the distance between the house and the edge of the woodland first.

A glance behind me, and I'm not being followed. They must not have discovered my father yet.

"Go, Sienna. *Go!*" I mutter to myself.

Then, I'm running towards the trees. Every part of my body jolts and screams with the agony of sore muscles and the concussion I suffered when my head hit the wall.

They won't find me in the woods. It's what keeps me going. I can climb a tree and shelter in the branches, or find a hollow and climb inside, or bury myself beneath a mountain of mulch. The possibilities are endless.

At least, that's how it seems until I hear the first gunshot.

I sprawl face-first on the sodden ground.

Peering behind me, soggy leaves clinging to my face, and hands, I realize that I'm still too close to the house. If the men follow me outside, it won't take them long to figure out that I'm hiding in the trees, and with my twisted ankle, they'll catch up with me before I've gone anywhere.

I drag myself back onto my feet and keep hobbling through the woodland.

More gunshots ring out behind me.

Angry yells.

They know that I'm missing.

I move erratically, staggering this way and that to confuse them, but certain that they'll be able to trace my footsteps on the soggy mulchy ground. I trip over an exposed root, and land heavily on the ground again, the oxygen leaving my lungs with a whoosh.

I roll over, half-expecting to find Nick looming over me with a gun aimed directly at my heart, but instead I find that I've covered more distance than I realized. The silence surrounding me, and the pitter-patter of the rain dripping from the dense canopy overhead and onto the ground would be peaceful were it not for the gunfire coming from the building.

Another shot cracks the air, making my pulse race.

I'm confused. It didn't sound as if it came from the property. It sounded more like it came from somewhere amongst the trees.

I remain on the ground, saturated and shivering, listening to the weapons being fired beyond the trees. I don't know how many men were in the house. Minus my father, I'm aware of

Nick and the Russian, but this sounds like a whole load of shots being fired back and forth.

The men aren't trying to frighten me.

They're defending themselves. And this can only mean one thing: Kyle has come to save me.

I feel safe here. No bullets have whizzed past my head, which means that the fight must be confined to the open space in front of the building. I scramble backwards and hide behind a wide tree trunk, hauling myself onto my feet and following the sounds of gunfire, back and forth.

With each shot that slices through the miserable night sky, I jump. I pray that Kyle doesn't get hurt. Or worse. He's only here because of me.

The silence is sudden. Shocking in its intensity.

All I can hear is the blood gushing through my veins and the thump-thump-thump of my heartbeat.

Just when I think it must all be over and I should head back towards the house to find Kyle, I hear another sound like a twig snapping. The forest is so wet, that I remain motionless, trying to hear above and beyond the rainfall. Perhaps I imagined it. But then, I hear another sound.

Closer.

I retreat deeper into the woods, stopping frequently to listen.

The rainfall seems to get heavier, harder, louder.

I stumble blindly onwards, my imagination turning the shadows amongst the trees into monsters that take the guise of Nick Morris and the dark-haired Russian.

I increase my pace. The rain is blinding. The dense darkness is becoming oppressive. When I trip over an invisible rock and land heavily on my swollen knee, I drag my knees to my chest and huddle my arms around them.

"Who's there?" My words are swallowed by the trees.

The wind howls through the woods like a feral animal, and my eyes dart back and forth, convinced that every twitch of a branch is one of my captors about to pounce on me.

I stand up. Only, once I'm back on my feet, I've no idea which direction I was heading in.

I turn three-sixty, inspecting the ground for the imprint of my footsteps like this is an imaginary childhood adventure through the jungle, but I was wrong. The ground is too wet, and any footprints I might have made are already filled with water. Everywhere looks the same. There are no distinguishing features, no odd-shaped trees, no markings carved by kids who once played here. Only the rain, and the howling wind, and the trees bowing under the weight of the storm.

"Is anyone there?" I hear the tremor in my voice.

A sound behind me.

I whirl around. Stare into the gloom. "Hello?"

Nothing.

Then another sound, but this time it's coming from the opposite direction.

My head spins with each movement, and I lean against a tree. "Kyle? Is that you?"

Still no answer.

I realize that I want it to be Kyle so desperately, that I've convinced myself that he came here to save me and has defeated the men who were keeping me imprisoned. But Kyle wouldn't scare me this way. Kyle would be yelling my name, telling me to wait for him to find me. Kyle would keep talking so that I could follow his voice until he appeared amongst the trees like an apparition and folded me into his arms.

The silence that follows each sound tells me all I need to know.

I'm not alone in the woods, and whoever is here with me, doesn't want to be seen.

I spot a glimmer of movement from somewhere nearby on my right. I strain my eyes to bring it into focus, but all I can see are branches swaying in the relentless clutches of the wind. More movement on my left.

I don't call out.

I move slowly backwards and around a wide, gnarled trunk, until I'm completely hidden, then I start running.

My painful ankle is forgotten. My head jars with every footstep. I keep running until the gusts grow stronger, trying to force me back inside the woods, and I can no longer feel my face with the icy rain.

I run until the trees stop and the ominous black sky starts.

I'm panting. My brain is trying to make sense of what it can see, and then I hear a voice behind me.

"There's nowhere else for you to run, Sienna."

I whirl around to find Nick watching me, his face in shadow, his hair like a wet black swimming cap fitting his head snugly. He raises the gun in his hand and points it at my head.

26

KYLE

Nick moves too quickly through the woods as if he knows the layout of the land and can navigate the trees with his eyes closed. There's something about the way he slithers into the overgrown foliage like a snake chasing food, that makes me send Patrick into the building to check out the basement. It's more than just a coward saving his own skin. His movements are predatory.

He is following someone.

Sienna.

I thought I'd glimpsed someone escaping the house when we first arrived, but the rain distorted my vision, and then they were gone. I should've trusted my gut. I should've gone after her myself, and now my hesitation may have cost Sienna her life.

She and Nick are standing on the edge of the cliff when I emerge from the shelter of the trees, the gale pummeling them, whipping their hair around their faces and trying to undress them. The brooding night sky provides a fitting backdrop. Because Nick's arm is around Sienna's neck, and his gun is pressed against her temple.

I can see the fear in her eyes as she watches me. I promised that I would never let anyone hurt her. I'm keeping that promise.

"Let her go, Nick!" I have to yell to be heard above the shrieking wind blowing in from the sea. "This has nothing to do with Sienna."

I lower my gun, crouching slowly, and place it on the wet ground at my feet. No sudden movements. I straighten again.

"Touching." Nick blinks the rain from his eyes and grins. "Kick the gun out of reach. Carefully. One wrong move, and I pull this trigger."

I kick the weapon sideways, just far enough that I can still lunge for it if necessary. I have a pistol tucked inside the waistband of my pants, but I have no intention of using it while he has her. I'll find another way to free her before I kill him.

I spread my hands wide, palms facing outward. "No weapons. Let Sienna go."

"Still think you can call the shots."

A gust catches hold of them, and they stumble forwards, locked together. Nick quickly regains his balance, but my heart has already lurched into my mouth. One more strong gust is all it's going to take to suck them both over the side of the cliff.

"I'm not calling the shots. I'm begging you to let her go. Sienna doesn't deserve this. She doesn't deserve any of it."

His eyes are dark, sunken into their sockets; he's playing a dangerous game, and he knows that if she goes over the side, he's going with her. He's dragging it out because this isn't about Sienna. This is about him wanting to be in control, about him finally having the power that his half-brothers have gained through hard work, loyalty, and respect.

The difference is, he expects to gain the same level of power by murdering an innocent woman.

My woman

My soulmate.

"Did you know that she's having your baby?"

His words punch a hole in my gut and stun me into silence. I feel the wind howling straight through me as if I'm nothing. A feather caught on a summer breeze.

My baby?

He's toying with me. Twisting the knife before he pulls it out and tosses me aside.

But when my eyes meet Sienna's, I know that it's true. Her eyes are pleading with me to save her, to save them both: her and our baby.

"Shame that it won't save them," Nick yells over the wind as if reading my mind.

"I'll give you the Titan," I yell back, my throat hoarse.

"No!" Sienna screams. "No, Kyle! Don't—"

Nick jabs the end of the pistol against her skull to shut her up. "Too late! We already have the Titan."

He's bluffing. He must be. There's no way Caleb would ever hand over any part of the Murray empire without fighting for it, and the fight has only just begun.

Well, two can play this game. "Name your price, Nick. Whatever you want. Whatever it will take to save Sienna."

Sienna's shoulders heave with sobs, her tears mingling with the rain streaking her pale face. But she's still standing tall, chin jutting, defiant as always. If only she believed in her own strength.

He flicks wet hair out of his eyes. "We have the Titan. It's only a matter of time before we take everything else the Murrays own. So, you see, we don't need her now. She's superfluous to requirements. Baggage that we can do without when we go back to New York and claim our prize."

I need to keep him talking. He hasn't loosened his hold on Sienna, and I need to get her away from him before I shoot the fucker. A bullet through the head will be too easy. I want to see the fear in his eyes. I want to watch him fly over the edge of that cliff, knowing that his death will be anything but quick and painless.

"Why?" I call out. "What's this all about?"

The demonic grin is back. "I thought you'd have figured it out. We're half-brothers. What's yours is mine, etc. Why should you get to live a life of luxury while I spend the rest of my life turning mutton into lamb. Do you have any idea how soul-destroying it is to watch you and your brothers parading your wealth around the city while I get nothing?"

We were right about Nick Morris, but it's no consolation hearing it from his own mouth. I remain silent and keep my hands by my sides. I'm hoping that his bitterness will keep him talking so that I can convey a message to Sienna with my eyes. If she raises her feet off the ground when I give the signal, he'll lose his balance, and it will give me a fraction of a second to fire a bullet into his leg.

"It's sickening," he continues. His mouth twists into an ugly sneer. "What have you ever done to deserve that life, huh?"

I can think of plenty, but I'm not about to share my life experience with him, not while he has a gun pressed to my woman's head. Instead, I switch my attention to Sienna. She's struggling. Her chest is heaving, trying to fill her lungs.

I hold her gaze and lower my eyes to the ground. She tracks my movement to my feet. I don't know if she understands what I'm trying to convey, but her captor is still speaking, and I need to keep him distracted now that he has begun his sour rant.

"My life!" I'm certain that if he had a free hand right now, he'd be thumping his chest dramatically like a deposed monarch of ancient times facing his executioner. "You stole my life from me! My mom died because of him, because of our father. You... You still get to speak to your mom every day of your life. What do I get?"

Through the squally lashing rain, I can see him withdrawing. His body is present, but his mind is elsewhere, reliving the traumatic childhood experiences that led him to this moment. This is dangerous.

We're running out of time.

"I get nothing!" The wind snatches his shrill voice and carries it over the cliff-edge and out to sea.

I widen my eyes at Sienna and drop them to the ground. I do this on repeat, until she mimics my movements. The timing has to be impeccable. I'll wait for Sienna to knock him off-balance, pull my gun from my waistband, and fire during that one-or-two-second window while he's figuring out what's wrong with her. I can't afford to miss my target.

This is the part that worries me the most.

I'm a lawyer, I'm not a violent man.

Pulling this trigger will be the hardest thing I've ever had to do, but Sienna's life is at stake here, and I'm trusting my heart to ensure that my aim is true.

"Well," he's still yelling, "that's all about to change. Right now!"

The world seems to freeze. The slanting rain is like a sheet of beveled glass separating me from Sienna and Nick as I watch her raise her legs and land on her knees in slow motion.

As predicted, Nick is caught off-balance as she slips from his grasp. The gun hovers somewhere above Sienna's head.

Moving on autopilot, I reach for the pistol tucked inside my pants. My fingers find the handle, but before I can pull it out, take aim, and press the trigger, a shot rings out and my entire body prickles. The sound reverberates inside my skull.

But my eyes are locked onto Sienna.

Realizing that he has relinquished control of the situation, Nick tries to grab her, and she rolls away from him. Then she disappears over the edge of the cliff.

"Nooooooo!" My hoarse scream is drowned out by the storm.

I'm running towards the edge.

Nick is lying spreadeagled on his back on the ground, blood seeping from the bullet wound in his chest. A guttural sound escapes his lips as I approach him. It almost sounds like he's calling for help, but I don't look at him.

Footsteps behind me.

A familiar voice screams, "Kyle! Come back."

My mom.

I don't know where she came from, or how she found us. I don't even know if she fired the bullet that will end Nick Morris's life. All I can think about is Sienna.

The edge is closer than I realized. My feet skid across the waterlogged grass when I try to stop myself from hurtling over the side, and I land on my back with a dull thud, pain shooting from my coccyx to the top of my spine. I roll over and claw at the soil, dragging myself away from the edge, soggy clumps of stringy mud coming away in my hands.

Great heaving sobs lodge inside my chest making it difficult to breathe.

"Sienna..." I murmur her name over and over, as I crawl closer to the edge on hands and knees, petrified of what I'm going to find.

I swipe rain from my eyes with muddy hands. The wind batters my face, forcing me away from the edge as if trying to protect me from the unimaginable horror below.

I sit back on my haunches, tilt my face towards the cloud-heavy sky, and yell, "Why? Why did you have to take her?"

"Kyle." My mom's eyes are dark, and her voice is firm as she crawls over to me. "Don't move."

She watches me closely, the wind whipping her hair around her face, until she is convinced that I heard her. Then, she flattens to her stomach on the ground and drags herself towards the edge, burying her hands in the soil as she peers down below.

My mom is lying there, motionless, for so long that my mind and my chest feel empty. Numb. Hollowed out. It feels as though someone slit me open and scraped my internal organs out with a spoon leaving behind an empty husk.

I already know what she has seen.

Sienna's bloody broken body on the rocks below.

My tears force their way out, hot and stinging, mingling with the torrential rain.

I drag myself onto my feet slowly. I find the gun that I dropped when Sienna disappeared and pick it up, surprised when the cold metal sends a shiver through me. I can still feel then. How is it possible when there's nothing left inside me?

Taking careful measured steps, I walk over to Nick Morris.

His breathing is labored. Blood trickles from the corner of his lips which are turning blue. His chest is concaved. But he's still alive.

Nick's eyes are like black holes in his ashen face. "I... What are you... Help me..."

I raise the gun and press the barrel against his temple the way he did to Sienna. There's so much that I want to say to him, but he doesn't deserve my words. He doesn't deserve a quick and painless death. But I'm not doing this for him.

I'm doing it for me.

I pull the trigger.

I barely notice the blood and gore that splatters my face to be washed away by the torrential rain.

"Kyle." I didn't even see my mom crawl away from the edge. But she's here now, and her hand is on my arm, and she's trying to tell me something. "She's alive. Sienna is alive, Kyle. She's alive."

27

SIENNA

Pain.

Flashing lights behind my eyes.

Something sharp digging into my cheek.

The wind venting its anger on the world, and the rain trying to rinse away all that has happened, to cleanse me of the vile memories.

I must fade in and out of consciousness. I don't know how much time passes before the pain returns with a vengeance, shooting through my arm, my spine, my face, my skull.

And with the blinding greedy pain comes the flashbacks.

Nick.

The gun pressed to my temple.

Kyle relinquishing his own weapon, promising Nick the Titan to let me go.

Nick was never going to let me go; Kyle knew this. He was trying to tell me something. A warning. He had a plan, a trick up his sleeve like a magician pulling a rabbit from a hat.

Another memory pops into my head. A childhood friend's birthday party. Cone-shaped hats, streamers, balloons, and a magician who could produce chocolate from behind the kids' ears. He hid playing cards inside his sleeves and guessed the card I chose as if he could read my mind. But there was something odd about him...

The memory fades as quickly as it appeared, morphing into Moira emerging from the woods like a ghostly apparition with a pistol in her hand. In the shock of the moment, I wondered if she was a figment of my imagination, conjured up by fear and dread and despair.

Kyle was unarmed.

We were too close to the edge of the cliff.

Nick's gun had already left an imprint on my skull that I would never be able to erase.

But they hadn't seen her.

I was the only one who knew that she was there, and suddenly I knew what to do. I knew how to get away from Nick and save Kyle.

In the moment, with my dice rolled in favor of the man I love, I was calm. Sinking onto my knees was the hardest part, the rest was simply the universe offering me a helping hand. I rolled towards the edge of the cliff. I heard the gunshot. I saw Nick lunging towards me, and then I was falling.

Falling.

Falling...

Choking sobs stick in my throat, clogging my airways and making my chest heave as I struggle to fill my lungs. Everything hurts. I need to move before the wind and the sea drag me away, but sitting up requires too much effort. My face feels as though it has been impaled on a sharp rock, and when I open my eyes, I find myself staring at a sheer wall of jagged stone.

Lying perfectly still, I begin with my toes, trying to get my bearings. I'm saturated from the rain, but I'm not submerged, which means that I'm not in the sea. I try to consider this a bonus, but it isn't much consolation. I'm lying on my stomach. I can move my feet, but I'm scared to go too far for fear that I'll start falling again.

The fingers on my left hand flex, scritch-scratching against icy rock. It's my right arm that sends spears of blinding white pain shooting through me.

Then a griping pain twists my stomach into knots, and a cry escapes my lips.

The baby.

I can't lose the baby. The universe can throw any kind of shit it wants at me, but not this. *Please, not this...*

On the edge of the cliff, I knew that I would do whatever it took to save Kyle, but now there's our baby to protect too. Kyle might call me his leoin, his lioness, but he hasn't seen anything yet. Because if anything happens to our child, I'll scale this cliff with my bare hands and rip Nick Morris's heart out of his chest myself. With my teeth if I must.

Gritting my teeth against the spears of pain, I drag my right arm close to my side and shield it against my body. Then, a fraction of an inch at a time, I pull my left arm under me and prepare to support my upper body. Another dull wrenching pain blossoms in my abdomen, and I force myself to ignore it.

If I can sit up, everything will be okay. I'll save our baby. All I need to do is sit up, get my bearings, and wait for Kyle to rescue me.

That's the mantra I repeat inside my head as I use my left arm as leverage to raise my head from its rocky pillow. Slowly. My face comes away from the sharp flinty point glueing me to the ground, and I feel the trickle of warm blood on my cheek. I'm facing the cliff, so the rain is pummeling my back, offering my face a momentary respite.

Until I twist my neck and peer out across the foaming choppy sea.

Every part of my body tries to curl up into a ball and pretend that I'm somewhere far away. With the needle-sharp rain still hammering the cliff, it's impossible to see where the ominous black sea and the storm-riddled sky merge. It's like a scene from a Gothic horror story where the main character is plunged into a world filled with shades of gray, and where every sound is a threat.

However, it seems that when I rolled over the side of the cliff, a ledge broke my fall and saved my life.

But the drop beneath me to the lethal rocks below is even more frightening than the view from the window of the mansion. Because now, all that stands between me and a certain death is a narrow bed of rock, and the wind is an angry fucking bitch who has just been cheated out of claiming my life.

My heart is pounding against my ribs, yelling at me to get the fuck away from the edge. In response, the wind unleashes its wrath and curls around me with the intention of dragging me over the side and hurling me to my death.

Panic takes hold. Sobs erupt inside my chest and lodge inside my throat, but I push myself backwards, staring out at the sea, praying that it will take pity on me. I've come too far to give up now. This isn't my time to die.

"It isn't my time to die," I murmur to the universe. Louder, "*It isn't my time to die!*"

If it was, I wouldn't be here now.

A cramp in my abdomen jolts me back to the ledge with a bone-shattering thump. I slide my left arm underneath my body, careful not to make any sudden movements or to raise my body too far above the ledge and let the gusty wind in.

I cradle my belly. "Hang on in there, baby. I've got you."

Another sound competes against the wind for my attention, making every hair on my body stand on end. I press myself against the rocks behind me, straining my ears.

Nothing.

Then I hear it. It sounds like voices.

"Sienna!"

I recognize it instantly, and a sob escapes my lips. "Kyle?" The wind snatches the name and flies away with it as if it too, knows this is my lifeline.

"Sienna! Don't move! I'm coming to get you!"

I can't be sure if this is what I heard or if I'm imagining it, manifesting my own escape route in my head. But I have no intention of going anywhere.

Instead, I close my eyes and pretend that I'm sitting on a sandy beach on a warm summer's day. The sun is high in the sky. The breeze is gentle, caressing my bare arms with the salty air stolen from the water's surface. I tilt my face towards the brochure-blue sky and soak up the sun's rays, feeling the energy coursing through my veins.

In my dream, Kyle wades out of the shallows, water dripping from his hair and his tattooed chest. My sex instinctively clenches at the vision. Other heads turn as he walks up the beach to where I'm sitting on a striped towel spread across the sand. He has eyes only for me, and when he smiles, I tingle from head to toe.

He lowers himself easily onto the towel beside me. He leans in, dripping water onto my shoulders and back, and kisses me on the lips as he slides a hand around my pregnant belly. Then he dips his head and kisses the baby inside me.

"Did I tell you I love you, leoin?" he mutters, his lips brushing mine.

I wrinkle my nose. "I'm not sure. Maybe I wasn't paying attention at the time."

He laughs and sucks on my bottom lip. "I could fuck you right here."

"With all these people watching?" I peer around exaggeratedly, expecting to find dads building sandcastles with their kids, moms rubbing sun lotion onto their kids' faces and warning them to keep their sun hats on, couples sunbathing, wraparound sunglasses shielding their eyes.

But we're alone.

"What people?" Kyle pushes me gently backwards, his fingers entwined in my hair, his tongue probing my mouth.

His hands are inside my bikini top. He exposes my nipples, tweaking them between his thumb and forefinger before lowering his head and sucking on them. I arch my spine, excitement already making me wet as he straddles my legs, squashing my breasts together, needing to suck them both at the same time.

"Do you want me, leoin?"

"Always."

He licks my lips. "Do you trust me?"

"Yes."

He drags my bikini bottoms down over my hips. My pussy reacts instantly to the sun's warmth, and I spread my legs wide. I don't care that we're on a public beach. I don't care about anything but feeling Kyle's tongue inside me.

"Close your eyes." He kisses my eyelids tenderly. "I'm going to make you come like you've never come before."

"Is that a promise?" I can't help smiling.

"For ever and ever, and then some."

He kisses my lips. His tongue traces a damp line between my breasts, down my swollen belly, and between my legs. He finds my clit and teases it, dragging his tongue back and forth, sucking on it, drawing my juices from me, the sunshine beating down on us from above.

My orgasm is about to explode when I hear my name called again through the icy ferocious wind, and I open my eyes, bursting the daydream like a balloon being popped.

28

KYLE

I flatten my body against the saturated ground and peer over the side of the cliff.

I can see her. Just about. The ledge on which she landed must be no more than a few feet wide. A freak stroke of luck, that the outcrop caught her and held on tightly. The universe is on our side. If ever I needed a sign that things would finally go our way, this is it.

"Sienna!" I call out, the sound plucked by the gale and carried God only knows where. "Sienna! Don't move! I'm coming to get you."

On my hands and knees, I crawl to the edge directly above the rocky shelf containing my future.

A heavy hand lands on my shoulder before I can turn around and lower myself over the side. Patrick. He doesn't try to pull me away. Instead, he kneels beside me and follows my gaze.

"The others are coming, lad." He gestures with his head

towards the gloomy mansion looming above the treetops. "We'll get her to safety, don't you worry."

"Kyle." My mom crawls closer, her eyes dark, her face paler than I've ever seen it. "I can't let you go down there."

I want to tell her that she can't stop me. No one can. Sienna is down there, and she needs me, and I made a promise that I can't break. But the adrenaline pumping through my veins is fading rapidly, and I can't seem to form the words and get them out there. My mouth opens and shuts, and my mom throws her cold wet arms around my chest and hugs me tightly.

The other men appear then, emerging from the woods and sprinting across the clearing towards us.

Patrick stands and waves his arms above his head, gesturing to the cliff's edge. Everyone else is still functioning normally, processing the danger, and doing what's necessary to keep us all safe. But their loved ones are not at stake here. For me, the stakes have never been higher.

"We checked the property." Damon faces me with his legs planted firmly apart, weathering the storm like a seasoned fisherman who has tamed the sea. "There's no one else left." He glances at Nick's corpse and back again, barely acknowledging it.

Patrick steps forward, taking control. "Sienna is about a dozen feet down on a narrow ledge. It broke her fall."

Damon's eyes flit back and forth between us. I know what he's thinking: she got lucky, but she isn't out of danger yet.

"Is she conscious?" he asks.

"Difficult to tell." Patrick spreads his hands towards the sky.

Cillian and his pal join us. I wait for Damon to explain the situation, their expressions never faltering. They're here to do a job; they won't walk away until it is completed.

They crouch on the ground and unpack the equipment stowed inside their backpacks. Ropes. Metal hooks that resemble anchors used for mountaineering. Harnesses. Without a word, the two lads step into the kind of heavy-duty harnesses used by professional climbers and skydivers. They fasten them around their bodies and attach the ropes to the metal hooks, then peer behind them at the woods.

A couple of men dutifully run with the ends of the ropes and fasten them securely around the widest trunks. It's a seamless organization, each understanding their role in the process.

"I'm coming with you." I yell above the wind and stand in their way.

"You done this before?" Cillian asks. There's no judgement in his tone, or none that I pick up anyway.

"Nope. But that's my woman down there."

He smiles and claps me on the back. "Stay here, pal. We'll take good care of her, I promise."

They don't linger on the cliff's edge. They don't give any instructions to the family members standing in the clearing. Without me noticing, several men have taken up position along the length of the two ropes supporting the climbers. Damon and his brother Aiden are lying face down on the ground, their heads and shoulders over the edge of the cliff, waiting to play their part.

Patrick and Mom flank me, and the two young men disappear over the side of the cliff. The ropes pull taut. I freeze. My ears strain to hear the signal that they reached her, but the wind appears to have gotten stronger, whipping the trees and our clothes into a shrieking frenzy.

I can't keep still. I need to do something.

"It should be me down there."

I don't even realize that I said the words out loud until Mom wraps a trembling arm around my shoulders, comforting me in the only way she knows how.

It feels like an eternity passes by before a head appears from behind the cliff. Damon and Aiden scramble closer to Cillian, while two burly men grab their legs and dig their heels into the soggy soil. They brace themselves, working as a team, everyone an integral part of the operation to rescue Sienna.

The two brothers half-disappear over the edge, head down, and my heart is in my throat. What if something goes horribly wrong? What if we lose them? They're only here because of me when they should be at home looking forward to the holidays.

Then they're being dragged backwards, and there's a bedraggled figure between them, and I'm running to Sienna, my mom and Patrick close behind me.

Sienna's body flops onto the ground like a fish out of water. Her eyes are closed. Her skin is gray, and her lips are turning blue.

"No. No. No." I lean my face close to hers, my cheek pressed against her icy lips. "Come on, Sienna. Don't die. I'm here now. I'm here..."

I can hear someone sobbing, my mom maybe, but I pay them no heed.

I rest my head on Sienna's chest, searching for a heartbeat. Behind me, I hear Cillian and his pal clambering back into the clearing. Patrick kneels on the other side of Sienna and takes her wrist in his hand.

"She's alive, lad."

That's when I hear the faint heartbeat.

I pull Sienna into my arms, transferring what little body heat I have to her, rocking her back and forth. "I've got you, Sienna. Everything's going to be okay because I've got you. I'm here, Sienna. I love you. Hold on to that, mo leoin. I love you."

The ambulance rushes Sienna to Letterkenny University Hospital. I go with her, cradling her icy hand in mine while the paramedics monitor her vitals. Her body is covered with a foil blanket to raise her body temperature. She opens her eyes several times, and her eyelids flutter, but she doesn't regain consciousness.

"She's going to be alright," I murmur to the paramedics. "She isn't going to die."

"Her body has gone into shock," one says. He's a middle-aged man with graying hair, and a kind round face. "Lucky you found her when you did before hypothermia set in."

Lucky.

This isn't the kind of luck I'm accustomed to, but if everything else from this moment forward goes well, I'll be eternally grateful that the universe chose to keep her alive tonight.

But there's one more thing.

"She's pregnant," I say. "Will the baby survive?"

"Gestational period?" The round-faced man raises his eyebrows questioningly. "How far is she?"

"I-I don't know." I've been back from Ireland for less than a month, so it isn't hard to calculate. "A few weeks."

He nods. "We'll do everything that we can. She's in safe hands."

Safe hands.

He probably says this to everyone who accompanies a loved one to the hospital. Comforting words. It's all part of the job.

But no one's hands are safer than mine when it comes to Sienna. I make a silent vow to the God I'm not entirely sure I believe in, to protect her for the rest of my life, or he can strike me down any way he sees fit.

When we reach the emergency room, they make me stay in the waiting room while the doctors treat Sienna. My mom and Patrick arrive shortly after Sienna is admitted. They get me coffee in a flimsy plastic cup that I don't drink. They sit on uncomfortable plastic seats in silence, surrounded by people with worried eyes and thin lips, while I pace back and forth, my clothes drying in the cloying heat and sticking to my skin.

It feels like I've been waiting for an eternity.

Time drags. People come and go. Faces light up as patients emerge from the bowels of the hospital and announce that they can go home.

I want to believe that Sienna will survive. I know exactly what she would say if our roles were reversed: stay positive and manifest the outcome that you want.

But it isn't that simple when you've recently witnessed the love of your life falling from a cliff in the middle of a raging storm.

"Kyle, why don't you sit down, love?" My mom's voice is tender.

I haven't even asked how she came to be at the property, carrying a loaded pistol. I'm grateful that she was. If she hadn't shot Nick when she did…

A medic in green scrubs approaches me then. She's young, surprisingly fresh-faced considering her profession, dark hair cropped into a short, blunt bob.

She smiles. "Mr. Murray? You can come through and see Sienna now."

"I can?"

Mom and Patrick are both on their feet. Mom squeezes my hand before I follow the young woman along the busy hallway to the room where Sienna is being treated.

She pulls back a green curtain, winks at me, and says, "I'll give you some time alone."

I step inside. My palms are sweating, and my eyes start twitching when I see Sienna in the raised bed, a drip inserted into the back of her left hand, her right arm strapped onto and supported by raised blocks. She's still deathly pale, there's a Band-aid covering her left cheek, but she smiles when I enter, and I know without a shadow of a doubt that she will always be the most beautiful woman in the world to me.

"Hey." I feel like an inexperienced teenager all over again, mentally tripping over what I want to say while my cheeks grow hot. I lean over Sienna and kiss her forehead, smoothing her hair away from her face. "How are you feeling?"

"Like I got hit by a truck." She pauses. "Again."

A small smile appears on her lips, and my chest floods with relief.

"They need to operate on my arm." She flexes her fingers which tap lightly on the thermal blanket. Her voice is hoarse. "It's broken in two places."

"Have they given you something for the pain?"

"Uh-huh. I have a concussion."

"From the fall?"

"Not exactly." She doesn't elaborate, and I don't press her. She'll talk about it in her own time.

I notice then that one of her legs is raised above the bed. "What happened to your leg?"

"Long story." She swallows painfully.

I fill a small plastic glass with water from the jug on the bedside cabinet, support her head with my arm, and raise the drink to her lips. There's a lump the size of a tennis ball on the back of her head, and her jaw is mottled with blue-black bruising.

"Sienna, I'm so sorry. This should never have happened to you. If I'd been on that flight—"

"Don't, Kyle." She settles back against the pillows, trying to get comfortable. "There's no point wishing you could change things. We can only do what we think is right for us at any given moment in time."

She is wise beyond her years, my leoin.

But I'm skirting around the question that I'm afraid to ask.

"Sienna, are you... I mean, the pregnancy, is it..."

I can handle a meeting with a renowned violent mafia don, the police commissioner, and the mayor of New York City, but I don't know how to ask the woman I love if she is still carrying our baby.

"The baby is fine, Kyle." Tears well in the corners of her eyes, and I catch them with my fingertip. "*Our* baby is fine." She sniffs loudly. "This isn't how I imagined telling you that you're going to be a dad."

I move in closer and kiss her on the lips. "We're not like other couples, leoin. But I promise you on my life—"

"No, Kyle. You should never swear anything on your life. Not even for me."

"Too late. I already did. I will always protect you and our child, no matter what it takes. I will never let anything like this happen to you again."

Her smile widens, even though her eyes are dark and heavy. "Thank fuck for that. Just keep me away from cliff edges, will you?"

"Deal."

She grows quiet, pensive. "The doctors have suggested that I take it easy for a while. Until the pregnancy reaches the second trimester. The effects of trauma can take some time to present themselves."

"Oh, don't worry. I won't let you so much as lift a finger if I can help it. Think of me as your slave for the next eight months."

"Slave, huh?" She slants her eyes. "Does that mean that I get to handcuff you and force you to pleasure me?"

"I don't need forcing, leoin, but you can handcuff me and throw away the key if it makes you happy."

Footsteps approach us from the corridor, and disappointment weighs me down. I'm not ready to leave her yet. But they keep on walking, and we both sigh with relief.

"You don't have to stay here in Ireland." I pull the visitor's seat closer to the bed, sit down, and cradle her hand in mine. "We can fly back to New York as soon as you're able to travel. You can move into my apartment, or we can find an apartment elsewhere. Whatever you want to do, Sienna. Wherever you want to go, I'll be right there with you."

I hesitate. Before she came to Ireland, Nick Morris had proposed to her, the gallery had been trashed, and our relationship was still teetering at the top of the roller coaster ride that began almost six years ago. Sienna might be having our baby, but we've never openly discussed how we feel about each other.

Pulse racing because I need to know, I add, "If you'll have me."

What will I do if she says no? What if she doesn't want me to be a part of this baby's life because she wants nothing to do with my family? What then? How will we move forward from this?

Sienna chews her bottom lip. "I think I'll stay here, Kyle. For now. I don't want to go back to the city."

I wait for her to enlighten me on where I fit into her plans. Outwardly, I must appear calm, but inside, I'm swallowing great ugly sobs that I want no one to ever see.

"With you," she says finally. "Because I love you too."

I kiss her on the lips while the words to the Sum 41 song 'With Me' play in my head.

I'd wait here forever, just to see you smile, 'cause it's true, I am nothing without you.

EPILOGUE

SIENNA

It feels like the scene at the end of the movie *Love Actually*.

Kyle and I are waiting at Dublin airport for everyone to arrive from New York City. Emily came over a week ago to spend the summer with us. It turns out that she has an artistic streak that she'd been keeping to herself since she was a child, afraid that her older brothers would laugh at her if she revealed that she wanted to be an artist. She loves animals too. So far, there are seven paintings of cows in my new studio, each one named, each with a personality of their own.

One day, I'll persuade her to sell them.

Kyle leans over my shoulder and kisses my cheek as he hands me a vanilla latte smothered in cinnamon and sits beside me. His hand cups my belly, and the baby reacts with a few well-placed kicks.

"I stand by what I said before: he's going to be a footballer." Kyle winks at Emily who is sitting opposite us in the arrivals lounge.

"*She* is going to be a prima ballerina." I sip my drink and hide behind my cup.

"What do you think, Em?" Kyle watches his sister, who snaps her attention back to the conversation.

She hasn't been watching the planes preparing for take-off, or studying the flawless blue sky for a glimpse of the family's private jet coming in to land. I follow the direction of her gaze to two young men sitting near the bar area of the lounge playing a card game. One, dark-haired, blue-eyed, classically handsome, glances over at Emily, catches me watching him, and looks away again.

I wonder who they're waiting for. Their parents? Friends? Girlfriends?

Everyone here is waiting for someone. We're waiting for Kyle's family to fly into Dublin for our wedding next week. It's been a few months since I've seen baby Holly, and although Victoria sends me pictures every day so that I can see how she's growing, I'm excited to spend some time with her before she forgets who I am.

Since the abduction and the subsequent deaths of Nick and my father, I've been spending most of my time in Ireland. Kyle bought a little cottage by the sea for me to stay in while I figure out my next move. It has small, low-ceilinged rooms, a wood-burner, an outside shed filled with freshly cut logs, and a garden filled with wildflowers.

My closest neighbors, in another cottage with pink climbing roses framing the doorway, are Kyle's security team. He thinks that I don't know about them. But I haven't told him that I still look for Seamus every day, expecting him to come marching up the front path and offer to give me a tour of the coastline. His death follows me around, and the guards' presence is like an invisible comfort blanket.

When the sun shines, the sea sparkles like a million diamonds, and when it's stormy, the sea turns moody-gray, the sea-monsters come out, and the wind shrieks around the cottage, a warning to stay inside.

I like the stormy days the best.

When everything outside is chaos and carnage, I feel a sense of inner peace that I'm not sure I've ever experienced before. The wind, the Irish Sea, and the baby growing inside me keep me company when Kyle is in New York.

He currently divides his time between here and the States, but I sense that it's becoming increasingly difficult for him to leave whenever he's needed in the city. His life is right here. He's connected to Ireland through blood, through his family legacy, and through me while I'm here. He wants to stay. For good. Build a life here with our child, open a new gallery, visit the local pub on a Sunday afternoon for a pint of Guinness, get involved in the close knit community.

I haven't told him yet that I'm tempted.

I don't have the same roots. The more I think about it, I'm not even certain that the roots I put down in the city are keeping me alive. But I finally feel like I'm starting to grow again.

I haven't painted since Nick and my father destroyed my artwork in the New York gallery.

I broke my right arm in two places when I fell over the side of the cliff outside the mansion in Donegal. Fortunately for me, there was a narrow ledge jutting out of the sheer cliff-face. It broke my fall and saved me from certain death on the rocks below, but it broke something inside me at the same time. My arm is healing well. The doctors say that there'll be no lasting damage, and that with continuing physical therapy, there's no reason why I can't get back into the studio.

But my heart isn't in it.

Not yet.

Kyle built a new studio for me. He thought it was what I needed to help me recover from the ordeal. But each time I pick up a paintbrush, I relive the moment when I discovered that everything I'd ever painted had been trashed.

Maybe I'm being melodramatic, but it feels as if all the tiny pieces of my soul that I mixed into the paint on those canvases were destroyed with them. I'm struggling to pick myself back up. I know I will in time—I've always bounced back before—but will I paint again?

Who knows?

Besides, I'm going to be a mom soon; the baby growing inside me consumes my every waking moment, and I'm happy with that.

"It has to be a girl." Emily's eyes gleam when she smiles at me, dragging me out of my reverie.

I spend too much time inside my own head lately, but that will change when everyone else arrives and we all move into the Murray family home for the next couple of weeks.

"Look at what she's already survived." Emily aims this at Kyle. "Only a female would be strong enough to fall off a cliff and keep hanging on. And besides, this family is still male-heavy. We could do with some more women on our side."

"She and Holly will be like sisters," I add, swallowing a mouthful of vanilla latte and furrowing my brow. "Did you add brown sugar to this coffee?"

"Aye." Kyle tries and fails to suppress a smile. "Not quite sweet enough for you, *leoin*?" He whispers his nickname for me; it's for our ears only.

I smile. "Can you get me some more? Please? My body is craving sugar."

"You see!" Emily squeals. "Definitely a girl. She's already building up to the chocolate cravings she'll never be able to satisfy when she gets older."

"Girls play football too, you know," Kyle tosses over his shoulder as he sets off to find some more sachets of demerara sugar.

With Kyle out of the way, Emily's eyes slide straight back to the two guys playing cards. A faint blush creeps into her cheeks.

"Why don't you go over there and speak to them?" The baby starts wriggling inside me and I shift in my seat to get more comfortable. "You see, even she agrees with me." I smile.

Emily's eyes grow wide. "I can't do that."

"Why not?"

For a strong, intelligent young woman with four big brothers looking out for her, she doesn't have half the confidence when it comes to dating that I had when I was her age.

Or perhaps the four big brothers are the reason why she holds back. I can picture them sitting her down before her sweet-sixteen party and warning her not to speak to any boys, and *absolutely not* to get close enough to kiss one.

I smile to myself. One day, she'll rebel, and I can't wait to see how her brothers handle it when she does.

"Can I?" She seeks out Kyle, realizes that he has his back turned to us, and stands up.

"Sure. Go for it. I'll cover for you."

I watch her join the two lads tentatively, shoulders hunched as though trying to make herself as inconspicuous as possible. If she only knew. Other heads turn as she walks past, and she's totally oblivious. The good-looking lad half-stands and gestures for Emily to take the seat beside him; once seated, he offers her a soda from the stash on the table. Emily doesn't even look my way.

She reminds me of Victoria when we were at high school together. Victoria never saw what other people saw when she looked in the mirror; she was always waiting for the next ball to roll down the alley and knock her down. So, she found it easier to set her goals too low. If only sixteen-year-old Victoria could've seen where she would end up.

"Where did Emily go?" Kyle has a handful of sachets.

"She's playing cards with some friends."

In response, Emily's laughter reaches us from the other side of the lounge, and I glance across to find her rosy-cheeked, her grin so wide I can see her back teeth.

"Do you know them?"

I place a hand on Kyle's thigh, luring him away from the potential threat of two young lads playing a card game with his sister. "Leave her be. They're not doing any harm."

Kyle plants a kiss on my lips. "You do realize that if this baby is a girl, I'm never letting her out of my sight."

"You do realize that if you never let her out of your sight, you'll have a rebellion on your hands when she's a teenager."

He chuckles. "Bring it on."

Through the window, the private jet catches my eye as it touches down on the tarmac. "They're here."

He squeezes my hand. "Are you nervous?"

"About us all being together in one house or about marrying you?"

"Both?" He winces, afraid of the answer.

"I'm fucking terrified." I raise his hand to my lips and kiss his knuckles. "But I wouldn't change it for the world."

I hear Victoria squealing almost before she appears through the sliding door to the arrivals lounge. She runs to me, throws her arms around my neck and hugs me tightly, then places both hands on my swollen belly and says, "It's a girl."

Caleb is close behind, Holly in his arms.

I don't think a child has ever resembled her father more. Holly is a mini-Caleb, with wide green eyes and a beautiful smile that lights up her face.

She holds out her arms for me to take her, and my chest swells with love when she rests her head upon my shoulder as if it's where she belongs.

"She remembers you." Victoria's eyes are damp. "Hormones," she adds, blinking. "You've got this all to come."

The Murray clan's arrival is like a tornado sweeping through the arrivals lounge.

Emily comes running over when she spots her parents and brothers. Terry pulls her into a bear hug and swings her around, her feet above the floor, while the rest of us hug and kiss and everyone tries to guess the baby's gender.

"It's a girl." Moira links arms with me, and we follow the men out of the airport to the waiting vehicles.

"Mom's always right." Cash winks at me from over his shoulder.

He looks older. I notice the first strands of silver in his thick hair, and he seems to have lost the boisterous energy that always followed him around like a wall-climbing shadow. Or maybe he has matured a little since his arrest. The charges were dropped—Kyle worked tirelessly to prove that all the evidence against him had been planted—but it must've been a wake-up call, nonetheless.

Bash is still Bash. Calm, laid-back, and eyeing up a blond woman in a halter-neck dress scrolling through her social media apps while she waits for someone to arrive.

"Are you sure you still want to go ahead with having the wedding in a meadow, Sienna?" Moira asks as we step out into the sunshine.

Summers in Ireland are glorious, I've realized; another reason why I'm tempted to stay. No pollution. No traffic fumes. No hazy artificial heat like the bubble that surrounds New York City through July and August. Just endless blue sky, green fields, and calm sea.

"I'm sure." I tilt my face towards the sun's rays.

I never really thought about the kind of wedding I wanted when I was younger, but it makes perfect sense now that we're here, like this was the way it was always meant to be. Like everything that ever happened to me, my father, my mom dying too young, the accident; it was all building up to this moment.

It was always going to be Kyle, right from the first moment I met him when he was Kenickie, and I was Wilma.

"What about your dress?" Moira continues. "Aren't you worried that it will be ruined? What shoes will you wear?"

"I'm getting married barefoot." I smile at Kyle who is holding open the passenger door to the MPV waiting to take us home. "So is Kyle."

"You can go barefoot too, Mom," he says.

"I will," Emily chimes as she climbs into the back seat of the car ahead of us. "Sienna, I invited Eoghan Byrne to the wedding. I hope you don't mind."

Her eyes are bright; I recognize that look. It's the same gleam that I see in Victoria's eyes whenever she and Caleb are together. It's how I feel whenever I'm with Kyle.

"Is that the guy from the airport?" I ask.

"Did I hear the name Eoghan Byrne?" Terry's expression is serious. "Declan Byrne's son? The same Declan Byrne who—"

"Terry." One word from Moira, and he presses his lips together.

"Dad, relax." Emily pokes her head back out of the car, "Do you have any idea how many people are called Byrne in Ireland?"

Kyle comes up behind me and hugs my belly, nuzzling my neck, his warm breath on my cheek. "You'd better get used to this, my love. The Murray men are a protective bunch."

I kiss the tip of his nose. "I wouldn't have it any other way."

And I mean it.

THE END

POST EPILOGUE

SIENNA

I wake up early with the sunshine streaming through the open curtains of the bedroom in the cottage. The window is open, and I can hear the waves slapping the shore outside, the gulls calling boisterously to each other between land and sea before the new day gets started.

I've grown to love these sounds. The shush of the water across the shell-littered beach. Kyle's key is the lock each time he arrives back from the States. His regular greeting, the one that makes my heart race: "I'm home, leoin." The click-clack of his footsteps across the flagstone hallway as he explores the cottage to find me.

When he gets back later, we'll take a picnic down to the beach and watch the sunset, and we'll walk back to the cottage, hips bumping, and Kyle's arm wrapped around me.

I cannot wait.

The lethargy that has taken over since our wedding a month ago and the family's subsequent departure, is still in full swing. I told myself that it was the excitement of the wedding celebrations. The constant chatter of conversation while everyone was there. The sightseeing excursions, the barbecues, the meal-planning and the relentless flow of alcohol and champagne that had left me feeling exhausted.

Not that I was drinking. I was happy to watch everyone else enjoying themselves while the baby performed somersaults inside me.

Our wedding day was blissful. Blue sky overhead, warm grass underfoot, and everyone we love watching us recite our vows. Kyle had never looked more handsome in his open-necked white shirt and silver-gray pants. No suits. No ties. No lengthy ceremony.

We wanted it to be intimate, filled with love and joy and laughter.

Moira kept her shoes on, but she looked young and fresh in a floaty chiffon dress and a wide-brimmed hat.

I wore a simple white dress that belonged to my maternal grandmother. I never met her. She died the year before I was born, but I keep a photograph of her and my mom in a silver frame beside my bed, next to a picture of me and Kyle.

The women in our family die young.

I try not to dwell on this, but it's always there, lurking in the back of my mind, just waiting for me to latch onto it and examine in more depth. Even though I keep the thought at bay, I wonder if it's contributing in some way to my lethargy, and my continued reluctance to get back into the studio. Like a silent voice urging me to enjoy every moment with my child when he or she arrives, because life is too short.

As usual, I counter this with the eternally grateful reminder that Nick didn't win. He didn't beat me. He tried to knock me down, but he failed because good always triumphs over evil, or at least, that's what the fairy tales would have us believe.

And I do believe in fairy tales these days.

Kyle might not be the angelic Prince Charming of ancient lore, but he is my prince. My soulmate. My happy-ever-after.

Shaking my head at my hormone-fueled musings, I plump the pillows up behind my head and haul myself into a sitting position. I reach for the novel on the nightstand, *The Wolf and the Dove*, an epic historical romance, the main characters of which are uncannily like me and Kyle in my head, as pain grips my abdomen.

I drop the book onto the floor and tears well in my eyes as my bookmark flies across the floor losing my place in the story.

I stare at my neon-pink toenails, painted badly because I can't reach my feet with my swollen belly in the way, no matter which position I contort myself into. I practice breathing, in through my nose ... hold ... out through my mouth.

I'm sweating by the time the pain subsides.

I'd planned on staying in bed for a while—I'm almost at the end of the novel, only fifty pages to go—and Kyle isn't flying back from New York until this evening. But I have to retrieve my bookmark, and the bottle of water on the nightstand is empty, and I need to clean the refrigerator.

Besides, there's no way I'm going back to sleep now.

The practice contraction has left a dull ache blooming in my pelvis, my pulse racing, and my thoughts mulling over all the stuff that I still need to prepare before the birth. I was putting it off until after the wedding, and never seemed to get around to it, but I guess today is as good a day as any. There's still a month to go, *but you never know*, as Moira keeps reminding me every time she calls.

I smile as I swing my bare legs over the side of the bed. I can almost hear the relief in Moira's voice when I speak to her later and tell her that I've packed my bag and the baby's bag ready for the hospital.

She was still trying to change my mind about having the baby in Ireland right up until the day they flew back to the States.

It was Terry who finally convinced her. "You were adamant that you were going to have Emily at home, remember, love?" He winked at me, like it was a private joke we'd concocted between us.

"Where did you have her?" I asked.

"At home." Moira said. "Just like I wanted."

"It wasn't my choice, you see," Terry continued. "But I wasn't going to argue the point with a pregnant woman."

Moira, realizing that she wasn't going to win, took my hands in hers and looked me directly in the eye. "If you want me to be here for the birth, you only have to ask, Sienna."

I haven't asked.

This is Kyle's last trip to the States until after the baby arrives. There's no way he's risking being on the other side of the Atlantic when our baby is born.

I walk barefoot through to the kitchen, fill a glass with fresh orange juice from the fridge, and peer out at the sea. It's like a sheet of shimmering blue glass. A butterfly flits around the wildflowers growing knee-high on either side of the path leading to the front door. I never imagined this would be my life one day; the universe clearly had other plans.

I rinse out my empty glass when I'm finished and stand it upside down on the drainer. Then I open the door to the fridge and start shifting the food from the shelves to the kitchen counter. I've already started on the salad drawer at the bottom when the next contraction rips through my belly.

Panting, I lean over the counter, eyes closed, and suck in deep breaths, trying to breathe through the pain which is unlike any of the practice contractions I've felt before. My belly is solid as a rock. It feels tight, like someone has wrapped a metal band around me and is tightening the screws.

When it subsides, I cross the room and sit down heavily in one of the chairs around the pine table, trying to rub the ache away.

"I'm not in labor." I say the words out loud as the fridge starts beeping at me for leaving the door open. "Okay, okay, I hear you." I go back and close it.

The food sits forlornly on top of the work surface, wondering what's next. Ripe, juicy tomatoes, locally caught salmon, a block of cheddar cheese, crisp apples, Greek yogurt, and jars of pickles.

I check the time on the oven clock. 6:15.

I fill the basin with soapy water, finish emptying the fridge of its contents, and spray it with antibacterial spray. When it's spanking clean, I replace the food, fill the coffee machine with water, and move onto the oven. Might as well be productive as I'm awake early.

The time reads 6:23 when the next pain hits.

This one is stronger than the last and leaves me feeling drained when it passes.

But, determined to finish cleaning the kitchen, prepare the new bassinet, pack the hospital bags, and run some errands before Kyle gets home, I crack on with the oven.

Then I start pulling everything out of the cabinets. The more I look, the more fingerprints and smears I find. Packets of biscuits that I've opened on a craving and left to go stale. Crumbs that I never spotted before. A squeezy jar of honey that has dripped onto the shelf.

I spray and scrub and work myself into a frenzy, stopping whenever a pain rocks my belly, withdrawing into myself, and breathing through the agony. By the time the kitchen is spotless, and my damp hair is clinging to my forehead and the back of my neck, the contractions are coming every five minutes.

The clock on the oven says that the time is 9:42.

I must be in labor.

I didn't want to acknowledge it, but the pains are getting stronger. I can feel them in my back as well as in my belly, and each one is lasting longer, leaving me drained as they fade.

I'm not due for another four weeks though.

And Kyle isn't due back in Ireland for another six hours.

Perhaps if I soak in the tub for a while, it will slow the labor down or even stop it completely.

I leave the faucets running and grab a fluffy towel from the rack. The smell of the lavender-scented candles in the bathroom soothes away the lines that I can feel between my eyes, as I drag my hand back and forth through the warm water.

It's fine, I tell myself. The information that I received via the maternity app said that the practice contractions would become more frequent closer to the due date. I'm worrying about nothing.

I drag the oversized T-shirt that I wore in bed over my head and am about to climb into the tub when water gushes out from between my legs.

It's followed by a pain that keeps me on my knees, panting, while I grip the side of the tub and wait for it to pass.

"Fuck!"

I clamber unsteadily into the tub and lean back, submerging my belly.

I haven't prepared my overnight bag.

The new sleepsuits that I bought for the baby have been washed and sorted into various piles according to size, but I haven't unpacked the bottle sterilizing unit or collected the stroller or thought about formula if I have problems with breastfeeding.

I feel my uterus tightening as another pain crashes through me. The warm water helps. A little. But there's no denying that our baby is too impatient to ride it out for the next four weeks.

At this rate, she isn't going to ride it out for the next four hours.

I have too much to do to waste time soaking in the tub.

Climbing back out, water puddling around my feet, I wrap the towel around me and wander back into the bedroom. I need to let Kyle know. He can't miss the birth. He'll be devastated if he doesn't make it home in time.

My fingers tremble when I unlock my phone and hit the green button on Kyle's number. The call goes straight through to voicemail. He's several thousand feet above the ground, of course he is. Even if I leave a message, there's nothing he can do that will get him back to Ireland sooner.

The next contraction leaves me feeling dazed and sore.

I can't think straight. I can't remember the procedure for being admitted into the hospital. But I need to get dressed, get my overnight bag ready, and clear up the mess in the bathroom from where my waters burst.

One thing at a time. I don't have the bandwidth to think beyond pulling on some clean clothes. Not with the image flashing in and out of my mind like a beacon of Kyle working on his tablet, mid-flight, oblivious to our baby's imminent arrival.

Dressed, I ride out the next contraction on my knees, leaning over the side of the bed, balling up the sheet in my fists. The instant it passes, I mop up the bathroom floor, empty the bathtub, and stuff toiletries, clothes, and underwear into an overnight bag.

Another contraction.

They're getting stronger. I've stopped timing them, and I remember that it's the first question the midwife will ask when I call the hospital: *how far apart are they?*

In the kitchen, I grab the notepad that I usually use to make grocery lists and note the time. I barely have a moment to remember where I left my phone before the next one rips through me.

"Shit. Shit. Shit."

Kyle isn't going to make it.

I'm overwhelmed, not with fear that I'm doing this alone, but with sadness for my husband. I can't even begin to imagine his disappointment when his flight touches down, and he realizes that he's too late. It's the kind of missed moment that stays with a person forever. I only hope that one day, he'll look back on this and be able to laugh about the terrible timing.

I call Emily next. With the growing certainty that the birth is happening today, right now, and that there isn't a chance in hell of slowing it down, I've achieved a clarity that I've been missing for longer than I can remember.

Emily doesn't pick up. She's in Ireland for the summer but has been staying at Eoghan's family home for the past few nights. I don't leave a message.

Without considering the time difference, I try Victoria next. She answers while I'm in the throes of another contraction.

"Si? Sienna?"

I suck in a deep breath and exhale noisily.

"What's going... Fuck! Are you in labor? You're not due for another month." She must cover her phone with her hand; I can hear her muffled voice speaking to someone else. Then, "Sienna, is Kyle with you?"

"No. He isn't due back until this evening." I'm shocked at how normal I sound between pains, almost as if they're happening to someone else. "I just wanted to check that he made the flight."

"He left earlier than scheduled, Si. Said there was something he had to do when he got back to Ireland." She pauses. "I thought he'd have been home by now."

"What? What did he have to do?"

"I don't know, Si."

I put the phone down on the bed and focus on my breathing through the next pain.

"Is Emily with you?" There's no mistaking the panic in Victoria's voice now.

"No."

"Where the fuck is she? Have you called the hospital? Or what about the security team? They'll take you, Sienna."

"The security team?" I'm only half-invested in the conversation now.

Where is Kyle? What was so important that he didn't even tell me he was flying back earlier than planned?

My phone vibrates with call-waiting. I don't even say goodbye to Victoria.

"Kyle?"

"No, it's Emily. Guess what, Sienna, I got married!" She squeals at me from the other end of the call.

My next contraction sucks the impact of her announcement out of me before I can even begin to process it.

"Sienna?" Her voice buzzes at me through the speaker. "Sienna, what's wrong? Oh no. Oh no, no, no, no. You can't be having the baby. Not today. Please tell me you're not in labor."

"I'm in labor," I pant into the phone.

"Is Kyle home?" Pause. "He's not back yet, is he?"

"Emily..." The contractions are so close together now that I can barely stop and think between them. "I've got to go."

"Sienna, wait—"

My fingers are slow and clumsy. I log into the maternity app, locate the number for the maternity unit, and press the green button.

I'm still on the phone, talking to a softly spoken midwife called Frances who is timing my contractions and talking me through what will happen when I arrive at the hospital, when someone opens the kitchen door at the back of the house and calls out my name.

"Sienna?" A ginger-haired man appears in the bedroom doorway looking sheepish. I recognize him from the security team's cottage; he stands out front every morning with a giant mug of coffee and stares at the sea. "I'm Paddy. Victoria called me. I'm going to take you to the hospital."

I'm in too much pain to argue.

He carries my bags and links his arm with mine to help me into his car, then he goes back to the cottage and locks up for me.

The journey passes in a haze of pain and panting.

By the time I'm admitted to the maternity unit and taken straight through to a delivery room, I feel as though I need to push.

"Just pant through this next contraction." Frances has a cloud of fine blond hair secured into a ponytail at the nape of her neck, plump rosy cheeks, and a permanent smile. She looks exactly how she sounded on the phone. "I need to see what's going on before we meet your baby."

"My husband..."

"Is he on his way?" Frances rests a warm hand on my belly as it grows solid again.

Inhale... Exhale...

I didn't even tell Kyle that I'm in labor.

"You're doing really well, Sienna." Frances drapes a cool cloth across my forehead. "The difficult part is done. We're ready to get this baby out now."

I experience a fleeting pang of sadness that Kyle is going to miss the most special moment of our lives, but then I'm riding the wave of the next pain, and Frances is telling me to push while another midwife grips my hand firmly.

Everything else is a blur.

With each pain, I squeeze my eyes shut and push. It's all I can think about. Even when Frances tells me that she can see the head, it barely registers that she's talking about our baby.

Then, I hear a familiar voice.

The door to the delivery suite opens, and Kyle is there. He comes over, kisses my forehead, and squeezes my hand. "I got here as soon as I could."

"Just in time, Dad." Frances smiles. "Ready, Sienna?"

Kyle sits beside my bed, cradling our baby in his arms.

Our son is cocooned inside a pale-blue baby blanket sleeping soundly. He looks just like his father, and I can already picture Kyle cheering him on from the sidelines at football practice when he's older.

"What shall we call him?" Kyle's eyes are gleaming.

I was so convinced that the baby would be a girl, I haven't given boy's names much consideration. I finish the last slice of toast on the tray in front of me and wash it down with a mouthful of lukewarm tea. I'm still ravenous.

"I like Skye," we both say at the same time.

We both blink and chuckle in unison.

"Skye?" In sync a second time.

I don't even know where the name came from, but now that it's out there, it feels perfect.

I lay back against the pillows and watch my husband and son. With baby Skye delivered safely and the midwives giving us some space to be a family, I replay today's events in my head. I poke about until I uncover the snippets of vague conversations that have been itching away at the back of my mind.

"Victoria said that you left New York earlier than planned."

Kyle peers at me, and I can visualize him dragging himself back to reality, to a world that only exists outside of this fresh tiny bubble we've found ourselves in. "I'm glad I did. I can't believe this little one decided to come a month early."

He's going to be an amazing dad. I already know that they'll be inseparable: my boys.

"Where did you have to go?" I ask.

His smile lights up his face. Kyle stands, settles the baby gently in my arms, kisses the tip of Skye's nose, and then pulls out a small plain keyring holding two silver keys from his pocket.

"The keys to our new house."

My eyes flicker back and forth between Kyle and the keyring dangling from his index finger. "New house?"

"Our son is Irish." Kyle shrugs. "I figured we should make a home here for him. Permanently, if that's what you want."

My chest is filled with so much love right now, I feel like I could explode. What did I ever do to deserve such a perfect life?

"It is." I lean closer to Kyle and kiss him on the lips. "I have everything I ever wanted right here."

"Me too."

Gazing at the beautiful baby boy in my arms, it occurs to me that we all guessed the wrong gender: me, Victoria, Moira, even Emily.

Emily!

I remember now. Something she said to me on the phone when I was in labor. Something about getting married. I must've been delirious with the pain; everyone will laugh when I tell them that's what I thought I heard.

Kyle perches on the side of the bed and takes a selfie of the three of us to send to his mom. He types the caption: *My perfect family*.

Thank you so much for reading my Kyle and Sienna's story, if you enjoyed it please leave me a review.

If you enjoyed Kyle and Sienna's story you will love Ruby and Harry's spicy read in forbidden Dark Vows.

Here is a preview...

Chicago 1987

Ruby

My mom straightens my coat collar, checks me out, eyes narrowed like she's disappointed I left home without applying lipstick, *again*, and says, "Smile, Ruby, for God's sake."

I stretch my lips upwards in a fake smile and roll my eyes at the same time. I can't help it. She clocks the eye-roll, and her mouth pinches into a tight buttonhole shape. "Remember why we're doing this."

We are not doing anything. What she means is, remember why *you're* doing this, Ruby.

"I didn't pay for all those ice skating lessons for nothing," she adds, her voice silky smooth while making sure that I understand we're in this together.

I work at the outdoor skating rink some evenings. I don't mind it. I like being outdoors. I like watching folks landing on their butts on the ice and leaping up again, laughing like they planned it that way. Like they enjoy making a total ass of themselves on a night out.

Sure, the boots stink sometimes, and I have to pinch my nose and hold them at arm's length when I shove them back onto the correct shelf, but it means I get to skate for free whenever I want. The rink gives off holiday vibes anyway, especially when we've had a frosting of snow in Chicago, and people are snuggled up inside their furry hoods and ski gloves.

The fairy lights strung around the rink twinkle behind my mom, highlighting her rosy cheeks and pink-tipped nose. I knew as soon as I saw the VIPs rock up in a black stretch limo that it would only be a matter of time before she showed up. I could've timed it down to the second if I wasn't so busy shoving boots into the hands of celebrities wanting to show off their skills—or lack of—on the ice.

I don't even know how she does it. It's like she has a built-in radar: *money alert, money alert, money alert.*

My dad had a stroke thirteen years ago, shortly after I started middle school. Before he got sick, he'd been a successful businessman. He started his company from the basement of his parents' house when he graduated from university with a master's in computer technology and an idea that he believed would make him a millionaire.

It did. And then some.

And then it almost killed him.

Well, not the business exactly, but the stress of running a company that was evolving faster than he could keep up with. I don't know what happened exactly—my parents don't talk about it—but I do know that a bad deal wiped him out and his business collapsed faster than a house of cards.

I watch my mom fussing over my hair, teasing strands over my shoulders and clicking her tongue like she could do with a can of hairspray right about now. Her hair is immaculate as always, her clothes old but still with designer labels attached to the inside. Her eyes skim my face, noting the state of play of the makeup and nothing else.

"It's fine, Mom," I say. "An extra layer of mascara isn't going to make any difference."

"It makes all the difference, Ruby." Her eyes finally meet mine. "I didn't bring you up to be the kind of girl who forgets to check her teeth in the mirror before she leaves home."

My mom applies two coats of mascara every day, more sometimes, depending on who she wants to impress.

She works in a beauty salon—I guess looking perfect comes with the job title. It's what she did before she met my dad and got swept off her feet and into the parallel universe of exclusive hotels, expensive champagne, and glitzy parties. Between her full-time job and my three part-time jobs, we cover the household bills now that my dad can't work.

She doesn't resent him for it—for better, for worse, until death do us part, right? But she misses the lifestyle they had before the business went bankrupt. She misses the doors money opened for her, the front row seats on Broadway, and the way people looked at her like she was somebody.

That's why she's here now.

She glances over my shoulder, and her eyes widen. "He's even more gorgeous in real life than he is in the movies." I see it in the slant of her eyes and the tilt of her head, flirting without even realizing she's doing it.

I have my back to the rink, but I saw Alessandro Russo arrive with a bunch of his wealthy friends. The boss served them. Only the best for celebrity guests—I guess he couldn't risk me trying not to gag as I handed over the bladed boots.

Mom thinks they ooze money.

I think they could do with oozing a little less arrogance and a little more authenticity.

So, maybe Alessandro Russo *is* Hollywood's rising star. Maybe his last movie *did* make him a bunch of dollars and first pick of the lead roles in next year's planned productions. But there's also the teensy little advantage in his pocket that his family is wealthy and associated with the Russian Mafia—if the stories are to be believed.

But I bet his shit still stinks.

"Don't look at me like that." Mom stands back and surveys her handiwork. AKA me.

"Like what?" I know that she knows exactly what I'm thinking.

You know how some moms say there's no point lying to them because they'll always catch you out? That's my mom. Celia Jackson. Lie detector extraordinaire. I swear it must've been her party piece when she was younger.

She places her hands on my shoulders, turns me around so that I'm facing the rink, and whispers in my ear, "Go catch yourself a Russo, sweetheart."

My dad used to take me fishing when I was a little girl when he still had time to spend doing family stuff. I never caught a fish because I couldn't sit still for more than a couple of minutes. I couldn't keep quiet either.

But more importantly, I never saw the point of trying to catch a fish using maggots as bait. It felt dishonest; those poor fish in the river never knew that the tasty maggot might be their final meal. They never knew that the meal came with a lethal hook, one that would sink inside their gullet and reel them in before they even knew what hit them.

This feels the same.

There's Alessandro Russo gliding around the ice without a care in the world in his black leather coat and shiny gold scarf. And here's me: the maggot.

The guy can skate, I'll give him that. He turns around so that he's skating backwards, legs crossed, body all sleek angles and swarthy good looks, grinning at his friends before he executes a simple toe loop and whizzes off, a trail of teenaged girls in his wake.

Ugh!

Of course, he's lapping up the attention like the cat that got the cream. He glides towards a couple of teenaged girls who are watching him from the edge of the rink, heads almost touching so that they can whisper about how hot he is, and hisses to a halt in the middle of them. I watch their cheeks turn pink as he offers them a hand each and leads them towards the middle of the ice where everyone will be able to watch the performance.

I don't even know how I'm supposed to get close to him.

A glance at my mom, and she raises her perfectly groomed eyebrows with a nod in the actor's direction.

Deep breath. I do a few laps of the rink, practicing my spins and salchows in time to the music and lose myself to the Friday-night atmosphere and the chill on my face. When I'm skating, I can forget everything else and pretend that I'm an ice princess, the way I used to do when I was younger.

The crowd around Alessandro Russo grows. I can still see his head above the girls trying to smother him with their autograph requests and their eager smiles, but he's obviously basking in their adoration like a lizard in the sunshine.

I skate away from my mom and stop at the edge of the rink, bending to fasten the lace of my left boot which has come undone. As I do, someone knees me in the side and performs a somersault over the top of me, landing on their back on the ice like an upturned beetle. I hear the whump of air whooshing from their lungs and flinch.

It sounded like it hurt. A lot.

"Are you alright?" I move closer and offer the guy a hand, and he takes it with an embarrassed smile. At least he isn't trying to fool me that he did it on purpose.

His hand is warm through his woolen glove, and his grip is firm, although he hauls himself upright and puts no pressure on me to help him.

He has a kind face, that's my first thought. My second thought is that his eyes are the color of the sea on a clear day in fall. Pumpkins pop into my head. Fiery orange leaves, steaming coffee, and log fires.

"Sore," he says, "but I guess that'll teach me to watch where I'm going next time." His gaze drifts towards the actor in the middle of the rink like a candy store owner handing out free sweeties.

"It's what happens when you choose to come skating on the same evening as someone famous." I shrug. "You should come midweek. You can practice falling elegantly as much as you like."

He smiles, and his whole face lights up. "Is that what you do?" Heat floods his cheeks. "I mean, not that I'm suggesting you can't skate. I've been watching you. Not like that, not in a pervy kind of way, just, well... You're good."

I can't help laughing. "My mom made sure I could skate. She said no one wants to be seen flat on their back with their legs up in the air, at least, not when they're wearing skates. She said if I didn't learn, there was always the possibility that someone else's blades would slice my fingers clean off."

He blinks, those cool blue eyes growing even wider. This man doesn't need an extra coat of mascara, that's for sure. "She said that?"

"My mom's full of life's important lessons."

He smiles again, his expression fading rapidly as his skates slide out from under him... While he's standing still.

I offer him another hand, only this time, when he grabs it, I can't help laughing. "On second thought, maybe you should stick to walking, or swimming. Although there's always drowning..."

He's laughing though. Which is a bonus. My mom always says I should try reining in the sarcastic humor when I'm in company because not everyone understands or appreciates it.

"Harry Weiss." He shakes my hand.

"Ruby Jackson."

"Do you want to—"

He doesn't finish because my mom has walked around the outside of the rink and is waving something at me. Harry follows my gaze, and I inhale deeply.

"Gotta go, sorry. Nice meeting you, Harry Weiss."

He nods. "You too, Ruby Jackson."

I feel mean abandoning him, but at least he can hold onto the side and pretend that he's taking a break. My spot beside him is immediately filled by another guy in a smart tweed coat, and I recognize him as one of the men who arrived with Alessandro Russo. Maybe Harry knows him too.

"Ruby!" My mom grabs my attention, and I shove Harry Weiss to the back of my thoughts. Wrong surname. Probably wrong background, too for what my mom has in mind. "What are you doing?"

"Being friendly to the paying customers?" I've spotted my car keys in her hand and try to grab them, but she snatches them away from me.

"Nu-huh. Not until you get out there and get yourself noticed."

"Have you seen how many people have had the same idea?"

She pockets my keys and sets her features into a this-is-me-you're-talking-to expression. "Other people are not you, Ruby. Other people can't skate right over there, grab his goddamn hand, and show him what you can do."

"What makes you think he'll be interested in what I can do?"

"He's a good-looking, hot-blooded young man, and you're a beautiful young woman."

That's it. That's her reasoning, and she doesn't even see anything wrong in the way she presented it like being a female is enough.

I don't tell her that I'm done being a maggot. He'll either notice me or he won't. And even if I reel him in, there's no guarantee that he won't flip straight back into the water to chase the fish already wagging their tails in his face.

"You're not getting your keys back until you do," she says, "so I suggest you start performing now." My mom walks away, her eyes on the prize who is currently autographing the back of someone's hand, a well-practiced smile on his face.

I skate around the group of fans, giving my best impression of someone who doesn't know that she's in the presence of movie royalty. I don't even look in Alessandro Russo's direction. I focus on the blades cutting the surface of the ice, and everything I ever learned when my mom dragged me to the rink as a child.

I sense, rather than see, the shift in the atmosphere. The music grows livelier, cashing in on the Friday night experience, and the crowd starts moving away from the celebrity, giving him space to strut his stuff. Two tunes later, and he's skating alongside me, hands behind his back like this was what he was born to do.

"Do you come here often?" He flashes me his most dazzling smile like that will seal the deal with minor effort on his part.

"Seriously? That's your chat-up line?" Sometimes, I can't help myself.

He laughs out loud. I bet it's won him a few dates before now with that laughter. "Shit. You got me there. You're good." He gestures to the ice.

Here's the point where I should tell him that he's not so bad himself. You know, flirt a bit, bat my eyelashes at him. But then I spot Harry Weiss in my peripheral vision, clinging for dear life to the side of the rink as my mom approaches him, says something, and then waits for him to make his way off the ice.

Whatever she said, it worked. He glances my way, once, but he doesn't smile or wave or even acknowledge that he almost took my fingers off. Nothing.

Then a new track comes through the speakers. 'Love is in the Air'. It's my dad's favorite tune, and it hits me like a jolt straight through my heart that I'm doing this for my dad. For us. To give us all a better life. And I smile at the hot actor.

Harry

It's late by the time I arrive at the InterContinental for Alessandro's birthday party. I didn't even see the others leave the skating rink—I was too busy changing the tire on Ruby's car. Her mom, Celia, told me that she'd noticed her daughter's car had a slow puncture and she didn't want her to be stranded in the city when she finished her shift.

I mean, how could I refuse?

I stumbled right over the goddamn top of her—changing her tire was the least I could do. Not that I was helping as an apology. I'd already made an ass of myself with that one.

If I'm honest, I don't even recall the physical process of the tire change. I guess I was shell shocked, or at least in a bit of a daze, reeling from my brief conversation with Ruby. Something about her...

Anyway, I study my reflection in the elevator mirror and realize that I have grease on my chin. I try scrubbing it off with the sleeve of my sweater and only succeed in spreading it further, so now I look like a kid who's just returned from summer camp. I smooth my hair back with my hands and sigh when it springs straight back up again.

The party is in full swing, buzzing with laughter and loud conversations that will only grow more boisterous as the evening progresses. I'll stay for a couple of drinks and then leave—parties are not really my scene, they're much more Alessandro's thing. I guess if we met now, rather than at Uni, we probably wouldn't be friends, we wouldn't even socialize in the same circles.

Carlos, Alessandro's brother, comes over and grimaces when he notices the smears on my face, and I subconsciously try to wipe them away with the palm of my hand. "What happened to you? Is this supposed to be some kind of camouflage so that no one will notice you? If so, it isn't working."

I check my fingers—they're grubby now too. "Just helping a damsel in distress."

He peers all around, his eyes twinkling. That's the thing about the Russo family—they all have that sparkle, a charisma that people literally find irresistible, and they're genuinely nice people with it. Must be why the universe smiles down on them.

"Where is she then, this damsel in distress?"

I can't help smiling. "She's the one that got away."

Carlos clamps a large warm hand on my shoulder and peers around at the guests.

Alessandro hired a function suite for the party, the ceiling heavy with crystal chandeliers that cast shimmering diamonds across the room. Waiters in crisp white shirts and black bow ties are walking around with trays of champagne. The tables lining the room are laden with platters of food and floral centerpieces.

Not the kind of place I'd ever have envisaged my friend hosting a birthday party, but he's drifting into a new lifestyle, and I wonder how long it will be before he leaves his old friends behind. I recognize a young actress from a recently released movie, wearing a gold dress that looks as if it has been poured over her. She's talking to a movie director who looks remarkably like Martin Scorsese.

I swallow hard, wishing that I'd at least gone back to my room to shower before making an appearance.

"I see Alessandro has finally met his match," Carlos says, dragging me out of my self-indulgent misery.

"Who?" I scan the room for Alessandro—he's taller than most people—and the air seems to leave my lungs for a second time this evening when I spot him across the room with a small group of people I don't recognize. Apart from the young woman standing beside him.

Ruby Jackson.

Do they know each other? Or did Alessandro dish out invitations like autographs at the ice rink? A quick glance around the room tells me that she's the only one here who isn't dressed to impress, so I guess he didn't bring a busload of folks back with him.

She's the only one.

A waiter comes over, and I accept a glass of champagne which I down in one go. And regret it instantly when the bubbles resurface almost instantaneously.

"Have you ever seen him like this?" Carlos nods in their direction.

He doesn't need to elaborate—I know exactly what he means. Alessandro is charming as always, steering the conversation, the wide easy smile a constant, but his eyes keep flicking to the woman at his side, the sparkle unmistakable. His hand snakes around her and settles on her lower back as he lowers his head to whisper in her ear, and she smiles up at him...

I signal for the waiter to bring more champagne and switch my empty glass for a full one. I sip this drink slowly.

I don't know why Alessandro inviting Ruby to his birthday celebration bothers me so much. Scratch that. I know exactly why it bothers me.

We've been friends long enough for me to understand that he'll woo her and then drop her like a lead balloon as soon as he gets bored. Alessandro is the classic chaser. He enjoys the challenge, and if my brief conversation with Ruby is anything to go by, she'll present the kind of challenge he'll be unable to refuse.

And Ruby Jackson deserves better than that. Fuck if I'm honest, I want her.

I swallow another mouthful of bubbly liquid. I need a beer. I'll never get used to drinking champagne and expensive wine that needs time to breathe before you can taste it.

How do I know that she deserves better?

I don't. At least, that's what I tell myself, as I turn away from the sight of my best friend nuzzling her neck while she chews her bottom lip.

"I think I need to meet the woman who has captivated my little brother." Carlos raises his glass to me in a mock toast and navigates around the guests to go join Alessandro and Ruby.

"Did you get into a scrape or something?" Ronnie comes over with a beer and eyes up my greasy face.

"Long story. Where did you find a beer?"

Ronnie taps the side of his nose. "I brought a secret stash. I can't be drinking that shit."

I follow him to the cloakroom, where he has hidden a crate of beer underneath a rail of glamorous but impractical winter coats. We crack open a couple of cans and follow the steady thrum of voices back to the function room.

Ronnie spots an old friend and leaves me standing next to a table filled with hors d'oeuvres, bite-sized morsels that smell overwhelmingly fishy. I'm so busy studying the swirls of pink mousse and crab claws and tiny mounds of caviar, that I don't notice anyone approaching.

"Have you recovered?"

I spin around to find Ruby standing next to me, a smile tugging her lips up at the corners. "Yes. Thank you. Yes, I always feel safer when my feet are touching the ground."

She nods. Too late, I realize that she has already spotted the black smears on my chin. "Another accident or did you read the newspaper on the way here?"

I can't help chuckling. She seems to have that effect on me, creating laughter that gurgles beneath the surface just waiting to erupt every time she speaks.

"I changed your tire. I should've gone back to my room to

shower, but I didn't think, and, well, you're not the first person to have noticed, so it looks like I'm stuck with it now."

She furrows her brow. "My tire?"

"Yes. Your mom said you had a slow puncture. It was flat as a pancake when I got there. She was worried about you getting home."

She nibbles her bottom lip with her front teeth and then says, "May I?" gesturing to my beer. I hand it over and she takes a long swig, wiping her mouth with the back of her hand before handing it back to me. "Thank you. For the beer and the tire."

Ruby moves closer and surveys the guests in their fancy clothes. "Are you and Alessandro friends?"

Alessandro... The name already sounds comfortable on her tongue.

"Known each other since Uni."

"Are you an actor too?"

She studies me intently, and I notice now that her eyes are green. I've never seen green eyes close up before, and I think I understand why cats are so bewitching.

"No. I work in oil. Petroleum. Fuel."

Her laughter caresses my cheek like a chiffon scarf. "So, you're used to getting your hands dirty."

I peer down at my empty hand and ball it into a fist to hide my grimy fingers. "Not quite. At least, not anymore."

Her eyes narrow briefly. "Not anymore?"

"I seem to spend more time in the office these days, managing numbers."

She gives me a curious sideways smile. "So, what, you're an accountant?"

I'm generally uncomfortable discussing what I do—most women turn their nose up at the word fuel—but Ruby isn't like most women. She's still here and she doesn't look like she's trying to escape. Yet.

"Not exactly." I swallow, the back of my throat clicking drily. "I'm the boss. I own my own company. It's still early days. We can't compete with the likes of BP or Chevron, but, well..." I glug a mouthful of beer. There's the dark family business but I'm not involved with it yet, and I don't want to scare my woman away. *My woman?* "What do you do? When you're not skating?"

"I read a lot."

I nod and pray that she doesn't ask me who my favorite author is. I haven't read a book since Uni.

"I studied literature," she continues without waiting for a response. Which is just as well really, as book talk isn't my strongest subject. "It was the only thing that I stood a hope in hell of passing, so I went with it."

She has an air of confidence that allows her to say exactly what she means rather than pussyfooting around. I like that about her.

"Favorite book?" I ask, because damn, I want to know.

"*Wuthering Heights*. I've lost count of the number of times I've read it. Doesn't everyone want to be loved the way Heathcliff loves Catherine Earnshaw?"

I must be gaping at her because the smile is back, but she isn't laughing *at* me.

"I guess," she continues, "if your next question is what I want to do with my life, it would be to write a modern-day *Wuthering Heights*. Not because I want to go down in history as the next Emily Bronte, but because if I can write about love with that kind of passion, then I'll be a very happy lady."

"Was Emily Bronte happy?" I ask.

She studies me coolly. "What a question, Harry Weiss."

A shiver travels down my spine at the way she says my name.

"You know, she probably wasn't. She died when she was thirty years old. Can you imagine what she might've gone on to write had she lived a full and healthy life?"

"There you are!" Alessandro is standing in front of us, his eyes sparkling for Ruby. "We're all heading down to the pool before we're too drunk to stay afloat." He entwines his fingers with hers and pulls her away.

"Are you coming, Harry?" Ruby doesn't move; she's waiting for me to answer.

"Course he's coming. Aren't you, Harry?" Alessandro raises his eyebrows at me, telling me to get a move on.

"Sure. I didn't bring swim shorts though."

"Who cares?" Alessandro guides her away from me. "No one did."

Ruby... Read Forbidden Dark Vows now free in Kindle Unlimited and available on paperback.

ABOUT THE AUTHOR

VIVY SKYS the author of Steamy Contemporary Romance novels, featuring smart, strong, sassy and witty female characters that command the attention of strong protective alpha males, from Off limits, age gap, bossy billionaires, single dads next door, royalty, dark mafia and beyond Vivy's pen will deliver.

Follow Vivy Skys on Amazon to be the first to know when her next book becomes available.

Printed in Dunstable, United Kingdom